ROSAMOND LEHMANN

THE
WEATHER
IN THE
STREETS

WITH A NEW INTRODUCTION
BY JANET WATTS

Published by VIRAGO PRESS Limited 1981
20–23 Mandela Street, Camden Town, London NW1 0HQ

Reprinted 1982, 1983, 1984, 1987, 1989, 1991

First published by William Collins Ltd. 1936

Copyright © Rosamond Lehmann 1936
Introduction Copyright © Janet Watts 1981

*A CIP catalogue record for this book is available from the
British Library*

Printed in Great Britain by
Cox & Wyman Ltd., Reading, Berks

INTRODUCTION

The poet – and the novelist – may prove to be a prophet. Genius, said William Blake from his own embattled position, is always ahead of its time. Rosamond Lehmann, who would be the last person to link that statement with her own work, nevertheless admits that *The Weather in the Streets*, her fourth novel, was 'not exactly contemporary. I think that many people felt that this was not true to their experience when it was published. A generation later, people were beginning to say: "This is speaking to me now."'

Rosamond Lehmann's best-selling first novel, *Dusty Answer* (1927), and its two successors, *A Note in Music* (1930) and *Invitation to the Waltz* (1932), had established her as a writer of an exceptional emotional intelligence, and by 1936 her fans were avid to welcome a new novel from her. In *The Weather in the Streets* Miss Lehmann gave them a love story, though for many of them it was not what they had expected or hoped. The love in this novel is that of a woman past her first youth for a married man, and its story is not an altogether pretty one.

Readers had met these people before. In *Invitation to the Waltz* they had watched Kate and Olivia Curtis, the daughters of a middle-class English country household, await and attend the coming-out dance of an aristocratic local neighbour. Olivia, valiant but uneasy in an ill-cut flame-coloured frock, smiles, suffers, and – wonderfully – survives a first dance that comes perilously close to humiliation and disappointment. Her evening is made magically all right by a meeting with Rollo Spencer, the debutante's glorious elder brother, and a few minutes' chat with him on the moonlit terrace.

The readers who had been enchanted by Olivia Curtis at seventeen now rediscovered her ten years older: thinner, sadder, and not apparently much wiser, with a failed marriage behind her, and ahead such miseries as they might have preferred not to witness. She and Rollo Spencer meet again in a train. Her marriage is over; his is unsatisfactory. They quickly fall in love and into an affair. Olivia looks to this relationship for the salvation of her life: but it brings her unhappiness, an unwanted pregnancy and a double loss.

A number of people were not pleased. Rosamond Lehmann's American publishers, anticipating the dismay of their readership in ladies' luncheon clubs, had implored her to remove the abortion sequence. The novel's publication – complete, on Miss Lehmann's insistence – won many good reviews, but (as she recalls) 'I also had very sour notices from male critics, saying "She obviously doesn't like men, and she doesn't understand them." Though the funny thing was that it was the male critics who were apt to say what an absolute cad Rollo was. Most of the women who wrote to me – and my readers have mostly been women – said: "Oh, Miss Lehmann, this is my story! – how did you know?"'

This sense of identification has perhaps been Rosamond Lehmann's greatest attraction for her women readers. In her books they have found themselves: their own confusions and pleasures, sorrows, passions and episodes of farce. 'It looks now as if I was writing specifically about the predicament of women, though I was not conscious of it at the time. I just wrote what seemed the truth in my experience, out of something inside me – an enormous complex of experiences and emotions, my own and other people's, that I had to give expression to.'

She has always firmly resisted the 'spotters' who have plagued her writing life with attempts to attribute the characters in her novels to real people in her own life. 'I suppose because much of what I wrote dealt with romantic and sexual love seen from a subjective angle, the detective squads were rampant; also the self-identifiers; also those with a so-called knowledge of my private life more beady-eyed than accurate,' she has written.

Rollo Spencer always particularly engaged their curiosity. 'I remember Cyril Connolly for one nagging at me: "Was it so-and-so? Well, who was it, then?" I said, "It's somebody you've never known, and never will know. He has got an original, but it's not what anybody's ever thought or guessed.' It was a man who loved her, with whom she never had an affair, who 'belonged to a very uncontemporary world that has gone now. He became, for me, almost an archetype; and he haunted most of my subsequent work.'

Rosamond Lehmann admits that people and experiences from her own life have certainly gone into her books: but in the books they have acquired a new and different reality. In writing this novel and *Invitation to the Waltz* she 'saw the image' of one of her sisters in creating a character; but she insists that she did not write about that sister's experiences. The fictitious reality takes off, floats away from the original image in a new life belonging to the book alone.

Rosamond Lehmann cannot be sure whether, when she was writing *Invitation to the Waltz* half a century ago, she already had in her mind the story's sequel. 'But when I came to the meeting between Olivia and Rollo on the terrace, I think I thought: I see! *this* is what all this is about! It's unrealised now, it's broken off – but this is what I've got to deal with later.'

What comes later for Rollo and Olivia, in *The Weather in the Streets*, is love. Rollo is rich, fashionable, secure in his social and business worlds, and unhappily married to the beautiful girl with whom he was already in love in *Invitation to the Waltz*. Olivia is alone, impoverished, part of a semi-bohemian London circle.

Neither in their separate worlds, nor in the larger world of their time, can the love between Rollo and Olivia have a public life. It can have no recognition, no expression, no allowed morality, no home: no existence outside their minds and hearts. Its reality is on the other side of everything else in their lives – their families, friends, work, interests. Olivia looks out from her love, their companionship, his warm car, and sees the other world – the real world. 'Beyond the glass casing I was in, was the weather, were the winter streets in rain, wind, fog . . .' Which is stronger? 'Go, go, go, said the bird', wrote T. S. Eliot: 'human kind / Cannot bear very much reality.'

This is a novel of tenderness, but also one of courageous investigation, in which Rosamond Lehmann explores the deep recesses of people's private lives. She follows Rollo home; she accompanies his mother on her pilgrimage to Olivia's doorstep. She trails Olivia on her lonely London circuits, takes her through the abortionist's consulting rooms, and afterwards back to her bed. She probes the cracks in the carapace that encloses the chaos in Marigold Spencer's soul. She exposes the thick thread woven by money and class and social position in the frail fabric of Rollo's loyalties and loves, without which a bond may fray away to nothing. She goes into the spaces of this love affair, and transmits to us the desolation of Olivia's weeks alone, or in the colder climate of her friendships, that cast a long shadow over her hours of delight in Rollo's company. Olivia is no more a grumbler in this novel than she was in *Invitation to the Waltz*, and sometimes we seem to experience her pain, in this affair, more sharply than she does herself.

'Even trimmed up with Rollo's flowers, that room never cracked a whole-hearted smile,' she reflects, in her straightforward way, about one of her London perches.

The thing is really, I don't like living alone. The wind gets up; or else I start wondering what the people were like who lived in the room before me; dead now, and soon I'll be dead and what's it all about? . . . I sit in a chair and do nothing, or lean against the mantelpiece . . . I was alone in that room more than I thought I'd be . . .

Olivia is not a masochist and Rollo is not a cad. Yet there is pain here. Yet there is pleasantness. Their affair balances as precariously as life itself between alternatives at once almost opposite and yet almost the same. Love shimmers between friendship and passion, resentment and affection, nostalgia, exuberance and regret. A benighted weekend swings between despair and the ridiculousness that rekindles laughter and warmth. A dramatic confrontation is undercut by prenatal nausea. The agony of a miscarriage is framed in the ambiguous comfort of an accidental reunion.

The love between Olivia and Rollo warms their conversations as much as their bed; and in recording these, too, Rosamond Lehmann affords her reader a remarkable double awareness. At once we feel what the lovers are both feeling – the tension and attraction and enjoyment between them – while we are touched by the writer's unwavering perception of their separateness: the differences in their thoughts, hearts, lives.

I'd have liked to go to the smart places where people eat, and to theatres and dance places. He didn't want to. Of course it wouldn't do, he knows all those well-connected faces, they're his world . . . He only wanted to be alone somewhere and make love. 'Where can we go?' he'd say. 'Can we go back to your room?'. . . . I told him he had only one idea in his head . . . I said to tease what I wanted was a soulmate. 'You don't, do you?' he'd say, rueful, coaxing. 'And anyway,' he'd say, 'I do love talking to you. You know I do. You're such a clever young creature . . . We have lovely talks, don't we?'

We did, of course, really, lovely talks . . .

There is a conversation one night in Austria, shaded by some chestnut trees. It is the high point, the centre of the lovers' closeness. Next day it is gone: not only bypassed with the fragmentation of their companionship, the splitting of their routes, but extinguished in the deeper death of their separate perceptions. Their memories of the same shared experience are different. Rollo's moment of commitment is to disappear into his mental repository of good times.

In the last moments of this novel, Rollo and Olivia talk for an allotted hour in his house. The conversation merges with all the others they have shared. Suddenly it seems only a step away from their chat on the moonlit terrace, or in the restaurant of the train where they met again; and only a step away to the next stage of their lives, whatever that is to be. They have loved each other, and left each other; perhaps everything that could happen between them has happened. Yet their talk, trembling between triviality and importance, is still full of the immediacy and uncertainty, the million possible differences, of a present that is about to become a future.

'Do you think she went on seeing him?' said Rosamond Lehmann, when we talked about this book. 'Yes, I suppose she did. I expect it all went on and on, I'm sorry to say. It never became a tragedy, exactly . . . it couldn't become one. And yet it was.'

Was it? Perhaps. Rollo Spencer confirms, in that last conversation, that separateness that is at the root of the pain of love. Yet his coaxing murmur doesn't belong to tragedy. It makes you smile. It makes you love him. It helps Rollo's reader – if not Rollo himself – bear a little more unbearable reality.

Janet Watts, London, 1981

PART ONE

1

TURNING OVER IN BED, SHE WAS AWARE OF A SUMMONS:
Rouse yourself. Float up, up from the submerging
element . . . But it's still night, surely. . . . She opened
one eye. Everything was in darkness; a dun glimmer mourned
in the crack between the curtains. Fog stung faintly in nose,
eyelids. So that was it: the fog had come down again: it
might be morning. But I haven't been called yet. What was
it woke me? Listen: yes: the telephone, ringing downstairs
in Etty's sitting-room; ringing goodness knows how long,
nobody to answer it. Oh, damn, oh, hell. . . . Mrs. Banks!
Mrs. Banks arrive! Click, key in the door; brown mac, black
felt, rabbit stole, be on your peg at once behind the door.
Answer it, answer it, let me not have to get up. . . . Etty,
you maddening futile lazy cow, get up, go on, answer it at
once. . . . Pole-axed with early morning sleep of course, unconscious among her eiderdowns and pillows.

Olivia huddled on her dressing-gown and tumbled down
the narrow steep stairs. Etty's crammed dolls'-house sitting-
room, unfamiliar in this twilight, dense with the fog's pene-
tration, with yesterday's cigarettes; strangled with cherry-
coloured curtains, with parrot-green and silver cushions, with
Etty's little chairs, tables, stools, glass and shagreen and
cloisonné boxes, bowls, ornaments, shrilled a peevish reproach
over and over again from the darkest corner: withdrew into
a sinister listening and waiting as she slumped down at the
littered miniature writing-table, lifted the receiver and
croaked: "Yes?"

Kate perhaps, fresh-faced, alert in the country, starting the
children off for school, about to say briskly, "Did I get you

5

out of bed?—Sorry, but I've got to go out. . . ." Kate knows I never could wake up, she condemns me and is pitiless. One day I'll be disagreeable, not apologetic.

"Yes?"

"Is that Olivia?"

"Oh . . . Mother. . . ." Mother's voice, cheerful, tired, soothing—her emergency voice. "Yes?"

"Good-morning, dear. I've been trying to get an answer. . . . I thought perhaps the line was out of order. . . .?"

"No, the line's all right. Sorry, I've only just—— What time is it?"

"Past eight." Mild, unreproachful: your mother.

"Oh, Lord! There's an awful fog here, it's quite dark. Mrs. Banks must have got held up."

"Dear me, how nasty. I do hope she hasn't been careless at a crossing. There's not a sign of fog here. It's dull, just a wee bit misty, but it looks like a nice day later. . . . Listen, dear. . . ." Her voice, which had begun to trail, renewed its special quality of soothing vigour, proclaiming, before the fatal tidings: All is well. "Dad's in bed."

"Dad? What's the matter?"

"Well, it's his chest. Poor Dad, isn't it a shame?"

"Bronchitis?"

"Well, dear, pneumonia. He's being so good and patient. Dr. Martin says he's got quite a good chance—if his heart holds out, you know, dear,—so there's no need to worry too much just at present. He's making such a splendid fight."

"Is he in pain?"

"Well, his cough's tiresome, but he doesn't complain. He gets some rest off and on. Dr. Martin's so kind—he comes three or four times a day. You know what trouble he takes. I'm sure no doctor in England could take more trouble. And I've got such a nice cheerful sensible little nurse—just for night duty. Of course, I do the day."

"When did it start?"

"When did it start, did you say, dear? Oh, just a few days

ago. He would go out in that bitter east wind, and he caught cold, and then his temperature went up so very suddenly."

"I'll come at once. Is Kate there?"

"Yes. Kate's here."

"Oh, she is!" Summoned sooner than me: more of a comfort. "I'll catch the next train."

"That'll be very nice, dear. But don't go dashing off without your breakfast. There's no need. Give Etty my love."

"I will. Have you had any sleep?"

"Oh, plenty. I can always do without sleep." Scornful, obstinate, rather annoyed in the familiar way. . . . Others may have human weaknesses—not I. . . .

"I'll catch the nine-ten and take the bus out."

"Very well, dear, we'll expect you. But do take care in this fog. Don't breathe it in through your mouth more than you can help, and if you take a taxi, do tell the man to *crawl*."

"Nine minutes," said an impersonal voice.

"Remember your breakfast. Good-bye, dear."

She's hung up hastily, she's on her way upstairs without a moment's hesitation. Nine minutes have been lost. Forward, forward. Too much can sneak past, can be unsupervised in nine minutes.

Between stages of dressing and washing she packed a hasty suitcase. Pack the red dress, wear the dark brown tweed, Kate's cast-off, well-cut, with my nice jumper, lime-green, becoming, pack the other old brown jumper—That's about all. Dress carefully—hair, lipstick, powder—look your best. Don't go haggard, dishevelled, hot-foot to the bedside—don't arrive like a bad omen. No need to worry too much just at present. *Not too much just at present:* ominous words. *He's fighting*—means *he's holding his own?*—means, always—*he's defeated.* . . . Is it his death-bed? Must I dye the red, the green, must I go into Tulverton, looking pale, and buy some mourning, must I buy black gloves? Wouldn't he manage to say, if he was still just ahead of the thing that was trying to overtake him, still able to preserve his own mixture, his particular one, sealed away from the universal ending, the lapse into the general death of people—wouldn't he be sure to say: If I catch you having a funeral. . . . Surely he must have said it some time or other. If not, if he hadn't bothered, if he hadn't had time, if Aunt Edith were to come flowing with all her veils and chains and overthrow him, if the Widow lurking in Mother were to triumph, or the cheerfulness of the nurse dishearten him beyond the remedy of malice and cynical resilience—then black and elderly women would prevail, black armlet for James, black-edged notepaper, and weeds and wreaths and Aunt Edith's smelling-salts; and there'd be nothing left of the important thing he knew, that he hadn't attempted to impart except as a kind of spiritual wink of an eyelid, barely perceptible, caught once or twice and returned without a word: something, some sense he had of life and death; the lifelong private integrity of his disillusionment.

She ran down to the next floor, telephoned for a taxi, then opened the door of Etty's bedroom, adjoining the sitting-room. Silence and obscurity greeted her; and a smell compounded of powder, scent, toilet creams and chocolate truffles.

"Etty. . . .!"

At the second call, Etty turned on her pillows and groaned "*darling* . . ." in mingled protest and greeting.

"Etty, I don't want to wake you up, but I've got to go home. Mother's just telephoned. Dad's very ill. I'm just off."

"Oh, *darling*. . . ." She switched on her lamp, lay back again with a heavy sigh. "*What* did you say?" She sat up suddenly in her pink shingle cap, pale, extinct, ludicrously diminished without her make-up and the frame of her hair.

"He's got pneumonia."

"*Oh, no!* The poor sweet. Oh, darling, have you got to *go*? How *devastating*. Oh, and I do so adore him—give him my love—*and* Aunt Ethel. Wait a minute now, darling, let me think, let me *think*. Half-past eight—oh dear! Where's Mrs. Banks? Not here, I suppose. Wait a minute, darling, and I'll help you." She whisked off the bedclothes; her brittle white legs and bony little knees slipped shrinkingly over the edge of the mattress.

"There's nothing to help about. I'm all ready. I've packed and all. Get back into bed at once."

She stood up feebly for a moment in a wisp of flowered chiffon, then subsided deprecatingly on the edge of the bed.

"Oh, darling, you must have some tea or something. Let me *think*—Yes, some tea. I'll put the kettle on."

"I don't want any. I'll have breakfast on the train. It'll be something to do."

"Will you really, darling? It *might* be best. Now *mind* you do. It's *no* good not eating on these occasions, one's simply *useless* to everybody. Oh, *is* there a fog again? How *vile*. It's simply—It's almost *more* than can be borne."

She huddled back into bed and shivered.

"Just one thing. Later on, about ten, if you'd ring up Anna at the studio and explain I can't come."

"I will, darling, of *course*. I *won't* forget. Isn't there *anything* else I can do?"

"No, go to sleep again, Etty."

"Oh, darling, I feel *too* concerned." She lay back, looking stricken. "So *miserable* for you."

"It may be all right, you know. He's stronger than people think. He's quite tough."

"Oh, he *is*, isn't he? I've always thought he's *very* strong really, invalids so often are. I do *think* he'll be all right. *Promise* to ring me up, darling. Let me see, I'm dining *out* to-night, oh dear, what a nuisance . . . but I'll be in between six and seven for *certain*. I *tell* you what, I'll ring *you* up."

"All right, do, Ett. Good-bye, duck."

"Can you *manage* your suitcase? Oh! . . . good-bye, my sweet."

Pressing all her cardinal-red fingertips to her mouth, she kissed then extended them wistfully, passionately. Above them her frail temples and cheekbones, her hollowed eyes stared with their morning look of pathos and exhaustion. Like an egg she looked, without her hair, so pale, smooth, oval, the features painted on with a stare and a droop.

"Lie down again and go to sleep."

She will too.

Olivia slammed the canary-yellow door of the dolls'-house after her, swallowed a smarting draught of fog, said "Paddington" towards a waiting bulk, a peak immobile, an inexpressive disc of muffled crimson stuck with a dew-rough sprout of hoary, savage whisker—and plunged into the taxi.

Out of the station, through gradually thinning fog-banks, away from London. Lentil, saffron, fawn were left behind. A grubby jaeger shroud lay over the first suburbs; but then the woollen day clarified, and hoardings, factory buildings, the canal with its barges, the white-boled orchards, the cattle and willows and flat green fields loomed secretively, enclosed within a transparency like drenched indigo muslin. The sky's amorphous material began to quilt, then to split, to shred away; here and there a ghost of blue breathed in the vaporous upper rifts, and the air stood flushed with a luminous essence, a soft indirect suffusion from the yet undeclared sun. It would be fine. My favourite weather.

An image of the garden rose in her mind—soaked lawn, strewn leaves, yellowing elm-tops, last white roses on the pergola, last old draggled chrysanthemums in the border; all blurred with damp, with a subdued incandescence, still, mournful and contented. And him pacing the path with his plaid scarf on, his eye equivocal beneath the antique raffish slant of a Tyrolese hat, his lips mild, pressed together, patient and ironic between the asthma grooves. He can't die. . . . She rummaged in her bag for mirror, powder, handkerchief, and attended minutely to her face. A speck or two of fog-black, and my eyes look a trifle weak, but not too bad. Various nondescript wearers of bowler hats sat behind newspapers all down the breakfast car: travelling to Tulverton on business probably; or through, on to the north. . . . Here came something in a different style—a tall prosperous-looking male figure in a tweed overcoat, carrying a dog under his arm, stooping broad shoulders in at the entrance. With a beam and a flourish the fat steward conducted him to the seat opposite Olivia. He hesitated, then took off his coat, folded it, put the dog on it, patted it, sat down beside it, picked up the card, ordered sausages, scrambled eggs, coffee, toast and marmalade, and opened *The Times.*

Rollo Spencer.

A deep wave of colour swept over her face: the usual uncontrollable reaction at sight of a face from the old days. At once her mind started to scurry and scramble, looking for footholds, for crannies to hide in: because my position is ambiguous, because I'm anonymous. . . . On Tulverton platform, in the Little Compton bus, walking down to the post office, the eye of flint, the snuffing nostrils, the false mouths narrowly shaping words of greeting, saying underneath their tongues: "Now, what's your situation? Eh? Where's your husband?"—whispering with relish behind their hands: "Poor Mrs. Curtis: it's hard she didn't get that younger daughter settled. Bad blood somewhere: I always said . . ."

I won't go outside the garden, I'll wear a disguise, I'll have a shell like James's tortoise. . . .

Carry it off now, carry it off—What do I care? Snap my fingers at the whole bloody lot. Who's Rollo Spencer? He won't recognise me. I'll smile and say: "You don't recognise me. . . ." Dad's on his death-bed maybe. . . . I shan't say that.

The dog stirred about on the coat, and Rollo said something to it, then glanced across and smiled the faint general smile with which people in railway carriages accompany such demonstrations. The smile sharpened suddenly into a kind of wary prelude to recognition; and then he said in quite a pleased, friendly way:

"Good-morning."

"Good-morning."

"Revolting in London, wasn't it? It's a relief to get out."

"Yes. It's going to be heavenly in the country."

Soon, an attendant brought steaming pots, dishes, plates, set them before him. He helped himself with leisurely liberality.

"Terrific breakfasts railway companies do give one. I always overeat distressingly in trains. There's something in the words scrambled eggs, rolls, sausages, when you see them written down. . . . One look at the card and my self-control snaps. I *must* have everything."

"I know. I feel the same about ice-cream lists . . . mixed fruit sundae . . . cupid's kiss . . . banana split . . . oh! . . . banana split!"

He laughed.

"I see what you mean, but you know, the sound of it doesn't absolutely fire me—not like the word sausage. I'm afraid I'm more earthy than you. I'm afraid you're not with me really?" He eyed her solitary cup of coffee. "I hope I'm not turning you up. . . ."

"Not a bit. I'm just not a breakfaster." And only got one and sixpence left in my purse.

"Hi, Lucy. . . ." The last mouthful went into the dog's pink and white, delicately hesitating jaws.

"What a pronounced female."

"What, this one?" He looked dubiously down. "Well, I don't know. Are you, Lucy?"

The dog quivered madly and blinked towards him. She had a coat like a toy dog and her eyes were weak with pink rims. Her nose also was patched with pink, and she wore a pinched smirking expression, slightly dotty, virginal, and extremely self-conscious.

"She's horribly sentimental," he said.

"I see it's one of those cases . . ."

"How d'you mean?"

"She thinks you and she were made for one another."

"Oh! . . ." He considered. "I believe she dóes. It's awful, isn't it? She's shockingly touchy."

"Can you wonder? Look at the position she has to keep up. Being a gentleman's lady friend——"

He burst out laughing; and she was struck afresh by what she remembered about him years ago: the physical ease and richness flowing out through voice and gestures, a bountiful-ness of nature that drew one, irrespective of what he had to offer.

"I used to see you—quite a long time ago—didn't I?" he said shyly. "At home or somewhere?"

"Yes. I used to come to tea with Marigold. *Ages* ago. I didn't think you'd remember me."

"Well, I do. At least I wasn't absolutely sure for the first moment. . . . I've got an awful memory for names. . . ." He paused; but she said nothing. I won't tell him my name. "And you've changed," he added.

"Have I?"

They smiled at each other.

"Got thin," he suggested, a little shyly.

"Oh, well! . . . Last time we met properly I was a great big bouncing flapper. I hadn't fined down, as the saying goes."

"Well, you've done that all right now." He looked her over with a warm blue eye, and she saw an image of herself in his mind—fined down almost to the bone, thin through the hips and shoulders, with thin well-shaped cream-coloured hands, with a face of pronounced planes, slightly crooked, and a pale smoothly-hollowed cheek, and a long full mouth going to points, made vermilion. No hat, hair dark brown, silky, curling up at the ends. Safely dressed in these tweeds. Not uninterest-ing: even perhaps . . .? "All those charming plump girls I used to know," he said, "they've all dwindled shockingly."

"Has Marigold dwindled?"

"Mm—not exactly. You couldn't quite say that. But she's sort of different. . . ."

"How?"

He reflected, swallowing the last of his toast and marmalade.

"Oh, I don't know. . . . Got a bit older and all that, you know."

"More beautiful?"

"Well, if you can call it—— Haven't you seen her lately then?"

"Not for years. In fact, not since her wedding."

She glanced at him. "I think that was the last time I saw you too. . . ."

"I remember."

"Do you? We didn't speak."

"No, we didn't."

She looked away. A bubble of tension seemed to develop and explode between them. He watched me from the other side of the room. I thought once or twice we looked at each other, but he was too busy, caught up in his own world, to come near: sleek, handsome-looking in his wedding-clothes, being an usher, being the son of the house, laughing with a glass of champagne in his hand, surrounded by friends, by relations. . . . And Nicola was there too, in an enormous white hat. I was still in the chrysalis; engaged unimpressively, without a *Times* announcement, to Ivor, and my clothes were wrong: a subsidiary guest, doing crowd work on the outskirts, feeling inferior, up from the country.

"I follow her career in the *Tatler*," she said. She smiled, thinking how often the face, the figure, almost freakishly individual, had popped up on the page in Etty's sitting-room, sharply arresting the attention among all the other inheritors of renown: the co-lovelies, co-dancers, racers, charity performers, popular producers of posh children: Lady Britton at Newmarket, at Ascot, at the point to point, at the newest night-club, the smartest cocktail bar, the first night of ballet, opera; stepping ashore at Cowes, basking on the Lido, sitting behind the butts, wheeling her very own pram in the Park, entertaining a week-end party at her country home; Lady

Britton with her dogs, her pet monkey, her Siamese cat, her husband. . . .

"Yes," he said, as if with a shrug, half-amused, half-cynical, "she does seem to be something of a public figure."

One never saw him or Nicola in the gossip columns. Some people seem to lose their news value with marriage, some to acquire it. Nicola, that once sensation, appeared to have faded out. What is the clue to this?

"She's a restless creature," he said. He drank some coffee and looked uncertainly out of the window.

"Is she happy?"

"Happy? Oh, well . . ." He raised his eyebrows, and made a faint grimace, as if the question were pointless or beyond him altogether. "She seems all right. She was always determined to enjoy life, wasn't she?"

"Yes, she was."

"So I suppose she does. Or doesn't it follow? . . ." He laughed slightly. "But to tell you the truth I haven't looked into it very closely. Brothers don't generally know much about their sisters, do they?"

"I suppose you don't feel romantic about her," she said, smiling. "I always did. In fact, the way we felt about the whole lot of you! . . . You were fairly drenched in glamour. Especially you."

"Me? Good God!" He burst into such a shout of laughter that the other occupants of the car peered round their partitions to look at him. "You're pulling my leg."

"No, I assure you. You floated in a rosy veil. Marigold was always feeding us up with accounts of you, and everything you did sounded *so* superior and exciting. You didn't seem real at all—just a beautiful dream. Of course it was a very long time ago. One gets over these things." She smiled, meeting the look in his eye—the kindled interest, the light expectation of flirtation. I can do this, I can be this amusing person till Tulverton; because after that we shan't meet again. The shutter will snap down between our worlds once more. . . . He's wondering about me. . . . A person with thoughts you don't dream of, going into the country I shan't tell you why. . . .

"Well," he said, sitting back. "I've done a number of things off and on over which I prefer to draw a veil—but I swear I've never floated about in a rosy one."

"How do you know what you've done? It's all in the mind of the beholder—*We* don't know what we look like. We're not just ourselves—we're just a tiny nut of self, and the rest a complicated mass of unknown quantities—according to who's looking at us. A person might be wearing somebody else's hated aunt's Sunday black taffeta, or look like a pink blancmange that once made somebody else sick—without knowing it. . . . Or—oh, endless possibilities."

"I see," he said seriously, looking first at her, then down at himself. "It hadn't occurred to me. Even a pair of brown plus fours. . . . Could they be so unstable?"

"Oh, yes. How do you know how they might look to Lucy, for instance? . . . Once I had a simple ordinary frock, not very nice, with rows of pearl buttons on it—and someone I knew turned pale when he saw it and rushed trembling away. I had to change. But I can't just have been wearing a frock with pearl buttons, can I?"

"Good God! Did he explain?"

"No. He didn't know why. He thought it was the buttons, but he wasn't sure. He went to a psycho-analyst but he never discovered."

"What a frightfully sensitive chap he must have been!"

"Yes, he was."

"Are all your friends interesting like that?" He leaned forward over the table, his eyes teasing her in a way she remembered. "I do wish I knew the people you knew. My life's terribly humdrum."

"Is it? That's hard to believe. What is your life?"

"Oh—just a City man. I left the army, you know. Three years ago."

She suggested rather nervously:

"And—you're married?"

"Yes, married into the bargain. Three years."

"I saw about it in the papers."

"Married man, City man. What could be more hum-drum?"

"Well, it depends——"

"I dare say. . . ."

She glanced at him. He was looking out of the window. The warm, trivial, provocative play of his interest over her had been suddenly withdrawn. A hint of moodiness about him, a flatness in his voice struck an echo; and in a flash she remembered the sculpturing moonlight, their voices dropping out on to the dark, answering each other in a dream. "I've seen you dancing with somebody very beautiful." His flat reply: "Oh, yes, isn't she?" "I dare say she's as stupid as an owl," he said moodily. These things of course he wouldn't remember, but I do. They had retained their meaningless meaning; were frozen unalterably in their own element, like flowers in ice. She came down the stairs in a white dress and held up her hand to signal to him; whereupon he left me and they met far away from me, the other side of the hall. Even then there had seemed a confusion in the images—a feeling of seeing more than was there to see: the shadow of the shape of things to come. Or was that nonsense? But he had married Nicola Maude: just as I knew then he would.

His face was turned towards her again now, in rather a tentative way, as if he might be going to ask: "You're married too, aren't you?" or some such question; which to prevent she said quickly:

"Don't you like being in the City?"

He answered in the conventional tone of mild disparagement:

"Oh—it's not so bad. It's boring sometimes, but other times it's not such a bad game. Anyway, it's the only way that presented itself of turning a necessary penny. And now that my outstanding abilities have raised me to the position of partner I give myself an occasional day off—which helps to relieve the tedium. To-day, for instance."

"I suppose you're going to Meldon?"

"Yes, going to murder a few pheasants. I meant to go down last night, but it was too thick. The woods ought to be looking good. . . . You going home, too?"

"Yes. . . . Yes, I'm going home. Just for a few days."

"D'you often come down?"

"No—not very often really. No, I don't." She stopped, feeling stubborn, choked by the usual struggle of conflicting impulses: to explain, to say nothing; to trust, to be suspicious; lightly to satisfy natural curiosity; to defy it with furious scorn and silence; to let nobody come too near me. . . .

There was a flat, weighted silence. He offered her a cigarette out of his smart gold case, struck a match for her. She watched his hand as he lit his own. The fingers were long and nervous; a ring with a blue engraved stone on the left-hand little finger; a well-shaped hand, not a very strong one. She said:

"Last time we met you told me to read *Tristram Shandy*."

"And did you?"

"Yes, of course." She smiled. "I started the very next day." It was clear as yesterday in memory: Kate gone to the Hunt Ball with the Heriots, me reading in bed, holding little brown calf Volume I. with a thrill of emotion, thinking: "I'm not bereft, I've something too": not *Tristram Shandy*, but a link with the grown-up world, the world of romance—of Rollo. "I was awfully disappointed and puzzled. I'm afraid I gave it up. But last year I tried again—and I enjoyed it a lot."

"Good!" he said. He seemed pleased and amused. "My favourite idea of heaven is still a place where there's a new volume every three months."

"I suppose you know it's one of the things men try to make one feel inferior about? They say only a man can appreciate it properly. Like old brandy."

"Do they?" His eyebrow lifted, he had an expression of humorous flirtatious deprecation. "Well, naturally I'd subscribe to that. I mean I couldn't be left out of a thing like that, could I? All the same, one mustn't be bigoted. I'd be prepared to say that every rule has an exception: and you may be it."

"Thank you so much."

"Not at all. I must have been perspicacious enough to detect it years ago." After a pause he added, "What a good memory you've got."

She sighed.

"For the old times—yes, I seem to remember everything. When one's young a little goes such a very long way. It's like being on a rather empty road with a few signposts simply shouting at you and a few figures looming out at you larger than life. At least, it was like that for me. One has so little and one expects so much."

He did not reply.

"Were you like that?" she said.

He said slowly:

"More or less, I suppose. I was awfully enthusiastic and foolish, you know, and enjoyed everything like mad . . . But I don't know . . . I've always been an idle sort of bloke . . . drifting along with the stream, knocking up against things. I don't actually remember my youth frightfully clearly . . . Just one or two things. . . .

"The way I made bricks out of straw! . . . It's staggering to look back on."

He glanced at her, glanced away again, said finally:

"I think you must have been rather a peculiar young creature. I thought so at the time."

"What time?"

"The time we talked. . . . Didn't we?" He hesitated, diffident. "At a dance we had . . . when I found you on the terrace. . . . Didn't I?"

"Oh—do you remember that?"

"I seem to. To the best of my recollection you were a thought depressed; and we talked about life."

"Oh dear! Yes, we did. I always did if I got half a chance. But how extraordinary!"

"What?"

"You remembering."

"You don't, then?"

"Yes. Oh, yes. Awfully well."

"Well, then, why shouldn't I?"

Meeting his eyes, she laughed and shook her head. She could think of nothing to say. He stubbed out his cigarette and gave Lucy a pat.

"But what I notice," she went on, feeling slightly perturbed, disorientated, as if she must re-establish a more impersonal basis, "is that things that have happened more recently aren't nearly so vivid. It's all a blur. Houses I've lived in—people I've been with. . . . There seems a kind of shutter down over a lot of things—although they should be more real. No images come. . . ." The difficulty of remembering Ivor with precision; or that cottage we had. . . .

"It's age creeping on," he said. "That's what it is. I suffer from the same thing myself. Though I shouldn't have expected *you* to, yet awhile."

That's the way he treated me last time. . . . She noticed a faint touch of grey at the edge of his thick chestnut hair, above the ears, a suspicion of reddening in his ruddy complexion. He must be thirty-five at least, and in the end he would look like his father. She said:

"I suppose it *is* age. Impressions pile up faster than you can sort them, and everything dims down and levels out. Not to speak of there being a good many things one wants to forget . . . so one does."

"Yes, there's that." He nodded; and after a moment said seriously: "Do you mind the idea of getting old?"

"Terribly. Do you?"

"Terribly, I'm afraid. Teeth dropping out, wrinkles, fat and slow and pompous. No more feeling enthusiastic and expectant. No more—anything."

"Yes." No more making love, did he mean? "And feeling you've missed something important when it's too late."

He nodded ruefully.

"It's the principle of the thing I object to. Being stalked down and counted out without a single word to say in the matter."

"I know. In a trap, from the very start. Born in it, in fact."

He said with a faint smile:

"I don't suppose we're quite the first people to resent it, do you?"

"No. And sometimes I think it may not be as bad as all that—that the worst is now, in the apprehension of it . . . and actually we'll just slip into it without a struggle, and accept it quite peacefully. . . ." After all, Dad had done this, and most people who grew old. . . . "We shan't long for our time over again."

"Don't you think so?" He stared out of the window.

"I think it. I don't feel it. But very occasionally I get a hint—that one day I might be going to feel it. I suddenly see the *idea* of it . . . like getting a glimpse of a place a long, long way off. You only see it for a second now and then in one particular weather; but you're walking towards it and you know it's where you're going to get in the end."

"That's a better way to look at it." He still stared out of the window. "I dare say you're right too. It *should* be like that. I expect it will . . . at least, if we've had a fair run for our money." He turned to look at her intently, and said with sudden emphasis: "And that's up to us, isn't it?"

"Yes."

"One's apt to put the blame on—other people, circumstances: which is ridiculous."

"And unsatisfactory."

"You've found that too, have you?"

Something about the way he said it startled her vaguely: as if he were insisting on an answer—a true one. What was in his mind? Wasn't he getting a run for his money? What did he want? He didn't look the kind of person to be gnawed by dreams and desires beyond his compass. . . . So prosperously handsome, so easy-mannered, so obviously pleasing to women. . . .

"I'm afraid I'm not very grown-up," he said suddenly.

"Nor am I."

"I should have said you were."

"Oh, *no*!" There was a pause; and she added nervously: "I've noticed people with children don't generally mind so much . . . about age, I mean. They seem to feel less anxious about time."

"Do they? I suppose they do," he said. "I expect it's a good thing to have children."

"You haven't got any?"

"No," he said. "Have you?"

"No."

They made it a joke, and laughed. . . . All the same, it was surprising he hadn't produced an heir. Couldn't, wouldn't Nicola? . . . or what?

"Then," she said, "there are the pleasures of the intellect. They're said to be lasting. We must cultivate our intellects."

"Too late," he said. "One ought to make at least a beginning in youth, and I omitted to do so. The fact is, I don't care much about the intellect. I'm afraid the scope of my pleasures is rather limited."

"Really?"

"Confined in fact entirely to those of the senses."

"Oh, I see. . . ." She answered his odd comically inquiring look with a lift of the eyebrows. "Well, I suppose they're all right. Only they're apt to pall."

"Oh, *are* they?"

"I was thinking of cake." She sighed. "It used to be my passion—especially chocolate, or any kind of large spicy bun. Now, it's beginning to mean less . . . much less."

He leaned back, laughing; the tension dissolved again.

"Hallo," he said, "the gasworks. We're nearly there. I've never known this journey go so quickly."

The steward advanced, pencil poised over pad.

"Two, sir?" He smiled, obsequiously arch.

"Yes," said Rollo.

"No," she said quickly.

"Please. . . ."

He scrawled out the double bill and shortly moved on, gratified by his tip. She laid a shilling in front of Rollo.

"Thank you," she said.

"Aren't I allowed to stand you one cup of coffee?"

"Yes, certainly, with pleasure—any time you invite me. But please take this now—for luck."

"I dislike feminist demonstrations," he said.

"So do I." She picked up the shilling and put it in his palm.

He looked at it and said finally:

"Right!" He flipped it in the air, caught it and slipped it into his breast pocket.

"And I'll hold you to that," he said.

"What?"

"That cup of coffee."

The train was slowing into Tulverton. The familiar roofs and chimneys, the clock tower slid by, etherealised in the first soft gold breaking of sunlight. In another few minutes they were alighting on the platform. There stood Benson the chauffeur, brass-buttoned, capped, dignified, greeting him with respectful fatherliness, looking exactly as he used to look twenty years ago fetching Marigold from dancing-class: a kindly man of character. Jovially Rollo hailed him. A porter was already dealing nimbly with the baggage. In the aura of cap-touching recognition and prompt service surrounding him, he appeared as with a spotlight on him, larger than life-size; the other occupants of the platform a drab background to him. Jocelyn would find in the scene a fine text for a sermon of snorting moral indignation; Colin would observe with his

best sardonic lip on, and afterwards act it; Anna would detach
herself and stroll off to look at the automatic machines. . . .
But I with my capacity for meeting everybody half-way stand
meekly within his orbit and feel gratified by his attentions.

"Good-bye, Rollo."

He turned towards her quickly, as if the use of his Christian
name had moved him.

"You're being met?" He took the hand she held out.

"No. Bus. I must fly."

"You'll do nothing of the sort. I'll drop you in the car,
of course. Where is it—Little Compton? It's practically on
my way. Here, porter, another bag."

Disregarding a feeble protest, he seized and handed over
her inferior suitcase, swept her along in his wake and installed
her beside him in the family Sunbeam, beneath an overpowering fur rug.

Away they glided, out of Tulverton through the narrow
high street, past the market square, past the war memorial,
between the more outlying rows of little red and yellow brick
boxes, past the Baptist Chapel, past the gasometers, beyond the
last lamps, over the bridge and skirting the duck pond—relic
of a rustic Tulverton, long vanished—out along the damp,
flat, field-and-allotment bordered, blue-flashing road that led
to the old village.

"This feels very grand," she said. "I do wish I had a car."

"D'you live in London?"

"Yes, I do."

"A car's almost more trouble than it's worth in London.
I find mine sits eating its head off in the garage most of the
time."

And of course that's the reason why I don't bother to
get one.

"Every time I come along this road there's a fresh outbreak
of bungalows," she said. "*Look* at that one! '*Idono*' . . . If
only I had the energy to set fire to every one of them in the
middle of the night . . . except that they'd go and put up

something worse. There's one somewhere called '*Oodathortit*.'"

He laughed.

"Don't you mind about them?"

He looked at her in some surprise.

"I suppose I do rather . . . when I look at them. Nasty little brutes."

"You ought to mind about them."

"Ah, but I never do anything I ought."

"England gets squalider and squalider. So disgraced, so ignoble, so smug and pretentious . . . and nobody minds enough to stop it."

"Nobody can if it wants to."

She felt his mild obstinacy hardening against her, deliberate, refusing to be lectured, quite good-humoured, half-teasing. He went on:

"It's all very interesting and degraded, I agree. But what's one to do?"

"Can't people be educated——?"

"But they have been!" he said triumphantly. "This is the glorious result: Art homes."

Oh, well, sit back in one's luxurious car then under one's great expensive, tickling fur rug and ignore it all—give one's mind to important things instead: like shooting pheasants. . . . She was dumb.

She stared out of the window and the flitting bungalows stared back at her, brazen, cocksure.

"I'd—just like to blow the whole thing up."

"Oh, anarchy! But that's not very constructive, is it?" He's laughing at me. . . . "You ought to have a remedy." Getting his own back. . . . "Personally I subscribe to the Society for the Preservation of Rural England, I think it's called, so you see I do more than you. . . . It's a magnificent object and I'm all for it. . . . I don't grudge a penny of it." He lit a cigarette. "And furthermore," he said, "I'm all for the League of Nations. But if people want war they'll have war."

"I see you're what's called a realist," she said, looking out of the window, playing with the hand-rest. People like him . . . well-padded, cynical. . . . Phrases from Colin and the rest clotted and obstructed her head, like lumps of used cotton-wool. . . .

He laughed quietly.

Some inner shock at the sound made her look round at him. What's it all about? . . . His eye was fixed upon her, alight, hard, with a sort of unconscious wariness and determination. . . . He's enjoying himself. . . . He's . . . he wants. . . . Her head whirled, snatching at questions, dissolving, her eyes stayed riveted on his. . . . What is it? . . . Fighting, subduing me. . . . What'll happen? He might hit me, kiss me. . . . She dropped her eyes suddenly. It was all over in two seconds. After a pause, she heard him say pleasantly:

"I'm afraid you must find a desert island."

"I don't want to."

I don't want to argue any more, or assert different views. *Please.* Forget about it; let everything be soothing, harmonious again. I don't know anything and I don't want to think now, to disagree with you. . . .

"What's the matter?" he said suddenly.

"Nothing." She wrenched out a narrow smile and presented it to him. "Can I have a cigarette?"

"Rather. So sorry. Dozens." His voice was kind, perturbed.

I shall cry. . . . Oh, God! God!

"The thing is really——" She applied herself elaborately to the match he held out.

"Mm?" He went on holding the match with care and patience.

"Why I'm coming home is—because my father is very ill——"

He was shocked. His hand went impulsively out towards her on the rug.

He's sorry now he had that argument, thinks no wonder I was a bit touchy, tiresome. . . .

"I say, I'm most terribly sorry. Why didn't you tell me? How awful for you. . . ." Such sincere sympathy, such a warm solicitous voice. . . . "I do hope you'll find it isn't so bad."

"Yes. Thank you. I expect he'll be all right. I mean—I feel he may be. . . ." I've betrayed him to Rollo . . . to excuse myself, to re-establish myself in Rollo's favour.

"I expect he will be, honestly I do. Daddy was most frightfully ill last winter—heart and kidneys and God knows what —all the works. They said he'd never be able to shoot or fish again, and have to live in an arm-chair if he ever left his bed again—and now you should see him. He's as right as rain— practically."

"Is he? I'm so glad." She could meet his eyes once more and smile. The shameful, half-hysterical emotion subsided. He's not to be sorry for me. "Do give him my love if he remembers me." Disarming of him so unselfconsciously to call Sir John Daddy.

"Rather. I will."

"Give everybody my love—specially your mother."

"I will indeed. I believe Marigold's coming down this week-end."

"Oh, Marigold. . . . How lovely it would be to see her again——"

"Well, why not? It isn't impossible, is it?"

She hesitated a minute.

"No, it's no good. . . . It's so long ago and——"

Beyond Benson's immobile cap, neck and shoulders appeared the village green, a cluster of cottages, the farm. There wasn't much more time. She said with an effort:

"You see your mother is a sort of symbol to me. . . . I can't quite explain. . . . When I was a child I wanted her approbation. She's stayed at the back of my mind—as a sort of standard for suitable behaviour. . . . Often,—when I was in the middle of an upheaval—a few years ago, she used to appear before me like a reproachful vision." She laughed. "Don't look so startled. It's quite irrational. But even now, when I've more or less—after enormous efforts—given up minding what people think of me, it would be distressing to feel I'd—I'd disappointed her. . . . Even though—perhaps—her idea of what's a—a good kind of conduct—might be—probably is—quite different—in some cases—from mine nowadays. . . . Do you see?"

"Yes," he said, after a pause. "I see. All the same I think you underestimate Mummy's wisdom. She's a strange woman. She lives by the most rigid standards herself—and has almost complete tolerance for everybody else. It's only that she doesn't let on. . . ."

"Yes. Yes, I can believe that's true. She's one of the people who've chosen a behaviour long ago and stick to it." Like the Queen's toques—unfashionable, monotonous: but reliable, distinguished, right.

"Besides," he said, "if she likes a person she doesn't change. I've never know her to. And I believe you were always a favourite of hers."

"Was I?"

Once again, a start of surprise went through her, not at the fact, if fact it were, but at his calm statement of it. A hundred questions stirred. I was—am still—spoken of? Rollo listened?—asked questions about me?

The turn of the drive was in sight. Benson was slowing down and changing gear.

"Tell him to stop at the gate," she said hurriedly. "Not drive in."

"Are you sure?"

"Yes, truly. You see, the noise . . . it might disturb. . . ."

"I see. Of course." He tapped on the window.

But it wasn't so much that. . . .

"Well, give him your bag. Let him carry it up."

"Gracious no, I wouldn't dream of it." She jumped out and seized it. "It's very light." Not a shadow of this meeting must colour my arrival. "Please——" She gave him her hand. "Good-bye, Rollo. Thank you for kindness."

He kept her hand in his, leaning forward. Benson stood discreetly behind the door, holding it back.

"I do hope so frightfully he's all right."

"Yes. Yes, thank you."

"I do wish there was something I could do."

"Oh, no . . . it's quite all right. It's sweet of you, but please don't think at all about it. . . ."

"Might I ring up? Would it be a bore?"

"It wouldn't be a bore, only *please* don't. . . . Yes, do—if you like, I mean . . . if you think of it."

"Then I will. I'd awfully like to know. We all would."

"It's very nice of you."

He let go of her hand, looking suddenly a trifle embarrassed.

"Who would I ask for?—I mean—if I wanted to get hold of you? I'm so bad at names, I never remember."

"Oh!"—she hesitated, her colour rose. "Olivia Curtis—I'm still that. . . . I mean—I *have* been something else—I've gone back to that—Good-bye."

She took her case and hurried up the drive without looking back, hearing behind her, through a perturbed flurry, the soft mounting roar of the car as it swept him on and away.

II

KATE was at the front door to meet her.

"Hallo."

"Hallo. Whose car was that stopped at the gate?"

"The Spencers'." Olivia went in past her and put her bag down in the hall.

"The Spencers'?"

"Mm. . . . I met Rollo in the train coming down and he gave me a lift."

"Oh. . . . I saw it from the window. I suppose he's come down for the shooting."

"I suppose so. Where's Mother?"

"With him." She looked Olivia sharply over in the familiar way, thinking: she's altered the coat. Not bad.

"No change, I suppose?" She said it in the casual way Kate would require of her, her heart beginning to beat thickly, in dread and anticipation.

"Not that I know of."

"How long've you been here?"

"Since Tuesday."

Four days. And not a word to me. Did they think I'd be hysterical, or a disturbing influence or what?

There hung his old hat, his cap, on their pegs, his woolly scarf and brown fleece-lined gloves folded on the table beneath them: poignant objects. They seemed to have taken on a life of their own; to be dumb, dark, monstrously urgent questions: as dogs are whose masters have gone away.

From the top of the stairs a muted voice called down:

"Is that Olivia?"

Down floated Mrs. Curtis, smiling, to kiss her.

"Mum——" Tears sprang, her throat tightened. But her mother said with cheerful calmness:

"It's nice to see you, dear. I didn't expect you for another half-hour. Especially with such a fog in London. I made sure your train would be late. What time did you get in?"

"Quite punctually, I think. But I'm early because I ran into Rollo Spencer on Tulverton platform, and he gave me a lift out."

"Did he? Mr. Spencer? How very kind of him. It's quite out of his way, too."

"I know. He insisted."

"A good three miles. Did he drive in?"

"No, he dropped me at the gate."

"I thought I heard a car. I suppose he was on his way to Meldon?"

"Yes. For a shoot."

"Ah, yes." She wafted Rollo towards his home, his recreations, with a gracious nod. Apprehension sank away again.

The lurking threats of change, of disaster, retreated before Mother's impregnable normality. Rather pale, rather drawn and dark about the eyes, but neat, but fresh, erect, composed as ever, preoccupied with the supervision—in retrospect—of the arrival, checking up on detail with nearly all her customary minuteness and relish. . . . Mother was being wonderful.

"Did you get plenty of breakfast?"

"Yes. I had some coffee on the train."

"Nothing to eat?"

"I didn't want anything. You know I hardly ever have breakfast."

"I know you're a silly girl. No wonder you're so scraggy." She looked her daughter over with dissatisfaction.

"Oh! Must we go through this old hoop again?" Olivia flung herself down on the oak settle, and studied her shoes.

"How is Etty?" Mrs. Curtis passed on smoothly.

"Fast asleep, I expect. She was snuggling down nicely again when I left."

"Does Etty ever do anything but sleep?"

"Never—in the mornings."

"Hmm——"

The special indulgent Etty voice was no longer used. Etty had not married—not even unfortunately. She both went to bed and stayed in bed too late. The whole thing was discreditable, suspicious. No longer was it tenderly remarked that Etty was such a frail little creature. She was as strong as anybody else: the trouble was that she'd been spoilt, she'd never had any backbone.

"If Etty would see to it that that woman of hers, Mrs. Binns, isn't it? who appears so very deaf over the telephone, came at a reasonable hour and cooked you both a good nourishing breakfast, if she's competent to do so, which I doubt. . . . How can you expect to do a proper morning's work on an empty stomach?"

"I don't do a proper morning's work—but it's no good putting the blame on my stomach. However full it was it wouldn't persuade people to let Anna photograph 'em, or pay their bills when she had——"

"You don't know——"

Olivia giggled, drumming her heels. Mrs. Curtis gave her a searching glance. No, not satisfactory, not sensible. . . . Not enough to eat, pretending to be warm enough in ridiculous underclothes. . . . Probably a mistake, this being Etty's p.g., though at the time it had seemed such an excellent plan: Etty just orphaned, with her little house and legacy, Olivia difficult, refusing to come back and live at home. . . . But if Olivia was out, did Etty know where? with whom? . . . when she'd be in? Never. Fatuously cooing into the receiver. . . . No attempt whatsoever at even the most tactful supervision. Idiotic . . . or deep? Slippery anyway.

"I must go back," she said briskly. "Dr. Martin will be here any minute—and Nurse must go off."

"Can I see him?" said Olivia.

"Oh, not just now, dear. He's having a little sleep. Later on you can just put your head in and peep at him. When he wakes up I'll tell him you're here. That'll cheer him up. Kate, dear, I was wondering if you wouldn't perhaps like to go for a little stroll with Nurse——?"

"Oh, were you wondering that?"

"I just thought it would be nice for her, instead of her going alone. You could take her the pretty walk. I tried to tell her yesterday how to go, but I don't think she quite took in it."

"I don't expect she wanted to. I'm sure she loathes pretty walks. She's all right. I've been quite enough of a pal for one day. I've already promised to cut out an evening dress for her. Turquoise blue satin. Scrumptious!"

"Oh, well—Fancy! I wonder what she wants it for. You wouldn't think she had many occasions to wear turquoise blue satin."

"I expect a grateful patient presented it—to match her eyes. He's going to take her out to dinner in it."

"Who is? Is he?" Mrs. Curtis was confused.

"A bottle of bubbly and a topping show," said Olivia. "Oo! I wish I was her. Is she a peach, Kate?"

"No. More of a jolly fine girl."

"Oh, well . . ." said Mrs. Curtis. "I must say it seems to me a bit cool to ask you to cut it out for her."

"It's all right, Mum, I offered. I'd rather cut out every stitch she wears for the next five years than go for a walk with her."

"Oh, well——" Really, this exaggeration and so forth . . . "Just as you like, dear. There's a fire in the schoolroom. And, Olivia, if you run through and just ask Ada she'll make you some bovril. She and Violet have been so good with the trays and everything. They're so anxious to help——"

Mrs. Curtis reflected an instant, then set off energetically up the stairs again.

"I don't want any bovril," said Olivia, low.

"Want must be your master," said Kate. "Can't you stop kicking against the pricks for *one* morning? Ada's to make it and Violet's to bring it up and we're to drink it and we'll all be doing our bit. I'll go and order it. Meet you in the schoolroom."

"Put a swig of something in mine. Port or sherry or something."

But the door had swung to.

Olivia went upstairs—ascending, ascending into the current of power. . . . In her mother's wake it seemed to flow; to concentrate at the silent threshold of his door. . . . He mustn't cough, I can't—won't hear it. But there was no sound, no odour of sickness, and the door seemed guarded. A strong resistant life was in that blank white panelled shutter, a watchful eye in the wink of the brass door-knob: Nothing shall pass here, said she from within. By the power of domestic habit, by the compulsion of household routine, death shall be elbowed out: there shall be no room for it. By the virtue of family reunion, by the protective assertion of common habits of speech, of movement and expression; by the serene impartiality of my outwardly distributed attention, by the colossal force of my inward single concentration—death shall be prevailed against. Meals shall be punctual, sheets aired, fires lit, bovril prepared and drunk, all at my bidding; and therefore nothing shall alter, not one unit of the structure shall collapse. My reserves are barely tapped yet: they shall be sufficient. By the exercise of my will. . . .

Briskly, the door of the bathroom was flung open, and out rustled a white figure, plump and crisp, across her path. Nurse. Ah, there it was, the lurking symbol, the menacing reassurance. . . . It was here, large as life, blocking the light, the efficient white flag of danger.

"Good-morning." Through the open bathroom door she saw bottles, white enamel vessels, and, on the floor, the shape of an oxygen cylinder, sinister. . . . Yes, it was here, all around. . . .

"Good-morning." The nurse held out a cool dry hand. "Are you the other daughter I've heard about?"

"Yes, I am." Eager, ingratiating, feeling sick all of a sudden. . . . Compact, short shape, broad face in its frame of white, clear full blue eye appraising her, fresh cheek, good teeth, lips strongly modelled, pale: a nurse's face, lesbian face. She devoured all in one glance. We are delivered into your hands.

"It's nice you could come. Your mother will be ever so glad to have you." Cool voice, with an edge of sub-nasal gentility.

"How is he?"

"Oh, he's quite comfortable. He's having a little snooze just now. I expect you'll be wanting to peep at him later."

"Oh, yes . . . please . . . if I might." Placate her, be obedient.

"I expect you could."

"Is he—I suppose he's—is he awfully ill, d'you think?"

"Well—pneumonia's always a nasty thing, isn't it? And at his age."

"Yes, of course . . ."

"Still, we must hope for the best. He's a good patient, I must say. Not like some. Of course he's been used to illness, hasn't he?—Makes a difference."

"Yes."

"Isn't it a glorious day? I was just going out for a little stroll round."

"Were you? Good. It's too lovely out now. I expect you're longing for some fresh air. You must be so tired being up all night. . . ."

"Oh, not too bad. Just a bit stale, you know."

"I'll see you later, then."

"Yes, that's right. Bye-bye."

Used to illness. Pneumonia's a nasty thing. We must hope for the best.

In the schoolroom, Kate was already bending over the table with pins in her mouth, the cutting-out scissors in her hand, and portions of blue material and paper pattern spread around her. She murmured through the pins, without looking up:

"I'll just slash about and she can do the rest. I'm damned if I'll fit turquoise satin over her fat bottom."

"Fat bottoms to you, Mrs. Emery—Don't trouble yourself, I beg. There'll be many only too pleased . . ."

Kate spun round with a jerk.

"God! I thought for a moment. . . . How d'you know how she speaks?"

"I've just been chatting in the passage."

"You nearly made me swallow ten pins." She bent once more over the table, and added: "Idiot."

Olivia flung herself down in the basket chair by the fire and lit a gasper.

"Still smoking like a chimney?" said Kate, through pins, beginning to cut.

"Rather, more than ever."

"How many do you get through a day?"

"Donno. It varies. Sometimes I do knock off for a day or two—if my morning cough gets too disgusting. Or if I'm short of cash."

"You simply choke up your inside with those foul fumes. No wonder you haven't any appetite. I believe that's what it is."

Cigarettes for supper, and a cup of coffee. Surprising how adequately they took the edge off one's hunger . . . how often, by oneself, when one couldn't be bothered to cook anything, or wanted to afford a movie instead. . . . Wouldn't Kate scold if she knew. . . .

"I suppose so. That, and the booze."

Above the scissors, Kate stole her a surreptitious glance. Nowadays it was apt to be a tricky business questioning Olivia. She was as touchy as could be. For the most part her immediate reaction was a sort of defiant irony, extremely boring. Anything would set her off, flaunting the no-lady pose, cracking low jokes—really awful ones— and God knows I'm no prude about language, not after eight years of Rob: but it does *not* suit females. Or else she'd simply hoot with laughter. Once, twice, dreadfully disconcertingly, she had burst into hysterical tears.

"We sex-starved women have cravings you comfortable wives and mothers don't dream of," remarked Olivia, blowing smoke-rings.

"And vice versa," said Kate tartly. She guided the crisp scissors in one unbroken line from edge to edge of the stuff.

After a pause, Olivia said:

"*She* seems to be bearing up all right."

"Who, Mother?"

"Mm. Full war paint."

Kate reflected. The words, the tone, conforming as they did to a filial convention of ribaldry for normal private occasions, wouldn't do just now—not in this crisis. Olivia showed a lack of sensibility. She said with seriousness, though without reproach:

"She hasn't had any sleep this week—not more than an hour or two. She's in and out of his room all night. She's simply amazing. I don't know how she does it. I haven't seen her fussed once."

"I suppose neither of you thought me worth informing till this morning?"

"Mother didn't want to take you away from your work if it could be helped. It was you she was thinking of."

"Oh, how very kind of her." She takes Mother's side nowadays.

"Of course we wanted you to come. . . ."

"I suppose it didn't occur to either of you I might have liked to see him before . . . I might have liked . . ." She stopped and bit hard into a thumb nail. "He and I've always got on all right. . . ."

"I know. . . . Of course. . . ." Kate was reasonable, irritated, distressed all at once. "Only you've said so often . . . You've often said it was difficult for you to get away, you were alone in the office or something."

Making that the excuse for not coming home, or cutting a visit short. . . . Oh, well. . . . That's enough of that.

"Is James coming?"

"No. Not at present, anyway. Mother didn't know what to do, but I advised not unsettling him if we could help it. She hasn't even told him. You know what he is. . . . Any excuse to be off. . . ."

What was James? He was a problem. The only male Curtis of this generation was rebellious, not inclined to conform, to settle. After the most brilliant conceit-inducing start at school, he had progressively disappointed; had failed to win the university scholarship which would have enabled him to defer the question of career for a time. Dispatched after this grave set-back to a mill-owning acquaintance of Mr. Curtis in Bristol to learn the business he had left without farewells at the end of six weeks; arriving at the front door at 1 a.m. after three days on the road, blistered, feverish, sullen. Natur-

ally that was the end of the Bristol experiment. Naturally his
wounded employer washed his hands. As for James, he explained nothing; and, though briefly bitter, not to say insolent,
about mills, voiced no preferences. At home he was disagreeable and spotty, refused all invitations to tennis parties and
dances, avoided everybody's eye, burst forth for day-long
solitary walks. In the evenings he sat in his bedroom, playing
Delius on his portable Decca and reading poetry: perhaps
writing it—nobody knew for certain: but he was known to
possess a thick furtive black copy-book. It was only a phase,
of course: boys did go like that. But it had seemed best, while
waiting for him to come on again, to send him to a French
family for a while. French was always useful; and then there
was a dark implication of the advantage of removing him
from the neighbourhood of Uncle Oswald, for whose society
he now showed an odd mingled distaste and fascination. And
then the discreet mixture of foreign emancipation and home
influence provided by Monsieur et Madame Latour of Fontainebleau might be just what was needed to soothe and settle him.
Certainly madame's elaborately eulogistic, maternally sympathetic, exquisitely penned letters about him appeared to
justify such a hope. As for James's own letters, though scanty
and reticent, they arrived regularly, contained no disquieting
P.SS. and altogether appeared the products of a normal English
youth accepting life as it was ordered for him.

But now and then Olivia remembered him that week-end
after his tramp from Bristol: sitting in the bathroom with
his trousers rolled up, soaking his swollen feet in a large bowl
of hot water and lysol; submitting to female ministrations,
silent, inhaling eucalyptus, drinking hot lemon, his masculinity
cast down, made ludicrous; his expression that of a performing
dog in a circus. He had made his gesture of independence, and
in the act of making it, he had let it crumble and be ridiculous.
Whatever savage amorphous plan for freedom had illumined
him at the start and driven him forth, he had, after all, come
home. He could do no other, he saw with incredulous rage.

He had proved nothing but his own futility, his servitude. He
would do no more. He would go into the mill. He would rot.
They had been tactful after the first shock; after the first
questions, they had attempted to conceal their profound
dismay. Nobody had brought him to book. He had been left
alone with his stubbornness and his hatred and his streaming
cold. To whom went the letters that he locked himself up to
write and took secretly to post? When the replies came, always
in the same small cramped hand, back deep, deep beneath its
surface his poor face had shrunk all day, so naked, so concealed,
fixed in a rigid frenzy, an agony of self-protection. He had
been alone. No friend had come with love and understanding
to cast forth his dumb spirit.

In the night, in London, unwillingly Olivia had thought
about him, banished him, seen him again; struck suddenly by
a crazy notion: that he now had no eyes. He had closed them,
sunk them; there were cobwebs over them. As a child he'd
had large eyes, intensely blue, of a notable shape and wild
brilliance. . . . Could I have helped him? . . . hit somehow on
the right word? . . .

Going once to his bedroom, on an impulse, the others all
out. . . . But he was not there. And oh, the room, so burdened
with him, stricken, sensual, poignant with his penned-up
mysterious youth, his harsh male unhappiness; the tidiness of
concealment everywhere, the locked drawers of the writing-
desk, the densely scribbled blotter, the poems of Eliot, Yeats,
Hopkins, Owen, the Elizabethan dramatists by his bed; the
Van Gogh landscape pinned up on the wall opposite, to comfort
him. . . . I didn't help. . . .

If Dad dies, they'll push him straight into the mill. . . .

"Kate, what do they think really? I mean, will he get
better . . . or not?"

"I don't know. I think he may."

"And we may know quite soon . . . to-day . . . ?"

"Probably." Kate went on pinning a piece of pattern to a
length of material. "In pneumonia, good nursing counts for

a lot, and he's certainly having the best of that. But of course it mostly depends now how his heart holds out."

"Have you seen him?"

"Oh, yes. These last two afternoons I've made Mother go out for half an hour, and sat with him."

"How does he seem? Is he dreadfully—uncomfortable?"

"Well, he's restless—and his cough hurts—but not too bad."

"Does he—does he talk to you?"

"Not much. Just occasionally. He wanders a bit."

"Does he. . . .?" She bit her thumb hard again. What does he talk about?—giving himself away . . . I don't want her to tell me.

"I've nursed pneumonia before. Rob had it, don't you remember? . . . the year after we were married,—when Priscilla was six weeks old?"

"I'd forgotten."

"And I fed her just the same all the time."

Kate laid down her scissors for the first time, smiled faintly, reminiscently.

Over her unconscious face spread the expression of her life, calm, yet half-rueful, just amused, just triumphant. Kate, that young, fresh, most virginal of virgins, was a shrewd matron, capable, experienced. What look is my life giving me? Any look? . . .

"I've never nursed any one. Once Ivor had a poisoned thumb, but I didn't nurse him. He was in such a stew he summoned his mother." She giggled. "So I went off to the seaside alone for the week-end. I stayed in a pub. It was late October, it was perfect. I didn't let them know where I was, and when I came back—my hat!—— How delicate he'd always been, and how he'd been a whole day alone in the house, and he might have had to have his arm off, and she knew someone who'd started with a boil on his nose and finally lost all his legs and arms and died raving. 'Ivor won't die,' I said. 'I'll try neglect, starvation, anything to oblige. I know you'd love to lay his death at my door. But Ivor's not the dying sort, though he does look so pale and wistful. He's tough—jolly tough. Like you.'"

Kate looked at her.

"You didn't really say anything of the sort, did you?" How hard her voice was,—unkind. . . . Poor Olivia. But after all . . . her husband; she would marry him. . . . She must have given him a time, despising him like that.

"No, I didn't really," said Olivia, after a silence. "I spend a lot of time devising these posthumous cracks."

"I hope they give you satisfaction," said Kate, and added, pinning busily: "D'you ever see him?"

"I saw him in Giulio's about a month ago. He was with a very powerful-looking middle-aged woman with a black Bohemian fringe and a cigarette holder and a deep motherly bosom. I think he must have been telling her about his unhappy married life. She gave me such a look."

"You didn't speak to him, did you?"

"Oh, yes. He said he was just off to France to write a novel. I expect she's got a villa there and she'll give him nourishing food till he's finished it. I said, 'I suppose it's about me,' but he said no, the girl in his book was short, with red hair and green eyes."

"Wasn't he embarrassed?"

"He didn't seem to be. . . . I don't know." Olivia was silent. "I wonder if that was a joke of his about the red hair. . . . I wouldn't put it past him. Damn! It never struck me. Perhaps he's one up."

"He deserves to be, I must say."

"What do you mean?"

"Well, how could you?"

"How could I what?"

"Go up to him like that—in a public place——"

"Why not?" She flushed darkly. "We're nothing to each other. Besides, it's much more civilised, isn't it? We haven't got a death-feud just because we're separated. Though I know you and Mother think we ought to have. . . . Makes it more *respectable*, I suppose."

Kate said nothing; and Olivia continued with bitter anger: "In a public place! . . . What a foul expression. You're as bad as Mother: ' Not in front of the servants.'"

Kate was a concentrated arc above the table and seemed not to have heard.

"Besides he knows Giulio's is one of my places. He knows I often go there with Anna or someone. I dare say he did it on purpose to make me feel beastly—bringing that antique cart-horse to glare at me,—just to see what I'd do."

"Keep your hair on, do. I'm not sticking up for him. I never could stand the man, as you know. . . . There, that's done, thank God." Kate flung down her scissors and stooped to pick up shreds and fragments from the floor; adding quietly, with her head under the table: "Only I just couldn't have done it myself, that's all. No offence meant."

Olivia sank back in her arm-chair and turned her face away. After a bit she said:

"Well, nor could I have—till I did it. So there. I can't explain . . . but that's just the worst of it." . . . Kate with her conventional, her sheltered successful life, tied to her husband by children and habit and affection and respect. . . . She couldn't possibly understand. . . . "He developed my nastiness from a mere seed into a great jungle. He made me so mean and bloody. . . . Well, I just am a bloody character, I suppose. And I always thought I was so nice."

"You're all right." What an idiotic way to talk. "Here, drink your bovril, I forgot it. It's getting cold." She brought the tray over from the window-seat, put it on the floor between them and sat down in the other basket-chair. They picked up their cups and began sipping.

"Only," said Kate, "as it was all so hopeless obviously from the start, I don't know why you don't want to snap out of it altogether. . . ."

"Why ' obviously '?" She fastened on the word—superior,

smug-sounding—stiffened inwardly. It hadn't been so obvious as all that, not by a long chalk. With his long-lashed greenish eyes, almond-shaped, his soft thick green-dark hair, the sweetness of his profile with its full lips and rounded chin, his pale-skinned, still-adolescent physical charm, his undergraduate's blend of verbal liveliness, shyness, sensitiveness, conceit: with all that, he'd been a natural person anyway to fall in love with.

"Well, no idea of doing any work or having a home or anything."

"He was too young."

And he was to have devoted his life to poetry. No good saying that to Kate. Those early poems, too clever, obscure, but with an individual something—they had promised, everybody said so. But the weakness in them was the weakness of his nature, basic and irremediable. They, like him, could never branch and toughen; but narrow, but dwindle and deteriorate, after the first graceful flowery outbreaking. I didn't help him. Nobody could, of course. . . . At least. . . . I think not. . . . She said with a sigh:

"We neither of us had the least idea about anything. How to behave or what things cost or how to set about anything. No practical technique whatever." His two hundred a year, my hundred had seemed any amount of money, for a start.

"I know. You never had. You always thought me earthy for saving up my pocket money." An old grievance soured Kate's voice.

"We're not all born with our wits about us like you, my love. But I bet I could give even you some tips nowadays about how to live on nothing at all. One learns if one must. But in those days I thought the Lord provided for people like us."

"One of you was to make daisy-chains, while the other coaxed the shy wild things to come around you."

"Exactly."

He was romance, culture, æsthetics, Oxford, all I wanted then. Oxford had been a potent draught, grabbed at and gulped down without question. To live the remainder of one's life in that condition,—towery, branchy, cuckoo-echoing, bell-swarmed—had seemed the worthy summit of human happiness.

"We just shouldn't have married, that's all."

"No, of course not."

"Of course not, of course not. . . . It's all very well to be so frightfully shrewd and sensible about other people's arrangements. You know as well as I do it's mostly luck. And one's first choice is more or less a matter of—of picking blindfold—practically at random, isn't it?"

"Sometimes."

"'Sometimes'! Don't you be so jolly superior. Rob wasn't your first fancy, was he? Supposing you'd married—the person who was . . .?"

"Well, I didn't," said Kate sharply; and she coloured, after all these years, and put on the look that accused one of tactless insensibility. It *was* rather a shame to bring it up. No doubt it was true too that Kate would have made a go of it, whoever she'd married. . . . That was her nature; that was just the difference.

"What we should have done was to live together for a bit. Then we'd have had a chance of discovering . . ." How short-lived desire could be; how there could be nothing, nothing left, overnight almost; only reluctance, heaviness, resentment, only the occasional, corrupted revival of excitement, and tears and nerves, and the unforgivable words, and the remorse. . . . "But you wouldn't have approved of that either, would you?"

"I shouldn't have cared what you'd done," said Kate with a yawn. "It was none of my business. The point is, *you* wouldn't have approved of it. It's no good pretending you were so frightfully unconventional and free-lovish—in those days anyway."

Olivia was silent. It was true enough. And the trouble is I'm the same now really: wanting to make something important enough to be for ever.

"Oh, no," she said finally. "I was all for regularity. I

must say for poor Ivor he had some qualms—but I hypnotised him We were in love so we must be married. I never thought of anything else. I suppose one never gets away from a good upbringing."

"One never gets away from being an idiot," said Kate. "*Not* speaking personally."

"I must say, it's funny considering how sure you all were it would turn out badly how squawky you all were when I left him. You ought to have been delighted."

"Nobody was squawky. It's entirely your diseased imagination. Naturally Mother was anxious. Wondering what the hell you'd do next. . . ."

"Why couldn't she trust me?" Wondering was there another man? . . . Wondering what will people say? . . .

"And no money," added Kate, treating the question as rhetorical.

"Well, I didn't ask any of you for any." Olivia lit another cigarette with unsteady fingers. The blood started to beat in her face. Damn them all.

"No, you didn't," agreed Kate mildly. "I can't think how you managed." Never thought she would.

"I've managed because I swore I would." Olivia smoked with frenzy. "But it's been no picnic, I can tell you."

"I bet it hasn't." Kate was reasonableness itself.

"I have a hard life——" Her voice quavered.

"I expect it's been much more satisfactory, being on your own. I should have done the same."

Olivia laughed suddenly.

"It isn't hard really. I don't know what I'm talking about. It's all comparative. It's taught me a bit anyway—about the way some people have to live, I mean. . . ."

"What's-her-name does pay you, doesn't she?—Anna?"

"Oh, yes. As much as she can afford—more, really. *And* commission. But that's not very frequent. Nobody seems to want to be photographed. Nobody I know can afford it."

"I must try and bring the children," murmured Kate.

"She's not very good with children."

"I shouldn't think she was," said Kate, with transparent meaning. "Besides, you know, she *is* expensive."

"She's far better than any one else." That's as may be, said Kate's silence. "However, you've done your bit, coming yourself."

"Oh, well, Rob wanted me done."

"She thought you were wonderful."

"She couldn't have." A flicker of scornful pleasure crossed Kate's face. "I know I was looking awful that day. I always do after that early train journey. And her beastly lights made my eyes water. Not that it mattered much one way or the other. The results weren't so bad, I must say."

"Anna's not used to fresh young matrons from the country. She was quite overcome."

"Oh! . . . Fresh young matrons my foot! I know my looks aren't what they were, so you needn't go on."

"Nonsense!" Nonsense it was. She glanced at her. Something was gone, but Kate was a striking-looking woman. "Anyway, compared with me you're still in your teens."

Kate said nothing. It was so untrue, yet so true on the surface, it didn't bear arguing about. Those infinitesimal lines beneath her eyes, the line one side of her crooked mouth, her thinness, really almost a frail look, blast her. . . . If only she'd feed up and preserve her energy with more underclothes. . . . She looks like . . . I don't know what: nothing to do with real age: like an old child. . . . Bother—Bother. . . .

After a while Olivia said:

"How are the children, Kate?"

"Flourishing. Jane had a touch of earache last week but it went off. She didn't have a temperature, so I wasn't too worried. I must ring up George at lunch-time. Oh, Lord! I've got a million things to do next week. It couldn't have happened more awkwardly. Can't be helped."

"Perhaps he'll . . . Perhaps you'll be able to get away."

"Perhaps."

"I could stay on another few days if necessary."

"We'll see." Kate got up and stretched. "When are you coming to stay?"

"I don't know, Kate. I'd like to."

"You always say that, but you never come. The children are always asking. You're popular, for some reason. Polly doesn't even know you."

"Sweet Polly—the flower of the flock, I thought, at three weeks."

Kate said with a funny look, as if she were saying something a tiny bit embarrassing, on the sloppy side:

"We think she's a little like you. She's got your eyes."

"Really? How flattering of you and Rob! . . . Family likenesses do seem such a compliment. . . . I don't quite know why. I suppose it's because they make you feel powerful."

"Hmm. . . . Rob ought to feel powerful enough after Priscilla, Jane *and* Christopher. All the dead spit. However, I suppose I ought to rejoice." Kate rubbed her eyes. "I did think Christopher might be different. You're always told the boy favours the female. . . ." She added with bitterness: "And Mother going on every time as if I'd done it on purpose. Raking their faces for the Curtis chin and the West nose. . . ."

"Anna was mad to know if the children looked like you. She got quite moral and indignant when I said no."

"Did she?" Kate's lip curled a little; but there was a glint of satisfaction in her eye.

"Not but what Rob is a fine well-set-up specimen. In fact I think he's jolly attractive."

"Thanks."

"The thing is really we're too special to be repeated. . . . Hadn't I better adopt Polly? Three's quite enough for you to go on with. When I see the prams in the Park, I simply ache to have one to push, and lift up the steps and leave in the hall."

Kate went suddenly serious. Standing on the clipped wool hearthrug, she pulled her skirt up to let the fire get at the backs of her legs, and said finally:

"Why don't you divorce him?"

Olivia laughed.

"I follow the train of thought."

"Well, why not?"

"Too much trouble."

"You don't want to go back to him by any chance, do you?"

"God, no!"

"One day you'll want to be free and he could make it awkward for you if he wanted to."

"Why should he want to?"

"Well, you never know. You say yourself how spiteful he is. You're bound to want to marry again one day."

"Oh—I don't know. Shouldn't think so. Don't know any marrying men."

"And what about *him* wanting to be free? He might start some funny business on the sly—to get evidence."

"Oh, Lord! You think of everything, don't you?" Olivia blew out a great sigh and closed her eyes.

"You can think me as nasty-minded as you like—but he might. He might land you in a mess."

"He might—but he'd be hard put to it. My life is blameless and chaste—worse luck!"

She began to feel horribly depressed.

"You don't seem to want to give yourself a chance." Kate was implacable. "It's all very well now to knock about London on your own like you do. But you don't want to do it for ever, do you?"

"Perhaps not." Perhaps not indeed.

"Even frightfully nice——" Kate stumbled: unusual for her: went on a trifle lamely: "I mean even the most broad-minded men are a bit—well, on their guard about a woman who's legally married to some submerged person in the offing. They don't want to get mixed up——"

"Don't they? Don't they really?" Olivia opened her eyes wide.

"No, they don't," said Kate sharply. "Look here, why don't you let Rob go and have a talk to him? I'm sure he would. The longer you leave it the more difficult it'll be. Rob would be able to sort of put it to him and suggest he should give you evidence without putting his back up. Rob's awfully good with people."

"I'm sure he is." Tactful. . . . Look here, old chap, we're men of the world. . . . Cool but amiable, standing no non-sense. . . .

Olivia burst suddenly into a loud vulgar chuckle.

"Now what's the joke?"

"I was only thinking of Ivor taking a tart to Brighton for the week-end. Oh dear, it would be funny . . . the conversation. . . ."

"You're hopeless," said Kate coldly.

Out of patience, she gathered up an armful of blue satin and tissue paper and left the room.

In disgrace, thought Olivia, left alone. She went and knelt on the old hard cocoa-coloured couch by the window, and leaning on the sill looked out. Away spread the blue damp garden—just as I imagined—lit with a ghost of iridescent mist. The leaves of the walnut were down, and Higgs was sweeping them up, all lemon-yellow, into a barrow. Soon I must go down and say charmingly: "Hallo, Higgs? How are you all?" At the end of the garden rose the elm-tops with a gold shout, plump still, full sailing, but thinning, black-branch-threaded. A flock of starlings pecked on the lawn, on the path. Up they flew all of a sudden and scattered; and she heard a car change gear, hoot, and turn out of the drive: Dr. Martin.

The telephone rang, faint to her ears: someone inquiring. Kate would answer. It couldn't be Rollo: not yet. Not ever, of course. Rollo would think about ringing up, sometime to-morrow maybe; and then he wouldn't do it. Because nice men don't like to get mixed up. . . . Rollo was undoubtedly in the category of nice men, broad-minded. They are on their guard. . . .

What a queer meeting, what a queer conversation . . . getting on so well, such a long way. . . . Or didn't we really? . . . What was it happened in the car? What did it mean? I was to be punished, subjugated. . . . He must dominate. What were we near? I couldn't have been mistaken. . . . Very near, very far. . . . He could be brutal. I want to, I must, shall I never see him again? . . .

Oh. . . . This mood, this time, will pass. This heavy weight shall be lifted. Whatever happens we shall all go jogging on again somehow. The dust will settle once again upon these fly-blown images. . . . Are these all my mind shall contain? Shall no piercing shock of resurrection dislodge their tentacles, crumble them for ever? Can it be that what I expect will never be?

The smutty window, the brown street blighted with noise and rain; the stained walls; the smell of geyser, of cheese going stale in the cupboard, of my hands smelling of the washing-up bowl, nails always dirty, breaking; the figures on the stairs, coming and going drably, murmured to reluctantly, shunned at the door of the communal, dread, shameful W.C. on the middle landing. . . . The despised form in the bed, nose buried, asleep at eleven o'clock in the morning, the sheets are dirty, he is my husband, this is my life, my shoes are shabby. I shall never have a child in the country. . . .

Rollo, it wasn't all my fault, I did try. If we'd both been different, if . . .

Rollo, this isn't me, cynical, flippant: you remember me: don't judge me by what I say. They befog me with their explanations and solutions, they lay my cards on the table for me, they disapprove, they sympathise.

If I could escape to a new country, I'd soon strip off these sticky layers, grow my own shape again.

The ordinary, the unnatural day wore on. The telephone

rang, was answered; rang again. Footsteps went up and down the stairs, along the passages, creaking, subdued. Meals were swallowed punctually; tags of conversation picked up, dropped, resumed again. Soon after lunch, Dr. Martin's car returned; and when the early, fog-breathing motionless dusk crept over, there it was still, looming black, extinct, monstrous in a corner of the drive. Kate and Olivia sat over the drawing-room fire, Kate knitting with rapid fingers, Olivia darning a stocking with slow ones: a couple of dummies performing automatic gestures. As darkness fell, they gave up talking; their ears were strained for sounds from above; their bowels stirred, breathing seemed arrested. They existed only in suspense. All else, all energy and emotion, had been drained out of them to concentrate in the silent space on the other side of the ceiling; and they were powerless as ghosts.

Kate got up and lit the lamp, Olivia poked the fire. They looked out. With the increase of light in the room the darkness without had grown suddenly complete, uncompromising. It's night. Mother's been away too long, I want her to come. . . . Draw the curtains. No. The waiting car won't let us. . . .

They sat down again. All at once they heard voices, the front door opening and closing. The black oppressive bulk in the drive became a normal car, throbbed, blazed, drew away with its old familiar long-drawn rising moan and settle on the change-up.

Prepare now.

The door opened, soft, precise: the white cap was there, stuck wide, angular, vivid in the doorway.

"Hallo! All in the gloaming down here, aren't you?" Her voice was brisk and level. "Don't you believe in having light on the scene then?" . . . She gave a little laugh. "His temperature's down. He's sound asleep—breathing ever so much better. Thought I'd just pop in and tell you. Why don't you draw those curtains? Make it more cheerful, wouldn't it? Bye-bye for the present."

"What about his pulse?" said Kate. But she was gone.

"Nice of her," said Olivia.

"She's a good sort."

"Isn't it *good* . . . ?"—Choking. "I suppose we'd better just wait." . . . Carefully steadied.

They drew the curtains and stood over the fire, exchanging a brief sentence now and then. Half an hour went by. The door opened again. There wasn't one particular moment when she appeared, but there she towered, alarming, triumphant, with an unfamiliar white incandescent face.

They faced her, speechless.

"Here I am, dears." She came forward to them, smiling in secret power and triumph. "He's through it. He's sleeping— such a peaceful sleep—like a child. His pulse is steady."

"That's good," said Kate, through pale lips; and she began to breathe deeply as if she had been running.

"Of course, he's not out of the wood yet. . . ."

"No," Olivia nodded, vehement, rigid. . . .

But he will be: you've brought it off, you extraordinary woman, you know you have.

"But Dr. Martin thinks he stands a good chance now . . . with every care, of course."

"Yes."

"Nurse is with him, now. She insisted I should come down for a short time. She's been such a treasure. This room strikes me as chilly. Not a very cheerful fire. What it needs is a log. Olivia, ring the bell, dear. Have you had tea?"

"No, we haven't."

"I think we could all do with a cup of tea."

III

OPENING his eyes, he saw brass bed-rails, blue curtains, drawn, shrouding the window; darkness, suffused with muffled faint illumination. Night then. . . . Who's here? Who lit the lamp? His lids fell down again, pressed upon by an infinite but gentle weight.

A clicking, a rustle,—alive, secretive, wary: that was coal shifting, settling in the grate. All was well. This sound, this darkened room were from the beginning. The bed, the muffled light, the blue curtains; tick, flap, hush-sh-sh, the fire in the grate, in the winking bed-knobs; wide, shrunk, wide, shrunk in the fluttering ceiling. All this I know. . . .

Someone in the room, just stirring. This also was awaited. . . . Call out, perhaps. . . .

Who's moving? Where's this room? In the far-sunk depths of him, time started a gradual, a reluctant beat. When is it? Who is this, lying in a bed? His own identity began waveringly to crystallise, close over him. Apprehensive now, he opened his eyes again, saw a figure move across and vanish from his line of vision. He moved his lips and a faint sound came from between them.

There was a soft, rapid forward movement; someone by the bed. A face. . . . Well, well, well! . . . The girl Olivia. His lids fell again.

"Awake, Dad?" A tiny voice.

After a long while he sighed out:

"Very weak." A quiver fled over his face.

"I know, Dad. It's a shame. Never mind. You'll soon be better."

Sounded odd: tearful?

"You think so, do you?" That was the line. "What you doing here anyway?"

"Just sitting here for a bit—in case you wanted anything. Do you?"

He waited. . . . Want? Want? Foolish, exhausting . . .

"Little drink?" she whispered.

"No."

"Mother's downstairs, writing letters. Shall I fetch her?"

"No. No." He waited. "The other one. . . ."

"Nurse?"

"Nurse." She saw amusement break far down below his face. "Very strong woman."

"Is she? I bet she is."

"Whisks me up and down, rolls me over . . ."

"I know. . . ."

"Like a blinking baby. . . ."

Weak laughter caught them both, shook them helplessly. Tears crawled down his cheeks. When the spasm had worked itself out, he sighed heavily, groaning almost, and lay like a log. She brought a chair and sat down close beside his bed, and wiped the tears off with a handkerchief. His wasted face with its six days' growth of grizzled beard, its mouth slack, mournful, cracked with fever, was hideous, strange, distasteful to her. It was a sick old man's face—not his. But he has his forehead still. Untouched, magnanimous, it rode above the wreck, as if informed with a separate, a victorious life of intellectual strength and serenity: saying: Behold! we shall all be saved. . . .

Is he alive? Has he died? Ought I to go for someone? If he's dead, I'll be blamed. . . I let him talk too much. . . . But he said suddenly:

"Olivia."

"Yes, Dad?"

"I thought you were dead."

"Did you, Dad? I'm not. At least I don't think so."

"So it seems. Tant mieux." He sighed. "Very bad dreams. Shocking."

"It was the fever."

"No doubt. How long . . . ?"

"About a week."

"Indeed."

"I turned up yesterday."

"I see. Family summoned." He smiled infinitesimally. "All here?"

"Not James."

He looked distressed all of a sudden and said, more sharply: "Oswald?"

"He's not here . . . but he shall come whenever you like. Don't worry about him, Dad."

"Poor old fellow." Another tear crept down.

"Mother didn't want to upset him. . . ."

"Why upset? He's a sensible chap. She doesn't want him here. Never did."

"He's coming, Dad, I promise you. Don't worry. I'll arrange it. Everything's all right."

Very slowly his hand came up from beneath the blankets, crawled in her direction. *Oh! Don't.* . . . She took it in hers and said, aching:

"You two shall stuff around and stump each other with *locus classicuses* and read boring books to your hearts' content. Don't worry. Don't worry about anything. Just get better quick."

He gave her hand the ghost of a pressure. The girl was a nice creature, she meant well. Oh, but so lugubrious . . . to struggle up and find yourself at the end after all. A laughable disappointment. . . . Give up, go down again? . . . No. . . . Too late. . . .

He drifted off to sleep again, his hand in hers. It felt brittle, dry, like a claw. . . . Oh, is it going to be worth it for him, after all? How in this spent declining frame could the vitality well up again to replenish him; restore this claw, this mask, to human warmth? . . . Sparing ourselves the funeral, the black, the money difficulties, only to offer him, after laborious days and nights, a rug, an invalid chair: imitations of living, humiliations; only a fettered waiting on life and death. . . .

His wife came in softly and stood by the bed. Barely perceptibly, her face altered, stiffened.

"He's asleep. He woke up and talked quite a lot, quite like himself, and then he dropped off again . . . a moment ago. . . ."

"Well . . . go and get ready for supper. I'll stay with him now."

I stole a march. I cheated. She should have had his first words, not I . . . I've betrayed her. . . .

Guiltily, under her mother's shuttered eyes, she disengaged their hands.

IV

"ARENʼT you going to drink your soup, Olivia? It's one of Ada's nicest."

"No, thank you, Mum."

"Oh, come now, do try it. It's all vegetables—so good for you. I found the recipe in the *Star*."

"I don't like soup much, you know, Mum. . . ."

"What a pity. Ada'll be so disappointed. She made it specially."

"Look at me," said Kate. "I'm drinking mine up."

"Yes." Approval and exasperation struggled in Mrs. Curtis's voice. "You're a sensible girl, thank goodness."

"You can't expect to have more than one satisfactory child, Mum," said Olivia. "Not in these days."

There was a soup-drinking silence. Olivia's cup sat before her in smug reproach with its cap and button on.

"And as a child," said Mrs. Curtis, "you were always the one to have a big appetite. Kate was the fussy one."

"And now I gorge," said Kate languidly.

"You don't gorge, dear. . . ."

"It's motherhood," said Kate.

"Dad never could bear a scraggy woman."

"I know, darling, you've said so before," sighed Olivia. "That's why he picked us a Ma like you."

"Well, it's not right, and what's more it's not becoming, I don't care what people say. Your grandmother always said: 'If you go against Nature you'll pay for it.'"

"*I* don't go against Nature," said Kate. "I'm nicely covered."

"You aren't fat, dear, not a scrap. You're just nice."

"Yes, that's what I said—just nice. Though, as a matter of fact, Rob really prefers them on the skinny side."

"Nonsense. Rob has far too much sense."

Mrs. Curtis's manner conveyed an arch benevolent unperturbed reproach: for Kate, cured of that early tendency to tart defiance, of that dreadfully nervy phase she'd had after Paris—disagreeable remarks, sarcastic generalisations, tears for no reason at all—Kate had long since turned out entirely sensible and satisfactory. Kate, bless her, had slipped with no trouble into a suitable marriage within easy motoring distance. As the wife of a young doctor with a good country practice, a solid man, a man with a growing reputation; as the mother of four fine healthy children she had established herself beyond question in all eyes. No doubt she was critical still, still impatient of advice; but all the same, sitting over the fire nowadays, each with her knitting, they were very cosy, very happy together. Talk flowed on, as warm, as refreshing as a good cup of coffee. The barrier between generations was dissolved. It was almost like being young: almost—though May was gone and that blank ached irremediably, a cruel amputation—almost like having a sister again. A comfort, yes, a comfort, now that Olivia . . . now that James . . . phases, we hope; phases, of course . . . above all, now that Charles. . . . Saved, but a ruin. . . . I know it. . . . Hush. . . . Pass on.

"Did I tell either of you, Dolly Martin's getting married?"

"It can't be true!"

"Who to?"

"Well, it seems it's a young missionary out in China. She

met him some years ago—when they were both doing work in the East End—and they've been corresponding for some time, so Dr. Martin tells me. She sails next month."

"Well, well, well! Good old Pudding-face! Who'd have thought romance was nesting behind those horn-rims all these years?"

"No wonder she always looked so conceited. It just shows where there's a will there's a way, and one never need be sorry for any one."

"She's such a capable energetic girl," sighed Mrs. Curtis. "She'll be such a help to him. But it does seem a long way to go."

"Let's hope the suns of China won't reduce her. She's a luscious morsel for a missionary."

"And a very primitive place, I understand, right in the interior."

"She'll be captured by bandits," said Olivia, "for a cert. She's got just the looks they always pick on. A few more years shall roll and Dolly'll be held for ransom in a bandit lair. I see her photo in the papers now."

"These missions do wonderful work," said Mrs. Curtis with a touch of severity: for why should everything be made a mock of? "It's a hard life and a dangerous one."

"Serve 'em jolly well right for interfering," said Olivia harshly.

"People must do something, I suppose," Kate yawned.

"His name is Potts," said Mrs. Curtis, passing on with determination to the particular. "Cyril Potts,—or was it Cecil? Not a very romantic name," she conceded, smiling; for of course they thought it funny—"But Dr. Martin says he's got such a particularly nice open face. Olivia, you might send her a line, I thought. She was always more your friend."

"I might."

"I've been wondering what I could give her that would really be useful."

"A cake-basket."

"A cruet-stand . . . or two cruet-stands."

"I thought perhaps a little cheque really, then you girls could give her a little something personal. From the two of you. You needn't spend much."

"No, we needn't," said Kate. "It's the thought that counts."

"Poor Dr. Martin, I'm afraid he'll miss her dreadfully. But Phyl's coming home to keep house for him. You know she's been sharing a cottage in Wiltshire with a friend, a Miss Trotter, and breeding—now what is it?—Angoras, I think."

"Poor old Phyl," said Olivia. "It's a shame she should have to give up her career. Hard on Miss Trotter, too. You don't find a pal like Phyl on every blackberry bush."

"Yes, Dr. Martin was a little unhappy about it, but she would. She never hesitated. Those girls have always been so devoted to their father."

"And she may be able to do something with rabbits here."

Oh, give it up! . . . Plain, cheerful Martins, companions of childhood, coping efficiently with their lives, sensible women. . . . Dolly would never wake up one morning in China and tell herself: My marriage has failed and my life is empty, futile. Not she. Dolly scored heavily.

"What a divine salad," said Olivia. "What's in it—Prunes? Can I have some more, Mum, please?"

A ray of simple pleasure shot across her mother's face.

"Do, dear. I hoped you'd like it. I told Ada to put a little cream in the dressing."

And cream was nourishing. And it was all part of the plan, thought out specially to tempt, to please. And she looks so worn. I hate myself.

"Has any one taken Mrs. Skinner's cottage yet?"

And after that I'll ask for details of Miss Robinson's complete breakdown. . . . And after that. . . .

Across the table they began to ply a peaceful shuttle between the three of them, renewing, re-enforcing, patching over rents and frayed places with old serviceable thread. They were tough still; they were a family. That which had chanced to tie them all up together from the start persisted irrevocably, far below consciousness, far beyond the divergences of the present, uniting them in a mysterious reality, independent of reason. As it was in the beginning, is now. . . . Only the vast central lighting-piece no longer stupefied the cloth with a white china glare. When the daughters came home, grown up to have ideas on becoming lighting, they had condemned it; and during their visits, four candles in elaborate Victorian silver candlesticks burned above the expanse of damask, around the silver fruit-bowl. The table floated, a stealthily-gleaming craft moored far from shore, between the beetling promontories of clock and sideboard, below the soaring lighthouse of grand-papa's portrait. Very restful and pleasant it was too, once you got used to the enormous areas of shade where anything might be happening: though Violet was a worry, always tripping up at the door with the tray: on purpose, Kate said. . . . How young, how pretty Kate looked; no more than a girl; and Olivia too, softened, glowing, as she always used to be . . . and I too helped, no doubt, more as I would like . . . as I was, before these wrinkles. . . . Mrs. Curtis finished her glass of claret. Delicious, reviving. . . . The girls had insisted; and certainly it had made a difference,—just for once. . . .

"I needn't go up just yet," she said happily, as they rose from table. "He's all settled for the night and Nurse is there. Isn't it a blessing he's taken such a fancy to her? There's something about her tickles him, though I can't see anything funny myself. . . . Let's sit in the drawing-room."

The fire blazed and the lights stared behind thin, white silk, rose-wreathed shades. Olivia stretched herself upon the white wool hearthrug, between Kate and her mother, facing each other in their arm-chairs. They knitted. Stockings for the children, jumpers for the children, babies' night-vests, coats, bootees—there was never an end. Kate had taken on and elaborated the theme unfolded in her own infancy by Mrs. Curtis. The little tables either side of the fireplace were choked now with photographs of the grandchildren at all stages:

straight-fringed, neat-featured, hygienic-looking. A number of the more rococo pre-war likenesses of Mrs. Curtis's own young—plumes, curls, ribbons, frothing frills—had been put away to make room for them. From time to time Kate laid down her needles and studied them closely, with a searching frown. From time to time Mrs. Curtis's hands dropped and she heaved a sigh: her vast unconscious sigh. But nowadays this no longer cast a blight upon her daughters. Olivia smoked, looked at the *Illustrated London News*. Over her head the two pairs of hands resumed their busy conspiracy, the two voices droned peacefully on. . . . The children, the servants, the children, Rob, Dad, James, the children. . . .

At ten o'clock the telephone rang in the hall.

"Now who can that be?" said Mrs. Curtis. "At this hour?"

"I'll go." Olivia sprang up with a sudden tingling surmise. "Hallo?"

"Could I—er—speak to—er—Miss Olivia Curtis possibly . . ."

"Speaking." Yes. It was.

"Oh, hallo, good-evening!" He sounded relieved. "This is Rollo Spencer."

"Oh, yes! Good-evening. . . ."

"I hope I'm not an awful bore ringing up. I wanted to ask how—if—how your father is. . . ."

"It's frightfully nice of you, Rollo. He's better—really better. We *think* he's turned the corner."

"Oh, I'm terribly glad to hear that—terribly glad." Warm, delighted voice.

"It is sweet of you to ring up."

"Not at all. I wanted to, I've been wondering a lot. . . . I didn't want to be a nuisance. Mummy'll be terribly glad, she was awfully sorry when she heard. . . . She wants to say a word to you. . . ."

"Oh, does she? . . ." Alarming. "How are you?"

"I'm extremely well, thank you."

"Are you, really?"

"Yes, truly. How are you?"

"Oh . . . in my usual rude health. . . ."

They laughed, waited doubtfully, embarrassed.

"Hang on a moment, will you," he said finally. "Mummy wants to speak to you. Hang on. I'll give her a shout."

"Right you are. I'll hang on."

Gone. That was all. Full, strong lazy voice, trailing away, inconclusive; nothing said one could fasten on to, or remember; current expressions of superficial sympathy. . . . Only the voice, promising something, raising an expectation. . . . Oh, well, that was that: finished with. All the Spencers had good manners.

"Is that Olivia?" Incisive ringing tones filled the earpiece.

"Yes, Lady Spencer." At once she felt meek and gratified, nestling under a wing: as of old.

"My dear, Rollo's told me the good news. I do *so* rejoice! We've been so concerned since Rollo saw you. I hardly *liked* to ring up but I've thought of you all so much. Do tell your mother this with my love. *What* an anxious time, poor dear. How is she?"

"Oh, she's very well. A little bit tired, but really marvellously well."

"*Is* she? How splendid. She must take care of herself— she'll feel the strain now the anxiety is less."

"Yes, I expect she will."

"Now, my dear, *are* we going to be able to get a glimpse of you, I wonder?"

"Oh. . . . I don't know, Lady Spencer. I'd love to. It's ages. . . ."

"I know. *Far* too long. Do you think your mother could possibly spare you to us for an evening?"

"I'm sure she could."

"That would be delightful. Well, now, we've got Rollo and Marigold with us till Monday—and they're *so* anxious to see you. In that case it would have to be *to-morrow* evening, wouldn't it? Would that suit you?"

"To-morrow evening would be perfect."

"It would? How delightful. Marigold will be so enchanted. Is Kate there?"

"Yes, Kate's here."

"Dear Kate. Give her my love." The voice fell a tone or two, seemed to reflect a trifle doubtfully. "Would she come too?"

"I don't know. If you wouldn't mind holding on, I'll ask."

Back to the drawing-room she flew, gave rapid messages.

"How kind of her." Mrs. Curtis was gracious, appreciative. No more than one's due, but thoughtful all the same.

"I won't go," said Kate quickly. "I'd truly rather not."

"Do go, Kate, dear, why not? It'll do you good."

"No, I don't want to. Go on, Livia, rush. I'll lend you my white. Tell her you'll come, but not me."

Back she flew.

"Kate is so sorry, Lady Spencer. . . ."

"I quite understand," cut in the voice vigorously, with sympathetic approval. "I felt perhaps your mother wouldn't *quite* like to spare you both. Well, dear, we shall expect you to-morrow then. Benson will be there at 7.30. . . . But of course, nonsense, I insist. . . . And we shall all look forward so *very* much to seeing you. Good-bye, dear."

v

BENSON drew up beside the portico, hopped out and pulled the bell while she waited inside the car. Stiff, ageing as he was, his limbs still moved not at their own pace but as if under an old persisting mechanical compulsion to look sharp now, look alive, bustle up for orders at a moment's notice. A lifetime of service, said his patient figure, standing on the steps, waiting: the last, no doubt, to wish to change his station; deploring each successive stage in the breakdown of the social scale; yet a man of intelligence, of dignity.

The heavy doors were flung open, the lights of the hall blazed out, the footman faintly returned her faint smile, she stepped inside.

"I'll just leave my coat here." Assume my image is still the one I saw in my bedroom glass: satisfactory enough. Another view might shake my equilibrium. She slipped off her mother's fur coat into the footman's hands, and gave a touch or two to the white dress. Floating, transparent and fragile, swathing itself lightly over breast, waist and thigh and sweeping backwards and out in a wide flaring line, it was a romantic, pretty, waltz-like frock. Inside it she felt drastically transformed, yet at home with it, able to suit it.

"There you see," Kate had said scoldingly. "In spite of you choosing to adopt the Bohemian consumptive style nowadays, the fact remains that this looks entirely apt on you, whereas on me it's on the kittenish side." She pulled in and tied the long flying airy bow in the back of the waist. "Look." She marshalled her to the long glass.

It was true. She looked a young girl, and a pretty one.

"You'd better stick to it," said Kate. "I fell for it in the sales, but I can't wear this sort of thing any more."

"Oh, you can. . . ."

"And may it be a lesson to you," said Kate.

Olivia followed the young footman's spruce, swinging, glittering back across the pillared spaces of the hall, down a corridor lined obscurely with supernumerary specimens of family portraiture—here a legal wig, red robes; there the dulled splendour of ancient regimentals; here a pink satin gown, a smirk, a rose, a long neck, a white hand and breast, there a towering Victorian group, exaggeratedly fertile-domestic-blissful. Now they were in the drawing-room. Empty. I'm too early.

"Her ladyship will be down in a few moments." He swung briskly away.

She went and stood by the fire where the logs blazed and

whispered rosily in the wide carved marble grate. She looked round. There it all was, not changed at all: the long elegantly proportioned prospect of white, of gold, of green brocade, the panels of glass, the screen, the Aubusson carpet, the subdued gleam of porcelain and crystal, the piano painted with light faint-coloured wreaths and sprays. Chrysanthemums, white, bronze, and rose-coloured, outsize, professional-looking, were massed in Chinese bowls, in vases and stands. The oval mirror above the mantelpiece gave her back a muted reflection; for the chandeliers were unlit and, except for the narrowly radiating wall-lights in triple-branched gold brackets, the only suffusion of light came from two tall porcelain reading-lamps by the fireplace. . . . Yes, and the Gainsborough ancestress was lit, the Romney boy and girl.

This was the scene—huge, flashing, stripped, a hall of ice in memory—of the children's parties years ago; of that last dance for Marigold's coming-out. After that, the parties had been in London: and we weren't invited. She left the fire, crossed over and craned her neck at the Gainsborough. Feet make no noise on the passage carpet. The room might be filling up behind me. . . .

"Hallo!" A voice from the door.

Rollo came towards her, alert and pleased-looking.

"Hallo. . . ."

He took her hand and held it, looking down at her with head held up, lids lowered, in a characteristic way. "This is a good idea."

"I'm awfully early, I'm afraid. Benson was so prompt."

"Benson is a very punctual man. Well, all the better."

"I'm glad you're first. I'm so frightened."

"Nonsense. Mummy's thrilled to see you again. So's Marigold."

"So am I thrilled, but—Is there a party?"

"Not my idea of a party." He laughed. "Not a lot of party spirit."

"But people?"

"A few."

"God!"

"Don't worry. I'll look after you." Their eyes met, smiling, acknowledging a secret united front. "Come by the fire," he said. "Have a cigarette. Have a drink. Shall I make a cocktail?"

He busied himself over a tray of bottles and decanters on the piano, and brought back two brimming glasses.

"Goodness, what a size," she said. "I shall be dreamy after this."

"Will you? But you're always dreamy, aren't you?"

She looked at him, slightly startled.

"Yes, I suppose I am. Is it so awfully noticeable?"

"Only to a close observer."

"Oh. . . ." She raised her eyebrows, glanced sidelong: an adaptation to his technique. "Well, when I'm really tight I get dreamier and dreamier. I do everything in slow motion. I lean and lean about and my words trail off and I smile and smile. . . ."

"It sounds rather attractive. Come on, drink up. Here's luck!" He drained his glass and scrutinised her again, attentively. "You're looking very well to-night. . . . I'm most awfully glad, you know, about your father."

"Yes, thank you so much. It's grand."

"I told you it would be all right, didn't I?"

"Yes, you did. I'm afraid I didn't believe you."

"Ah, you see, you should. Poor dear, you did look so small-faced. I couldn't make out what was bothering you. I didn't like it."

"It was nice of you. . . ."

"I hate gloom, don't you? For myself or any one else. . . . It's so uncomfortable."

"Yes, it is." She laughed. "I can't do with it at all."

"Yet some people enjoy it. It's a fact. I know someone who does." He made a rueful grimace and she said in mock surprise:

"You don't really, do you?"

"Yes. My mother-in-law. You wouldn't credit what a lugubrious woman she is. Give her a really large-scale disaster in the morning papers and she's renewed like that bird. Not to speak of private croakings and prognostications of doom."

"I know the type."

"Do you? I suppose it's fairly common." He looked a little depressed.

She said rapidly:

"I had a mother-in-law. She was just the same."

"Ah! . . ." He hesitated. "You had. I *have*. . . . Has yours passed away?"

"Far from it. They never pass away. But—but we're dead to one another, as you might say. At least I hope so. Worse than dead, I suppose I am to her. Though it's what she always worked for."

He nodded, sighed dolefully.

"My case is different," he said. "We are far, far from dead to one another. We meet with outstanding frequency . . . in my house. . . . I suppose we always, always shall. . . ."

"Can't you make a stand?"

He said after a moment of silence:

"No, I can't. I'm a weak selfish easy-going character, and all I want is a quiet life." He glanced at her with a smile. "Don't you?"

"It's not *all* I want. . . ."

He shrugged his shoulders and looked away, whistling softly between his teeth.

"However," he said, " let's not dwell on unwholesome subjects. Have another drink."

"No, thanks."

"Why not?"

"I don't need any more support. I feel fine now."

His eyes travelled intently over her and he smiled to himself. She looked up at him. Yes, all was well. For this evening some illusion was being breathed out, some reflection thrown back of a power as mystic, as capricious in its comings and

goings as it was recognisable when it came. No need for
anxiety now: it would carry her through. I shall enjoy myself.

"Well, I need a good deal more support myself." He strolled
over to the piano and mixed himself another drink.

"Who'd have thought it?"

He looked handsome, fresher than ever in a plum-coloured
velvet smoking jacket; and the prosperous aroma clung to
him: cigars, expensive stuff on his hair, good soap, clean
linen . . . a rich mixture.

"You're right," he said. "I don't feel too unhealthy, and
that's a fact. Two days hoofing it in the open air—blown some
of the cobwebs away. Shooting's not among the more intellectual of my recreations, but it suits me quite well all the
same."

"Do you think I might be sitting next to you at dinner?"

"I do think so. I've reserved you."

"Oh, good!"

She beamed on him whole-heartedly.

"Olivia! It is!"

Lady Spencer was in the doorway, was bearing down, full-
rigged, confined in an ample severity of black, with diamonds,
with heroic shoulders bare, with white, austerely sculptured
cheeks and hair, with both hands outstretched. "My dear! This
is delightful!" She kissed her warmly on both cheeks. "We all
felt we *had* to see you—when Rollo told us of your meeting.
. . . Let me look at you. . . . Yes, it's our same Olivia. But thin!
. . . Naughty girl." She gave her a loving, scolding pat on the
hip; then laid a hand on Rollo's shoulder.

"I am so glad to see you. . . ." Olivia felt the tears prick
under her lids. . . . Absurd. . . .

"Dear. . . ." Lady Spencer looked affectionately absent,
musing. There was something. . . . Ah, yes. . . . "And your
father is *really* on the mend? That does make me so happy.
. . . Do tell your dear mother . . . Jack!" she called: for Sir
John himself had entered, had creaked down the room to join
the group . . . and she was calling out to him in reassurance,

to cover his entrance . . . because there was something wrong with it; because one couldn't help watching, with faint uneasiness, his ponderous leaden-footed progress. . . .

"Hallo, Daddy!" said Rollo.

"Hallo, m'boy. . . ."

"Jack, dear, you remember our friend Olivia?"

"Who?"

"Olivia Curtis, Marigold's friend, you remember?"

Lady Spencer addressed him with a careful encouraging firmness that spoke of habit, her eyes made blank, long ago refusing to consider impatience or acknowledge dismay.

"Ah, yes, yes! How are you? Very glad to see you."

His hand was dry and stiff.

"Olivia's come over from Little Compton to dine with us."

"Very friendly of her. Some good shooting round Little Compton. Nice spot. . . . Know it well?"

"You remember Mr. Curtis, Jack, Olivia's father, at Little Compton. . . . We used all to meet in the old days—more than we do now, I'm afraid."

"Curtis? Are you the daughter of my old friend Charlie Curtis?"

"Yes, I am."

"Bless my soul! How is he? Haven't seen him in years. . . ." For a moment the look she remembered broke across the thick inflexible surface of his face—the mastiff look, kindly, amused, mildly titillated. "So you're Charlie Curtis's girl. . . ."

His mouth dropped open, he looked vaguely round the room. "Er . . ."

"Where are the dogs, Daddy?"

"Shut them in the library. They're all right. Both got their baskets." He smiled at Rollo, the expression of faint bewilderment smoothed out.

"That reminds me, I must have left Lucy in my room. She's probably cooking up a deadly grievance under the bed, waiting for me to kneel down and implore her to come out. . . . Shan't be a moment."

Laboriously his father's gaze went after him, clung to him as he strode out of the room. Yes, Sir John was altered. He was so slow, so heavy, standing beside his wife, she seemed somehow to be supporting his dead weight. Both had aged; her hair was white, her face hollowed under the cheekbones, the delicate skin scored with innumerable fine papery lines, the Queen Mary curves had lost perhaps the ultimate edge of opulence; but she was erect, imposing as ever, and an ageless vitality flashed from the pale blue, enigmatic, clear-gazing jewel-like iris. But he had gone old irrevocably. Below his smooth forehead and thick brown young-man's hair, the spark was extinct in the bloodshot eyes and the broken-veined dusky cheeks; and though his frame still carried him upright, broad and tall, it seemed embedded in some petrifying semi-solid material; as if too much of earth, too little of live flowing blood informed it.

People were coming in now. Almost perceptibly the energy began to well up in Lady Spencer. She began to draw them all towards her, to relinquish them with care and set them in motion towards one another. For the millionth time in this drawing-room, by such a fire, effortlessly, she was designing the social process, and nothing should be left to chance: no one left out, no one obtruded.

"My sister, Lady Clark-Matthew—Blanchie, I wonder if you remember our neighbour, Olivia Curtis, such an old friend of Marigold? . . . Do see to this hook for me, there's a dear, Doris always misses it. . . . My niece, Lady Mary Denham. . . . Mary, dear, I looked out that address you asked me for—*and* the recipe: remind me to give it you. . . . Mr. Denham: Harry, did you get a game of billiards? . . . Sir Ronald Clark-Matthew . . . Ronnie, have you pronounced yet on the Wilsons? Jack was going to ask your advice—weren't you, Jack? . . . Mr. Bassett, Miss Curtis. . . . Well, George? Did you have a nice nap? . . . Oh, yes, you did, my dear, it was quite audible. Never mind, we're all apt to drop off now and then as we grow older. . . . *Henriette!*"—stooping to shout in the ear of an apparition newly arrived upon the hearth, shapeless and formidable in a casing of lilac and silver brocade with trailing skirts, festooned like a Christmas tree with chains and bracelets, head wrapped in black lace shadowing a mad frizzle of frosty fringe and two dark star-pierced pits of eyes ringed with smudges of mascara. . . . "Ma chère! Je voudrais te présenter une jeune amie. . . ."

"Qu'est ce qu'elle me dit-là !" . . . Toneless croak of interruption, addressed to nobody in particular.

Once more, *fortissimo*:

"Une bien chère amie, Olivia Curtis. . . . Marigold's dear godmother, Olivia, Madame de Varenne. . . ." *Sotto voce*: "She's rather deaf. . . ."

"D'où donc arrive-t-elle celle-là ?"

Again the remark hung on the air, in utter detachment, like a statement picked up on the wireless.

"Now where's that bad girl ? Late as usual, I suppose. . . ."

"She was in her bath a few moments ago," said the one who was to have the recipe. "I heard her singing. I just gave a tap on the door and called out the time, but I didn't get any answer."

"I dare say not." Rollo was back, followed self-consciously by Lucy, had come straight to stand beside Olivia, smiling at her, conspiratorial. "I dare say the singing got louder, didn't it, Mary ?"

Mary gave him a pained, slight, patient smile, and turned away.

Olivia bent to pat Lucy, who winced away, hostile and cringing.

"She doesn't like me."

"That's odd."

"She hated me on sight in the train. Is she always like this with strangers ?"

"Not always—she has an unerring instinct."

"That sounds rather impolite."

He laughed.

"I don't think you quite follow me." He gave the woolly

body a soft push, saying: "She sets up to be my conscience, you see. . . ."

"Well, we won't wait," said Lady Spencer, turning from conversation with the tall, spare, rosy, white-moustached pronouncer-on-Wilsons, and putting a finger on the bell.

Expectation sharpened perceptibly in the air. Ha! A good meal coming, another good dinner: one of hundreds before, hundreds to come—anywhere, any time they liked. Not one grain of doubt, ever, about the quality, quantity, time and place of their food and drink. . . . In prime condition they all looked: no boils or blackheads here, no corns, callouses, chilblains or bunions. No struggle about underclothes and stockings. Birthright of leisure and privilege, of deputed washing, mending. . . . Can they sniff out an alien upon this hearth? Or is it disguise enough, simply to be here, in an evening-dress?

Marigold . . .? Where is Marigold?

"Dinner is served," pronounced an official voice.

They started to file out, through the double doors, across a space of hall towards the dining-room: Olivia last, with Rollo.

Someone was running down the spiralling, shallow staircase. Out of sight still; round and round; would be swept out on it into the hall in a moment, just behind us. . . . A figure swayed round the last curve of the balustrade, and came arrowing down the last flight in one straight skim, ran silently to her side, caught her and clutched her hand at the dining-room door.

"Marigold!"

"Olivia!"

She said rapidly, panting a little, barely glancing at her:

"You haven't changed a bit. Oh, I'm so glad. . . . How's Kate? I've changed, haven't I? Hell, I did mean not to be late. Nannie would wuffle on, and make me change my stockings. . . . Are you all right?"

"Yes. . . . Marigold." They still held hands, tightly, half-inclined to laugh, to cry. She was so different. She was exactly the same. "You do look wonderful. . . ." Her hair, her mouth, her neck and shoulders . . . and such a dress. . . .

"Do I? D'you like my fringe? It's new. Darling, I'm so pleased to see you. . . . I've got two children. . . . Can you imagine? . . . Oh, you *have* changed, as a matter of fact. You're lovely, and you weren't. Kate was. Is she still? P'raps not. . . . She is lovely, isn't she, Rollo?"

"She is . . ." said Rollo. He was watching them both with an absorbed expression, smiling and narrowing his eyes. They had the same eyes, though with variations—longish with full lids, the pupils dilated, the iris deep, peculiarly blue, electric-looking.

"D'you remember the Dance of the Wood Nymphs?—with shot chiffon scarves? And Monsieur Berton's ear-trumpet? And the passion he had for you?"

"And Miss Baynes drinking tea all through our music lessons?"

"I wonder if it *was* tea? She used to get awfully hazy and mop her eyes a lot after a cup or two. . . . How eccentric everything was, wasn't it? Every one of our instructors cracky. No wonder I'm backward!" She gave a high shout of laughter. "But you're not. But then you were clever, you and Kate. . . . Oh, look, they're all beginning to masticate. . . . Where are we at this dismal board? Miles apart, I suppose. Never mind, we'll talk afterwards. You're over there, by Rollo. Good-bye."

She waved her hand in the remembered gesture as she left them, and ran to slip into her place.

Now the scene had shifted on to another plane, unrealistic, strange and familiar. It was as if Marigold's appearance had somehow co-ordinated diverse ordinary objects, actions, characters, and transmuted them all together into a pattern, a dramatic creation.

Now all was presented as in a film or a play in which one is at one and the same time actor and infinitely detached spectator. The round table with its surface like dark gleaming ice, its silver and glass, its five-branched Georgian candlesticks, the faces, the hands, the silent, swift circulating forms of butler and footman, the light clash and clatter, the mingling voices . . . all existed at one remove, yet with a closeness and meaning almost painfully exciting. This element I am perfectly at home in. Now all would unfold itself not haphazard but as it must, with complex inevitability.

Rollo on one side, Sir Ronald on the other. Whom had Rollo on his other hand? The one called Mary . . . and Sir Ronald had the Wicked Fairy. He was leaning towards her ear speaking French with an accomplished Foreign Office accent, scarcely raising his voice. She could hear now all right; she looked lively, rejuvenated, disconcertingly intelligent. Marigold was diagonally opposite, sitting beside her father: no doubt—with the aid of Aunt Blanche on his other side—to spare him social effort. Her hand was laid on his, she stooped forward with a soft rounded thrust of bare shoulders, curving her neck towards him, towards George on her left, animating them both, seeming to caress them, talking with the old mobile lip movements, screwing her eyes up. Her dress was made of some curious thick silk stuff, faintly striped and flecked, greenish whitish, with a gold thread in it, plain and clinging, taken back in a sort of bustle and cut right off the shoulders. Two white magnolias in the front of the bodice touched the table as she leaned out over it.

Drinking clear soup, she said to Rollo:

"It is exciting to see her again."

"Marigold?"

"Yes. It's so nice when the years haven't made a person dim out. I was a tiny bit afraid she might have. You never can tell with those uncertain, shifting faces. Sometimes it's all over in no time. They just bloom out tentatively and wither off. I suppose it depends what happens inside them. . . . She's more extraordinary than ever. She's really beautiful."

"Beautiful?" He looked across at her. "Could you say that

quite? It's such a funny little snouty face—indiarubbery—isn't it?"

"Well—it all depends what you like, I suppose . . . what you look for."

"What do you like?"

She said ardently:

"I like what's uncertain—what's imperfect. I like what—what breaks out behind the features and is suddenly there and gone again. I like a face to warm up and expand, and collapse and be different every day and night and from every angle . . . and not be above looking ugly or comic sometimes. . . ."

"I see. . . . It sounds interesting—but not awfully restful."

Nicola was the other kind, of course—flawless, unimpeachable.

"Is your wife still as lovely as she used to be?"

"Nicola?—Yes, I suppose she is." His voice was rather flat. "She hasn't altered much. But she's not what you so eloquently describe, you know. She doesn't give you surprises every half-hour."

"Seeing her once was a lovely surprise."

"Was it? That's nice. You didn't meet her properly, did you? You must some day." He was silent, his mouth falling into a heavy line. He added abruptly: "It's a bore when people aren't strong. . . ."

"Isn't she strong?"

"No. . . . Always seems to have something wrong with her, poor dear. She's always taking—having to take to her bed."

"I'm so sorry. How wretched for you."

"It is. . . ." His expression was grateful. "You see, she's awfully—I don't know—highly strung, I suppose. At least, so her mother tells me. . . . It's a thousand pities, isn't it?"

"It is."

"One's apt to feel such an insensitive brute—always being with a highly-strung person."

"I don't suppose for a moment you need to feel that . . ."

Was that going further—saying something a little less in

the fencing style—than was expected? She felt a qualm. But he said, in the same doubtful, depressed voice:

"Well, I don't know. . . ." He helped himself to fish before saying with a rueful twist of an eyebrow: "I can't bear women to cry. I do deplore it."

"Yes, it's a bad habit."

He said quickly:

"That's what I think——" checked himself; added vaguely: "No. . . ."

"What does it make you feel when people cry?" she asked lightly. "Sorry? Irritated? or what ? Does it melt you, or freeze you?"

He thought a moment.

"Donno. A mixture, I suppose. Damned uncomfortable anyway. I want to rush off *miles*. . . ." He made a grimace, sighed. "It's a very sad thing how much men make women cry." His voice became personal again, light, flirtatious.

"Do they?"

"Don't they?"

"Well. . . ." She hesitated. . . . Oh, yes! . . . Memory flashed *mal à propos*, all out of key. . . . Far back, in the early love-making days with Ivor: so far away, so almost unremembered. And he'd cried too, had needed to be comforted. . . . But that was to be buried. . . .

"Perhaps I'm not much of a crier. . . ."

"Oh, but it's such a luxury!" he exclaimed with that curious sensual mockery and harshness she had noticed before. "Don't you know what a luxury tears can be?"

"Well. . . ." She felt at a loss. "P'raps I've still to find out."

"Are you a puritan?"

"No."

"No, I don't think you are. . . ."

"So what?" She met his eyes.

"I'm not sure. . . . You don't give away much, do you? Wise woman."

"No, I'm not that."

"Don't tell me there's nothing to give away. . . ."

"It's just that my life's . . . not peculiar, I don't mean, or mysterious . . . just rather unexplainable. . . ."

"Is it? Try."

"But it's not like *any* kind of life!" she cried out, in a kind of helplessness and distressed reluctance. "Not like any that comes your way, I'm sure."

"How d'you know what comes my way?"

Not that kind of waking anyway, and getting on a bus, and mornings with Anna; not bed-sitting-rooms and studios of that sort; not that drifting about for inexpensive meals; not always the cheapest seats in movies; not that kind of conversation, those catch phrases; not those parties and that particular sort of dressing, drinking, dancing. . . . Most particularly not those evenings alone in Etty's box of a house, waging the unrewarding, everlasting war on grubbiness—rinsing out, mending stockings for to-morrow, washing brush and comb, cleaning stained linings of handbags; hearing the telephone ring: for Etty again; and the ring before, and the next ring. . . . Not the book taken up, the book laid down, aghast, because of the traffic's sadness, which was time, lamenting and pouring away down all the streets for ever; because of the lives passing up and down outside with steps and voices of futile purpose and forlorn commotion: draining out my life, out of the window, in their echoing wake, leaving me dry, stranded, sterile, bound solitary to the room's minute respectability, the gas-fire, the cigarette, the awaited bell, the gramophone's idiot companionship, the unyielding arm-chair, the narrow bed, the hot-water bottles I must fill, the sleep I must sleep. . . .

"Should I be shocked?" he asked with a comic look of hope.

She burst out laughing.

"No, I'm afraid not. . . . No. I don't mean to sound interesting. There's nothing to tell. It isn't anything."

She cast about in her mind. . . . Amorphous, insubstantial. . . . Leaning against Etty's mantelpiece, head pressed down on the edge, till forehead and wood seemed part of one another, thinking: Do I exist? Where is my place? What is this travesty I am fixed in? How do I get out? Is this, after all, what was always going to be? . . . One couldn't explain that to him.

"Let's take it step by step," he said. "What do you do in the mornings?"

"In the mornings I go to work. . . . But that gives a wrong, busy impression. I help a friend who's a photographer. Her name's Anna Cory. She's very good. I'm a sort of secretary; and sometimes I help her with sitters, when she's tired or bored."

"Sounds interesting," he said conventionally.

"Occasionally it is, but often it isn't. Nobody comes, or Anna gets sick of the faces and won't take any trouble. . . ." And is so casual, not to say contemptuous, that they go away flustered, bridling, and do not recommend her to their friends. "She's a painter, really, a good one, only she says not good enough; and she's only interested in beautiful people."

"She sounds rather petulant and exacting. I don't think I'd like her to take my photograph."

"I've made her sound awful, but she's nice. And you should see her when she *is* interested. She'll take endless trouble. Only of course it isn't a commercial way of going on. I expect it'll come to an end soon."

"And what'll you do then?"

"Don't know. Look for something else, I suppose—goodness knows what. I shan't be snapped up." He looked faintly disturbed and she added gaily: "The rest of the time I mooch about and go to the pictures, and see people and play the gramophone and talk. . . . Just like other people, in fact. So there really is nothing to tell, you see. What I enjoy most in the world is my hot bath. I'd stay in one all day if it weren't so debilitating."

"What a horrible confession."

"What do you enjoy most in the world?"

He considered, raising his eyebrows:

"I really only like one thing." He said it in a momentary general silence; laughed to himself and added: "Tell me where you live."

"I live in the house of my cousin, Etty Somers. P'raps you remember her?"

"Lord, yes, I remember Etty Somers. We were debs together. What's happened to her? Hasn't she married?"

"No, she never married. She still floats about—just the same. Does some little odd jobs and goes lunching and dining and night-clubbing. . . ."

"She was very attractive."

"Yes. She is still: only she's got a bit teeny-looking—shrunken. And somehow she doesn't fit these earnest down-to-bedrock days. She's a pre-war model left over, really. She says garden parties and parasols and blue velvet snoods, and a stall at society bazaars and Lily Elsie . . . and the *Dolly Dialogues* and airs and graces. Poor little Ett! Though I don't know why I say poor. She seems quite safe and happy. . . ." She had her own money, and people with a bit of money were all right. "She never wanted to marry. She could have a dozen times over."

"I see," he said. He was looking at her closely, amused. . . . Wondering about me. She said on a sudden impulse, flushing:

"I married years ago—I'm really Mrs. Ivor Craig. It didn't work. We separated two years ago. . . . However, perhaps you know all that by now."

"Bad luck," he said quietly.

"Oh, no. Stupidity. Only myself to blame."

"Oh, don't do that," he said quickly. "Don't blame yourself. Or any one else. I never do." He was serious, saying something he meant. "People do what they must," he said, staring at his plate.

"Yes," she said, with a kind of internal start. "I think that too."

It was like a surrender. She felt acquiescent, supported. Now he's the person who's said that to me.

As if some obstacle to general sight and hearing had suddenly been removed, she became aware again of the room and its other occupants. Voices, faces by candlelight opened out on her once more. She saw Marigold shaking with laughter, heard her talking shrilly, rapidly, down the table to George and beyond George to her mother, to the man called Denham on her mother's further side. They seemed to be chaffing Lady Spencer. All were turned laughing towards her, and she was countering their sallies with a quick tongue and a sparkling eye. Dear, dear Lady Spencer, enjoying herself, being teased. . . . Even George looked almost lively. He doesn't remember me. He looked quite blank when I murmured we'd met . . . as if he couldn't have heard aright. He hasn't changed much . . . a little less of the flat brown hair on the small round, unintellectual head; frame a little heavier, expression a trifle more stunned, opaque. . . . "D'you remember, Mr. Basset, when you were obliged to correct me for calling pink coats red coats? . . ." Oh, dear, the mortification. . . . The one called Denham's got a horrid face. And so has his wife. A coupling of monsters. . . . Rollo ought to talk to her now, she looks constricted, conveying: "Don't mind me. Being ignored doesn't upset me in the slightest. I have my own thoughts. . . . Nowadays of course one's used to bad manners. . . ." Plump, buttoned-up face, baby-blue eyes close-set, turned-up nose, banal obstinate mouth in grooves. . . . Beyond her, the impassive, steadily-chewing macaw's profile of Aunt Blanche. . . .

Now for Sir Ronald. She turned towards him, breaking the ice with a radiant beam. He said in a surprisingly high, feminine register:

"I feared vis uvverwise delightful meal was going to slip by in vain proximity."

"I feared so too." She continued to beam, disarming him. In case he thinks because he's old . . . or because I'm too engrossed. . . .

"Better late van never," he said. His eyes were as limpid, as innocent as a couple of dew-washed periwinkles: the girlish eyes of the British general, the Imperial administrator, the pioneer explorer. . . . He gave a jerk of his head towards his other neighbour, and murmured: "Wonderful creature. . . ."

"She must be. Such an appearance. It's fabulous, isn't it?"

"Ve wittiest woman I ever knew," he pronounced solemnly, "and ve most truly cosmopolitan. And what a musician! . . . What a musician! . . ."

Olivia took a look across him at the gaunt aquiline profile set in a dark remotely-brooding immobility, neither eating, drinking, looking nor listening.

"She seems to embody Gothic grandeur. . . ."

He considered this.

"I fink raver of ve great French style," he said. "Zélide. . . ."

"Ah yes. Zélide. . . ." To reassure him about the extent of my culture.

"In vese days," he sighed, "a glorious anachronism . . . a blessed anachronism. . . ."

"Ah, yes." Time to change the tone. Culture will fail me. "No pudding?" She raised her eyebrows at his empty plate.

"No. . . . No . . ." he said doubtfully, rather anxiously. He stuck his eyeglass in and eyed the pink-and-white cherry-scattered *volupté* she was engaged upon. "No, I fink not."

"It's so good,—you can't imagine. Angel's food."

"Between you and me," he murmured, leaning towards her confidentially. "I don't care much for sweets. Never did. I shall reserve my forces for ve savoury . . . I suppose vere is a savoury?" He looked anxious again. "I can't read ve menu at vis distance."

"'Croûtes aux champignons à la crême,'" she read encouragingly.

"Ah! Yes—good. Croûtes aux champignons à la crême. Always delicious in vis house. Vey've had veir cook close on twenty years here—did you know? I fink I must be acquainted wiv the whole of her extensive repertoire. She's a wonderful creature. Of course, she has her weak spots like all artists.

But she has a way of doing veal. . . ." He cast his eyes up. "It's like nuffing I ever tasted in vis country. . . . Croûtes aux champignons à la crême. I shall reserve my forces for vat and enjoy vis course vicariously."

"I love puddings," she said, in the style of pretty confession. "In fact, I love food altogether."

"Excellent! So do I. I like to hear a lady admitting to a healthy appetite. From what I gavver, it's rare in vese degenerate days." His eyes travelled mildly over her, and his thought was plain: Not that these curves are as they should be. . . . Tastes formed in the Edwardian heyday, when Aunt Blanche had, presumably, dazzled him with her upholstery, revolted from modern concavity. Ah, Blanche and Millicent Venables, notable pair of sisters, graceful, witty, majestic! . . . And all the others. . . . Alas! a mould discarded. These contemporary silhouettes, not only unalluring but disquieting, like so many other symptoms in the sexes nowadays. . . .

"My very dear sister-in-law, Millicent Spencer," he went on, polishing his eyeglass, "has always understood to a remarkable degree ve art of living . . . somefing of a lost art nowadays, to my mind . . . decidedly a lost art. It includes, I need hardly say, a forough understanding of ve principles of gastronomy . . . a forough understanding. . . . Her table is still one of ve best in England . . . one of ve best." He turned round in his chair and sniffed yearningly towards the serving-table. Still no savoury?

"I adore her," said Olivia, gazing at her hostess. "I've known her since I was a child. Marigold and I did lessons together."

"Did you indeed . . . did you?" That sends me up a place or two. "What a charming child she was! Dear me, yes; exquisite. . . ." He stuck his eyeglass in, and blew out a reminiscent sigh. "But she'll never be what her mother was. Never."

"No, I suppose not. The scale's entirely different for one thing, isn't it?—the difference between—say a lyric and an

ode: an Elizabethan lyric and a grand rolling Miltonic ode."
Another blow for culture, at a venture.

"Precisely. Very apt." He was pleased. "Both rare and
precious in veir degree—in veir degree—— Or, to make a more
general comparison, let us say between ve romantic and ve
classical. My personal taste has always leaned towards ve
classical. Particularly nowadays," he added mildly, "as I
descend gradually towards ve brink of total decrepitude, do I
find its austerities and formalities a consolation. . . . But in
youf," he added, smiling with charm, "in youf we can afford
to dally wiv caprice and irregularity."

"Reason has moons . . . you know," she cooed, feeling more
and more exquisite.

"What is vat? It seems unfamiliar. . . ."

She continued to quote in a dainty voice:

> *Reason has moons, but moons not hers*
> *Lie mirrored on her sea,*
> *Confounding her astronomers,*
> *But oh! delighting me!*

"Delighting me too, I'm afraid." She gave him a slightly
wistful smile.

"Ah!" He meditated, surveying her, owing to the monocle,
with one libertine's orb, and one seraphic one. "A very pretty
little case for it. Whevver or no we subscribe to ve doctrine
. . . whevver or no. . . ." He sighed. "Even a horny old
crustacean like myself is capable of a sharp unmefodical twinge
on spring or autumn evenings . . . or in ve company of ve
young and fair." Another old-world smile. "*Le cœur a ses
raisons.* . . . I often fink of vat. It's one of ve trufs we haven't
outgrown yet . . . not yet."

No end to the tossing back and forth of this fragrant
nostalgic æsthetical cowslip-ball. . . . In what career had he
doubtless distinguished himself—lisp, monocle and all? The
aura of authority was around him; drawing-rooms of taste,

cultured evening parties seemed his obvious setting; upper-class Egerias his natural companions: all gracefully, spaciously, securely à la recherche du temps perdu. Connoisseur of . . . collector of . . . He suggested that sort of thing.

The savoury was before him now, rich, succulent. He was respecting it with silent gravity and concentration.

"What a pretty room this is." Deep sea-blue walls, panelled, picked out in gold leaf, elaborate moulding, ceiling a slight finely turned vault, painted with tumbling sea-nymphs, and glowing wreaths, shells, tritons, and Venus emerging among it all. "It's such a nice shape."

"A gem," he said with satisfaction. "Unique, I should judge. Although of course vere's Holkhurst—know Holkhurst? . . . Ah, you ought to go to Holkhurst. Glorious place. I was vere last week-end. Now, ve dining-room vere—ve small dining-room not ve large one—is after ve same style. Fought to be a copy. Ve detail is distinctly coarser—distinctly coarser." He spared a moment to stick his monocle in and survey the ceiling; continued: "I sometimes ask myself whevver ve work doesn't show traces of more van one hand. It's uneven. Ve painting of ve right-hand group in ve corner, for instance. . . . Vat's always seemed to me a *fought* crude. . . ."

"Yes." She examined a few wantoning nymphs. "I see what you mean . . ."

"Ah, vese treasures are a goodly heritage!" He shot out his monocle with an elastic flick, wiped his moustache and squeaked with sudden violence: "And what's to happen to vem all? Look at Holkhurst! Look at Hilton! Closed free-quarters of ve year!"

She hazarded tentatively:

"I suppose it's the end of a chapter . . .?"

"Yes, ve end of a chapter! Ve end of all æsfetic standards! I ask myself: who'll care a hundred years from now for art and letters . . .? I ask myself who. . . ."

"More people perhaps?" Careful now, careful. . . . His eye

was glinting with a fixed fanatical inward spark. . . . Soothe him. ". . . with more leisure, better education . . .?"

"Ach . . .!" He controlled himself, swallowed, brought his voice down an octave. "Potted! Re-hashed! Distributed cheap to all consumers. Yes, yes, yes. . . . No doubt. Museums plentiful as blackberries. Ve long gallery at Holkhurst railed off wiv greasy ropes, guides in attendance, ve cheap excursions disgorging at ve gates and shuffling frough. . . ." Overcome yet assuaged by the drama of the conjured vision, he added with quiet and mournful solemnity: "Yes. Sometimes when I look round I tell myself: Yes, all I care for's well-nigh had its day, and so have I, fank God. . . ."

It was best to smile deprecatingly, sympathetically. One more false step and he might leave the table; or at best awake with indigestion in the night.

He continued with nobility:

"One must try to take ve long view—ve historical perspective. . . . But what goes to my heart"—he leaned towards her, and muttered—"is to see *vem* so hard up. It does indeed. Ve worry tells on vem. Vey put a brave face on it but ve worry tells. It's told on him." He jerked his monocle in the direction of Sir John.

"I'm afraid it has. . . . An estate like this must be a terrible problem these days."

"Parting wiv ve Rembrandt was a terrible blow. And heaven knows what'll have to go next!" Another jerk, towards Rollo. "What's to happen in his time I can't imagine. Unless he contrives to make some money. He's very able—oh, very able. . . . Of course, a—an advantageous marriage would have helped matters, but vere it is. . . . We couldn't wish vat uvverwise. Wiv a young man of his mettle, ve highest fings come first. . . . Dear Nicky. . . . Do you know his wife, his Nicola?"

"Only by sight."

"Beautiful creature, charming creature. . . . Ve most devoted couple. . . . No, one cannot wish vat uvverwise. . . .

Only"—he sank his voice to a mutter—"one could wish her stronger."

"Is she so very delicate?"

"Raver delicate, I fear. Very poor helf. Poor dear. Hmm. Pity." He cleared his throat and continued in stronger tones: "Ah, but when I call to mind ve way life was lived once here! ... in ve old days ... before ve War.... What happy times we had, to be sure! Everybody came here in vose days. Veir week-end parties were famous.... She had vat extraordinary knack of getting ve best out of everybody...." It was like reading a *Times* obituary notice. "Ah dear!" He laughed wistfully. "I shall never forget some of ve charades. Quite elaborate dramatic performances vey used to develop into: everybody used to dress up and have a part: even ve butler and ve ladies' maids. Dear me! I remember a maid of my wife's wiv ve most remarkable soprano—untrained, of course, but really charming. Vere was some idea of paying for her training.... I don't fink anyfing came of it.... I was always called upon to provide ve musical accompaniment. Hours I spent at ve piano ... very small beer, you know—I was never a composer—but it served, —it served. My wife and Millicent—Lady Spencer, you know— bof had pretty musical voices, trained voices, and vey used to sing duets.... Why does nobody sing nowadays?"

The image came up sharp to her mind's eye: Blanche and Millicent, in white, with hour-glass waists and rosebuds sewn all over their flounces, standing up together by the piano, all splendid curves and sparkle, opening their unpainted lips and warbling out duets. Dear me! ... And there sat one of them, opposite, elderly, powerful and sober, frowning a little, giving some view with obvious trenchancy: practical farming perhaps or the housing committee; the other, a few places up, cracking a walnut with deliberation, unwieldy, rather torpid, stertorous-looking: both in black. Dear me! ...

"I remember so well—little Guy, as Eros, in a classical charade—wiv his little winged cap, and a bow ... and nuffing else on ... how enchanting he looked.... How it shocked

some of ve neighbours. . . . Dear oh dear! Did you know Guy?
What a dear handsome boy he was! . . ."

"No, I never saw Guy. I suppose I was just too young."

"Yes, yes, of course. I was forgetting. Yes. Of course. It
was long before your time. . . ."

"I've seen his portrait often. He looks wonderful."

The charcoal head of him as a boy, by Sargent: an Edwardian dream-child with romantic hair, and one of those
long necks in an open cricket shirt. . . .

"Ve flower of ve flock. . . ."

But he died for England: going over the top, at the head of
his men, shot through the heart. . . . All as it should be. And
they'd done what could be done: worn white for mourning;
put a memorial window in the church; collected his letters
and poems and all the tributes to him, had them printed for
private circulation. All bore witness—nurses, governesses,
schoolmasters, broken-hearted friends—all said the same: gay,
brilliant, winning, virtuous, brave Guy: pattern of the eldest
son. . . .

"I remember—a very handsome boy, a cousin—called
Archie——" she hazarded. For of course he must be Archie's
father: yet one never knew: Archie might have died, or turned
out a problem or a disgrace. . . .

"Ah, you knew Archie, did you? My young hopeful. . . .
Young scamp vat he was. . . ." His voice seemed to lose
warmth, to suggest dissatisfaction, perhaps reluctance. "Yes,
he spent a good deal of his time here as a schoolboy. His aunt
was extraordinarily good to him . . . extraordinarily good. She
had a weakness for him. . . ." He shook his head. It was clear
that Archie was no part of the pink sunset glow of the past.
"We had no settled home in England ven of course. . . . It was
during my last governorship. . . ."

"Oh, yes, of course. . . ." So that was it. But where? Where
are Governors? . . .

Sir Ronald turned to his other neighbour.

"Cigarette, Olivia?"

"Thank you." She turned joyfully to Rollo. The way he said "Olivia" sounded pleasant and strange, setting up a kind of echo in her ears. She met his eye, ironical, over the lighter he held out to her.

"The point is," she murmured, "nothing is as good as it was before we knew about it."

"And any one dead is automatically superior to any one alive. . . . All the same, if he was telling you what a much better person Guy was than me, you can believe him. It happens to be the truth. Dear old Guy, he was a good chap, he really was. He had that dead right touch. . . ."

"Do you miss him very much?"

"I did once. Mostly I forget him now." He relit his cigar. "Occasionally I still feel a vague impersonal annoyance when I reflect on the waste . . . and the inferior article's aptitude for survival. Mine I mean."

She said nothing. After a bit he went on in the same colourlessly reflective voice:

"He loathed the war, it shocked him, he believed in God. I'm never shocked. I dare say I'd have taken very kindly to the war. . . . Dash it all, most people did, didn't they?"

"I suppose it was easy to get apathetic. . . . One can't keep up horror and indignation. . . . They're too wearing."

"They're no good anyway."

"Why not?" There he goes again. . . . "Surely one must believe *something's* some good?"

"Oh, rather. . . ." He puffed away at his cigar, narrowing his eyes; then continued: "What I should like is to be able to keep my head—sort of on the sly—wouldn't you?—whatever I found myself involved in . . . I feel that might be some good."

"Some satisfaction, you mean. Awfully superior feeling."

"Well, no." He nibbled his forefinger, frowning a little. "It's a *kind* of belief, really. . . ."

"Living privately—no matter how publicly . . .?"

"Something of that, perhaps. . . ."

Marigold called across the table:

"Rollo, *haven't* you got a foul temper?"

"Foul."

"Mummy's saying none of her children ever quarrelled. Did you ever! I can remember when I was about four, looking down from the top landing and seeing you and Archie trying to throw each other over the banisters."

"Marigold, what nonsense."

"Well, I did. Didn't I, Rollo?"

"Don't remember. I dare say you did, though."

"I was thrilled."

"It was a game, you silly girl," said Lady Spencer, almost annoyed.

"Well, it wasn't. Because they didn't make any noise at all. It was like a fight in a film. That's how I suddenly realised they meant it. I've never forgotten it."

"You dreamt it."

"Well, fancy not wanting us to have tempers," said Marigold, subsiding with a pout. "We're not eunuchs."

There was laughter; and the table broke up again, into separate pieces.

"What's happened to Archie?" said Olivia, low to Rollo.

"Oh, he hangs around. . . . When did you last see him?"

"At Marigold's coming-out party. He made rather an impression."

"Oh, did he?" Rather harsh, hostile voice.

"He was the beautifullest young man I'd ever seen."

"Was he? He's gone off a bit, I fear. He's put on a tummy and his hair's a bit thin."

"Oh, how sad."

"Terribly sad. I'm afraid he's worried."

"Also he was the first drunk person I'd ever talked to. It was a shock."

"Oh, was he a bore?"

"It wasn't so much that. It was something more general—more important. About people changing and forgetting—and not meaning what they said. . . . It turned life suddenly into such a *black* problem—too much to go through with almost. When one's young and gets a knock, all humanity seems involved. . . . As a matter of fact that was why I went out on the terrace. . . ."

"Where I also had gone for a breath of air. . . ." He stared at a wine-glass, turning it in his hand. "Very odd."

They were silent. . . . And when we came in again, Archie was shouting for Nicola. Rollo shouldered him out of his way, it was clear then, the impact of their dislike and jealousy. . . . Nicola came down the stairs and held her hand up.

"And ever since then," he said, "I've wanted to see you again."

She looked quickly away from him, round the table. It sounded preposterous—like a voice in a dream.

"So have I. . . ."

Change was in the air. The wheels were running down. Lady Spencer and Aunt Blanche were on their feet. Rollo stood up and pulled her chair back without looking at her at all. Lady Spencer held out a hand affectionately as she passed and drew her on into the doorway.

Replete, at ease, smoothing their hips, warming their backs, the ladies stood round the drawing-room fire. . . . Now Marigold and I will talk. . . . But no. Marigold, wandering absently, touching things with vague fingers, sketching fragmentary smiles, powdering her nose without looking at it, said suddenly:

"Mummy, I must dash up and see Nannie. I promised I would. She's got hurt feelings because we haven't had a heart-to-heart, and you know what that means . . . purple patches on her neck and hell for the housemaids. I shan't be longer than I can help."

She darted out of the room without so much as a glance in Olivia's direction. As if she'd forgotten my existence. Nothing could have been more disconcertingly typical. She hadn't changed at all; still restlessly appearing and disappearing, suddenly attentive, suddenly remote; like a cat.

"Poor old Nannie." Lady Spencer looked thoughtful. "She's getting very difficult. She's *so* rheumatic and crotchety and trying with the young servants. . . . But what's one to do?"

"Can't you pension her off?" said Aunt Blanche.

"That's what I'd like to do, but where's she to go? She's hardly got any relations left—only one old married sister somewhere in Wales, and they don't get on. And she won't just take it easy here and potter about. It would break her heart to feel she's not useful any more. And of course she *lives* for the children's visits. Marigold's so sweet to her."

"I often think," said Cousin Mary, sitting down and drawing a piece of tapestry work from a large black silk bag, "what a sad life it is to be a Nannie. I'm sure I don't know what I'm going to do with mine. John goes to school next term and the guvvie will take on both girls in the schoolroom. There'll really be nothing for the poor dear to do. I suppose I might keep her on for sewing. She's very clever at loose covers and so forth. But Harry thinks we shouldn't afford it." She sighed complacently, threading a needle.

"And then of course you do so much sewing yourself." Aunt Blanche sat down with a heave and a creak, knees spread, legs planted foursquare on a pair of incongruously elegant narrow feet.

"I make most of the girl's clothes, of course," said Mary, in a modest voice.

"Marvellous."

"It's a saving, of course."

"What's that you're on now?" Aunt Blanche put up a lorgnette and leaned forward tremendously to peer. "Jolly colours."

"Do you like it?" Mary smoothed out the canvas, appearing to deprecate it. "It *is* rather a nice design. Tudor."

"Mary always did lovely work," sighed Lady Spencer. "Do

you remember, dear, the cushion you did for me, years ago?
It's in my boudoir to this day."

"Oh, that!" She looked scornful. "Quilted. I remember.
It wasn't a bad pattern."

"I wish I was clever with my fingers."

"I can't bear having idle hands," Mary confessed gently.
"I got the children's winter jumpers finished, and stockings
for John, so I thought to myself, well, why shouldn't I give
myself a treat and do something in the ornamental line for
a change."

"What's it going to be, dear?"

"Oh, it's just for a chair. I'm doing a set of eight for the
dining-room."

"*What* a labour for you?"

"I think it will be gay," she said meekly, holding up
the square with her dear little old-fashioned head on one
side.

Nothing you did or conceived of could ever be gay; and
do your children know yet they hate you?

"What's *your* masterpiece, Blanche?" inquired Lady Spencer
as her sister also opened a work-bag, a massive and handsome
one of crimson damask, and drew from it a stout pair of wooden
knitting pins, a ball of violet wool and a curious knitted oblong
to match.

"Oh, my dear, it's just a garment. For my needlework
guild. You know—everybody makes two and the things go
to the Workhouse for Christmas. It's a sort of bed-jacket, I
think." She looked at it in a brooding, doubtful way.

"It'll be nice and cheerful," said Mary with gracious
interest, conscious of superior powers. "What's the stitch,
Aunt Blanche?"

"Oh, my dear, just plain. Purl's too much for my feeble
brain."

"You'll never finish it, Blanche."

"Not a hope, my dear. Tucker'll have to unpick it all, I
expect, and knit it up again. Still. . . . I thought I'd start it.

Poor old dears, they do so appreciate it if they know one's made the things oneself."

Olivia sat down on a low stool beside Aunt Blanche.

"What a gorgeous bag," she said. The look of it lying richly on that bursting lap made her feel weak, yielding and protected. Aunt Blanche looked down at her in a plethoric kindly way from under her full, fowl's lid.

"Rather jolly, isn't it? I got it at that Blind place in London. Do you ever go there?"

"Oh, yes, I know," said Mary. "They do wonderful work. I always make a point of doing my Christmas shopping there. Only, of course, they're so dreadfully expensive. . . ."

What's the Blind place. . . . What's become of the blind man. . . . Timmy his name was; and he and his wife kept hens, and he had a child called Elizabeth. . . . Sharply she remembered him in this room, ten years ago: waltzing round and round with him to the Blue Danube, his fingers quivering; . . . feeling him listen for Marigold hour after hour. . . .

"Do you do needlework, Olivia dear?"

"No, I'm afraid I don't. It's as much as I can face to mend my stockings. Kate was always such a natural-born sewer, I felt defeated at the starting post and never bothered."

"Dear Kate, how is she? I always admired her so much. Has she still got that exquisite skin and hair?"

"Yes, still very good."

"Olivia's sister," explained Lady Spencer, "had the most exquisite fair skin and hair."

"Kate's exactly the same," said Olivia. "Only of course quite different."

Mary uttered a deprecating tinkle.

"Like all of us." Lady Spencer smiled with a sigh. "And is she happy, dear Kate?"

"Yes, I think she is. I think she'd say she was happy on the whole."

"She was always such a splendid capable girl." The sensible sister . . . the one who'd avoid getting into trouble:

so different from the younger one. . . . "And *how* many children is it?"

"Four. Beautifully spaced out."

"Four! How delightful. The ideal number for a family. I hope they look like her?"

"No, they don't. They look like their Pa, but they're quite nice. Three girls and a boy. The youngest a baby."

An extraordinary bleating sound, something between a gasp, a groan and a coo, came from Mary.

"Oo-o-oh! *How* old?"

"About eight months, I think. I can't remember."

"Eight months! The *lamb*! How I do envy her. Every time I hear of any one with a tiny baby I feel quite *green* with envy. Oh dear! If *only* they'd stay wee and cuddly and *never* grow up. Personally I think up to a month old is the sweetest time of all. . . . Oh dear, when I think of mine, the great long-legged things!—I can't bear it."

"Can't you really?" said Olivia. "I should have thought the only point about producing them was to encourage their growth. Or isn't it like gardening?"

Mary ran an eye over her. . . . Ringless hands, flat hips and stomach. . . .

"I don't think it's quite the same," she said with cold firm amused gentleness, making allowances. "Not for mothers anyway."

"Of course I've never had any," said Olivia clearly, "so I can't tell."

"I always found their companionship such a joy as they grew older," said Lady Spencer, breaking in with tact. "But of course, one misses the babies too."

"Personally I always disliked babies," said Aunt Blanche, struggling with a dropped stitch. "All the same, I do wish Archie would marry a nice girl and make a grandmother of me. I find I quite yearn to be a grandmother, Millicent. I suppose it's old age."

"It's very pleasant," sighed Lady Spencer. "Marigold's two

are such darlings. Of course grandmothers have to know their place, and *never* give advice or interfere."

"You must find that a little difficult, dearest."

"Not as difficult as you'd find it, love."

"Are you the mother of Archie?" said Olivia, playing with the ball of wool. "I remember him. We used to dance together at the children's parties." She smiled up at Lady Spencer. "I remember teaching him the baby polka and he thought it was so funny. He simply stood still and cackled with laughter. I couldn't think why. And once I said to him: ' What lovely blue eyes you've got,' and he said, ' Oh, d'you think so? Yours are brown, aren't they? I do prefer blue myself.'"

Aunt Blanche shook to the depths with a chuckle. "The wretch!" She was delighted. "I hope you snubbed him."

"Not I. I was much too madly in love with him. I was a fearfully amorous child. But even at that, I think he must have been irresistible."

Mary gave a trifling laugh in the top of her nose: deploring the tone. . . . I must always have been a nasty-minded girl.

"He's always been very good to his old Ma," said Aunt Blanche. She gave Olivia an approving, it seemed almost a grateful look. She likes me anyway. . . . Without a word said, it was all plain: Archie, far from satisfactory, on bad terms with his father, tapping secret supplies of money, of love, comfort and indulgence from his foolish mother. . . .

"He's a dear boy," said Lady Spencer, looking unusually abstracted.

"Do you see much of him these days?" inquired Aunt Blanche, a touch of something in her voice,—embarrassment, apology. . . . "He's got so many friends, I really don't know. . . . He's out so much. . . ."

"Oh, no, I haven't seen him for years. He'd never remember me. We're in quite different worlds now."

Lady Spencer broke in quickly:

"What is it exactly you're busy at nowadays, dear? Your mother did tell me——"

"I work in London." It seemed a futile effort to explain it all again; but she did so, briefly.

"How interesting," said Lady Spencer, approving the principle of labour. "It sounds delightful work."

"You must give me the address," said Aunt Blanche. "Not for myself—God forbid!—But I do think Archie ought to be done. I haven't got anything nice of him since Eton. Don't you think Archie ought to be done, Millicent?"

"What sort of prices do you run?" said Mary.

"Absolutely top prices."

"Oh, really? What a pity! I mean I do think it's rather a pity not to come down these days when everybody's coming down—don't you? I mean everybody's so badly off. . . . It sort of keeps people away, doesn't it?"

"Oh, yes, it does keep people away." This is the personal touch in salesmanship—counts for so much: dine out in the best houses, use your charm, and the rest's child's play.

A dance orchestra flooded the room suddenly, noisily.

"Gracious! Where can that come from on a Sunday?" said Mary.

"Some low foreign station," said Olivia.

Silently, Marigold came back through the open doors from the ante-room, and stood in front of the fire, listening, nibbling her fingers—the same trick as Rollo.

"What a jolly tune," said Aunt Blanche.

"Couldn't you turn it down just a little, dear?" said Lady Spencer. "We can't hear ourselves speak."

"No, no," said Aunt Blanche. "It's cheerful. Makes me want to dance." She tapped her feet and swayed about from the hips in her arm-chair, humming loudly.

"I haven't danced for years," sighed Mary. "Harry just won't go out in the evenings. He's getting *such* an old stick-in-the-mud. I tell him he's just letting himself get middle-aged—and me too. We'll soon be just a dull old stay-at-home couple, sitting over the fire." She made a pretty, girlish *moue*. "And I do so *love* dancing."

"Why don't you find a boy-friend and go on the tiles?" said Marigold.

"Oh, Marigold!" Mary bridled and tinkled. "Aunt Millicent, isn't she awful? What next?"

Marigold dropped suddenly on her knees by Olivia's stool and leaned a cheek against her shoulder.

"What next? What next?" she murmured.

After a moment she moved away lightly and knelt by the fire, staring into it. Something seemed to happen in the room. Beneath the incongruous assault of drum and saxophone it appeared frozen suddenly in a gleaming fixity. The group by the fire had a static quality, as if anæsthetised. The needles paused. The ladies leaned their heads upon their hands, stared in front of them.

Only Lady Spencer stood up erect, majestic, upon the hearthrug: as if to stand thus were her sole purpose and function: as if the pose were an heroic assertion. Time drew a circle round the scene. It was now: it was a hundred, two hundred years ago. . . .

Nothing essential is changed yet. . . .

"What a lousy din," said Marigold suddenly. She sprang up, seizing Olivia by the hand, and led her rapidly away through the doors into the ante-room.

She switched off the wireless, flung herself on the sofa and pulled Olivia down beside her.

In the ensuing vacuum of silence Aunt Blanche's unrepressed voice rang out, clearly audible from the other end of the next room.

"What an attractive gel, Millie. Where did you get her over from?"

Olivia kicked her legs towards the door, kissed both hands with a flourish.

" We can—hee-ee-ar you!" Marigold trumpeted through her fists in a loud ribald whisper. They giggled.

A low murmur was going on from the inner sanctuary, inaudible now. . . . Laying fingers to lips, raising eyebrows, nodding. . . . *Most unfortunate.* . . . *Really?* . . . *Who was he?* . . . *And is she* . . . *? Dear, dear!* . . . *Pity.* . . .

Discreet, guardedly regretful.

Marigold sprang up again.

"Oh, come on."

Olivia caught her up in the corridor among the dark bloodshot pictures.

"Let them cackle their heads off," said Marigold. "God, how I do hate women. That Mary needs a bomb under her—and I wish I could be the one to set it off. . . . Olivia. . . ." She stopped short and gave her a hug. "I'm *extraordinarily* glad. . . . Why don't I ever see you? Why haven't you ever looked me up in London? You are a pig. I think of you so often—you and Kate. Oh dear! How we used to laugh! Didn't we? Mm? D'you remember?"

"Yes, I do."

I suppose we laughed. . . . Yes, we did. . . . Only what I remember seems much more complicated: exciting, emotional —melancholy, somehow, on the whole. . . .

"Such fun. . . ." She went on walking apparently at random down one passage and at right angles into another. "You must tell me all about you. My dear, I've got two children. Did you know? Can you imagine? I've done my duty, haven't I? They're rather sweet. Oh, and I remember you wrote me a divine letter when I had Iris, and I don't believe I ever answered."

"It doesn't matter. It didn't need an answer."

"Oh, but I meant to! Only I'm so hopeless about letters. I don't know what comes over me. I *can't*. And there were so many," she added vaguely.

She opened a door at the far end of the passage: they were in a wing of the house Olivia had never penetrated before. She switched on a light and they went into a small, close uneasy-shaped room with red walls and dark red curtains and heavy Victorian furniture. Various antlers, foxes' brushes, heads of animals were nailed about the walls; and in a case on the table was a stuffed otter, snarling on a rock among greenery, with bared teeth and scarlet tongue. Silver cups and other athletic trophies adorned the mantelshelf; and above them hung photographs of horses and fish, and sporting and school groups. A thick smell of polish and green baize pervaded the room.

"Ugh! How murky." Marigold wrinkled her nostrils. "Never mind. It's sequestered anyway. They'll never guess where we are. I must telephone." She closed the door behind them, switched on a stark rail of electric fire in the grate, and looked about her. "My God! What a nightmare of a room. I never noticed before. Its name is the telephone room. It's a secret extension known only to the family and you, and everybody comes here to put their secret calls through. The footman mostly, I should think, judging by the smell." She took up the receiver from an old-fashioned instrument screwed to the wall behind the door, and gave a London number. "Sit down, Livia. Make yourself at home. I promised to ring up Sam. You don't mind, do you?"

"Shan't I go away?"

"No, of course not. It isn't private. . . . Beside I want to talk to you." She leaned against the wall, holding the receiver in a vague half-hearted way. "Livia. . . . It *was* fun Rollo running into you like that. He was so thrilled. Isn't he a darling? . . . I do love him. . . ." She stiffened suddenly and said: "Hallo! . . . Oh, Lang? . . . It's me. . . . Tell his lordship, will you, please? . . . Not there? . . . Oh. . . . Wasn't he expected? I thought he said he'd be dining to-night. . . . I see. . . . Yes, p'raps he did. . . . No, no message. At least . . . No, never mind. Good-bye, Lang."

She hung up with a crash and stood gnawing at her fingers, her eyes very narrow beneath the fringe. "His lordship telephoned at seven o'clock to say he'd been unavoidably detained in the country," she quoted. "Just—as—I—thought. Damn his eyes. The fur *will* be in the fire. . . . Well, he can stew." Her eyes darted, looking at nothing.

"What's the matter?"

"Oh, nothing really. . . . Only he'd arranged to dine in London to-night with his aged parents. It was all fixed up. He was going to do the clean breast and ask for some money. We're so in debt. And they're so touchy, they'll be furious and bitterly wounded and everything, I suppose. Bang goes our last hope. He *never* does what he says he will. *Never.* I've never known him to." She laughed. "Oh, well. . . . What the hell? . . . It doesn't make much odds. We've been bust for years, but we seem to go on in comparative afflatus, not to say luxury, like everybody else. . . . Sam's fantastic about money. You wouldn't believe. And I'm not awfully economical either. . . . What's to be done? . . . I wonder if Mr. Ponds would like to put me in his harem. . . . What, jib at a couple of double gins?—not Lady Britton. . . . Shall I offer myself for five hundred?" She began to walk up and down, fingering and shifting objects. "You know, I wouldn't a *bit* mind being poor. I truly wouldn't. I know I wouldn't. It's one of the few things I'm certain of . . . though everybody laughs if I say it. I mean —if I was in love with a person—and we wanted perhaps to go off together—I wouldn't mind *one scrap* if he hadn't a bean— it would never occur to me to be refrained by that. *Heaps* of women I know, quite nice ones, simply say, ' No money, no go, my boy '—and that's that. But personally I'd be glad . . . yes . . . I'm almost sure I'd prefer it. It 'ud make one feel one was doing something *real* . . . wouldn't it? I often think about living in a little house and doing the cooking and saving up for treats and——"

"Oh, Marigold! *What* a day-dream!"

"Why?" She reflected, seeming to be taken aback. "Are you poor, Olivia?"

"Pretty poor."

"I know, someone told me." Her eyes flew over Olivia from top to toe; and the latter said, smiling:

"Don't I look it?"

"No, you look marvellous. But then you always did, you and Kate. It's your figures, I suppose."

"It isn't amusing to be poor, darling. You wouldn't like it, honestly. Unless you mean something different from what I mean. I expect you do. . . ." Well on the safe side of the line, with somebody to fall back on and a guaranteed overdraft. . . .

"I don't know what I mean. Never do. I suppose I'm talking through my cocked hat, as usual. But I just feel anything would be better than this frittering futile. . . . I'd like to have to work—have my day filled up from start to finish and come home too weary not to be peaceful." She leaned against the mantelpiece, brooding. "Tell me, Livia, do you ever feel as if you weren't real?"

"Often."

"Oh, do you ? I shouldn't have thought you would. It's a beastly feeling. Everybody has a solid real life except oneself. One's a sort of fraud . . . empty." She spoke the last word with a slow lingering emphasis. "I thought having babies would cure me: it's one of the few things you can't pretend about all the way through. However prettily and unsickly you start, you're jolly well for it in the end. But I don't know. . . . It turned out to be another sort of dream. They gave me so much dope I sailed through the worst of it as if it wasn't me. And there I was again: the young mother. Touching. Money for jam for the photographers." She laughed suddenly.

"I'd love to see your children."

"Oh, yes, you must! They're divine." Her voice was vague. After a moment she went on, differently: "I adore them, of course, but I must admit I'm simply *amazed* every time I see them, wondering where on earth they came from and why they've taken up their abode in the house. And then . . . Bennie's so frightfully naughty and unbridled—absolutely a *gangster*. When I see him in one of his moods I think to myself —*look* what you've done . . . and I simply *long* to abolish him. It seems the only way out."

Olivia burst out laughing; and Marigold's rapt ferociously

frowning expression relaxed gradually into a look of puzzled, faintly amused relief.

"I suppose it'll work out all right," she said vaguely; adding after a pause: "I wonder if dying'll be a sort of dream too? Don't you? I can't believe it'll seem like *me*, *me* dying. . . . Ugh! Have I really got to?" She opened her eyes to their widest, and they looked blank and blind with their dilated pupils, like eyes made of glass. "I get moments when it sweeps over me—in the middle of the night or when I'm by myself in the house—and depressed. It's like dropping through a trap-door unexpectedly."

She turned round and leaned her arms along the mantelpiece and her head down sideways on her arms. Her curls tumbled over out of their sophisticated dressing, and looked irresponsible, childish. What the years had done to her looks became suddenly evident. The face, that sketch in a few light lines, had acquired not precision exactly, not an adult cast, but a curious clarifying and definition of each one of the old tentative ambiguities and contradictions. Enthralling, paradoxical interplay of planes and surfaces seen momentarily in repose: cold, sensual, tender, adamant . . . transparent, dissimulating . . . moving romantic creature. . . . Sinister creature. *Mad, bad, and* . . . No, what nonsense! . . .

"Are you often by yourself and depressed?"

She lifted her head and looked round at Olivia out of the corners of her eyes.

"No, no, not I." She looked slightly sheepish, slightly mocking, as she used to look in the Shakespeare class when they caught her drawing rude Skinny Gingers. "I'm practically never alone and I enjoy myself *frightfully* practically always. Don't you? It's so silly not to, don't you think? . . . Livia, darlin', tell me more about yourself. I've been talking too much about me. Why *did* you go and drop out of my life? I wish people wouldn't do that. I hate it. I was so excited when Rollo told me. . . . He was quite determined you were to be got to come—not that he needed to be determined, because of course we all wanted. . . . Only it was funny of Rollo, he doesn't often. . . . I was so glad. I do hope you like him. Poor sweet, it's time he had a break."

"Why? Does he need one?"

"*I* think he does. He's just *wasted*. Only he's so kind and easy-going it 'ud never occur to him. Between you and me, and any one else who cares to listen, that Nicola's no damn' good." She made a grimace, and came and flung herself down in one of the leather arm-chairs opposite Olivia. "There! That clinches it: this chair smells of Albert's hair-oil. I suppose he wantons in it with the housemaid. I always thought this room had a sort of lustful atmosphere."

"Why do you say she's no good?"

"Who? Oh, Nicola? Oh, she's a bitch. She loathes me and I loathe her. She's jealous. Mummy can't do with her either, only of course wild horses wouldn't drag it out of her. . . . All this family bunk! Of course, Rollo won't hear a *word*. . . . He adores her—or he thinks he does. My only hope is that somebody'll enlighten him one of these days."

"You mean you don't think he does really?"

"No, it's only he's so loyal. . . . She doesn't give him a thing. . . ."

"I don't believe that makes much difference. . . . In fact, quite the contrary sometimes." Why do I go on? Why feel embarrassed—almost guilty? . . . and pleased as well? "Is she double-crossing him or something?"

"Oh, no, not that! She'd never have the guts. . . . If only she *would* do something definite, like have a lover or take to drugs, there might be some hope. Oh, I don't know. There never was such a witless die-away ninny. And not an ounce of humour. She had a miscarriage once, quite an ordinary one, at least two years ago, and instead of going ahead and trying again she's decided she's an invalid—or her mother has. Her mother's a proper sabre-toothed tiger. I bet she's told Rollo Nicola's too delicate to take any risks with and he mustn't go to bed with her. She's always lying on sofas and if she's crossed she cries and her mother says her nervous system's ruined. . . . Poor old Rollo. . . ." She took up a tiny silver-framed snapshot from the table beside her and examined it through screwed-up eyes. "Who's that pursy infant? One of us, I suppose." She put it down again, thrust out her gold-sandalled feet and examined them, wriggling her toes. "The point is . . . she's awfully sweet in some ways. She's just an infant, a spoilt one. And of course she's quite, quite lovely. One can't help rather cherishing her. There's no vice in the girl. . . . Not like Sam, he's full of it. Livia, you must meet Sam. You'd like him. Women always do. He's terribly attractive and he's rather sweet too, only he's got a lousy temper, specially when he's a bit tight. . . .

"He's sort of unexpected too: he's very musical and he goes to concerts by himself . . . and he gets worked up about Ireland: he's Irish, you know, so of course he's got the gift of the gab and he's not awfully reliable." She sprang up again, looking restless and undecided. "I must say I'd like to know what he's been up to this week-end. . . . I *thought* there was something in the wind: he was so emphatic about being bored to death where he was going. . . . Shall I ring him up and give him a glorious surprise? Shall I? Now?"

"If you like."

She looked at Olivia in a vague yet insistent way. . . . Ringing up Sam an act of hostility to which I'm to lend support. . . .

"I jolly well will." She started towards the telephone, stopped. "No, I won't. . . . I don't know where he is, and that's a fact. I meant to ask him, but I forgot." She went off into one of her silent laughing fits. "Livia, marriage is the devil, isn't it? It's too degrading. . . . It suits me all right though, really." She looked suddenly sobered: remembering my ambiguous state. "Livia . . ." she said with affectionate vagueness.

"Mine turned out to be a non-starter. My marriage, I mean." Olivia coloured and giggled.

"You laugh just like you used to. . . . Darlin', I'm sorry. It's a gamble and no mistake, to put it in an entirely original way." She spoke uncertainly, as if wondering what to say.

"Oh, it can't be helped. I shouldn't have married him. . . . I dare say I'm not particularly suitable to marriage."

"Aren't you? Why not? Come to that I don't know who is, on the face of it. Perhaps Mary. Marriage or murder. . . . I know which I'd put her down for. . . . God, what a week-end, really! They make such a point of my coming down, and of course I do love to—only *why* will Ma collect all these specimens—rattling their bones and reeking of moth ball? Talk of feasting with skeletons! . . . Tante Henriette's all right—the French one—she's got some kick left—she's a devil—only she's deaf and ill. . . . But as for the others! Can you imagine when you're old wanting to sit round like they do and track down all your relations and relations by marriage, known and unknown, all ages and generations, and whether they've inherited the family squint or hammer-toes or whatever it is? . . ."

"I know. My mother's just the same. I suppose it makes them feel safer . . . as if they weren't going to disappear altogether."

"I suppose so." She looked sober. "Poor darlings. What with Daddy being so ga-ga. . . . I don't think they feel awfully cheerful any more. Everything falls flat. Have you noticed he's not frightfully bright? It is a shame. There's nothing to be done. He's best with old friends that don't notice him."

"I expect he's quite happy really, you know. He doesn't notice. He looks very peaceful."

She said with grateful eagerness: "Yes, he does, doesn't he? He didn't when he first got ill, he looked so melancholy I couldn't. . . . But now he's quite serene. And he still makes his little jokes, and he can do a bit of fishing and let off his gun. . . . Only there must be moments when——" She stood and stared. "He really was rather a good person. I'll tell you what he was—magnanimous. People aren't often." Suddenly she put out a foot and switched off the electric fire. "What are we doing in this most unprepossessive room? Let's go back." She drew Olivia close to her, an arm round her waist. "Darlin' Olivia, it's lovely talking to you again. How thin you are. Like a boy. Are you all right?"

"As right as rain."

They leaned against one another. Marigold said abruptly, her voice pitched at its highest: "Do you know any queer people?"

"Lots." Olivia laughed. "Nothing but . . ."

"What I meant was—you know—what d'you call 'em—Lesbians and things. . . ."

"Oh, I see." Olivia made a slight involuntary movement away. "Oh, a few, I s'pose."

"Do they fall for you?"

"No—not particularly. . . ."

"I wonder what it would be like. . . . I don't *think* I should like it. I've never felt inclined that way . . . but I once knew someone who was. You never know. . . . Lots of people are, aren't they? Far more than one realises. . . ."

"I expect so."

"Have you ever felt attracted like that?"

"No, I never have."

"I bet if I were like that I'd make a pass at you." She patted and stroked Olivia's hip with a light clinging touch.

"Thank you. The same to you." Olivia put up a hand and ran it quickly over the curls. . . . But I feel foolish, uneasy. . . .

"D'you remember that time you stayed the week-end and we slept in the same bed and pretended to be a married couple? How old were we, I wonder? About fourteen? . . . Innocent fun. . . ."

"I remember."

A silence fell. The smell, the weight, the darkness of plush, mahogany and leather seemed to Olivia to swell out around them, closing them in suffocatingly. What's she driving at? She turned and looked at Marigold and said: "But that's not why my marriage didn't work."

"No, of course. . . . I didn't meant that. . . ."

Oh, didn't you. . . . But why? My looks? A rumour? A sudden, reckless shot of her own at random?

"Not a lover of any sort," said Olivia, laughing. "Nothing romantic. It was more like getting on and off a moving bus very clumsily with the wrong foot and being left sprawling in the road with your hat crooked and your stockings muddy, feeling a fool. . . . For weeks I wasn't sure whether to go back or not. But I just didn't. I drifted away somehow. There wasn't what's known as a clean break."

"Well, I think it was frightfully brave of you," said Marigold vaguely, losing interest. "I'd never dare. . . ."

She pushed her hair back carelessly with one hand and it fell once more into its apparently careless, inevitable arrangement of curls. She took a few steps towards the middle of the room and stood still again, with the dull yellow light from the ceiling full on her fresh silvery skin and greenish gold-shot dress. In this claustrophobic lugubriously human room she looked strange, nymph-like, imprisoned. Her unfathomable individuality of appearance belonged to no period of fashion in looks, seemed independent of care, effort and artifice. She hasn't once glanced in a mirror or fussed with her frock the whole evening. . . . What's she thinking about?

"I s'pose we must rejoin the giddy throng," she said finally.

She sighed deeply, slipped her hand through Olivia's arm, and walked with her up the long empty passage, humming softly. They said nothing more. There was not another word to say.

She's rather bored with me, after all. . . . She made a false step with me. So she's finished; indifferent now. It's ten years ago, and these efforts to recapture . . . a mistake, really. She'd like to yawn. It's been a failure, she won't try again.

This is the last time we'll ever be alone together.

The gentlemen had rejoined the ladies in the drawing-room.

Rollo. . . . He was leaning against the mantelpiece, talking to George. Directly they came in he glanced towards them, glanced away again, went on talking with apparent absorption. The other men were standing about: the evening had not settled down yet. Lady Spencer was sitting opposite Aunt Blanche at the backgammon table, in the middle of the room. Busily they rattled their dice, not looking up. This is the first time I've seen her relaxed, absorbed in a private diversion, not on the *qui vive*, not ready aye ready, official and in control. She looked less old and worn now, her pale face had smiles beneath it. She's beating Aunt Blanche.

Madame de Varenne was in the room again now; sitting in an upright, high-backed chair, not far from Mary, smoking a small cigar and staring at the fire.

Rollo? . . . Surely he hasn't finished with me for the evening. . . . The old familiar sense of loss, of insecurity swept over her.

"Oh, there you are!" cried Mary, laying down her work and staring at them. Her face with its prettyish, loose, trivial moulding seemed to reach out like a sea anemone. "I thought you'd been spirited away."

"Did you?" said Marigold, with marked languor, taking up *Country Life* and examining a page of properties for sale.

"Up to mischief?"

"Mm, rather. We've been arranging a murder, haven't we, Livia? I've often thought I should make a first-class murderess. It's all a question of selecting a victim. And I *think*—I *think* . . . I—have selected—mine. . . ."

Rollo, still leaning against the mantelpiece, turned his head slightly, as if listening. Olivia caught his eye; he smiled, almost imperceptibly. The French eyes had shifted too, were resting on Olivia and Marigold, but there was no flicker in their blackness. Could she hear? Was she observing?

"Marigold! Rollo!" called Lady Spencer from her table, shooting a casual arrow of duty without looking up. "Does any one want to play bridge? . . . Double."

"Does any one want to play bridge?" repeated Marigold gloomily. "Hands up for not on your life," she added in a mutter to Olivia, flinging up an arm in a ribald waving gesture.

"Yes, now, who's game for a rubber?" called out Mary, looking hopeful. "Harry'll play if he's needed, won't you, Harry? Who else is feeling energetic?" There was no answer, and she added winningly: "Who'll be my partner?" She put her head on one side and looked up at Rollo.

He detached himself from his support and lounged across to Olivia's side.

"Play bridge?" he said.

"No, I don't. Don't know how. But don't bother about me. I shall be quite happy."

"With a photograph album," said Marigold.

"Must I play bridge with Mary?" groaned Rollo under his breath.

"No." Marigold leaned against him, fingering his studs, looking dreamy. After a moment she said: "Stay and talk to Olivia and seem as if you weren't paying attention to anything else in the room. Don't take your eyes off her, and if Mary calls out, be deaf."

"I can do all that."

She left them rapidly and went over to the fireplace.

"She'll manage it," said Rollo. He turned his back on the company, and leaning an elbow on the piano, bent an amused unwinking gaze upon Olivia. "Please look as if we were discussing philosophy ... or something. ... Olivia, are you enjoying yourself?"

"Yes, Rollo."

"Tell me something else. Shall we meet in London?"

"Yes, Rollo. Yes."

"Good. Good. Now ask me something."

"Where's Lucy?"

"You've got that dog on your mind. Sh! Asleep in her maiden basket behind the sofa. She turns in at ten sharp, thank

God, no matter what's happening. So after the hour has struck, I can range at will."

"I noticed you seemed freer."

"Much freer. Is anybody noticing us?"

"Your father. He looks as if he'd like to talk to you."

He turned quickly at that, and Sir John who had come to a halt in his slow walk towards them, as if uncertain of his welcome, now trod ponderously forward again and joined them.

"Hallo, Daddy."

"Hallo, my boy." He stood in front of them, creaking, breathing deeply.

"What you going to do with yourself?"

"Absent me . . . absent me from felicity." The last word was almost imperceptibly blurred.

"I should."

"I might go and smoke a pipe in the library. Then bed, I think, eh?"

"That's right, Daddy. Cut along. I'll look in on you later."

Affection flowed between them, warmly, as in the old days, but now its quality was changed; was protective, indulgent, tender in Rollo, and in his father tinged with a sort of doubt and appeal, as if he felt a bit lost, liked simply to be near Rollo.

He stood as if weighted down into the carpet.

"We were discussing the Polish question," said Rollo.

"Ah," said Sir John. "Ticklish . . ." and the melancholy inert mass of his face lost its fixity, lifted and became mobile with amusement over its whole surface. Now they smiled all together, feeling at ease, intimate, making an isolated, conspiratorial ring in the room. If Mary had noticed, she'd have called out: "What's the joke?"

Sir John said, without warning: "Do you like heliotrope?"

"Very much."

"So do I."

"I don't seem to see it often nowadays."

"Nor do I. I don't know how it is. Old-fashioned taste, I suppose. . . . We bring forth this sort of thing by the ton." He jerked his head towards a large tub of chrysanthemum and poinsettia. "Elaborate vegetation . . . Not flowers to my mind."

"Well, I admire them awfully. Only perhaps a bit too prosperous. . . ."

They laughed.

"A bit too prosperous." Indistinct again. "Yes," Sir John meditated, his eyes on her. . . . Wondering where on earth I've sprung from, if he knows me. . . . What about the women in *his* life? He must have been a handsome man, virile, well set-up, like Rollo. What memories were shut in his head, or what had he forgotten? *Dear dead women with such hair too.* . . . What old once-battering secrets between him and her alone? Or was it all plain sailing?—a straightforward uneventful history of monogamy, duty, fatherhood . . .? It was all nearly over. His time was past.

Answering her smile he said finally: "Know this part of the world?"

"She's a neighbour, Daddy." Patient voice. "Little Compton she lives."

"Ah, yes. Little Compton. . . . So you live at Little Compton. I don't often have occasion to go that direction nowadays. If I remember rightly, my old friend Charles Curtis had a house there."

"Yes. He still has. He's my father."

"What, you Charles Curtis's girl? . . . Bless my soul, how time flies. Well. . . . Very nice for my old friend Charles Curtis."

"Thank you." She gave the correct smile.

"Very able man . . . and what's better and rarer, a very witty man. Used to be. Sorry to hear not so fit as he was."

"No. Poor darling, he's a great invalid these days."

"Ah, very sorry indeed to hear that. Hard luck for an active fellow like him. Can he—can he get about pretty well, eh?"

"No. Not very well. Not just now, anyway."

He shook his head in melancholy. "Poor fellow. You give him my greetings. . . . Mm."

"I will indeed."

He was thinking: I'm still active on my feet: not like Charlie Curtis.

He laid a large lean vein-corded hand on Rollo's shoulder and said:

"What about a ride to-morrow?"

"Yes, Daddy, thanks. I rather thought of a short one before breakfast if the weather holds up."

"Good. I'll get a message to Naylor."

"I did, Dad. Save you trouble."

Sir John nodded.

"Wish I could come with you." His face puckered into a smile, unconscious of pathos. "Think I won't, though."

"I shouldn't. I wouldn't be so hearty myself, only I must get back to London by lunch-time."

"Must you? Hoped you could stay over to-morrow. Sure?"

"Afraid it's impossible, Daddy. I've got an appointment."

"Pity. Ah, well. . . ."

Sir John nodded again and raised a hand, sketching an awkward gesture of farewell. His face drooped again; carefully he set himself in motion and disappeared through the double doors.

Marigold caught Rollo's eye and made a reassuring grimace; and he and Olivia went back to the fireplace. Mary was stitching away, her eyes bent on her work, her mouth pressed in a sour twist. Marigold was lying on the arm of her godmother's chair, one arm flung across the lean purple-brocaded shoulders. The cigar was puffing furiously. Sir Ronald was in the act of dropping his monocle and putting on a pair of glasses to examine the Gainsborough—a long-necked young woman in rose-coloured satin, with high arching brows and protuberant slanting eyes; graceful, lively, fragile.

"Beautiful bit of painting," he murmured. His large up-

turned pink-moon face looked beatific. "You know, Rollo,
m'boy, I consider vis the finest fing in the house—one of ve
finest examples in England, what's more. On a small scale,
but it's masterly. I'm not sure vough—I'm not altogevver sure
it's hung in ve right place. I've never been sure it does itself
ve highest justice here. I've an idea I'd like it on ve end wall
vere between ve cabinets. . . . I've an idea I would. . . ."

"Would you?" said Rollo politely.

"By Jove!" cried Harry, with awestruck frantic zest, "I do
believe you're right."

He stared first at the picture, then at the wall, then at the
company, his jaw dropping with the intensity of his interest.
But his enthusiasm fell flat into a disregarding silence. He
continued to stand and stare, straddled on his little thick legs,
stretching up his short red neck until the roll of fat above his
collar swelled out like inflated rubber.

Scenting collapse, mistrusting her children, Lady Spencer
now called once more through the click of counters: "No
bridge to-night?"

"Not to-night, Mum. Everybody's lazy," called Marigold
quickly; adding, to deflect attention: "Who's winning over
there?"

"Your mother," said Aunt Blanche, with bitterness. "She's
had every scrap of the luck. I never saw anything like it."

"*Luck*, dear?" said Lady Spencer sweetly, shifting and
discarding with intent glee.

"You always were *revolting* at games."

"How pretty it looks," said Olivia, looking across at the
board with its long narrow red and black triangles and piled
shining counters.

Marigold leaned forward and pulled her down beside her
on the broad chair-arm. Madame de Varenne turned her head
and, through the faint smoke-screen of the cigar between her
teeth, scrutinised her unwinkingly. After a few moments she
remarked in a harsh crackling monotone:

"C'est un visage assez bien fait."

"N'est ce pas?" cried Marigold, nodding vigorously.

"Mais l'autre là bas. . . ." She jerked her cigar towards Mary. "Je la trouve assommante, hein?"

Again Marigold nodded, her eyes dancing. She put her lips to her ear and said:

"Specimène très mal réussi."

"Quelle banalité. . . . Mon Dieu!" She removed her cigar, and a long sigh, as of unutterable scorn and boredom, stirred her shrunken, padded-looking breast. After a moment she continued:

"Mais qu'est-ce qu'elle vient donc faire ici, cette petite?"

"Aha! Aha! Voilà!" cried Marigold, leaning on her god-mother's shoulder, playing with one of her ornaments, a heavy cross of diamonds and topaz. "Voilà ce que je me demande!"

She laughed at Olivia out of the corners of her eyes. . . . Not saying: She is my friend of childhood. . . . Not including me in her laughter . . . leaning away, remote, mocking, estranged. . . . Now she looks like a pretty rat.

A cold menacing wind blew round the hearth. These people are not my people. I don't want to come here any more. . . . Rollo. . . . I'll tell him I must go. . . .

Harry had buttonholed him and was saying cheerily:

"I say, old man, you know all about these things . . . be a good chap and give me a tip. . . ." Something about a shooting syndicate. . . . But Rollo was cool, off-hand.

Poor Harry, he wasn't at ease either in this house. Looks of indifference, of suppressed irritation, well-mannered rebuffs appeared his lot. Was he aware? Did he complain in the bed-room, over the collar studs, the black tie; worry away on his side of the double bed? Did Mary rally him, comfort him?— or snub him impatiently, with scorn, deploring her mate, wishing in her heart for another face upon the pillow? . . . A natural bore: every gesture and intonation revealed him pure-bred, true blue; but something more separated him from the rest of them: something deeper: Harry was not out of the top drawer. . . . Mary—possibly a little past her first hopeful bloom—had married out of, say, the third drawer down: her father's agent?—her brother's tutor?—her mother's secretary? . . . Relatives had turned the smooth public face of acceptance upon her choice, for the sake of the family, for dear Mary's sake . . .?

He didn't look a happy man, but on the whole he looked more assertive, more gratified than anxious. Tufts of sandy hair sprouted out of his ears and nostrils; and his thin lips stretched smirkingly beneath the bags of his cheeks and the pink beaky little nose. . . . What could it be like to go to bed with him? . . . Something tough, reptilian, was in him, something scaly and resilient, something between a turtle and a salmon. . . . He and she had the same light blue eyes, pouchy, rapacious.

"Il est beau, Rollo, hein?" croaked an abstract voice behind her ear.

"Très beau."

"En voilà un au moins qui n'a rien d'ignoble de sa personne. A votre âge il m'aurait fait faire des folies."

Olivia looked at her, dubious, smiling; and all at once she smiled back, an irresistibly moving smile, spontaneous, friendly, humorous, lighting her face, her past. . . .

"Elle est gentille," she remarked to Marigold after a pause, making the bare statement.

Olivia put out her hand and gave hers with its long fingers and encrusted rings and bracelets a quick pressure.

Warmth started to creep in again round the hearth. It was all right after all. Only one of those moments. . . .

"Comme on est triste ce soir!" Her voice was lively, taunting. "Ronald, viens donc ici me raconter quelque-chose. . . . Et toi, Rollo, qu'est-ce que tu fais là a te gratter le menton? Voici une demoiselle qui s'ennuie horriblement auprès de moi. Tu n'a rien a lui proposer?"

"Mais beaucoup de choses. . . ."

Ceasing to yawn and rub his shoulders against the mantelpiece he leaned forward and pulled Olivia to her feet, keeping his hand through her arm.

"Zero hour," said Marigold.

She jumped up suddenly and went to George, saying:

"Darling George, come and see the kittens."

"Kittens?" said George. "Rather, Marigold."

"Nothing jollier than a two-months old kitten," said Harry.

"Oh, these haven't got their eyes open," said Marigold. "They're not worth seeing, only George loves kittens."

"Harry," broke in Mary sharply, "you might fetch me my jacket from my room, will you? The black velvet one. It's in the wardrobe. I feel a bit chilly. I don't know if there's a draught or what. I may have caught a chill this afternoon. I got my feet so wet in that long grass, and I always get a chill if I get my feet wet."

"Better turn in with a hot-water bottle," suggested Harry.

"No." Peevish. "I'll be all right. Just fetch my jacket."

"Right."

Dutifully, without alacrity, Harry made off.

"Try a hot lemon and whisky," said George kindly. "Nothing like it."

"Ugh! no." She made a face of disgust. "Lemon always upsets me, and I simply can't *touch* whisky. It makes me sick."

"Who's got a cold?" called Lady Spencer from her table, not looking up. "Ammoniated quinine. . . ."

"Oh, come on," said Marigold, still with her arm through George's. "We don't want to keep the poor kittens up till midnight."

"Are you interested in kittens?" said Rollo to Olivia.

"Very interested."

"They're only ordinary little tabby ones," said Marigold, "but you shall see them."

Mary followed the departing procession with a goggling stare.

"Oh, what time is it?" said Marigold yawning, collapsing

on a chair in the ante-room. "It feels like three o'clock. I want to go to bed and pick my toes."

"I must go home," said Olivia.

"No, no," said Rollo quickly. "Marigold's remarks were purely rhetorical, weren't they, Maggie? Now we've managed to shed the husks at last, we can start the evening."

"Then I must have a drink," said Marigold, with her eyes shut. She's so bored she could die. Hopeless, all of them. . . .

"Where are the kittens?" asked George.

"The kittens? . . . Oh, the kittens!" Marigold sat up, looking tragic. "Oh, George! There was such a disaster. I didn't like to tell you before. Those poor little darlings . . . ten of them . . . they were all born dead."

"Good God!" said George, shocked, fond of animals.

"It was for the best, George."

"The fact is, George," said Rollo, "they didn't really come to anything, poor devils."

George looked blank, then his face cleared.

"Oh, I get there. . . ." He broke into a slow prolonged guffaw. "Aaah, ha, ha, ha, ha, ha, ha! Subterfuge, eh?"

"Aren't we ones?" cried Marigold. She got up and gave him a hug. But when he tried to keep his arm round her, rapidly she detached herself.

Olivia said to him: "Do you still hunt?"

"Me?" He looked surprised. "Oh . . . off and on, you know. . . . Whenever I can."

"George is a man of affairs nowadays," said Rollo. "Sport's loss has been the city's gain."

"And the fox's opportunity," said Marigold.

"You don't remember me." Olivia beamed on him.

A spasm went over his face. He gathered himself together suspiciously, stubborn, alarmed.

"N-no. . . . I'm afraid. . . . I can't say I do."

"Never mind. I'm glad. Because the last time we met you were obliged to correct me. You did it very kindly considering. I've never forgotten."

"Good Lord! . . . Me? . . . You must be thinking of some other bloke, eh?"

"George never spoke harshly to a woman in his life," said Rollo, "unless she'd done something unpardonable in the hunting-field."

"This was in the hunting-field. A bad toss."

"Another leg-pull, eh?" George's face cleared, ready for a laugh.

"What are you talking about?" said Marigold with another yawn. "I want a drink. Drinks in the hall."

She sprang up, opened the lid of the wireless cabinet, turned knobs, swooped through a range of snarls, whoops, wails, and opened out full blast on a jazz band.

"Hamburg."

She floated out in front of them, pausing for a second on her way to snatch up a large, smiling, plump débutante's photograph of herself and whisk it face to the wall.

In the hall, among the antlers and skin rugs, the Spanish chests and chairs, the music beat insistently through the open door. Marigold began to hum and sway, glass in hand; then draining it and setting it down, put both hands on George's shoulders and danced him off.

Drinking a whisky and soda, Rollo watched her a minute or two, standing beside Olivia. Then:

"Dance," he said, putting an arm round her.

After a turn or two he gave a sigh, as if weary or impatient.

"Why do you sigh?"

"Did I? Sorry. Bad habit."

He went on turning and swaying with the soft, subtle balance and rhythm of a good dancer. After a bit he said suddenly:

"Let's get away . . . mm?"

It sounded so rapid, toneless, odd, in spite of the questioning inflection—as if it had slipped out unawares, unconsciously almost. . . .

"Get away. . . . Do you want to?"

"Do you?" He looked down at her, not smiling. Uncertain, disturbed, she hesitated; and after a moment he gave a brief laugh.

"No. Never mind. Don't know what I'm talking about. ... One can't, anyway, can one?"

"I suppose not." I'm not helping him, I'm stuck. . . . "At least I suppose one can . . . a bit . . . if one wants." . . . Careful, be careful. . . . But he's waiting. I must say something. "It depends if one has ties—that are going to stop one. . . ."

"*That* depends on oneself, doesn't it?" he said quickly. "Whether one's going to let 'em. . . . They needn't. . . ."

"Needn't they . . .?"

"There are occasions—very rare ones—when I personally shouldn't let them. . . . It would be all right, absolutely, from my point of view. . . . What about you?"

"Well, I can't judge. I haven't any ties."

"None?"

"I'm on my own—entirely."

"You're lucky."

"I don't always think so. *You* are. . . ."

"I'm not sure."

"Why not?"

"Well, I want something—and I'm not sure if I'm going to be able to get it."

"I expect you get most things you want."

The voices were so light, quick, toneless, answering each other, they might have been repeating something trivial learnt by heart. They went on dancing, mechanically, not looking at each other now. She felt her heart beating and his hand just quivering. What's happened? All's been said. Hush, put it away now, not another word. It's not to be true yet.

Presently he said in a drowsy peaceful voice:

"People do manage to come across each other once in a blue moon. . . . It beats me how, considering the population of the globe."

She laughed, feeling happy suddenly, peaceful too.

"The whole thing beats me," he said. "It isn't as if one went about sort of looking for it in a business-like way. . . . One had given up worrying too much about all that—given up feeling young and excitable and all that. . . . Put the stopper on. Told oneself to lock up and turn in."

"Who's one?"

He laughed. His words, his new soft easy alarming manner burrowed and lodged, hiding in her mind, too insinuating—decisive—too . . .

"I ought to go now."

"Yes. I'll take you home now."

"Are you going to take me?"

"Of course I am."

So it's going to be true. I can't stop it.

She became aware again of Marigold and George. They were at the drinks table and Marigold was saying in a quarrel-some, insistent way:

"Why shouldn't I? I'm not tight. What makes you think I'm tight? George keeping an eye on my drinks! I like that, I must say! I should hide the next one or pour it away. Save me, George, save me! The demon drink's got me!" She drank off a stiff whisky and soda and said more peaceably: "I am a bit tight—but no more. I wish I was blind—and I would be if I was anywhere but in my own home. There's something about the roof-tree that makes it impossible to get absolutely roaring. I must confess to you, George, I've had enough to make me, what with one nip and another—but it's working the wrong way or something. I'll be sick if I go on or start to boo-hoo and you'll have to put me to bed. And you'd hate that, wouldn't you, George?"

"I wouldn't mind," he said.

"Well, I would. I don't want to be beastly, but I *really* would. You *are* one of my oldest, dearest friends, George, but I simply would *hate* to be put to bed by you. Oh dear! I don't feel a bit witty or exulting or anything. . . . Don't let's dance any more, for God's sake. It's *too* idiotic padding round and round and round . . . like those two. . . . Oh, no, they're not any more." She handed her glass to Rollo. "Give me another, Rollo, darlin'."

Rollo took the glass.

"Just a minute," he said mildly. "Olivia wants one."

"Sorry, sorry, Livia! . . . Manners." She shook her head.

"I don't want anything, thank you," said Olivia.

"Try a drop of this," said Rollo, firmly, pouring out Irish whisky. "Good for you. Warm you up for your drive. Look, I'll mix it with a dash of ginger ale and you'll love it."

"Gimme the same," said Marigold, sitting in a high-backed arm-chair, with her eyes shut.

"Right."

He poured out half a glass of neat ginger ale. "Here."

She took it, drank it, waited a moment and suddenly laughed.

"You old stoat," she said. "You're enough to make a cat laugh."

"Marigold, I must go now."

"Is Rollo going to take you?"

"Yes, I am."

"If it isn't too much bore."

Marigold lay back again, eyes shut, rolling her head to and fro on the chair back.

"Oh, *no*, it's not a *bore* for Rollo. He's looking forward to it. And you'll be *perfectly* safe with him because he's *dead* sober—and never does anything he oughtn't. He's so tactful too—quite extraordinarily tactful and temp—temp—what's the word?"

"Temperamental," said Rollo. "Tempestuous."

"No. Not that. That's petticoats."

She opened her eyes, sat up and smiled sweetly at all their watching faces.

"Well, I don't give a hoot," she said, "you're a lot of old

cows. You ought to wear caps and mittens. I don't want a
drink anyway. And when I do I'll have one."

She sat there smiling to herself, curving and lifting her
spine, her long full neck, serpentine, secretive—like a smooth-
fleshed strong serpentine white and green plant—indescribably
shrouded and somnolent-looking—like an arum lily. . . .

"Must you really go, darlin'?" She got up, stumbled a
little and giggled. "I wish you wouldn't go."

"I'll just look in on Daddy," said Rollo, "and bring the car
round. While you do the good-byes."

"Don't hurry the girl," said Marigold. She put an arm
round Olivia. They were the same height, dark and blonde.
"We'll go entwined," she said, "like two dearest female friends
—as we are, as we are. Livia, you might keep your arm round
me unob—unobstentatiously. I don't want to fall down at
Ma's feet. Do I reek? Give me a cigarette. There now." She
went off into helpless laughter. "*Don't* look so helpful and
understanding. I'm as sober as an owl. Good-bye, George!
The party honestly is over, darlin', and you might as well
stagger off to bed."

"Right you are," said George equably. "Good-night. Just
help myself to a night-cap."

"My aim is to lose George," murmured Marigold, glancing
backward as they left the hall.

He looked lonely all by himself, receding at the other end
of the enormous room, his simple round oil-sleeked head
gleaming, his stiff shirt stark and blank, his neat shoulders
rigid above the table, patiently squirting a siphon—expecting
nothing after all these years of being in love with Marigold;
waiting for nothing but his drink.

In the drawing-room, Sir Ronald was playing a gentle
Scarlatti tinkle upon the piano. Madame de Varenne had gone
and so had Mary. The sisters were still at the backgammon
board, but play was over. They were piling and putting away
counters, and talking in low sisterly gossiping tones.

"Olivia's come to say good-bye," said Marigold.

"Oh! . . . Olivia dear. . . ." Lady Spencer got up and took Olivia's hand in both her own. "My dear, this has been such a very great pleasure. Now we've found you we're not going to lose sight of you again so easily—are we, Marigold? Next time Marigold's with us we must try and arrange . . . we must telephone. . . ." She looked a little vague. "I expect you'll be coming down quite often, won't you, dear—to see your father?"

"Yes, I shall try."

"That's good. Your mother must be so glad to have you within reach. I know what a difference it can make. . . . Now I wonder if the car . . . Marigold, does Benson know, dear?"

Marigold, leaning on the piano, absorbedly watching her uncle's hands, was deaf, and Olivia said, with some loss of confidence:

"I think—Rollo said very kindly—he'd take me home."

"Ah! . . . Rollo's taking you. . . . *That's* all right then."

But did it quite do? . . . Not quite. Barely perceptible, the contraction of tone, the addition of emphasis to simple cordiality. . . . Or is it my guilt?

"I do hope he doesn't mind. It seems such a bore for him."

"Oh, no, I'm *sure* it's not. Rollo so enjoys a spin . . . and then I dare say he thought. . . . Dear old Benson, he's getting old. He's been with us thirty years. . . it's hard to realise. . . . Rollo's so considerate."

So considerate. . . . All the same if there weren't something not quite . . . not quite about me—something that's such a pity and explains why I'm not living with my husband—I'd have shaken hands all round in grateful affection and been removed according to formula by the chauffeur.

"How I wish," said Lady Spencer, "you could have met our dear Nicola."

Rollo came in, looking large and powerful with his overcoat on; and she said, laying her firm, strong white hand on his shoulders:

"I was just saying, dear, if only Nicola could have been with us. I should so have liked her and Olivia to meet."

"Yes," said Rollo, in a filial uncoloured way.

"She has such horrid headaches," Lady Spencer sighed. "I want her to see this new Austrian doctor Aunt Blanche has been telling me about."

"Oh, really?" said Rollo pleasantly. "I should think she'd love to. . . . Seeing new doctors is Nicky's pet hobby."

"I hear he's done some wonderful cures. He does all these modern scientific tests, you know. I always feel they *must* be on the right lines. I think they'd give her confidence. Well, Olivia dear——" She bent forward and bestowed a kiss briskly, closing that unfruitful passage. "My love to your mother—and dear Kate."

"Look me up in London some time, do," said Aunt Blanche. "Be jolly to see you."

"Tell Parr not to wait up for me," said Rollo to his mother. "I'll let myself in and lock up."

Marigold, murmuring "Wait for me in the hall," darted ahead and vanished.

Olivia went out with Rollo at her side. Glancing back for a moment at the door (but Lady Spencer was not looking, not sending after her a last smile), she took in the scene once more as in a painting—static: interior with figures. Now I've fixed it, to remember. In case this is the last of it for me.

"Marigold said wait," said Olivia by the front door.

"What for?" said Rollo. "This your coat?" He took up her mother's musquash from the settee where it lay folded. "It goes against the grain to extinguish you," he said, holding it, staring at her. "I love white. Dark ladies in white dresses."

He helped her into the heavy unyielding old coat and wrapped it round her.

"I wonder how one acquires these tastes," he said. "They seem to get into one's system unawares."

"I expect you once had a nice dark nurse in a white apron."

"I never thought of that. . . . Of course, that explains it."

Nicola wore white satin . . . with her knot of dark polished hair.

Marigold came running downstairs, wrapped in a long mink coat, the broad full circular collar turned up over her curls in a kind of hood. She called out hurriedly as she ran, to counteract Rollo's look of unwelcoming surprise:

"Rollo, will you go out by the south gate and drop me?"

"Drop you where?"

"Just a little way on. I'll tell you."

Avoiding their eyes she came on and opened the front door.

"What d'you want to do? Go for a walk or something?" He was annoyed.

"No. I want to see somebody."

"Who?"

She turned on him irritably. "Oh, can't you do what I ask without—— It isn't much to ask." She went down the steps, got into the back of the car, and said from within, reluctantly but more quietly, "As a matter of fact I want to see Timmy. Now come on, do."

"Get in, Olivia." He settled himself behind the steering-wheel, started the engine running, and said, still crossly: "Who on earth's Timmy?"

"Blind?" said Olivia.

"Yes." Her voice was grateful. "Olivia remembers. You know he's ill, I suppose—or didn't it penetrate?"

"Oh, Lord, yes. The chap they were talking about at lunch to-day."

"Yes."

He said more mildly: "But, Marigold, surely you can't go visiting an invalid at this hour?"

"Yes, I *can*!" she cried in a frenzy. "You don't suppose he *sleeps*, do you?—with a cough like he's got. . . ."

"Is he expecting you?"

She flung herself back in rigid screaming silence; and in silence they started off.

The moon was near the full, the night was windless, clouded, grey, with a smell of mist in the air, and decaying leaves.

Through the park, out by the south lodge, then between hedgerows along a narrow winding road.

"Stop here," said Marigold suddenly.

He slowed down and pulled up.

"This doesn't seem to be anywhere."

"Yes, there's a stile, look, and a path through the field into the side of the garden. I don't want to stop with a flourish at the front door, do I?—and blow the horn?"

"All right, all right."

She got out of the car and stood in the road.

"What a queer night. . . ."

She lifted her head, breathed out a great sigh. Above the frame of fur her face floated insubstantial, a livid papery disc, phosphorescent-looking, marked in with black stains for eyes, lips, nostrils. . . .

"I don't know yet if I'll go," she said. "I don't quite know what I'll do. I'll just see. . . . I might not feel like seeing him after all. You go on."

"Do you want to be picked up again?"

"No, I don't. I want to walk home."

Their voices dropped out flat on to the air, answering each other in the distilled, impersonal, mourning way of human voices at night. Still looking upwards, Marigold called absently:

"Good-night, Olivia."

"Good-night, Marigold."

He put the clutch in and slowly, softly drew away from her. She stood by the roadside, not moving, and the corner hid her.

"What'll she do?" said Olivia.

"God knows. . . . There's the house in there."

They saw a light burning in what appeared to be a kind of wooden hut or shelter on the lawn, and farther back the white shape of a small square house, half-concealed by fruit-trees.

"There's a light."

"I saw him once, I remember him very well. He came to that dance, and I danced with him. What's the matter with him?"

"Lungs. Started about a year ago. They're frightfully badly off. Mother tried to get him to let her send him to Switzerland—or a sanatorium somewhere, but he refused point-blank. He won't move. She had the hut built for him and he just lies there. Won't be nursed or let anybody do anything for him. Won't see his child and keeps his wife away as much as he can."

"Doesn't he want to get better?"

"Doesn't sound like it." He made a movement of discomfort. "He's pretty bad, I believe. Poor devil. I never saw much of him, but he seemed an awfully nice chap. . . . I don't suppose he clings madly to life. . . . Though you're always told the blind are so cheerful."

"And consumptives so hopeful."

"I didn't know she knew him as well as that. . . ."

"I don't know how well she knows him. . . ."

No one would ever know.

A sudden impulse? . . . a deliberated plan! . . . Out of love? . . . pity? . . . curiosity? . . . No one would ever know what had been, what was between them. Emotional images, fragments of dialogue came to mind. "Timmy, it's me. . . ." "Marigold! I knew you'd come." "Of course I came." "I wouldn't let them move me, in case you did. . . ." "Timmy, darling, I love you, you're not to die. . . ." That kind of thing? Or was she hurrying away now, panic-stricken, from his death, from the destructive element? . . .—which is hers too, which she'll never escape, which they recognised in each other, long ago, dancing and joking. . . .

"What a witless thing to do, though," muttered Rollo.

"Probably finish him." He was silent, than added, "I'll say for my sister, she knows how to make herself felt."

"What can it be like to be married to her?"

"What indeed? Beats me how any one had the nerve to take it on. Plenty of quite sensible people seemed to want to though. . . ."

"Of course. Everybody would want to. You see, it's the illusion she gives. . . ."

"What illusion?"

"Of being free, I suppose. Escaping, getting free. People see she's got loose, she's off. . . . They want to run after her, make a grab to catch her. . . ."

"You've been reading *The Green Hat*," he said after reflection. "Though I see what you mean . . . All the same she won't really come a cropper. She's a jolly sight too clever. Besides, she likes Sam. They hit it off, more or less. Couple of lunatics. . . ."

"Are the children nice?"

"The children are divine," he said briefly.

Easy to imagine Rollo as favourite uncle—tossing them up, stuffing their money-boxes, generally indulging them. Surely not Rollo's choice, or fault, being childless? An obvious begetter. . . . He doesn't want to talk of Marigold any more. Dwindling now, she still obstructed them; left a vacuum they could not fill. They hung separated, cold and light—hollow people.

Down into the valley. Far below to the left, a sprinkling of late lights still spoke in the mist, from village windows. On the right, the beech coppice ran down steeply to the road: when Kate and I used to come on our bikes with a picnic tea, and sometimes the Martins came; or Marigold was allowed to meet us, riding over on her pony. We cut our initials with a penknife, each choosing a different tree, and said we'll come back to look in twenty years. . . . And I climbed, and Kate dug up plants—she never cared for climbing; and we brought our books and ate nut-milk bars and turned somersaults over the railings, and free-wheeled home again down the hill in the evening with primrose and white violet roots in our bicycle baskets, and dead leaves stuck to our backs and stockings; and the sunset going on, different every time, the other side of the valley. . . .

. . . All that was important: had made an experience of emotion more complex, penetrating and profound, yes, than getting married. . . .

Round the corner on the hill known in the family circle as The Bad Turn: perennial object of foreboding and suspicion to Mother, though innocent still of disaster. Down, past the first cottages, round past grandpapa's houses—those triple-fronted stucco eyesores. In the middle top window a light—the usual light that burned all night—the window of the youngest Miss Robinson. She was in there, hare's face, soft, narrow, ignoble, peering perhaps from behind the lace curtain with her wild, full, harmless eye, or lying flat on her back, whispering to the ceiling; or pacing up and down her room, laughing, crying by turns. Not dangerous at all: only very trying turns. She wouldn't do her hair or bother to dress. Go out, even for a second into the back garden, she would not; and write anonymous letters she occasionally did; only the post office Miss Robinson was generally able to intercept them: not obscene, but calvinistic, minatory, or in the style of warnings—straight tips from God's confidential agent: certain damnation pronounced on Winnie Pratt, the stationmaster's daughter, fornicatress; a message from the Lord to the young milkman; a hint, no more, to the vicar about Miss Sibley, his housekeeper, instrument of Satan. . . . Also they'd had to lock up the piano with its rose-silk fluted bodice, she made such a din on it in the middle of the night, at dawn—waking the neighbours. She'd cried bitterly at that—oh! how she'd cried! They'd thought of doing away altogether with the piano to spare her feelings, only it had always been there like in Dad's time and his father's before him: the place would seem funny without it. . . . Then she wasn't to be trusted with scissors—

not that she'd do herself a harm, but seemed as if she had to lay about with them on any bit of stuff—slicing, snipping, shredding—romping through the length and breadth of it. In fact it was with the cutting-out scissors the crisis had exploded five years back: Mrs. Uniack's new black moracain victimised all of a sudden one morning, just after the second fitting; Miss Robinson's professional career brought to an abrupt full stop. ... But she ate well: oh, yes, she enjoyed her food. Some days she felt a king.

Dark crouched the two old cottages facing the green, housing on the one hand Miss Toomer and Miss Mivart, sleeping light, never quite warm enough in bed, poking their noses up at the sound of a late car (what faces if they could see one coming back at midnight with Rollo); empty on the other of Major and Mrs. Skinner.

Oh, dear, awful Major Skinner, you're under the earth, you were never allowed to teach Kate or me to play golf. We never went to tea in your cottage among Mrs. Skinner's gold and purple cushions. ... Brazen Winnie, scornful, ruthless girl, finished him off—sapping his means and strength with trips to Tulverton—shops, movies, cafés, movies, shops. Seeing her home late on foggy winter evenings was what got him down at last. The chill settled in his kidneys. "Rubbish: fit as a fiddle," he'd said the first week. "Cracked up, done for, good run for m' money, look after the dogs," he'd said the second; and during the third, Mrs. Skinner unostentatiously buried him, and vanished from Little Compton, leaving dozens of empty whisky bottles in the kitchen.

Nearly there now. ... Is this all? Can't we get back to each other? Isn't it to be true after all?

"Straight on?" said Rollo, his voice sounding brusque after the long silence. He slowed down at the cross-roads.

"Yes, and then the next drive on the left, where all that shrubbery is. You won't drive in, will you?"

He drew up close to the fencing, under the laurel hedge; switched off the headlights.

"There. . . ." She waited a moment. "Good-night, Rollo. Thank you so much for bringing me. . . . It was a lovely evening. . . ."

He sat still and said nothing. He took out his case and lit a cigarette with deliberate movements. Then he said:

"When shall I see you again?"

"When do you want to?"

Answering him, with fingers already on the door-handle, she felt unwillingly flippant, rather shrill. He put his hand out and snatched hers back into her lap, saying with a hint of roughness:

"As soon as possible."

Overtaken, caught, punished. . . .

"All right," she said at last, sighing it out.

She turned slightly to look at him—the dark bulk beside her, head in profile, staring straight ahead, the short, high-bridged nose, small thick moustache, full rounded chin; the hand shadowy on his knee, holding a cigarette. The smoke wreathed up. Slowly he stubbed it out into the ash-tray. He said:

"Do you want to see me again?"

"Yes." I suppose so. . . .

"That's all right then." He took her twisting hand in his warm dry firm-clasping one. "You remember what I said— that I wanted something I wasn't sure I was going to get?"

"Yes, I remember."

His voice was so quiet, so calm-sounding, one had to listen, answer in the same way. . . . Think, think. . . . But there aren't any thoughts.

"Well, shall I?"

"Yes. . . . At least. . . . If you're sure. . . ."

"I'm sure. But you must be too."

I must be, too. . . . I must be sure. . . . What's the answer? . . . He said, more hesitatingly:

"Do you think you might be able—to like me a bit?"

"Oh, *yes*. . . ."

He whispered, "Oh . . . *darling* . . ." and pulled her towards him and began to kiss her.

Self-conscious . . . reluctant . . . appalled: Rollo Spencer, married man, Nicola's husband, stranger practically, Rollo *Spencer*. . . . What'll they say—Lady Spencer, Sir John . . . Mother, Dad, Kate. . . . All watching. . . . Wrong, disgusting —naughty girl, leading him on, a married man. . . . An enemy. . . . Ivor wasn't. . . . Why do I think of, stop thinking of Ivor . . . ?

He went on kissing her, whispering to her, floating her away. Names, faces, times and places slipped off the reel into darkness. Only his voice, face, hands, unknown—recognised—remained.

Head on his shoulder, as if it was all quite natural, quite suitable. . . . Dumb.

"You're so *young*," he said. "I never knew anything so young." His voice was full of pleasure. "You're like a young, young girl. . . ."

What did he expect? . . . A woman on my own, I said, not so young in years. . . . A woman of experience? . . . What did he suppose? Anxiety brushed her, the faintest breath, there and gone again. . . . He's not young. . . . So certain, so un-diffident. . . . Expert.

"I must go in now." Still my own voice.

"I'll see you to the door."

They got out of the car. He took her arm, keeping her close, and walked with her along the drive, his step on the gravel crunching out loud and firm. At the bend in the shrubbery, where the house came into view, he halted, looking towards the square solid shape of brick outlined with its stout neat chimneys in the moon.

"Is that your home?"

"That's my home."

He stood and looked at it. The bushes gave a momentary shallow stir and twitch, and an owl hooted.

"I'll say good-night to you here."

He pulled her gently out of range of her home's blank

square rows of eyes, put his hands along her cheeks and tilted her face up.

"What are you thinking about?"

"Nothing. I can't think."

"You're not afraid, are you?"

"No." She sighed.

"What then?" He had a kind, safe voice.

"I suppose I just can't believe it."

He smiled.

"You will soon, you know. You'll believe it in no time— I'll see that you do—and then you'll be used to it . . . and then perhaps you'll be tired of it. . . ."

"Don't say that. . . . Why do you say that?" She felt quickened, awake suddenly.

"It does happen, you know. . . . You might get bored with me in no time. . . ."

"So might you with me. . . ."

They kissed each other, in sad voluptuous disbelief, denial, acknowledgment.

"When did you think of this?" she said, smiling for the first time.

"As soon as I saw you." He smiled too.

"What d'you mean?"

"In the train. Just as I'd finished ordering the sausages—— No, before that, to be honest."

"When?"

"The first time we met. At that famous dance."

"I don't believe it!"

"Yes. On the terrace. I nearly kissed you then."

"Oh! You didn't! What nonsense!"

"Well, I certainly toyed with the idea. . . . I did think you were rather sweet."

"I'd as soon have thought of being visited by the Holy Ghost."

"Now who's talking nonsense?"

"Well, it *may—just—*have occurred to me it would be nice.

. . . But entirely on the Gary Cooper level. . . ." Laughter, confidence came easy now. "Specially as I was so peculiar that evening—so in a flux. . . . Seeing myself in dozens of distorting mirrors. . . ."

"You looked all right to me. You seemed like something cool and kind." His voice was serious, almost unhappy. "Like the wind on the terrace. Restful. . . ."

"Darling. . . ." Incredible, miraculous words.

"What's more, after that I even thought about you— definitely thought about you. Not often. Say twice a year. For no reason at all. Getting into the tube—or shaving—or talking rot to my neighbour at dinner. . . . You'd pop into my head and I'd think: ' I'd like to see her again. . . .'"

"I thought about you too. I always knew I should meet you again. It was like feeling excited suddenly in the middle of a sunny day—or a wet one—for no reason you can think of. . . . It's queer—this doesn't seem sudden a bit to me—does it to you?"

He laughed.

"Not in the least."

"We don't quite know where we're going now—do we?"

She waited. . . . Say: She doesn't count, she wouldn't care, that's over, I'm free for you. . . . But all he did was to shake his head quickly, faintly.

She said hurriedly:

"It doesn't matter." She had a pang of love for him. It was the shake of the head, helpless-looking.

"You see——"

What? He stopped, lifted her hand up and kissed it instead. Leave it alone.

"Are you happy?" she said.

He turned her hand over and kissed the palm; nodded.

"Of course I am."

"I always meant to be happy," she said. "I always thought some day I would be. I believed in it. . . ."

He took out his pocket-book and by the light of the match

she held, wrote down her London address and telephone
number.

"I'll write to you," he said. "And if you want to get hold
of me——" He scribbled on a blank page, tore it out and gave
it to her. "That's my office. . . . Ring up there if you want me,
will you?"

She took the paper. He means: there, not my home. Don't
speak to me at my home.

"Lots of other engagements, I see." She smiled, seeing
various jottings as he flicked the pages.

"They're nothing. They can all be scrapped. Nearly all."
He shut the book. "My memory's rotten, I have to write
everything down."

Nicola tells him what dinners and things to put down. She
gave him his little book. A full social life, of course, lots of
engagements—not like me. She dropped the match.

They kissed again. She listened to his step going tramping
back again down the drive, so loud, collected, unconscience-
stricken; waited for his car to start away; ran back into the
house.

There was the awaited envelope, sitting on the hall table.
Put chain on door and remember landing light. The variations
had been slight, all these years. The jar of biscuits, the plate
of apples and bananas. Only no thermos now, except when
James was home. He liked Ovaltine, but the girls wouldn't
touch it. A nice cup of cocoa then? Hot milk? . . . So good
for you. . . . No, thank you, Mum. Not even Horlick's, which
Olivia used to be really greedy for, which had so undoubtedly
helped her to pass her Oxford exams. with flying colours. Of
course, neither of them did much brainwork now. A pity,
particularly in Olivia's case. A married woman with children
has plenty to occupy her without improving her mind; but
a pity all the same that neither of them appeared to take any
interest in politics or the deeper kind of thought: still prefer-
ring Pip, Squeak and Wilfred, or that ridiculous Beachcomber,

or any gossip column, to *The Times* leader or the foreign news. Pity. They were both girls with plenty of brains, if they cared to use them. Mrs. Curtis herself and Aunt May, too, had always believed in keeping abreast of the times in the broadest sense.

His hat, his cap and muffler on their pegs: no longer dumb creatures in pain, but homely symbols, their virtue restored, dozing peacefully, guarding the hall.

Nibbling a biscuit. . . . Around me the furniture frozen into night silence, friendly, estranged. . . . Kate, Mother, Dad, the maids asleep upstairs, the nurse, too, dozing in her chair probably—all of them unconscious of me, unconscious of the male step in the garden, the alien form by the shrubbery, deaf to branch listening, gravel speaking; to the two forms murmuring, clasping; to me hurrying away alone; flying from him, back to my home, back to myself, away from the two shapes in shadow; leaving them there: to be there now for ever, clasped, as I dreamed in the beginning they would one night be. This is with whom it was to be, and this is the night. Now I am back at the beginning, now begins what I dreamed was to be.

My own bedroom waiting, awake for me. . . . Peep in on Kate. Then a hot bath: float in water, warm water, softly dissolve; without one thought sink into sleep.

But something rustled on the landing: nurse going by on heelless slippered feet with a stir of starched skirts. . . . Without seeing she saw the broad haunches, brisk and trim, swinging down the passage, the broad short feet going hard down, flap flap on the heels in those blue bedroom slippers, trimmed beads and black fur.

She switched off the hall light, went softly upstairs, along the passage. At his door stood the white figure, waiting.

"Hallo! Had a nice time?"

"Lovely, thank you."

"That's right. It's nice to have a little change—good for you." The blue stone eye scanned Olivia up and down. . . .

Probably heard the car stop when it did, start again how long afterwards? . . . goodness knows. A good hour . . . perhaps two? And my face must be different. . . .

"How is he?" Anxious suddenly.

"Oh, all right. He's just had a little drink of hot milk with a drop of brandy. . . . He's been asking for you."

"Has he? Oh! Since when? Shall I go in?"

"Yes, I should. Just pop in for a tick. He'll settle off better."

The lamp, muffled with mother's dark green silk scarf, shone on the table by the fire. The bed in shadow. He lay on his back, propped on three pillows, eyes closed, exhausted. She went and stood beside him.

"Hallo, Dad——"

His eyelids lifted with an effort.

"Oh, it's you, is it?"

"I've been out to dinner—just back."

"Thought you'd gone away. . . ."

"No, no. Just to Meldon—to the Spencers. They sent you heaps of messages. They're so glad you're better."

"Hm. Jack Spencer. . . . Sick man. . . . Hm. . . ."

His unfamiliar grizzled sprouting jaws worked a little. . . . Presently he said, with his eyes shut:

"Let me see now. . . . How many children has Kate?"

"Four. Nice ones. I don't think you've seen the baby yet, have you?"

"No, I have not. . . . At least, I think not. . . . That husband of hers . . . he's all right, isn't he?"

"Yes, Rob's all right. He suits Kate. They understand each other, and get on."

He breathed out a deep sigh between his slack thin lips. Presently he said:

"Are you all right?"

"Yes, Dad. Of course I am." Still on his mind. "Don't you worry about me. I'm fine."

After a pause, he said with extreme diffidence:

"I forget for the moment what the exact position is. . . ."

He's been leading up to this.

"Between me and Ivor, you mean, Dad? Well, you know I don't live with Ivor any longer. It's all over. We separated —some time ago."

"No chance," he said apologetically, "of coming together again?"

"No. It was a bad mistake. We're best apart."

"Pity."

"Yes."

"To the best of my recollection he was a decent young chap. . . ." His voice was very weak.

"Yes, he was." Dad had taken to him, the few times they'd met. "Only we oughtn't to have married, that's all."

"I dare say you know best." Another sigh. "It seems unsatisfactory though. I wish . . ."

"Don't worry, darling. It'll work out. I'm awfully sorry to have been such a nuisance to you."

He waited; made a statement:

"I want you to be happy."

"I mean to be," she said quickly, moved. "Get better, and I'll be perfectly happy."

"Oh! . . ." He sighed irritably. "What's that got . . ." Soothing him, putting him off; when he was so tired too, when it was such an effort to say anything. . .

She bent down and said carefully:

"Listen. I will be happy. I promise you."

His eyelids moved slightly, as if in approval. He said, in a blurred way—rather like the other, like Rollo's father:

"No need to go regretting . . . suffering for things. Morbid. Remorse's nasty habit. Bad pol'cy. All make mistakes. You've got 'r life b'fore you."

"Yes, I know I have." Oh, yes! . . .

He tried again; but his mind, a burden painfully sustained on a bare knife-edge, began to topple. He couldn't quite finish. Feebly pompous, he pronounced:

"You can r'ly 'pon my co-operation. . . . Should've informed you sooner. . . . But I pr'cras'nate. . . ."

"Thank you, Dad. I'll remember. Good-night. Go to sleep now."

She kissed his forehead. . . . What a different kind of kiss . . . went out, closing the door noiselessly. He did not stir.

In the dressing-room adjoining, the white poised wing-spread of cap in the arm-chair by the fire. A tray with sandwiches, a thermos beside her. A book, the papers.

"Got all you want?" Olivia stood in front of the gorgeous fire and warmed the backs of her legs. . . . "She doesn't stint herself of coal; I must speak to her," said Mother. "Surely *half* the quantity these mild nights . . . ?"

"Yes, thanks, I'm all right."

"I can't think how you manage to keep awake."

"Oh, well, you get used to it, you know. I do get a bit yawny-like towards morning. But I have a wee doze now and then. He doesn't need very much seeing to now."

"How is he, do you think?"

"Oh, he's all right. He's doing quite nicely."

"He's awfully patient."

"Oh, yes, he's quite good. I always say I'd rather nurse men when it comes to anything bad."

"He's so terribly weak."

"Oh, well, he would be that, of course. I dare say he'll pull up gradually. He'll have to go slow, of course, and take it easy. He won't ever be what he was before, I don't suppose."

"He looks much iller now than he did. But I suppose that's natural at this stage. . . ."

"M'm. . . ." That was enough about the patient. Anxiety in relations was natural, but a little went a long way. He was all right, she'd said so. "What a noise those owls do make here at night."

"Yes, we've always had a lot of owls—ever since I can remember. Don't you like them?"

"Can't say I do. Creepy sort of noise. I suppose you'd have nightingales here too, would you?"

"We once had a nightingale.... Every May, in the shrubbery by the drive." ... Just at that place. ... "But he doesn't come any more now. I don't know why. I suppose it's getting too suburban."

"M'm. Suburban you call this, do you?" She uttered a brief sharp laugh. "Of course, the country's all right for a bit—but I shouldn't care for it for long. My goodness, I should get blue! Specially in winter. I couldn't stick it. Give me London in winter. I love London."

"Do you? It's exciting, of course, but I don't love it. I'd far rather live in the country. Most of all in winter."

Oh, stop, awful voices, glib words rubbing, rattling against each other without hope, without illumination. ... Is it true, can it be true, what was said, felt, half an hour ago? Are the shapes still there, perfect as we left them, in the November night, in the garden just beyond these windows? Is the night still beautiful as it seemed—penetrated with moon, with warm leaf smell, cold smell of mist, secretly dying and living? Is it all nothing? Can it be defaced, deformed, made squalid by a voice? Could it be seen in some other way—in her way, not mine? ...

"I hope my next case will be in London."

"I do hope so. It must be dreadfully boring for you here."

"Oh, it's all in the day's work. You can't pick and choose."

"I suppose not."

"That's a nice frock. Suits you, that long line. I like white. Not that I wear it myself—get enough of it on duty—white, white, white—so I always go for a colour. But I always think white looks distinguished. You always notice a woman in white—I mean a well-dressed woman."

"I'm glad you like it." Oh, enough, enough. ... She yawned elaborately, stretched. "I'm sleepy, I must go to bed. Good-night, nurse."

"Want to undress here and warm your toes a bit?"

"Oh, thank you so much—it's sweet of you—but my sister told me to look in on her."

"I see."

The blue eye screwed down, cold, speculative, obscene. . . . Now what have *you* been up to? You're not the stand-offish sort, I know you. Come on now: no flies on me either. *Men! We* know 'em. . . . All after the one thing. I could tell you some spicy bits. . . .

Wasn't it what I thought? Was it coarse, furtive? Was it making myself cheap and allowing liberties? Was it a passing lust that he indulged, was it something with obscene words for it?

Quick, quick, get away. . . .

"Well, good-night, nurse. Have you got everything you want?" Ingratiating smile.

"Yes, thanks. Night-night."

The eyes stared, dropped, fastening quickly on the news-paper. . . . Baulked.

Kate.

She turned the handle and looked in. The bedside lamp was switched on, but Kate was fast asleep. She'd meant to stay awake, but sleep overcame her. She lay curled up on her side, the bedclothes tucked well round her, her face pink, childish, peaceful, pressed into the pillow, squashing her nose a little.

Why is she so touching—what makes her so adorable?

Nowadays, away from her own home, Kate slept soundly, taking a rest. In the bosom of her family, the broken nights, nights of light sleep—tremulous, full of queries: Did a child call out? Was it a night bird? Cattle lowing? Would that car starting up, those late loud voices wake the teething baby? . . . Yes? No? . . . Prepared to leap up in a flash, assuming calm alertness. . . . Yes? No? . . . falling into thin sleep again.

All the same she won't like it in the morning when she finds she succumbed unawares and left the light on; and that

I came in and switched it off without waking her. She'll think there's been a mean march stolen: she won't like it at all.

What luck she was asleep—married, innocent Kate. To-morrow I shall have grown a more solid mask, there won't be a crack in it.

My own bedroom, my bed. She stretched out her limbs, relaxed, heavy from the hot bath. One blessing about Dad's illness: the boiler got a late stoking, the water stayed hot all night. Safe, alone at last. Now, can I think about him, can I see what it is, what it will be? . . . Is he in yet, out of the dark? Is he falling asleep too, and thinking? . . . One or two images floated up, sharp, and gone again, bewildering: as if one had been shocked into paralysis, recovering now slowly, making a tentative sequence little by little. Or like coming round from an anæsthetic, repossessing by degrees one's identity. . . . Springs, long dry, beginning to stir, to flow again; the blood beginning to assert its life again; after years of unsharingness, of thinking: It isn't so important; no hardship to do without and not feel starved, repressed . . . at least, not often. . . .

Rollo, I haven't had a lover. There was nobody I fell in love with, I didn't try experiments: it was never worth it. Not because I'm cold, only because of love—because I believe in it, because I thought I'd wait for it, although they said schoolgirlish, neurotic, unfriendly. . . . It was because of you. . . .

I shall tell him all that. I'll tell him. . . . He'll say: I feel the same, it's worth not spoiling. . . . He'll say: Darling, I'm so glad. . . . If he were here now. . . . I want him here. . . . Once Ivor . . . I don't want to think of Ivor. . . . Once we stayed out very late on the river, we took off our clothes and bathed from the punt, he said how lovely you are, you're so smooth and white; it was the first time seeing each other naked. . . . Afterwards he cried a bit, why did he, it was a failure for him somehow, I had to comfort him. . . . I won't think about Ivor. . . . Once I went to bed early and he came up late from reading, and when I opened my eyes there he was looking at me: his face so moved, and sort of pitying, tender, watching me sleep, and I held my arms out. . . . We were married. Rollo's married to Nicola. . . .

Why do I, I don't want to, I won't think about Ivor. . . .

Rollo'll write me a letter. I'll find the envelope in London, and it'll be true, it'll be from Rollo. What sort of writing does his hand make, will it be speaking in his voice; saying darling, saying Olivia, darling, will you. . . .

Yes, I'll say. . . . Yes. Anything you say. Yes.

PART TWO

IT WAS THEN THE TIME BEGAN WHEN THERE WASN'T ANY TIME.
The journey was in the dark, going on without end or beginning, without landmarks, bearings lost: asleep? . . . waking?
. . . Time whirled, throwing up in paradoxical slow motion a
sign, a scene, sharp, startling, lingering as a blow over the
heart. A look flared, urgently meaning something, stamping
itself for ever, ever, ever. . . . Gone, flashed away, a face in a
train passing, not ever to be recovered. A voice called out,
saying words—going on, on, on, eternally reverberating . . .
fading out, a voice of tin, a hollow voice, the plain meaning
lost, the echo meaningless. A voice calling out by night in a
foreign station where the night train draws through, not
stopping. . . .

There was this inward double living under amorphous
impacts of dark and light mixed: that was when we were
together. . . . Not being together was a vacuum. It was an
unborn place in the shadow of the time before and the time
to come. It was remembering and looking forward, drawn
out painfully both ways, taut like a bit of elastic. . . . Wearing. . . .

There were no questions in this time. All was agreeing,
answer after answer melting, lapsing into one another: "Yes";
"Yes, darling"; "Yes"—smiling, accepting, kissing, dismissing.
. . . No argument, no discussion. No separate character any
more to judge, test, learn by degrees. He was like breathing,
like the heart beating—unknown, essential, mysterious. He
was like the dark. . . .

Well, I know what it is to be in love all right. . . . What
happened to the person I was beginning to know before—
going home that time, going to dine with the family at
Meldon? . . . Suddenly, the connection snapped. . . . I remember
him well: agreeable, easy-mannered, with a kind of class-

flavour to his flirtatiousness and wit; friendly: and then not friendly: hostile, obstinate, on his guard. . . . Does being in love create a new person? Did I know him then, and not now? Have I swallowed him up? *Vénus toute entière.* . . . No, no! Nobody could say Rollo was a victim. . . . Could they? . . . Except that he's a bit weak and in a muddle. . . .

Beyond the glass casing I was in, was the weather, were the winter streets in rain, wind, fog, in the fine frosty days and nights, the mild, damp grey ones. Pictures of London winter the other side of the glass—not reaching the body; no wet ankles, muddy stockings, blown hair, cold-aching cheeks, fog-smarting eyes, throat, nose . . . not my usual bus-taking London winter. It was always indoors or in taxis or in his warm car; it was mostly in the safe dark, or in half-light in the deepest corner of the restaurant, as out of sight as possible. Drawn curtains, shaded lamp, or only the fire. . . .

In this time there was no sequence, no development. Each time was new, was different, existing without relation to before and after; all the times were one and the same.

The telephone rang in the morning. I was just going out.

"Look here." He always said that on the telephone. "What are you doing to-night?" He was always guarded on the telephone, crisp, off-hand, he never spoke for long—only to make quick arrangements. He never said anything nice.

"Well, I was having dinner with some people, and going to a film or something."

"I see."

"But I could get out of going——"

"Well, I've got to dine in myself."

He was always like that on the telephone—non-committal —grudging it sounded: rather putting-off till I got accustomed and could tease.

"Oh. . . . It doesn't seem much use then. . . ."

"I was rather wondering if we could meet afterwards? I

can get away by ten. We might have supper or something?
Unless you're fixed up?"

"I'm not fixed up. That'll be fine."

It was a funny sort of half-hearted-sounding invitation. . . .

"Shall I pick you up somewhere or what?"

"Well, I don't quite know where I'll be. I'll have dinner
with my people, you see, and not go to the film. . . . Of course
I don't mind a bit, I've seen three films this week." I had—it
was all I could do. "The best thing'll be if I come back here. . . ."
Quickly planning it all. "Call for me here."

"Right, I will. Ten o'clock then."

It sounded so very ordinary and above-board—a bleak-
sounding sort of date. I couldn't think at all or feel excited—
not consciously. The only thing in my mind was Etty would
be out; I'd have the flat to myself.

It was supper in Simon's studio, which is one of the things
I like best. Simon cooked and Anna helped, they know about
cooking like most painters. I brought some of those little
cigars, they were pleased. It turned into a kind of celebration,
I don't know why; every one in good form, amusing and a
bit light-headed. Adrian brought a new discovery, Ed, a boxer,
very handsome and mild, with beautiful manners, absolutely
charming, we all said, a fascinating character, we said. We
all took Adrian aside and congratulated him on Ed; and
Adrian said, the point is, my dear, his extraordinary shrewdness and capacity for irony, we must hear his stories about life
in the ring. He did say a few things, a clipped mutter up in
his nose, we all said absolutely fascinating. . . . I've forgotten
them. I got on well very with dear Ed, we held hands towards
the end, very kindly, not desirously. I thought: he's like Rollo,
somehow—the power, the goodness sealed up dark in them,
an unknown quantity, exciting—not spilled about all over the
place, or thinned off, gone through the tops of their heads with
taking little samples so often for public analysis and discussion.
I saw Rollo through Ed, clear, for a moment; their separation

from, magnetism for women. . . . No comradeship there. . . .

Every mouthful of food and drink tasted sharp and good, and all their faces, movements vivid, absorbing, and I noticed things in the room I'd never noticed before—not really to take them in: the design on the hand-blocked grey linen curtains, a cushion worked not very well in bright wools—a pattern of shells; a small lead figure of a woman high up on a shelf, a painted jug with Woolworth flowers stuck in it, a joking sketch of Simon examining his cactuses, one or two small paintings, still lives, I'd never noticed before, a mask Colin must have done during his mask period—wherever the eye fell some mark of liveliness, some kind of wit, selection, invention—the vitality of shape, pattern, colour making an æsthetic unity—the creative hand, the individual mind mattering—the dirt, untidiness, poor materials not mattering at all. Thinking: the room lives; their rooms are dead, full of dead objects. I meant Meldon. Wondering what would Rollo think of it, what kind of rooms Nicola'd made, and Marigold. . . .

Colin hadn't shaved for days, he had a butcher-blue shirt and a red scarf round his neck, no collar, he looked more like a miner, a stoker, than ever with his muscular neck, haggard pronounced features and jutting forehead with the lock of hair over it. He was explaining to us about music in relation to painting and writing, and then explaining why it was impossible to explain it. Anna was beaming quietly, her mouth open a little showing her front teeth like she always does when she's happy, running backwards and forwards to the kitchen trying to do everything for Simon and wait on every one. . . Simon was very white, his eyes incandescent—flitting, darting about, then sitting in that noiseless light way of his . . . as if he'd been checked, as if he was patient, waiting to be gone again. . . .

Sometimes when I see Simon going about, he seems the only person who *moves*, other people fumble. I've noticed it coming out of cinemas. We linger and jostle down the stairs, jammed in the crowd, talking, stopping, caught up with all the other lumpish bodies and clumsy slow limbs; but Simon always goes straight forward, threading his course delicately through the jumble, and you find him standing waiting on the edge of the pavement, looking ahead of him. It's as if he'd one of those flexible steel measuring rods slipped into his back, keeping him so upright, sheer without rigidity, balanced so neatly. . . .

It was nine when they said what about a film? And Anna said there's a French film at the Academy I want to see, and I got up and said, "I must go, dears." There was expostulation, and I said, "My cousin that none of you believe in is in bed with a feverish cold, and I swore I'd come back at nine and look after her." Soon we were all out in the street, Simon, Colin, Adrian puffing at their cigars, Adrian in his new, enormous, black felt hat from Paris. Ed said:

"You don't have to go, do you?"

"I wish I didn't have to." Mournfully looking at him.

"Be a cad," said Simon.

"Shall I? Shall I? No, I can't, I can't."

"She can't, it's her trouble," said Colin.

Calling, "Good-bye, dears," taking to my heels in the opposite direction. In the square I hopped into a taxi, panicky, I might be late, Simon's clock slow, I might not have time to prepare, do things to my face. . . . I was back at half-past nine.

Ten. Ten-past ten. Ten-fifteen. Twenty-past ten, and a car came round into the street and stopped, and next moment the bell rang. Starting up weak in the bowels from waiting, starting downstairs in a flurry, then making myself go slow, in a calm way, opening—and there he was on the doorstep. His long, big, black car seemed to stretch from here to the pub on the corner, a notable vehicle, not one to come covering one's tracks in.

"Hallo! May I come in?"

He stepped into the midget hall, his voice sounded so loud in it, sonorous, his shoulders blocked it, his head grazed Etty's phony little chandelier. He took off his overcoat and hung it up, genial, easy, deliberate in all his movements; at home wherever he goes. He was in a dinner-jacket with a soft shirt, pleated silk, rather a shock, I had the black studio dress on.

"How are you?" he said, going up the little stairs. "You're looking awfully well. Sorry I'm late. This residential area is most baffling. I've been up and down half a dozen little streets I've never heard of."

"It is rather mythical," I said. "It's every taxi's Waterloo."

He went into the sitting-room. "Very nice," he said, looking round. He walked up and down, looking amused rather, looked out of the window, picked up a pink crystal elephant on the mantelpiece.

"It's rather a snug little nest, I'm afraid. This is all Etty's. I just have a room upstairs. Etty's out somewhere."

"Etty's out, is she?" he said vaguely, looking at the huge, signed, fuzzy photograph on the writing-table, to Darling Et love Mona in a round fat female hand with a flourish—Etty's dearest girl-friend. That signature gets me down sometimes, but Mona's not bad, you never could mistake her for anything but what she is, a good-lookingish Englishwoman about thirty-five in the right hat worn not quite right, and small string of pearls, who's divorced a husband and has one little girl called Averil. She's always very friendly if I look in when she's come to tea with Etty—she's interested in Bohemian life. She once had a flutter with a Russian count, an artist. . . .

"Cigarette?" I said.

"Thanks so much. I've got masses on me. Have one of mine. I'm afraid it's a queer sort of time to call," he said. "I had to dine with Marigold. She had a party and I promised to do host, Sam's away. I do hope it wasn't a bore my coming at this hour. . . ."

"Not a bit. I couldn't have dined, anyway. I was dining out too. I've just got back." He wasn't to think I'd been sitting waiting. . . .

"They've gone on to some Charity Ball affair or other. I had her permission to sneak off. I can't stand these galas and festivals any more." He always had rather an ornamental special style of talk.

"You look very smart. . . ." It was all I could think of; and not able to look at him quite, feeling stiff, self-conscious, awful . . . wondering: Is it a ghastly mistake? . . .

"Sorry about that too," he said. "I had to. I hate this formal clothes business, don't you? It's such rot. . . . All the same it's rather nice after the city, you know—get out of your office suit and have a bath, and feel a bit cleaner. . . ."

"I like changing for dinner," I said. "At least, I should like it if I ever had occasion to. . . . I'd like to make a long ceremonious *toilette* every night and appear looking fancy as the Pope. I hardly ever see the inside of an evening-dress nowadays. . . ."

"People don't dress up like they used to," he said vaguely. "At theatres and things, I mean—do they? . . . Much more sensible. . . ."

"When I came to Meldon last week was my first full-dress event for—oh, months!"

"Was it? That was fun, that evening. . . ." Catching each other's eye, not knowing whether to laugh or what, looking away again. . . . Fun indeed!

"What you been doing since then?" I said quickly.

"Oh, nothing much. . . . As a matter of fact, I seem to have had rather a full week. Don't quite know what it's all been about. Nothing particular. It's always the same in London, isn't it? It's appalling, really, if you stop and think about it."

"It is."

He came to the fireplace where I was standing—standing up straight as always when I'm in a stew—threw his cigarette on the fire—electric fire—treating it like a coal one. He stood beside me, an elbow on the mantelpiece, played with the elephant and the three ivory monkeys and the cloisonné box, fiddling like Marigold. A stranger. It was all heavy, laborious, flinty, it was like having to break stones . . . wondering: Has he come to unsay it, call it off?

"Rollo, will you have a drink?" And my voice cold, sharp, smooth. "I'm afraid there isn't much in the house. There's some beer . . . or some gin?"

"No, thanks awfully. I really won't just now."

I sat down on the stool. "I say, how's your father?" he said.

"*Much* better, thank you. Sitting up in bed and eating more and stronger. I rang up this evening."

"Oh, excellent. I'm so glad. . . ."

Being with Rollo, even thinking about him at that time always made me start worrying about Dad, feeling guilty. I'd had to ring up twice that day. Mother'd been pleased but a bit bracing the second time—an extravagance, unnecessary now.

"Are you going away this week-end again?" I said.

"I think I am. Are you?"

"I'm not quite sure."

"Nicola went down to Cornwall last night—to her mother. I may go down and join her—just for the week-end—get a bit of shooting. . . ."

"Oh, will you?" Hell of a way for two nights, I thought—the expense—but that's nothing to him. . . . I thought: How devoted-sounding.

"She's going to stay a bit," he said. "I'll be a grass-widower."

"Oh, will you?"

Suddenly he said: "I came as soon as I could. . . ." Trying to break down something, making an appeal; as if saying: I had to wait till she'd gone, surely you see. . . .

"Thank you for your letter. . . ." Able to say that now, look at him with a bit of smile unfrozen.

"Not much of a one, I'm afraid."

"It was very nice." By the last post Monday night, and this was Thursday . . . three lines in his small, thick writing, uneven and not too legible, running downwards on the page;

saying, "Darling, I've been so happy all day, you were so sweet to me. How do you feel? I'll ring up as soon as I can.—R."

Read and reread. . . .

Getting up from my stool to take another cigarette, nervouser and nervouser. . . . He struck a match for me, saying very softly, in a funny, diffident, plaintive voice: "I've thought about that evening such a lot."

"So've I." Looking at the cigarette, puffing furiously.

He put his head down suddenly to give me a light, quick kiss on the cheek. No good. What can break this down? How to melt, how to start? . . . Because here he is, he's come for what I promised, it's got to be made to be . . . standing up side by side in Etty's crammed room. . . .

"Darling, are you glad to see me?" Coaxing. . . .

"Yes, Rollo."

"Don't be frightened," he said.

It was all over before now, it could still be nothing, never happen. . . . I don't know how, there wasn't one moment, but he made it all come easy and right as he always did, saying: "She won't be coming in, will she?"

"Not before midnight, anyway. . . ."

His head looked round the room quickly, over my head. "Not here," I said. If it had to be it must be where it was me, not Etty. . . . It must be more serious and important. . . . "Wait. I'll call."

Running upstairs, one flight, past Etty's bedroom, another flight, my bedroom, my own things. That was better. Bed, books, dressing-table, arm-chair, my picture of people sitting on park chairs under a plane-tree, sun-dappled—a woman with a pram, another with a red sunshade—my picture I bought with Ivor at the London group, with a wedding cheque, and was so excited, that was still all right to live with, though not so good as I'd thought. I turned up the gas-fire and switched on the bedside lamp with the shade Anna did. I thought: He must think everything nice, not tartish, undressing quickly, and my red silk dressing-gown on, tied tightly, it had to be wonderful, not sordid, thinking: This tremendous step, I must tell him, explain. . . . But it was already the space in between where no deciding is, and no emotion. . . . His loud step came up the stairs, he came in quickly as if he knew the room. "I couldn't stay down there any longer." Not looking round, but only at me. That's the thing about him, it always was, from the beginning—his directness—no constraint, awkwardness or head-doubts about what he wants, acting on a kind of smooth, warm impetus, making it all so right and easy. . . . Saying: "Oh, darling, I knew you'd be beautiful." Delighted. . . . "It's rather a step," I tried to say, but already it wasn't any more.

Then it was afterwards. He said, whispering:
"I'm your lover. . . ."
I thought about it. I had a lover. But nothing seemed changed. It wasn't disappointing exactly. . . . The word is: unmomentous. . . . Not wonderful—yet. . . . I couldn't quite look at him, but it was friendly and smiling. His cheek looked coarse-grained in the light from the lamp. I saw the hairs in his nostrils. . . . I was afraid I'd been disappointing for him. . . . Thinking: Aren't I in love with him after all then? . . . We hadn't said love once, either of us. . . . Thinking: It's happened too quickly, perhaps, this'll be the end. . . . I thought of Simon, of Anna and the others at the cinema, seeing them so clearly, thinking: What a contrast: a different make of face even, a different race altogether. Where was I between the two? Rollo with Anna would be unimaginable. Simon and I . . . I love Simon; but that's different again, never to sleep together, that's certain. . . . All the same, just then I thought: I love Simon, not Rollo—thinking I'd done something against Simon, somehow . . . it was mad of course . . . thinking it was siding with Etty and Mona and people like that, against Anna and her kind of feelings about love, to have Rollo for my lover. . . .

He said: "Isn't it nice being all quiet and peaceful afterwards?" He was so kind and gentle.

"Yes," I said . . . thinking how one's alone again directly afterwards.

"What time is it?"

I hadn't an idea. It might have been half an hour, two hours. . . . He looked at his wrist-watch.

"Half-past eleven."

"I'm so afraid Etty may be back sooner than she said."

"Oh, Lord, that wouldn't do, would it?"

I said, "I'm hungry." We laughed. "Let's go out and have something to eat." I dressed. He sat on the bed and smoked a cigarette, seeming quite at home. I thought: Has he done this sort of thing before, then?

"Nice room," he said. He was taken with the lamp-shade, thinking the horseback-riding ladies lewd and funny. He said he'd like one like it for his dressing-room. He walked about in his way, and smoothed his hair with my brush, stooping to peer into the mirror. It felt so domestic. . . . Being married to Rollo, which would never be. . . . Thinking that was the worst of my marriage; not enough money to have privacy, places of one's own; Ivor's clothes and comb and toothbrush mixed up with mine, Ivor lying in bed, bored, watching me dress. . . . Rollo and Nicola wouldn't know what that was like, did they have separate bedrooms or what? . . . I smoothed out the bedclothes and pillow, which amused him, and tidied everything, opened the window to let out the smell of his cigarettes—to blow it all away. Turn down the fire, switch off the lamp. There! He's vanished. Hypocrite room, deny it all! At the door he put his arms round me and kissed me—a different kiss from any yet—tender, grateful and protective.

"Darling," he said.

We went downstairs and put out all the lights. Then we went out into the empty street, into the car, and we drove away.

Rules's was rather empty that night. There were a few theatre people vaguely familiar, and an unaccountable party of stout thick people with indistinct standard faces, women by Derry and Toms with artificial sprays pinned on, and big, black, leather handbags with fierce clasps and handles; men with thinning, sleeked hair, stiff collars, face and neck in one; all with false teeth; all silent or speaking in undertones. No one we knew. We went through into the farther part and got the corner table, and sat on the red plush side by side. Opposite us were two young men, blonds, smoothing their hair and saying rather elaborately: "The point is . . ." They didn't take much notice of us. When they left, with a toss of their heads, settling their ties, we were alone behind the partition and we held hands. All the junk round us, the prints, the marble busts, oil-paintings, the negress with the lamp, the plush, the rather murky yellow light, the general stuffiness—all this made an atmosphere of a sort of sensuality and romantic titillation—the kind that lurks and lingers in curiosity shops and old-fashioned music-halls; the harsh, dark, intimate exhalation of hundreds of people's indoor objects and sensations, unaired, choked up pell-mell for years with no outlet. . . . It was just right then. . . .

We ordered sausages, and Rollo a lager and I a big cup of coffee. He felt in his breast pocket and took out a coin and showed it me on his palm. "I told you I'd hold you to it," he said.

"To what?"

"This cup of coffee."

"Is that my shilling?"

"It is."

"D'you mean to say you really kept it?"

"I did."

"We didn't imagine this sort of cup of coffee, did we?"

"I did," he said. "I've got lots of imagination. . . ." Thinking to himself *then*: I will too? . . . flipping, pocketing my shilling—planning the joke? . . .

"You're very business-like," I said. "Do you always get on so swimmingly?"

"Ah, now don't," he said, coaxing, plaintive. "Don't say things like that, will you, darling? I'm the luckiest man in the world. You don't know how proud I feel. You don't know what you've done for me. I'm so grateful and so proud. . . ." We held hands and smiled into each other's eyes; it was all tender, relaxed now, drowsy and smiling, the last of the bars fixed so stiff against him gone, and all of me acceptance, pleasure, like floating in warm lit water.

He said, "My God, I was nervous when I walked into your house to-night."

"You concealed it," I said.

He said, "You were like a statue. I thought I'd never be able to bring you to life."

"I was afraid you wouldn't too," I said. "But you made it all right for me."

He said, "You feel all right about it now, don't you, my sweet?" His voice has a particular way with endearments—irresistible.

"It was *wonderful*," I said; I seemed to realise suddenly . . . wishing we were back now in the room, and it could all be again and me different, more welcoming . . . I did wish it.

We went on talking softly, saying it had to happen, didn't it? We were always to have this kind of meeting. . . . At least I said so, he agreed. We could have sat on all night, but we didn't stay so very long. It was just as easy to part. . . . He was going down to Cornwall to Nicola next morning, but that didn't matter at all; just then it didn't seem particularly important to arrange for our next meeting; everything would glide on without our worrying and be all right. . . . It's strange how incurious, unpossessive we both were then. It might have finished that night. It might have been enough . . . or couldn't it have been, really? . . .

We dropped the shilling into the vase of scratchy, dry chrysanthemums on the table, so that we'd never know what happened to it next. I went home in a taxi by myself. I didn't want the car announcing me sensationally in the tiny street, in case of running into Etty. . . . Darling, *whose pluto*cratic *auto?* . . . We waved good-bye through the taxi window, and I kissed my hand to him on the pavement looking at me, and drove off. I was home before Etty after all. I was glad, it took away the last bit of fear of her noticing something different in the house. . . .

He used to say: "I don't believe you'd ever make a scene." He said that often in that time. "You're the only woman who doesn't go on about things. You leave people alone. It's so refreshing. . . ." "But of course," I'd say. "That's not odd, is it? Unusual?" "You don't know how odd it is," he'd say, wrinkling his forehead. . . . But what have I got to go on about? I used to think then. I've got everything. . . . He's my lover. . . . It was enough. Enough belongs to me. . . . Perhaps not possessive like some women, I'd think, smug. Congratulating myself, saying: "I don't think I've ever been very jealous. I suppose it's not my line." . . . The time I said that he shook me, saying: "I'd like to make you then" . . . and making love, we played a game of jealousy, saying things to provoke and tantalise, and in the game I was pierced for a moment as if truly pierced with jealous rage. I saw what it was like . . . but only till it was afterwards, and then it all slipped away among the words and feelings of that plane, so disconnected from the everyday ones, one hardly can imagine them. I only thought it had been exciting. . . . He was always giving me to understand he was a jealous person. "My God yes!" he said; and I thought, Nicola?—and I couldn't ask. In that time Nicola was hardly mentioned. We kept his life apart from me separate, we suppressed it; or it didn't seem to matter. Yet often she was why he couldn't meet me, or had to get home early. . . . I was incurious—or I made myself so—or I thought I did. . . . "Now I've got you," he'd say, "nothing else matters—all the things I *couldn't* see how to cope with.

. . ." Always very vague, but I felt he'd been sad or dissatisfied for a long time in his private life and I wanted to comfort him without asking too much. . . . It was enough he put his head down on my breast. . . . I wonder how long that time lasted. . . . Perhaps not long at all . . . a few weeks perhaps. . . .

It was understood when she was in London it was difficult to meet, but that winter she was away a lot. She went to Germany to see a doctor, or else she went down to her mother. I got a picture of someone perfectly helpless, with a maid to do everything, and every one gentle to her, and trays in bed, and wonderful nightdresses and wraps—the kind in Givan's window or the Ladies' Royal Needlework place. I saw her under a white satin quilted bedspread with pink and apricot satin cushions, monogrammed, propping her head, and a blue satin and lace wrap on, being visited by assiduous doctors exuding that restrained pervasive hygienic sex-appeal that is so telling. . . . I put her like that, a wax figure immune in a show case, to account for her, to make her harmless. . . .

I wouldn't let him give me clothes, though I longed for new things to wear for him. He wanted to buy me frocks, but I said no. It was partly not liking to dwell on how much I needed them, would like them—he couldn't bear to feel I was poor and had to work—partly the impossibility of appearing suddenly in new things and everybody wondering, guessing; but also it was pride. I wouldn't be a kept woman. He seemed surprised about this, but he partly liked it too, saying, "You're such a frugal little thing." . . . Though he was so generous, lavish, he was pleased I didn't want to spend his money. . . . I thought indignantly: He's got bills enough, paying for her négligées. . . . But he gave me wonderful stockings, and flowers, and all the books I wanted. I suppose I thought nobody would notice these. I don't know if anybody did or not. . . . Then of course the ring on my birthday—a square emerald set in platinum, deep, flawless. God knows what it must have cost. I was aghast. I looked and looked at it, and it said Nicola, Marigold, not Olivia. It said nothing about us, just brilliant, unimpeachable, a public ring, saying only with what degree of luxury he could afford to stamp a woman. . . . I didn't know what to say. He said, "I did so want to give you an emerald, darling, because I love emeralds. Do you?"

"I do. Oh, I do," I said.

"Look," he said suddenly, "I thought this looked like you. I don't know why—I had to get it too."

He put it in my hand, and it was the ring I wanted, our ring—a ring for the little finger, early Victorian, I think, a peridot set round with little pearls, in a thin elaborately turned gold setting. Made by hand and special. I loved it at once. "I'll wear it always," I said, "and the important one I'll wear at night alone, or when we dine together at the Ritz—when you want to flaunt me." I put it away in my jewel-case in the top right-hand drawer of my dressing-table and there it is now. Sometimes I look at it, thinking: that's an expensive thing. I'm worth something now if I'm ever in a fix. . . . I haven't even looked at it for weeks now. I suppose it's still there. . . . My darling little ring, I never take it off. I said to Etty and Anna it belonged to my grandmother, and to Kate and mother, Anna gave it me, it was her grandmother's.

The white lacquer and onyx cigarette case with the marcasite mount was his Christmas present. "Love" engraved inside it in his small crooked writing . . . but it never seems mine in spite of the inscription. I use it when I'm with him or by myself, I don't think anybody's noticed it . . . though Kate's bound to spot it sooner or later. . . . It's nice, I must say, to go about with somebody well off for a change. I wonder how rich he is, there seems no limit to what he can spend, yet they're all supposed to be badly off nowadays. It's all relative, I suppose. . . . People like him can overdraw and no questions asked.

No one must ask questions, no one must find out. It dashed me a bit sometimes at first, Rollo being so cautious, always in a stew for fear he'd be seen, recognised; always saying safer not, better not go here, do this or that; not ring up too often

at the office. . . . Quite soon I got infected with it. . . . At
Christmas when he went away with Nicola he had some cheap
yellow office envelopes typed with his name and address, and
gave them to me for my letters to him.

"Did you burn them at once?" I said.

"Yes, darling," plaintive. . . . I minded rather. . . . "I did
adore them," he said coaxing. "Such lovely letters. . . ." I'd
hoped he'd say, "I meant to burn them, but I couldn't. . . ."

I kept his. I had to. But I didn't tell him so. They weren't
lovely long ones full of everything, like mine; they were
slap-dash and sketchy, and about taking exercise with perhaps
one little loving sentence at the end, shamefaced looking. . . .

I did think once or twice had he done something of this
sort before and got into trouble, to be so afraid of being found
out? . . . I suggested it, teasing, but he was upset: he said did
he seem like an experienced seducer. . . .

"Well, I'm not sure," I said.

"No," he said seriously. "It's just that I could *not* bear it
to be spoilt. The world's so bloody, people are so revolting—
you're so precious."

I said once, "Tell me truly, does it make you feel miserable
really to be practising a deceit? Do tell me, darling. It would
me."

"I'm afraid it doesn't," he said in his funny rueful way.
"What people don't know about can't hurt them, can it? I'm
not hurting her as long as she doesn't find out, am I?"

"I suppose not," I said. "Only if it was me I think I might
worry. I do see how difficult it is for you," I said, awfully
understanding.

He said nothing. "You see——" he began, then stopped.
After a bit he said differently: "Women are dreadful creatures.
They will want to have their cake and eat it too. It's what
they call being honest. If my wife had a lover I hope to God
she wouldn't see fit to tell me so. I call this confession and
all-above-board business indecent." Saying "my wife" it didn't
seem like Nicola.

"That's because you'd feel it was such rotten luck for the other chap to be given away," I said. "You'd mind that almost as much as the unfaithfulness. It wouldn't be cricket. . . . You don't like women really, do you?"

"There's one or two things I quite like about them," he said in that beginning voice, kissing my ear. . . .

Searching back into that time, it seems confused with hiding, pretence and subterfuge, and covering our tracks . . . though it didn't seem to matter then. But now I see what an odd duality it gave to life; being in love with Rollo was all-important, the times with him the only reality; yet in another way they had no existence in reality. It must have been the same for him. Our lives were occupied, arranged without each other; the actual being together had to be fitted in, mostly with difficulty, carefully spaced out and always a time limit. Etty might come back or he had to go and dine, go away for the week-end, he was delayed at the office, I had to go and see Dad. . . . I thought once of our private debating society at Oxford—all of us b.fs. sitting on the floor in my room debating away sententiously without a ghost of a smile, the subject being: Love is the occupation of idle minds. I was against the motion. . . . But now I saw how busy people can be without love, and once or twice I got panic: Where is the time and place for this? Where is it? Supposing Rollo were to die, my out-ward life wouldn't alter one jot. Where, how should I do the crying? . . . I wonder how many women in England in such a situation. . . . Their lovers killed in an accident, or dying in hospitals or something, and nothing they can do, nobody ever knows. They go to work, they cut up the children's dinner, and choose their spring coats and go to movies with their husbands. . . . I was always thinking something awful would happen to Rollo, he'd be snatched away from me behind an official barricade of lawful friends and relations. . . . Because I loved him he was threatened—by life—by me—I don't know. . . .

Going into restaurants, one tried to be invisible; walking

with one's eyes fixed ahead, looking only at the table; then after a bit summoning courage to look round and about in a calm way. It's so sad, because I'm so proud to be with him, so fine and handsome, I wanted to be seen and envied. . . . I'd have liked to go to the smart places where people eat, and to theatres and dance places. He didn't want to. Of course it wouldn't do, he knows all those well-connected faces, they're his world. . . . He only wanted to be alone somewhere and make love. "Where can we go?" he'd say. "Can we go back to your room?" Sometimes I'd say, "No, I'm afraid not to-night. . . . Mrs. Banks is staying late; or Etty's gone without her latch-key, she'll be back early," rather than risk it; then he'd look gloomy, sulky nearly . . . cursing London and Mrs. Banks, and Etty and everybody else. . . . I told him he had only one idea in his head. . . . I said to tease what I wanted was a soul-mate. "You don't, do you?" he'd say, rueful, coaxing. "And, anyway," he'd say, "I do love talking to you. You know I do. You're such a clever young creature. . . . We have lovely talks, don't we?"

We did, of course, really, lovely talks—specially in the place we always lunched on Mondays. Every Monday, without fail. I was always early, so as to be sure to get our table right at the back, in the darkest corner, almost a separate little room. Coming from the city, he was often late. I sat and smoked and had a cocktail while I waited and read my book and looked at all the glinting wine bottles, all shapes and sizes, ranged round the room on a shelf. The darkness was the chief reason why we liked it, we felt safe; that and the emptiness. I can't think why it was so empty, considering the delicious food. Too expensive, I suppose—really beyond all bounds; but Rollo never cared what he spent on a good meal, he'd never eat anywhere inferior or female. He's a sybarite. There'd be one or two business men, motor-car people they looked like, and an occasional guards' officer and girl-friend, or an American, and some dark-skinned people, French, who'd come in late and lunch with the dark proprietor; friends or relations of his, I suppose, who got the left-over food. Our waiter was French, old, he looked like old Punch cartoons of Mr. Redmond, but wickeder. He called Rollo "milord." Rollo said, "Hallo, you old villain," and it was an understood thing the bill was roughly double what it should be, and Rollo would put the pencil through the total and pay something quite different, though still enormous. We were very happy together there, side by side at our table. Only once, just as we were going out, someone called "Rollo!" behind us, and Rollo turned and said in his easy way, "Hallo, old boy! Haven't seen you for ages. Where've you been lurking?" and I strolled on to the door to wait for him, after smiling a bit the way one should, seeing out of the corner of my eye a fair, rather stout young man with a pink face and a toothbrush moustache, and a quiet cool Scotch-looking girl with amused eyes and a short neck and silver fox furs. When we got into the taxi, "Who was it?" I said, and Rollo said, "A chap I was at school with. Dickie Vulliamy. That's his new wife. Rather nice, I thought." . . . I wonder why that made me so depressed . . . I felt left out. They were all safe except me, she was his new wife, not his new mistress, they were against me. . . .

Thursdays we lunched at another place, not a dark, voluptuous lunch, nice in another way. It was right off our ordinary beat, usually pretty full, but not with the people either of us knew; residential faces from S.W.1 and 3, youngish men with museum faces, one or two actors, the healthy public-school type, actresses,—real ladies, with the minimum of make-up. One got a comforting feeling there of the world being liberal-minded, cultivated, unsuspicious. Men and women could lunch together and no insinuations. The waiters were impersonal and everybody else indifferent. . . . Even one's relations wouldn't have suspected one there. Behaviour was agreeable and sterilised. And good food. I thought a lot about food in that time, I was always hungry. It came nearer being a public relationship, a reality in the world there than

anywhere else. Almost, the split closed up. We talked about
the city and about our families. I told him stories about our
childhood to amuse him. He'd explode in a roar of laughter,
he liked my jokes. He asked questions about my friends, he
was always curious; he said he wished he knew them, they
sounded more sensible and interesting than the people he
knew; but he supposed they were too highbrow for him. He's
got the most awful nonsense in his head about painters and
writers; awe and suspicion and admiration, and envy and
contempt all mixed up. I spoke of Ivor, too; it was odd how
he seemed to understand how it had all come about—he's very
intuitive, and never will judge, never blame. He was sorry
for us both. . . . Oh, Rollo, you're so tender-hearted. . . .
Magnanimous. . . . Occasionally he spoke of Nicola too, but
in a semi-impersonal, detached way, indulgent—how much
she'd minded about the baby, such a blow for her, poor sweet
—things like that. . . . He seemed to assume nothing could be
expected of her after such a catastrophe, it excused any mood
or collapse. I didn't say why doesn't she pull herself together
and try again, of course, because of not being able to bear to
envisage that . . . him getting her with child . . . I preferred
to assume—I mean I assume—I'm sure—a child's out of the
question now, they don't sleep together any more, it's not a
marriage. . . . A beautiful protected doll is in his house, not
a wife. . . .

He never spoke of his own feelings about the baby, he never
has; just said once, of course it didn't affect a man in the same
way. . . . I don't think he knows himself how much he minds;
it's obvious to me. When I said once how I'd love a child of
his . . . I only said it once, never again, it made him worried
and depressed. "Oh, darling, it wouldn't do. . . ." His children
must be legitimate, they must have the orthodox upbringing
and inherit. . . .

Occasionally after lunch he'd decide he needn't go back to
the city, and we'd drive to Richmond Park. First he'd ring
up his house and get his car driven to the nearest parking place,

with Lucy in it. We'd come out after allowing enough time, and there would be the car and Lucy sitting inside, all perked up, knowing what was coming. It was a relief to see that shrewish, anxiety-gnawed female throw etiquette and responsibility to the winds, and re-dog herself and go screeching after rabbits. Even to me she relaxed her fixed antagonism and bounded up on to the seat afterwards beside me with quite an amiable indifference. We'd walk a bit over the grass, and see the deer in the spacious silent blue-misted drives; it was sunny and still the times we went; hoar-frost on the bracken.

Driving back he'd say: "Is there *nowhere* we can go?" . . . He suggested a hotel, and I wouldn't. Then he said couldn't we take a room, why didn't I let him rent a flat for me or something. But, no, I said, no. . . . In his heart of hearts I don't believe he wanted to either. I didn't want even the shadow of a situation the world recognises and tolerates as long as it's *sub rosa*, decent, discreet; that means a word in the ear, a wink, an eye at a keyhole. . . . My idea being we were too fine for the world, our love should have no dealings whatsoever with its coarseness, I'd spurn the least foothold. . . . What was my idea, what was it really? We must be honest. . . . Was it that thing he said women do . . . wanting to have their cake and eat it? . . . It may have been I wanted to assure myself I was in between still, not choosing more patently than I must against Simon. . . . Not that Simon would ever have known or ever minded in the least whom I chose, what I did. . . . How surprised he'd be to know he's a sort of mystical private touchstone to me of—of some perfectly indefinite indefinable kind of behaviour . . . spiritual, if the word can be whispered. . . . He wouldn't like it at all.

Of course I had dreams of being Rollo's wife. . . . Sometimes we'd say, "If we were married," but in a pretending way, or joking about how it would be. . . . He always knowing what he wanted and intended, I suppose; I being content, I suppose, with a kind of permanent dream, keeping it intact from interference by reality. . . . One must face facts. . . . I think that's how it was.

Lord, I was happy! . . . Never so happy. Happy for the first time in my life.

No. . . . It wasn't exactly being happy. . . . We asked each other so many times. . . . "Oh, *yes*. Are you?" "Yes, yes, of course I am." He didn't by any means always have a happy face . . . only just at moments, afterwards, peaceful, utterly relaxed; or when I made him laugh. . . . I see I was more actually happy than he . . . more capacity for it, I suppose; a happy nature, as they say. . . . Then of course I wasn't having a double life to deal with in the same way. What do people. mean about being happy, there's so much talk about it, as if it was the one aim and motive—far from it; it doesn't affect anything, as far as I can see, it isn't the desire for happiness that moves people to do what they do. . . .

I suppose Simon's a happy person; not from trying to be —he never tries to be or do anything. . . . An inherent quality —a kind of unconscious living at the centre, a magnetism without aim or intellectual pretension. . . . Simon seems to cause an extremely delicate electric current to flow between people when he's there; they're all drawn in, but he's just one degree removed from it all, he doesn't need anything from anybody. . . . He's like Radox bath salts, diffusing oxygen, stimulating and refreshing. . . . Dear Simon.

He said more than once, "Darling, don't care too much about me, will you?"

"Don't you want me to love you then?" I said.

"Yes, yes, I do, terribly. Only you mustn't sort of think too much of me, will you? I'm not much good, and mind you remember it. Don't expect a lot of me, will you? I've never been any use to any one. . . ." He was always running himself down, warning me, not in an emotional way, quite matter-of-fact, laconic, almost—not exactly—evasive; as if he wanted to dismiss himself, shrug off the responsibility of being himself. . . .

Not like me. When he said so often, "You're the nicest person I've ever known," I thought, "I expect I am." I never contradicted . . . I did say once I was a coward, though.

When I try to think over it, the times we were alone together weren't so very many. After a bit I began to think the walls and windows were full of eyes when he came back to Etty's. There was his big car, and twice he put down cigarettes and forgot them, one burn on the sitting-room mantelpiece, one on the table by my bed. Mrs. Banks said what had come over me, was I in love . . . and then I began to suspect she didn't go home, but watched from the pub window on the corner. I dare say it was only my imagination, or even if it wasn't she'd never have breathed a word, she'd be delighted to encourage both Etty and me to have lovers, she's all for a good time and no Paul Prys or Mrs. Grundys, she thinks it's deplorable the half-hearted spinsterish finicky way we live. But all the same, I began to hate and fear her small sharp Cockney eye, I thought of her nosing in my room for signs. . . . The house always seemed to me so weighted after he'd gone with his strong male physical life. . . . I made more and more excuses for not taking him back.

He didn't come there any more, I don't think, after we'd had our week-end together. The week-end was the end of the first stage.

It must have been January. Extraordinary to think it wasn't till then we managed it. There was always some reason that prevented it; his week-ends were so booked, he's very popular. . . . And then Nicola of course. But in January she went off to Switzerland for three weeks. Marigold and Sam had gone too, and George and a good many of his circle. Altogether the air was less thick with his friends and relations and he felt safer, had more time for me. . . . What a pity it was never the other way about. I'm always accessible, waiting for him.

He called for me with the car on Saturday morning. Etty'd gone away the evening before, I'd told Mrs. Banks not to bother to come. The sun was coming out; it was mild weather, my favourite kind. When he turned up about ten I was making coffee. He poked about in the kitchen, very cheerful. He said he was hungry so I sent him out for a couple of sausages and fried them for him. That delighted him. "You are a domestic little creature, aren't you?" I suppose he'd never seen a woman put on a kettle or use a frying-pan in his life, it moved him: like Marigold—romantic about the simple life . . . we sat on the kitchen table together and drank our coffee and felt light-hearted. It was a happy start. I felt specially well and pretty that day, everything was without effort. We drove to his club to get some money, and I sat outside the important-looking door and felt it was quite all right, I belonged where I was, I'd be equal to any one who came out down those steps. One young man with an O.E. tie did come out, he glanced in at me, I smiled at him, and he at me—recognising Rollo's car, I thought—saying to himself, "She looks all right, wonder who she is . . .?" Rollo came out, running down the steps—he didn't often hurry, nearly always deliberate, on the heavy side, and said, "Darling, come along in and have a drink. There's nobody about." He took me to the room for the lady guests of members and we sank in vieux rose brocade arm-chairs with jade green walls panelled and decorated with plaster bunches of trophies and gilt-framed mirrors around us, and the ceiling above us bulging with fat moulding, and in the discreet expensive spaciousness we drank champagne cocktails and talked in the kind of voices that come over people in clubs. I heard the ping-tock of a game of squash going on somewhere underneath.

"It's quite lively in this room round about six and onward," he said.

"*Really?*" I said. It didn't seem likely.

"Yes. You know—chaps and their girl-friends. . . ." I saw wholesome young chaps and nice, well-brought-up pretty girls sitting together, talking in their pleasant, arrogant, standard voices about dances and horses and house-parties; temperately smoking and drinking cocktails, mildly flirtatious or just jolly good friends. . . . Well, why not? I was jealous, really. . . .

He ordered two more champagne cocktails and went to cash a cheque. I looked at the *Bystander*.

He was rather a long time, and I began to feel muffled, weighed down by thick stuffs and silence. I thought: He'll never come back; and when he did his figure seemed to come at me from very far away, dream-like and dwindled, making his way back along a tunnel. . . . I dare say it was champagne at eleven in the morning. I remember the waiter's face who brought the drinks—pale, with high cheekbones and fine features, faintly smiling, as if Rollo was a favourite.

It was such a heavenly day. We seemed to float out of London on the sun—champagne again, I suppose. We had no plans except to make for the coast and wander till we found somewhere we liked. It was one of those days when all the landscape seems built up of intersecting planes of light and shadow; the tree trunks' silvery shafts wired with gold and copper, violet transparency in between the boughs. The hills looked insubstantial, as if you could put your hand through them. The damp roads flashed kingfisher blue. I remember a line of washing in a cottage garden—such colours, scarlet, mustard, sky-blue shifts, petticoats—all worn under grey and black clothes, I expect—extraordinary. I remember light dazzling on rooks' wings as they flew up; and an ilex-grove at a crossroads, and red brick Queen Anne houses on the outskirts of old villages—nothing more fitting, more serene, could ever be invented. Oh, I was happy that day. I kept saying: "Look! . . ." The air was like April. It smelt of primroses, I said.

In the afternoon we came to the Dorset coast: through Corfe and out along the road that goes to Swanage. He knew

where we could get down to the beach; we left the car and
walked down, down, a long way, a rough, steep, scrambling
winding path. In all that sunlit green immense descent we
were the only people. The sun was getting low. I remember
only the great space, the swelling green, the evening shadows
folded in the hollows, the iron-dark cliffs, towering, tumbling
in phantasmagoric outlines, the sea spread out below, and us
going down, down, down. . . . It was half-tide and perfectly
still, the narrow, grey waves collapsing with a light noise of
summer. We walked along the beach, and he played ducks and
drakes, and I picked up some shells and bits of agate, saying,
"Look!" "Lovely, darling," he'd say in his indulgent voice,
not much interested. We sat on a rock; and it got dusk, and
cold. The big round pale stones of the beach were so cold.
Our feet sank in, slipped about on them with a grating, harsh
rattle and crunch—it gave one a dismaying futile feeling to
toil through them. We walked up the cliff again, slowly, arms
round each other, stopping to kiss. Oh, how wonderful! . . .
Going up along together in the dusk, peaceful and safe, stopping to kiss. It's a terrific climb, and if there's one thing I
hate it's that: but this was effortless: like being drawn up by
ropes invisible . . . my breath came and went so easily, without
strain. The gulls were crying. Near the top we stood and
listened to them. "Hundreds," he said. . . . It was nearly dark.
I can hear them now. It was too much suddenly, too much
space, and too sad. We were threatened . . . we wanted to be
indoors. Back in the warm car again, leaning against him, the
rug tucked round, I felt better. We were hungry, we'd had
only a snack at a roadhouse for lunch, wanting to get on. "I
feel like a rattling good dinner and every comfort," he said.
So did I. We got to Swanage, but it looked all gloomy and
deserted, so we went on, past the lights of Poole Harbour, into
Bournemouth. We asked an R.A.C. man the best place to dine,
and he directed us through sandy roads among pines, past
astonishing brick and stucco residences with towers, turrets,
gables, battlements, balconies—every marine-Swiss-baronial

fancy—to the new first-class modern hotel on the front. It was carpeted in pink, and there was an orchestra in the vast dining-room, and pink and gold chairs and rose-shaded lamps. The atmosphere was refined luxury, and the women dining looked expensive, flamboyant and respectable. The dinner was good, we enjoyed it very much. People looked at us, but there was nobody we knew, although Rollo had a qualm about the back of one man's head. After dinner, having coffee in the rectangular and zigzag chromium-fitted modern beige lounge, "Well, shall we hang up our hats?" he said. So he strolled away to the office where they were most eager and affable, I could see from my arm-chair, and he came back and said he'd booked a double room with a bath, was that all right? "I'd better go and put the car away and be done with it," he said. "You go up." And while I was standing waiting for the lift and the suit-cases, the frock-coated, brass-buttoned gentleman at the desk suggested most suavely I should sign the register now to save troubling us again. "Oh, yes," I said cordially. I took up the pen. For the life of me I couldn't think of a name on the spur of the moment. Every surname except Spencer went out of my head. It must begin with S because he had a huge R.B.S. on his suitcase. It wouldn't do to hesitate. I scribbled Mr. and Mrs. Spender, London, in a rush. The "d" came to me after I'd embarked on "Spen." "Thank you, madam," he said, and took a key and personally conducted me in the lift to the second floor. It was a grand room—gilt and cane twin beds with fat pink eiderdowns and a balcony overlooking the sea, and a bathroom next door with a smart built-in bath.

When he came up we laughed about the register. . . . We stood on the balcony for a bit in the mild, dark, starry night, and looked at the bay and the lights, and heard the sea whisper-ing. We felt calm and tender like the night. . . . I had a bath and went to bed. We were both a tiny bit embarrassed. I thought chiefly about my new nightdress, whether it would look nice enough. . . . It was queer seeing him in blue silk pyjamas, cutting a broken finger-nail with my scissors. But when we put the light out, all night we were quiet and gentle, as if we'd slept together for a long time. Not the kind of night I'd imagined, but lovely; and waking up in the morning was smiling and drowsy and close. We had breakfast in bed, and then I wanted to be up and gone. I didn't like the way I thought the waiter smirked when he brought the trays in. Rollo went down first in case of being spotted—we'd got that on our minds again—and paid the bill, a whacking one, I bet, and after a bit, when I thought the car would be round, I walked down by the staircase looking straight ahead, willing my form to be obliterated. . . . Doing that has become such a habit I don't think I'll ever get out of it. Very bad for my poise. . . .

"Did you run into any one?" I said when we were in the car.

"Faith an' I did," he said. "A big stiff called Podge Hay-ward I was at Sandhurst with. He appeared in the lounge with a very hot bit indeed—a redhead. Something told me he didn't want to be publicly acclaimed any more than I did, so we passed each other discreetly by. . . ."

"Podge," I said. "Etty had a great friend called that. She brought him to your dance. I'm sure it's the same. . . ." He would be here, I thought.

"Lucky you weren't with me, darling," said Rollo lightly, dismissing Podge as we drove away. But I couldn't. I remem-ber his awful patronising laugh and bulging opaque eye . . . hearing him say to Etty, "That little cousin of yours is quite sweet, but she needs teaching. . . ." *Needs teaching.* . . . Why should he crop up again to blight me? I felt almost nausea to think he'd been there last night with a very hot bit indeed. I couldn't bear Rollo saying that. It turned love, passion to derision and lust and squalor. I thought: I'll remember him saying that more than I remember our night, so after about an hour of moroseness which he didn't notice, I told him the trouble, and he was astonished, but he made it all right, and we came cheerfully to Weymouth.

It clouded over at lunch and a soft misting rain began to fall. We turned inland after lunch, through a wild, open country of moor and gorse and heather, with patches of tawny grass and marshland, and groups of pine and birch. The noiseless thin rain went on blotting out the distance. I told him, *O Western wind when wilt thou blow? That the small rain down may rain,* and he adored it and said it after me till he knew it. The darling, he's so sentimental. I don't remember much about the day. We drove in a dream, he steered with one hand and held mine on his knee with the other. Once or twice we stopped and smoked a cigarette. In the evening we came to a town with a cathedral, and bells ringing. It must have been Salisbury. We had dinner at an hotel, and decided to stay there. We drank burgundy at dinner, and afterwards brandy; we drank a good deal to make up for the horrid food. I felt hot and dazed going upstairs. It was one of those country-town hotels with rambling, uneven passages and shallow stair-cases winding on to broad landings, with palms in stands, and a coloured print of King Edward, and sets of old prints and warming pans hung up along the passages and stairs, and objects of china and Indian brass and carved wood by the score on every available surface, and stuffed birds and fish in cases and pampas in giant vases, and dark-brown and olive paint, and a smell of hotel everywhere—dust and beer and cheese, and old carpets and polish. . . . I don't know what. . . . The bedroom was big and square and colourless and stuffy, with thick draped lace curtains and an enormous architectural suite of light-brown furniture, and a white honeycomb coverlet on the staring hard high double bed. We had a fire lit and put out the screaming light above the dressing-table and then it was better. The fire piled up high with coal made a curious glow over us in bed and over everything. . . . And the wine, and the queer frightening room, so unconnected with any kind of room we'd ever known, and the rain outside, sealing us in together. . . . Oh, Rollo! Who were we? . . . There wasn't ever another time like that. . . . Crazy. . . . Footsteps went up and down outside on the pavement all night it seemed; late cars passed and clocks in the town chimed every quarter and the fire was still yearning out red over the ceiling when I fell asleep at last.

We went back to London early next morning. He put me down at Hyde Park corner and went on to the city, and I took a taxi back to Etty's, dropped my suitcase and went on to the studio.

After that week-end things were different. I couldn't go back to those furtive snatched half-frustrated meetings. I couldn't think what to do, but we didn't worry just then—still nourished by the week-end. We met for lunch nearly every day and dined together twice too that week and went to cinemas. It was a peaceful week. I see us talking, smiling in warm, calm intimate affection, almost without desire. It seemed so easy! . . . Is that what's called halcyon days? . . . They didn't last. He went away next Saturday, a week-end he couldn't get out of, he said, so I went home. Mother was glad to see me, relieved because I had some colour and looked well. I told her stories about Etty and Mrs. Banks to amuse her, and asked her advice about clothes and pushed Dad round the garden in the bath chair and read to him for hours, he didn't take in much, he dropped off asleep all the time. That was the first time I realised he wouldn't get any better in mind or body. . . .

I didn't go back to London till Tuesday, the day of Simon's party. We were looking forward to it, there hadn't been a real party for ages. I'd arranged with Rollo to drive with him first and go to Cochran's new revue. For once it would be me going on to a date I couldn't miss, I was elated and excited. I even thought I might take him on with me. I wore the white frock, my lucky frock. I told Etty I was dining with Marigold and her husband—that Marigold had asked me. She was thrilled for me, and twittered about while I dressed and made me take her silver coat lined with green velvet. We dined at Boulestin's and felt very festive. Rollo looked so fine and handsome, and it was romantic wearing the white dress again, I could see from his eyes he was feeling in love with me. He said he'd enjoyed his week-end in Wiltshire, he'd been in the right mood to enjoy himself. "Thanks to you, darling," he said. "You're so sweet to me and make me so happy."

"Were there any lovely girls to flirt with?" I said.

"Well, yes," he said, eyebrows up, coaxing and plaintive. "There was one rather nice one, darling. She's a sort of distant French cousin of mine—a great-niece of the old girl who was at Meldon, d'you remember? . . . Very young and awfully enthusiastic and spontaneous and unspoilt—and the prettiest figure I've seen in months—bar yours, darling," he added. I made a disbelieving grimace. "Honestly, truly, darling," he coaxed. "She *was* nice, but nothing like as nice as you. I was comparing you with her all the time to your advantage. I do much prefer you, darling." He took my hand under the table-cloth. I wasn't a bit jealous then. I asked some more questions and agreed it was nice to meet a pretty French cousin unexpectedly. Attractive cousins were extremely advantageous—in fact, the only possible kind of relative for pleasure. I'm sure I didn't feel one jealous twinge at the time.

I enjoyed the revue madly, the brilliance and frivolity, and sitting in the third row of stalls with Rollo and walking about with him between the acts. There was no one he knew, except one or two by sight. In the second half, just before the end, there was a girl dancing with a partner—a swooping, whirling, flying waltz. . . . I shall never forget. . . . She was terribly exciting . . . her long blue chiffon skirts swirled out, clinging, swirling—her long, slender legs showing and vanishing, her long, white, serpentine hips and back twisting, bending backwards, her face drugged-looking, mysteriously smiling with long, pointed lips and eyes under a standing-out cloud of white-fair, short, crinkled hair. Her name on the programme was Thalassa. That means the sea. She was enough to make any one hold their breath; I did, and I could feel Rollo spellbound. He didn't say a word afterwards, but clapped and clapped. I looked at him, smiling enthusiastically, and clapped too. But a terrible feeling came down to me . . . like sour thick carpet dust in my chest and windpipe. . . . The worst feeling of my life.

We went out with the crowd and found the car, and got in.

"My God, what a figure!" he said, moving out into the traffic.

"Yes," I said. I knew when he saw her he'd wanted her. After a bit I said in a bright thin voice, "You seem to have got figures rather on your mind to-night."

"I always have," he said; it seemed like a quick hit back, straight across the chest, a ghastly pang, but he thought we were laughing, he was quite unaware. . . . It's not the only time there's been a lag before he realised a change in atmosphere; in some ways he's not sensitive. . . . The blue shape played on by lights went on provocatively turning and smiling before my eyes. "Where now?" he said. I gave him the address in Fitzroy Square. I felt terrible, but I said nothing. We drew up and got out, still not having decided whether he should come or not. He wanted to rather. "Shall I?" he said. I felt too rigid, stifled to squeeze out more than a word or two, I couldn't say yes or no. I just went on in with a nod or a shrug —I don't know which—and he followed. We went in silence along the passage and met the blare and glare full blast in Simon's doorway. . . . Sailor trousers, shorts, berets, stoker's caps, scarves, grey flannels, peasant blouses, little velvet jackets, stark tailor-mades; Myra in pink satin and pale blue gloves, Mrs. Cunningham stately and noble in an ancestral frock of maroon velvet and old lace, ineffably posed against the wall, Gil Severn in tails and a monocle, Billy Meaker in a complete suit of white tights, his hair and eyebrows shaved off entirely, covered in wet white, and a white glazed cotton vine leaf, the smell of whisky and flesh and powder, and all, and all . . . the mixture as before, moving, struggling about in a mass blocking the doors—the party in full swing and no error.

"Coming?" I said, feeling less awful already, faced by the crowd.

"Good God!" he said, staring over my head; I thought for a minute it was horror at the party. "There's Marigold." I looked and it was; in a backless plain black frock and a wreath of metal flowers in her hair, dancing with David Cooke and looking pretty bemused. There's always a few of their kind at Simon's parties; one corner of his world slides over into Mayfair-Bohemia. It was a shock, I must say. Rollo was suddenly furious. "Who's that cad holding her up?"

I told him. "You know, the gossip-column person."

"He looks it," he said. "Dare say he'll give her a write-up. . . Give you all one, I expect. . . ." His jealousy evaporated mine, I felt nearly all right again. "I'm off," he said, hard, sullen. For a moment I thought I'd go too. But Anna dancing with Ed had just seen me and was waving, and I waved back, saying:

"Oh, there's Ed!"

At that he turned on his heel, and said, "Well, good-night," and went off down the passage. I debated a moment and then I had to run after him, he was going down the steps when I caught him up and took his arm.

"What are you going to do?" I said.

"Go home to bed, I suppose." He looked moody, wretched, childish.

"I won't stay long, I promise," I said. "Do let's meet afterwards, do!"

"Will you come along to my house then?" he said defiantly.

"All right," I said quickly.

"I'll wait up," he said, and I kissed him and went back in and swam straight into a nest of cronies all together round the drinks.

"You do look a lady," they said.

I said, "I've been dining with a wealthy benefactor."

I drank some gin and felt better; Ed put his arm round me to dance. We got on fine. He said:

"You're the quiet sort, aren't you, same as me. . . . I liked your style the first moment I clapped eyes on you."

"And I liked yours," I said.

"They're a funny lot," he said. "Funny idea of having a good time. . . . There'll be some nasty heads to-morrow." He cracked a quiet smile looking round. "Anna's very nice," he said. "I like her very much. Simon's very nice, too."

He picked me up and made a few remarks and lost me again at intervals for about an hour, then he went home. I looked for Marigold, but she'd disappeared. Simon was seeing to the gramophone and the drinks and everything, Anna helping him now and then; he was drunk, that means amused, deft, rapid, lightly caressing. He kissed me, saying, "I wish I saw you more." It didn't mean anything, but I was very pleased. Colin was dramatic-drunk, with a loud, wild, forced heartiness; his hair all over his forehead in heavy locks, his eyes glassy. He seemed to be flung from one person to the next, all supporting, embracing him. When he got to me he said the oak trees are cut away by the salt tide, the seaweed grows right under the cabbages and cornfields. "That's a symbol," he said, throwing the word at me as if I'd never heard it.

"I know."

"You don't. You're a woman. You know nothing about it."

"I know all about it," I said stupidly; he looked at me in a hostile way and laughed contemptuously.

"If you did," he said, "if you *did* . . . you'd understand the whole relationship of sex to life. . . . I could explain, I *could* explain, but I won't. You're a woman. You'd be *bored*. . . ."

I said, "Colin, I'm in love. . . ." But he tumbled on, shouting:

"Come on! Come on! Come on!"

Adrian bowed over me with a tumbler of whisky, portentously solemn, saying, "My dear, I'd very much like to have a word with you about Miles and Rachel. I hear they're *separating*. My God, how trying these couples are! Having at *last* found a real out-and-out bullying devilish character like Rachel, why can't he be content with her? After all, she *does* know how to spend his money. . . ."

"Yes," I said, "we shall miss her. . . ."

"My *dear*, yes," he said. "None more than I. . . ." He saw me laughing and went away in a huff, saying, "You're a *beast* to laugh, Olivia." I heard him complain to a group with Colin in it: "My dear, Olivia *laughed* at me." And Colin cried out, "Olivia laughs at us all!" and he turned and fairly hissed at me. I moved away, feeling depressed and lonely, there seemed so much hostility about, and suspicion. There was a young man from Cambridge standing against the wall, looking aloof and self-conscious, he reminded me of Ivor, who wasn't there; he looked grateful when I went up to him, thinking I seemed one of the respectable ones, I suppose.

"How are you getting on?" I said. "Are you amused?"

"It seems to me desolating," he said, clipping his words, precise, soft and haughty.

"Perhaps," I said, "we should drink more. Then we'd stop watching and blend."

"Not necessarily," he said stiffly.

"Do you feel isolated?" I said.

"Don't we all?" he said with a slavic shrug. He looked suddenly amused and youthful, and said, watching Colin's antics, "Perhaps not Mr. Radford. . . ."

Colin was shouting, "Lights! More lights!"

"Perhaps not," I said, thinking: You fool! Colin most of all.

Gil Severn came up and began talking about hotels in Spain. The young man knew all about them and after a few minutes I slipped away and left them talking, thinking: The lad won't feel his evening wasted, he'll have talked to the eminent critic, Gil Severn. . . . Desmond Fellowes was sitting on a sofa with an artistic-looking girl on his lap. She had ear-rings and a string of huge coloured beads round her short neck, and a little jacket with emerald and orange chenille flowers on it; she was plump and dark and springy and she had a kitten on her shoulder. He's always discovered sitting like that at parties, where does he get these girls, what do they talk about; they look so incongruous against his spare, fastidious, unrelaxingly intellectual-looking form, his beard and glasses. The kitten was the crowning touch. . . . Peter Jenkin turned up, of course, he's a hardy perennial, under a pile of sub-revellers, teeny actors and things, he didn't see me or wouldn't—more green-faced, spiteful, wizened than ever. To think of Oxford and the way he poisoned my first year—that note I got: "It's a pity you didn't think fit to save me, good-bye," in a shaky hand—and when I rushed round trembling faint to his rooms a cocktail party in full swing, and him drunk and perky, calling out, "Sorry you've been troubled, dearie. . . ." Billy was making odd noises dancing with voluptuou contortions by himself and snapping his fingers, he'd almost passed out, the wet white gone streaky, the vine leaf gone. Anna was wandering entwined with Mrs. Cunningham's beautiful son Peter, they were having long kisses. She's always adored him for his beauty, so I was delighted to see she'd got him for the evening, she looked quite pretty, flushed and sparkling. . . . Then suddenly Marigold was there again, with David Cooke. She was going round the room saying with earnest formal politeness, "Excuse me, have you seen half my bracelet? You haven't? . . . Thank you so much." David came up, sleek, black and flashing, and said:

"Olivia, my dear, if a section of old paste and ruby bracelet turns up it belongs to Lady Britton. . . ." How he did relish saying Lady Britton. "Can I rely on you to take charge of it? It's an heirloom, she so values it. I must take her home now."

"Yes, it's about time," I said.

He went away, and I looked down and round, and there it was just by my foot, under the piano. I picked it up and followed her into the passage; she was leaning up against the banisters, very pale, her eyes fixed.

"*There* you are, Livia," she said, looking cornered, evasive. "Why didn't you come and talk to me before?"

"You disappeared," I said.

"Oh, well . . ." she said. "There was such a noise and crowd. . . ."

"Here's your bit of bracelet." I put it in her bag.

"Thank God," she said. "I thought I'd left it upstairs, far, far up among all those twanging springs. . . . The day springs from on high. . . . Whose room was it, I wonder? *Too* extraordinary. . . ." She giggled suddenly and drew in a sharp breath, her eyes flew. "David's pocketed the other bit. I s'pose he's honest. Isn't he sweet, I adore him, don't you? Though he's been a bit of a broken sepulchre to-night. He's taking me home, that's a meretricious act, anyway. . . . He's just gone to fetch my coat. I really *could not* fetch it . . . Livia, what an awful party, isn't it? Or isn't it? I don't know how I got here. David brought me. Why do they wear such dirty clothes? Have you seen Rollo at all? You ought to ring him up. I know he'd love it. Nicky's in Switzerland, breathing the bracing mountain air."

"I thought you were too," I said, forgetting myself.

"So I was, but I came back," she said. "Sam's still there."

"I saw your photograph in the *Tatler*," I added hastily, but she didn't notice.

David came back with her mink coat, surprised, I saw, to find me talking to Lady Britton, specially when she said, "Good-night, darlin'," and gave me a lingering kiss with her arms round my neck, saying, "David, isn't Olivia sweet?" Then she said rather frantically, "For God's sake come on now, if you don't get me home soon I won't answer for me." He enveloped and surrounded her, soothing, important, and they started down the stairs. Half-way down she began to whimper, saying, "Oh. . . . Oh, David. . . . Oh. . . ." I wondered whether to go to her, but I thought better not; I heard him say: "It's all right, my dear, you'll be all right. . . . I've a

taxi waiting. . . ." I think he'd got more than he bargained
for taking Lady Britton out. He fairly swooped her out of
the door and into the taxi. It was one o'clock. I went back
to the party. The more repressed people were beginning to go,
the pot was boiling over nicely; people leaning and lying
about, and dancing in heavy stumbling groups, looking intent.
Dick had snitched that blonde called Muffet, Jasper's property—
he was glowering and glaring at Dick, his face working like
the villain in an old-fashioned film, it looked so faked I wanted
to laugh. Someone had been sick in the grate and someone
else said, "Rum on top of whisky. *Fatal*. . . ." Simon was
dealing with it, looking patient as Christ on the Cross. Fat
old Cora Maxwell had fallen down and cut her head open
somehow, there was a crowd round her bandaging and mop-
ping. Simon came with a glass of water and put his arm
beneath her shoulders, holding her up to sip. . . . Her red,
congested face, the handkerchief tied crooked over one eye,
the knot sticking askew on her peroxide mop, her fat hips and
little legs prone on the floor, stumpy toes turned up, and
Simon stooping above her, pale and clear, his beautiful mouth
folded so gently, blinking a little, holding the glass to her
lips. . . . I found Jocelyn, he'd only just turned up from writing
late, we sat in a corner on top of a table and had a quiet
talk. He made a cool island in the room. He wrote down his
address in the Tyrol for me, he was just off for six months to
write his book; he said why didn't I come out and join him,
and do some writing too. He always thinks I could write,
since those sketches I showed him. He said too I could have
his room to work in after he'd gone, he wasn't letting it, he'd
post me the keys. . . . Dear Jocelyn, you're my friend, you make
me sit quiet and consider ideas—that injustice matters and
unemployment, and the power and hyprocrisy of rulers, and
revolutions, and Beethoven and Shakespeare and what poets
think and write. . . . Things like that, not individual relationships and other people's copulations and clothes and motor-cars,
and things. . . . Not that it lasts. . . . But Jasper came prowling

up and put his paw on my wrist, and drew me away reluctant
to dance. "The virgin," he announced, meaning my white
frock. After a bit of his usual style, clamped against him,
dancing around with deep swoops and squeezes, and sharp
stops, my frock clutched up at the back like when I was sixteen
and always got those hard-breathing, hot-handed partners who
showed the backs of one's knees, he looked at me under his
brows like a seer, more like a lecherous old bison and announced, "You've got a lover. . . ."

"Have I?" I said. How I loathe him—all that mystic
intuitive prophetic bunk and sententious blood-wisdom about
Women; fancy his parents calling him Jasper of all suitably
bogus names. . . . The worst is he does hit the nail on the
head by accident sometimes. . . . " Have I?" I said, raising my
eyebrows, innocently surprised; but suddenly I couldn't bear
it any longer, I must go to Rollo, there were cigarette stumps
and ash everywhere, and empty bottles and marks of dirty
shoes, and a pool of something on the oilcloth by the lavatory
door, and everybody still going through their dreary old paces.
I thought: I don't want them, I'm superior, I've got someone of my own, I haven't got to stay. I sent Jasper for a
drink and ran for my cloak. The last I saw was Billy with a
broom sweeping the rubbish, pulling down the paper decorations and making a heap of them in the middle of the floor
and putting a match to them, and Colin with an efficient level-
headed expression squirting at them with an empty soda-water
siphon. I suppose Simon saw to it. . . . Jasper loomed up
behind me as I went down the stairs, he started to follow me,
muttering—but I escaped and was in the street. It was two.
Would he have gone to bed? If I couldn't see him what was
I to do? I told the taxi to put me down at the corner of the
street where it led into the square. I'd only once been there
before, when I walked past his house out of curiosity. . . .
That part of residential London behind Bryanston Square is
unknown country. There was a cold wind blowing. I shivered.
There it was, Rollo's house, number two on the corner, the

hall light showing through the fan; lights in a room on the
right of the door, the curtains parted a bit so that I could
see in, and I saw him. Standing up by the mantelpiece, smoking
a pipe. From outside the room looked warm, rich and snug—
a first-class comfortable home. I saw that. . . . I leaned over
the railings from the step and just managed to knock on the
bulging Regency window. The taxi I'd left went past and
stared at me. . . . Rollo, my darling, you opened the door
and drew me in and shut the door again, and there we stood
clasped in the hall of your house . . . murmuring: "Oh. . . .
I did *so* want to get to you. . . ." And, "I nearly gave you up.
I couldn't have borne it if you hadn't come. . . ." And,
"Forgive me. I'm sorry. . . ." "It's all right now. . . ."
Loving each other very much and both comforted. He took
me into the room and I sat on his lap in the arm-chair by
the fire to get warm.

"I mustn't stay here," I said.

"Well, I'm not going out into the streets with you at this
time of night," he said. "What's there to worry about? Everybody's gone to bed hours ago. I'm all alone."

So I hid myself against him, hiding from his home. It
wasn't a personal room we were in—more like a comfortable
office with a big, manly desk with a telephone on it and an
ABC and *Debrett* and *Who's Who* in a case and a high bookcase
with a glass front and smart editions of the classics bound
in calf behind it, and a dark-red and brown colour scheme. Over
the mantelpiece was a shockingly bad pastel portrait of Nicola
with a smirking bow mouth and an elongated goitrous neck—
the kind they always seem to have of their wives in these
houses: too meaningless to be upsetting. The first thing he
asked was about Marigold; it had been such a shock to see her,
thinking she was in Switzerland. I said I'd spoken to her
for a minute, she was all right, only a little drunk, she'd left
early.

"She told me to be sure and ring you up," I said. We
laughed. "She seems to think it's time you had a fling."

"The fiend," he said. "It's not safe to tell her a thing. She's had this hunch you'd only got to persevere to compass my ruin ever since we met in the train."

"You don't think she knows about it, really, and isn't letting on?" I said.

"No," he said emphatically, after a second. "She can't possibly. Nobody knows. We've been so careful." And I saw him give a quick look round, as if thinking: This isn't careful. He asked if I'd enjoyed myself, and I said:

"Oh *no*, I hated it all. They all seemed so futile and drunk and squawky. . . ."

"I don't expect they were really," he said in that tranquil way he does when I make sweeping generalisations about people, putting me right without snubbing—although it always makes me feel accused of pettiness. . . . "They looked very cheerful. Fancy-dress party, wasn't it? I expect you weren't in a party mood."

"The fact is," I said, "one shouldn't go to parties when one's in love. . . . It makes one act aloof and superior and they distrust you."

"I dare say that's it," he agreed softly, stroking my shoulder. . . .

It was like a reunion after danger, a reconciliation without the soreness and recriminations of an actual word-quarrel to get over. . . . After a bit I said:

"She was wonderful, wasn't she?"

"Who?" he said.

"That girl, Thalassa—the dancer," I said. "I can't get her out of my head."

"Oh, yes. . . ." he said in an ordinary, almost vague voice. "Was that what she was called? . . . Yes, she was good at her stuff. . . ."

That's all we said about her. I didn't let on. . . . Seeing him in this new setting, which was his own, made him in a way a stranger again—undiscovered, terribly significant, as he seemed at Meldon; and wearing the white frock again—and

the lateness, the silence, the keyed-up mood we were both in
. . . it was like being back at the beginning again. . . .

"This is a damned uncomfortable room," he said. "Come
upstairs."

We went up to the next floor—the stair carpet's chestnutty
brown and the paint deep tawny yellow, nice—and opened a
door, and switched some lights on.

"It's a lovely room of its kind, it really is. . . ." I exclaimed,
and he said:

"Yes, it's nice, isn't it? We knocked two rooms into one
to make it." That "we" was rather painful. I saw them
planning it, doing it together, to be a background for Nicola,
pleased with it together, showing it off to their friends—never
thinking I'd come and look at it. . . . I told myself rooms
made by a couple, joint possessions, don't matter, they're not
a real tie, not important. . . . But they are, they're powerful.
. . . The light came indirectly from three long shallow-scooped
niches in the walls, and these had tall white glazed pots in
them, elaborate Italian shapes, filled with artificial flowers—
brilliant, bright-coloured arrangements, formal but not stiff,
seeming to have a kind of rhythm in them. I thought: If
Nicola did these she can do something. . . . But I expect somebody in Fortnum's or somewhere did them. . . . The room
was long and empty and simple with cool luminous colours
like the insides of shells—the low, straight-lined, broad chairs
and sofas covered in white brocade, and the woodwork pinkish
grey. It really was a good modern room. There was only one
picture, a long, horizontal panel in the end wall, contemporary, though I can't be sure who did it—two seated
monumental figures of women on the seashore playing on
guitars, a group in the foreground lying with stretched
listening limbs, the colours rather pale, blues, browns and
greys. It surprised me, worried me rather. I liked it. But I
can't remember it clearly—or anything else; only the first
pang it all gave me, and a general impression of whiteness
and space. . . . We were there a long time. I lay on the sofa

with my eyes shut, sunk into the cushions, and heard the white clock ticking. . . .

"What's that?" I whispered suddenly.

He listened. "What?" he said.

"I thought I heard a creak . . . as if someone was outside? . . ."

"Couldn't be," he said. He got up and smoothed his hair and went softly over to the door and opened it. Nothing of course. The landing was empty, and I saw the empty staircase winding up. "Why are you so nervous?" he said, coming back. I sat up on the sofa with my feet tucked under me and saw Rollo walking about in his drawing-room, looking for a cigarette. Something was changed—far down, below all conscious layers. Yes, something began to change then. . . . It was that I began to lose my feeling of security. . . . Rollo had a nice house and a life of his own in it, and dependents, responsibilities. . . . I knew it after that. It's hard to face facts when they go against you.

I said, "I must go now."

"Next floor, darling, if you want to," he said. "Up two little steps and straight in front of you. I'll be downstairs." He gave me a kiss and I went up . . . thinking: the first door will be her bedroom. . . . I stood and waited by the first door on the right. . . . I remember the glass door-knob. The silence was dark, rigid. . . . I got a crazy feeling eyes were looking at me from above, looking over the banisters out of darkness. I opened the door of Nicola's bedroom, switched on a light, looked in . . . came out and shut the door again. Dust sheets over the quilt on the broad, low, silver-headed double bed, the mirror laid flat on the dressing-table under sheets of newspaper, pale-blue walls, blue curtains with a magnolia pattern, a drawing of Rollo, young, over the mantelpiece, two flower pictures, irises and pink lilies, pretty, a door leading into what must be Rollo's dressing-room. Shrouded, deserted. . . . The mistress of the house is away. . . . I went on into the bathroom and washed and dried my hands on her pale-pink towel, as soft as silk, and saw her blue glass jars for bath salts and powder and stuff, and saw Rollo's big bath-towel on the hot rail. The farther door must lead into his dressing-room too. . . . A married couple's suite . . . perfectly charming, extremely well appointed, every convenience. . . . What have I done? Why did I? How could I? . . . I didn't dream it would burn on, on, hot and sullen . . . as if a dull gong had been struck that will go on echoing for ever.

I ran down. Rollo was standing at the foot of the stairs, a glass of beer in his hand, looking up. The light was on in the dining-room, to the left of him—where he and she have their meals together and have well-dressed dinner-parties.

"I've been foraging for refreshments," he said. "But all the biscuits and fruit and things seem to have been put away, and I'm blessed if I know where, though it is my own house. . . ." My own house. . . . I wasn't hungry. I was shivering again. He made me drink some beer from his glass, holding me close to him. We went out and found a taxi on the rank and he took me to Etty's door. It was five o'clock when I got to bed. Dead beat. . . . I've seen Rollo tired, but never without his warm, dry, vital hand, never without his clear eye and fresh ruddy skin. His health is glorious. In his arms I feel an electric glow pass from him to me. How can Nicola be an invalid, living by such a warm source of vigour? If she slept with him. . . . But she doesn't, of course—that's what it is. . . . She won't. Poor Rollo. . . . But I comfort him, I always will.

Then came the next week-end, the last we could have together for goodness knows how long; she'd be back the week after. Etty was in, so he didn't call for me. I went with my suitcase to Paddington and sat on a bench on Platform One, and waited. He was half an hour late—a depressing start—A man in a bowler hat and stiff collar with wet lips and eager teeth sat down beside me and tried to engage me in conversation. He spat when he talked. An elderly crumpled woman with a brown stole and pince-nez walked up and down eyeing

me, I got a mad idea she was the Girls' Friendly or the Rescue
and Preventive come for me; and when I saw Rollo at last I
went to meet him in a stiff flurry as if everybody was looking,
and guessing what we were up to. He only said, "Sorry I'm
late. I couldn't help it." I was prim with unuttered reproach.

What a day—dark, sodden, ruined with rain since early
morning. We drove west. There was something between us,
heavy, that wouldn't disperse. We lunched in Oxford at the
George; it was funny to go back there with Rollo. Afterwards
we went into Blackwell's and looked about. Rollo bought a
huge illustrated book about Greek art, and I ordered a volume
of poems by a new young man Jocelyn had told me about. We
went on through Stow on the Wold—on. . . . All that spacious
sad green country with its beech groves and stone walls was
beaten out by rain. It was like the end of the world; there
seemed no way to deny or disregard its declaration of catastrophe. We wanted not to go to an hotel this time. I couldn't
face the register, and hotel faces staring again, we got too
much attention. Rollo has the kind of English appearance and
manner that makes waiters and porters press forward wherever
he goes, expecting his tips to be liberal and his name quietly
distinguished. He could never look like a medium-price
standard traveller staying around with his wife. . . . Our plan
was to find a romantic little inn or a farmhouse that took in
guests, and have two wonderful peaceful nights in rustic
solitude, with perhaps cows and chickens and rural voices in
dialect to wake us, and rosy-cheeked open wholesome country
faces round us. . . . Blue remembered hills, and perhaps the
wood in trouble; never this infinite thick soup of rain. . . .
Oh, the rain!

When it began to be dark we were far out on a country
road the other side of Tewkesbury, the car began to splutter
and check, going on the wrong number of cylinders. We drew
up under trees and I held a torch in the rain while he did
things inside the engine for what seemed ages. Then he went
on; but soon she started to halt and cough again. "Poor dear,"

he said. "She's got a chill in her tummy. We'll just have to crawl to the nearest garage if we can." We crept on in low gear and after a mile or two we had the luck to find a lonely roadside wooden garage and workshop with a light on, and one man inside. We drove in under shelter and Rollo and the man poked about in the engine and fetched tools from the oily bench, and had a technical dialogue while I sat inside half in a stupor watching them stoop, straighten up in queer lights and shadows, seeing their lips move, hearing the hum of their voices like in a dream. He opened the door finally, and said:

"There's nothing for it, darling, we'll have to leave her here till to-morrow. There's quite a job of work to do on her, and he wants to knock off, it's his Saturday night." He spoke with indulgent regret; I knew he was quite pleased to be fussing with the engine, looking forward to more to-morrow. "He says there's a little pub place about two miles on where they'd put us up. He'll run us up in his tootler. He's a nice chap. Shall we go and see what it's like, darling? . . ."

The man's car smelt like Walker's taxi used to, going to Meldon or Tulverton parties. The pub looked all right in the nearly-dark—square and whitewashed with a low dim stuffy bar full of wrinkled, grizzled men with pipes on wooden benches, and two young chaps throwing darts. Women weren't allowed in the bar and I waited in the parlour beyond—a dun-coloured airless box with a table with a green plush cloth and an ash-tray on it saying "Smoke Player's," and a calendar for 1920 saying "Guinness" hung on the wall, and a pink egg-cup on the mantelpiece. Our man took charge for us in the bar, and there was a calling out into the kitchen and a consultation and a woman came in, and said doubtfully:

"We 'ave got a room. . . ."

So I asked to see it, and she showed me up. It wasn't too bad, just small and stuffy with a cottage smell, a mountainous iron bedstead and a tiny window looking out over fields. We'd be quite happy in it, I thought, with a fire and the window open. The woman had by no means an open apple-face, she was raw-boned and harsh and crooked, with untidy despairing hair-wisps and a pale long face both tense and vacant. The man came up from the bar and looked in—a little sharp man with false teeth and a cap on—and was familiar, perky, obsequious. Not a sympathetic couple. The dialect they spoke was Cockney.·... No bath, of course, I did long for one. When I went down again, Rollo was having a drink with his car chap in the bar, looking very cheerful and matey, so I went back to the awful parlour and waited. Soon I heard him say, "Well, good-night, and thanks so much. I'll be along to-morrow morning. . . ." And he came and joined me, and said again what a nice chap he was.

"I think we'll be all right here, darling, don't you?" he said coaxing, in case I might be going to grumble—of course I didn't, I never did with him. He often said I was the only woman who never did, his theory about women is they expect every damn' thing and complain without stopping. I wonder does Nicola nag. . . . How I loathe women who expect consideration because they're women and give nothing back; who insist on the chivalry and yet hoot about sex-equality. I suppose with Ivor . . . I did go on at Ivor sometimes. . . . Yes, I did. But there was tremendous provocation. ·. . .

Rollo soon got things going, as he always did; a fire in the parlour and drinks and supper ordered. The woman said she supposed she could cook us something, the man said: "Anything you fancy, you've only to mention it." We had fried eggs and bacon, they tasted good with beer, Rollo had cold beef and pickles as well. I went up to bed, he stayed down and played darts with a local lad, making himself so popular with them all. . . . Affable condescension like his mother and the rest. . . . No, no, *no*, he's not like that—never. . . .

The bed was remarkable—appalling, the sheets made of thick cottony stuff—is it twill?—faintly hairy and with a special smell. They were a bit damp. Outside in the black night the rain went on teeming. . . .

I don't know what happened. I can't remember how it

started; I try, but I never shall. He was asleep long ago, I couldn't sleep, I was so uncomfortable, and the other side of the wall someone snored, snored, hour after hour, a dull rhythmic boom with now and then a choke. It sounded so difficult, destructive, hostile, as if someone coarse and angry were hating human sleep, defiling it. And the rain going on seemed to be piling up something irrevocable around us—a doom. Rollo slept on his side, soundly, turned away from me. . . . I started to cry, first quietly to myself, I was so on edge and tired—then sobbing and snuffling to wake him, he must comfort me. At last he turned over, and after a bit stirred and made a sleepy protesting noise, and murmured: "Oh, darling, don't. . . . What is it? I shouldn't crý. It's all right, you know. Go to sleep . . ." wanting not to hear, to be left in peace. I wondered if that's how he talks to Nicola. . . . I couldn't let him not hear, I sobbed louder.

Suddenly he woke right up, astonished, incredulous, horrified. Poor Rollo. It was the first time he'd seen me cry, except for a few voluptuous tears. . . . At Meldon he'd said so queerly: "Oh, but it's such a luxury! Don't you know that?" "Perhaps I'm not a crier," I'd said demurely. . . .

"What's the matter?" he said. "Why are you crying? Olivia!" He shook me. He never called me Olivia, always darling or something, the sound of it sobered me down. It all came out in a howling jumble—I couldn't go on like this— I couldn't—I loved him. . . . Why should I stand aside, why should I never count? I realised now what his life was. I was outside and had nothing. I should lose him. In spite of boo-hooing so madly I felt quite clear in my head, not saying things I didn't mean. Didn't he know what love was? I said. Did he think I was satisfied, as he apparently was, seeing him once a week by stealth—did he ever think of it from my point of view? . . . Sobbing into the pillow till it was soaked, part of me thinking all the time of that horrible couple awake perhaps, listening, nudging each other, whispering: "Something funny up. . . . I told you so. . . ."

Poor, poor old boy, he was appalled. "Stop, stop," he kept saying, trying to turn me over. He lit a candle and got up and fetched his hanky to blow my nose. I blew it, and then I saw his face by candlelight, calm, thoughtful, severe almost; and I stopped crying. Was it worse than I thought then? Had I said something final, irrevocable? Would his voice say: "If you feel like that we must stop?" I shrank up into myself, flat on my back, to receive the blow he'd deal.

"I must be very blind," he said. "I'd no idea you weren't happy, Olivia."

"I am—at least sometimes. . . ."

"I thought we were so happy."

"Perhaps we are really. . . ." Imbecile, wanting to unsay it all now. "I know we are really."

"Why didn't you tell me all this before?"

"I didn't know I felt it."

"Then what's happened?"

I couldn't say it. I couldn't. . . . Jealous. . . . I've seen your home, she's real, I'm jealous of her; having said always I'm not jealous, not possessive. I said, "I suppose it's been boiling up underneath. I've tried to suppress it, not worry you. . . . But I get so frightened. . . ." And I let out some more sobs.

"You see——" He stopped. He'd said it before once, just like that, and stopped. I waited, terrified. The snoring went on and he seemed to hear it all of a sudden for the first time. He listened, and said, "God!" and gave a laugh. So I did too. After that it was easier. He took my hand and started stroking it, speaking very quietly.

"Listen, darling. You know what my life is. . . ."

"Yes. . . ." It began to be like being spoken to for one's good by a kind firm elder, someone who expects you to be sensible enough to see their point of view, and there'll be no appeal. . . .

"I'm married."

I could have cried out, hearing him state it like that, bald and direct for the first time.

Anguish. I dug my nails into his hand, it must have hurt him, but he went on stroking.

"Yes. You're married."

"Well, there it is," he said after a pause, and we were silent. There it is, there it is. He's married. That was a fact when we started. . . . It'll teach you to get mixed up with a married man.

"I can't hurt her," he said.

"No." Why shouldn't she be hurt? I am. . . .

"And—whatever happens—as long as she wants me to stay —I couldn't leave her."

"No." She's his wife, she comes first. "She does want you to stay then?" . . . Torture, getting that out.

"Yes, she does."

"I see. . . ." Well, there it is. After a bit I wrenched out, "Have you—have you ever talked of *not*, then?"

Poor Rollo, he was suffering too. He didn't know what to say, he was in an awful fix.

"I suppose most married couples do some time or other . . . when they have difficulties. But she knows I never would— unless she wants it. And I don't think she . . . she may some day, but I don't think . . . She wants—she needs—to have someone she can count on. . . ."

"Yes, it's nice for her. . . ." I couldn't help saying.

We were silent. What was plain was what hadn't been said. Never once, not even in the joyful, grateful, amazing beginning days, had he . . . no, not once . . . put her second—broken a plan made for, by, with her to stay with me. . . . Not once. Nothing explicit said ever. Nothing crude or marital to hurt my feelings, but—well, there it is. . . . I should have thought of it all before, I should have gone on being content with a half-share. I shouldn't have gone to that house. . . . He sat on the edge of the bed, holding my hand, his shoulders droop-ing forward, his face set, heavy and mournful-looking in the candle-light. Perfectly exhausted now, bled white, wanting only to rest, I said what hadn't been said, knowing I wouldn't feel any more pain much:

"You love her."

"Yes, I do love her."

"Although she doesn't—although it doesn't work very well?"

"No, it doesn't work well at all."

He was struggling with things to say, not to say. It was agony for him, the whole thing, poor boy. He said:

"But I thought you knew—I thought you understood all this."

"I suppose I did. One doesn't think—tries not to. . . ."

He beat his fist in his hand, saying:

"I've been the most bloody selfish swine that ever . . . You made me so happy. I never dreamt . . . I suppose I took it for granted you were happy, it was all right for you too. . . . What am I to do?"

"Don't worry, I *am* all right. It doesn't matter. As long as you . . ." Stopping, in case it was forcing him to say what he couldn't say . . . what he did say.

"Olivia, I love you." Hardly ever saying it quietly like this. Often, "Darling, I *do* love you," making love, but that's quite different.

"You do believe it, don't you?" he said. "You must. Listen. I can't change anything. I can't change myself. I can't shatter her. But I love you, I expect I always shall. If it's worth it at all for you, don't quite leave me."

The misery and despair were draining away like smooth dark water pouring away noiseless, without check, into a tunnel, gone. . . . Life turned itself inside out again, like after a bad dream, showing its accustomed unsinister face. I thought I'd been mad. What on earth was the fuss?

"I'm terribly happy," I said. "If you love me nothing else matters. I can do without other things. And I promise," I said, "I'll never make a disturbance again." I said, "Forgive me."

"Some day," he said, "you won't want me any more. Why should you? You'll be fed up with me. Somebody will come along and marry you, and take you away from me. It'll be only natural." He was very sad. "You should marry again, I know you should. I tell myself so."

"It won't happen," I said.

"Yes, yes. It will. You should have a home, you should have children. It's such a waste you shouldn't." Terribly unhappy voice. "I'm so afraid of getting in the way of that. I dread it. You might want to marry and not like to tell me. *Promise* to tell me. . . ."

"Who on earth could I marry?" I smiled, pleased, he was feeling a qualm about losing me; it was that way round now.

"That Simon you're always talking about or someone. . . ."

I laughed out. He was jealous too. Why did he pick on Simon, I wonder? I hardly ever talk about Simon—more about Colin and the others if at all.

"*That* won't occur, I can guarantee. I could never persaude Simon to want to marry me, I'm afraid."

"Oh, I hope not!" Holding me. "I hope nobody will! I could *not* bear it. I wouldn't be any good at being noble and unselfish. I want you for myself."

So that was all right. I was exalted. The way he spoke of the future made it sound as if it was a thing going on till we were old: a woman on her own, I saw myself, with brave sad smiling eyes and a secret. Never any children. I thought I could manage. Rollo would die and I'd step forward afterwards and say I loved him too, and Nicola would turn to me for comfort, we'd set up together, I'd look after her. . . . God knows what muck went through my head. . . .

"Perhaps when we're very old," I said, "we can be together."

"On my seventieth birthday," he said, "we'll have a night together, for old times' sake. Is it a date?"

We laughed about that. He soaked my sponge in cold water from the jug and brought it and bathed my swollen face for me. We lay with my head on his shoulder and went to sleep. What I must, *must* know hadn't been said: I didn't say it till next day. The threatening images faded and were harmless. ... But waking up was clouded, heavy. Of all things, I'd had to go and dream about Ivor and his mother: I was at her house and she came out of the front door to meet me, I was propitiatory, full of plausible explanations about why I'd left Ivor, she was friendly, and smiled a lot, I looked for sinister thoughts behind the smile but found none. I woke thinking: Well, I'm glad I've got that straight at last; and there was Rollo, up, half-dressed, wanting to get to his car.

He was kind, but a shade off-hand, his mind on the job of work he was going to do. The rain had stopped, the day was dark, grey, cold and gusty—one or two tattered blue holes blown into the sky for a moment, then over-blown again. Flat fields out of the window. The features were a shed of pink corrugated iron, telegraph wires, some chicken coops and a new yellow stucco bungalow. He told me to rest, I looked pale. I took a look in my mirror; my God, I was a sight; dead looking, no eyes, even my lips pale, puffy.

"Poor little one," he said, absent, soothing. "You'll be all right later:" making it plain what a bad business I was. He kissed me and went off cheerfully, saying he'd tell them to bring my breakfast up. I bathed my face and got it a bit deflated and put on rouge. After a bit the woman came in, harsh, with her noisy raking stride, and plunked a great unappetising tray on my bed. She stayed a bit and gossiped, but not in a friendly way—disgruntled, dyspeptic, whining. They'd only been there a year, they were Londoners, she hated the country. She was ugly, she made everything raw, strident, ugly. I dozed a bit more, but one couldn't be comfortable in that bed, I ached all over. I was just dressed at lunch-time when Rollo came back, in good spirits, his hands black with oil. We'd have the car by three, he said; it was more of a job than he'd thought. We had a cut off the joint in the parlour, I could scarcely taste, all my senses numbed; I remember noticing my own voice gone light and small, my movements inert, languid. I'd meant to walk with him back to the garage, but a storm of rain came on, he went off again alone. I dragged myself upstairs and lay on the bed, and looked at his Greek sculpture book. Nearer four than three I heard the car; he came up and sat on the bed, and asked how I felt.

What I *must* know I hadn't asked yet. I asked it then. I shouldn't have, but I had to. . . . Whether he and Nicola—ever nowadays . . . my arm over my face, very quick and calm. . . . He waited a moment, I didn't look at him, it seemed for ever before he said: "No."

That was all I wanted to know, my mind was at rest. At least more so. . . . I asked him to forgive me, I had no right, but I had to know.

He nodded his head, and lit a cigarette. I said: "Let's go," and jumped up and packed very energetically, wanting to get away. It was after five when we started, lugubrious swollen clouds rolling up from the west.

"Couple of sharks," he said, amused, annoyed, as he got in the car. But he wouldn't tell me what they'd rooked him; he never will let me see any bill. I didn't feel right: on edge, a crashing headache coming on. He wasn't in good form either —a bit morose and distant. We turned towards London again, not having any plans. About dinner-time we found ourselves in Oxford and stopped at the Mitre for a meal.

"Shall we stay?" he said afterwards. "Or push on to London?"

"Just as you like, darling."

"Well, I've got to be back so frightfully early to-morrow it 'ud really be better perhaps if we pushed on. Getting up at crack of dawn is so grim—one gets back feeling like hell. What do you think, though, darling?"

"Let's push on," I said. I don't remember caring particularly. What with all those tears and the rain and all, the week-end was submerged, finished. We couldn't have revived it.

He was tired too. We only wanted to be alone and sleep. We drove on to London.

It's funny, after that week-end there seems a gap for a long time. We didn't see each other much, I'm sure of that. The problem of where to go got more and more acute. The snatched snips and fragments had become hateful to me—though he didn't feel it in the same way, and once or twice went away sulking when I said no, impossible. It was getting on for spring, he gave me freesias, mimosa, tulips. It must have been in early March that Jocelyn sent me his keys as he'd promised, with a note saying he was just off to Austria, and wouldn't I try to come out for a bit later. I rang him up and said would he mind if I lived there say for a month, and tried to do some writing after studio hours. He was delighted—telling me where he kept his sheets and towels, and about the geyser; and did I want his charwoman to do breakfast for me? I said no, I'd look after myself, but she was to come in for an hour every morning while I was out. It's a lot of washing up that gets me down. I explained to Etty, saying I just needed a workroom of my own for a few weeks, I knew a publisher who was interested, she was thrilled of course; she's marvellously uninquisitive and unobservant, I must say. Mother was suspicious at first, but pleased on second thoughts. She always thinks it's such a pity I dropped Writing after being in print so much at Oxford. She thought at last I might be going to settle down and Do Something. Poor Mum; she doesn't trust Etty, or Anna—or me either for that matter. So my tangled web was nicely woven. I didn't say a word to Rollo. We lunched together the day I moved in. I said I'd something to show him, and directed him where to go in the car after lunch, opened the door with my own latch-key, walked him upstairs, very mystified, and ushered him in. A grand surprise. The sun was streaming in at the window, and he was so beautifully pleased and excited. I thought I'd be very happy there. I like that part of London too, off the Fulham road. After he'd gone, masses of flowers arrived, and in the evening a great hamper from Fortnum's, full of those delicacies—fruits in brandy, foie gras, pickled figs and things—that are a bit of a worry really; one never can decide at what meal to eat them, and it seems such a shame to open the jars. A bottle of Calvados too. The sad thing was he couldn't have dinner with me, he'd got to dine out, he'd come round afterwards, if he possibly could. . . . Sometimes I remember what he said that time I got a glimpse of his engagement book: "They can all be scrapped." It wasn't often they were. . . . He can't help it . . . I couldn't be bothered to cook dinner for myself. I had a banana and a cup of coffee and went out and saw a bad film at the Forum. I came back and sat by the gas fire and waited. About midnight the bell rang, he was there. He stayed with me an hour or two, it was heavenly to feel secure against disturbance. He left and I heard his step go down the uncarpeted stair. . . . I felt lonely then and oppressed. The room seemed quite the wrong shape—too high—square—what? . . . I don't like bed-sitting rooms, specially at night. I can't sleep properly. The building seemed utterly empty except for me. A German couple lived on the ground floor, but in between me and them on the first floor, were empty rooms. A painter had one, but he lived in the country and only came up and used it if he had a portrait commission. He didn't have one while I was there. . . . And Jocelyn's windows, large, bald, vacant with his long dismal unlined butcher-blue curtains, trailing down like a giant's boiler-suit. . . . He hasn't any taste in decoration; not that he's indifferent, he likes his room; he just hasn't any eye. Writing young men often haven't. Not like painters: whatever the mess and squalor their rooms are generally alive. But serious young authors like Jocelyn are apt to live in impersonal apartments with a good deal of brown and blue casement cloth, and oak sideboards, and wicker chairs their mothers have let them have from home. Not uncomfortable, or downright ugly; undeveloped more, student-like. Not puritanical exactly, but, anyway, a hint of a moral attitude. . . . Jocelyn being against possessions at the moment, he'd given away a good many of his books, and the only things in the way of pictures were two photographs, one of Gaudier-Brzeska, one of D. H. Lawrence, cut out of books and framed in black passe-partout; and one lithograph, quite good—a nude. The walls were distempered in fawn, the bed had a Paisley shawl over it by day. . . . Even trimmed up with Rollo's flowers, that room never cracked a whole-hearted smile.

The thing is really, I don't like living alone. The wind gets up; or else I start wondering what the people were like who lived in the room before me; dead now, and soon I'll be dead and what's it all about? . . . I sit in a chair and do nothing, or lean against the mantelpiece. . . . I got to know Gaudier and Lawrence well, and the ugly bit of Victorian-Gothic church the window showed. I was alone in that room more than I thought I'd be. It was disappointing. Nicola stayed in London the whole of the time; I hadn't thought of her doing that. I used to think why didn't Rollo urge, persuade her to go away for a few days. He could have if he'd tried. I wanted him to spend a week-end there with me, or at least one whole night, and he wanted to too.

"But I *can't* suggest her going," he said rueful, his eyebrows up. "It seems so mean, doesn't it, darling? Don't you think it does?" It was one of the kind of little things he just can't do. . . . He told me she was much better, had more energy, wanted to go out so much more, and enjoyed things. I said I was so glad.

He was in such good spirits all that time, so sweet to me, I couldn't bear to let him see I wasn't in form myself. I'd promised I'd never complain or make a scene again; I never have. The Other Woman mustn't make too many demands: Rule the first. . . . Sometimes I thought—I still think—he was loving in a different way during that time. . . . What was it now? . . . More spoiling, more attentive. . . . As if he was apologising, wanting to make up to me. . . . I suppose because he wasn't seeing me as often as I'd hoped. . . .

He'd manage to come for dinner once a week. I cooked it in the tiny cupboard of a kitchen, and he laid the table, awfully pleased with himself. I shall never like cooking, I'm not talented enough, but it was nice cooking for him, he appreciated it so. I bought a stylish little new cookery book and dished up all sorts of mixtures. Sometimes when he couldn't have dinner with me, he'd ring the bell late, about one o'clock. I never stayed out anywhere after midnight in case he did. It was rather wearing, the waiting; often after one had struck, I'd listen for the half-hour, then two, then the half-hour again; still keyed up for the door-bell, the telephone, hearing in my brain his car come down the street and stop, sitting frozen in my chair—a listening machine. . . . I asked him how he explained when he came late. "I go to look up old George," he said. I knew George was an habitué of the house—Nicola's friend—it didn't seem safe; but he said George had had standing orders for the last ten years to provide an unhesitating alibi on all occasions with an element of doubt in them. George could be trusted. He was a very useful chap, never been known to ask a question.

His father and mother came to stay with them for a week during that time. Sir John was having some new sort of treatment from a specialist. That week I scarcely saw him, and when he did come he seemed to bring Lady Spencer with him—which was appalling. I thought: Her son. How dare I. . . . How wrong. . . . I thought how she'd disapprove, and I worried, thinking whoever Rollo can deceive he won't get past her. . . . Whenever the bell rang that week I had a mad fear it was Lady Spencer come to say all was discovered, I must give him up at once. I saw exactly what her hat would look like, I heard her voice ordering me off with majestic uncompromising finality—like the Queen at Ascot sacking improperly dressed ladies from the Royal Enclosure. My heart used to beat, going down to answer the bell. Dotty. . . . It just shows how guilty I really feel.

I did try to write now and then, I got about half a sketch

done, but I kept losing my way in it; and the listening and waiting interfered. A person in my state can't work. . . . Oh! Sometimes I wish . . . no . . . yes, sometimes I wish I could be free again, able to belong to myself. . . . The burden is too heavy, there's hardly a moment to fit in the happiness of loving. . . . And I would like to do something definite with my life. . . .

What it came to was that the evenings I knew for certain he wouldn't come were a kind of relief. Etty trotted round once or twice, and Anna, of course, and once Kate came up and spent the night. She took me to a theatre and I made her up a bed on the other divan and she enjoyed herself, though she criticised the geyser a good deal and got up horribly early and alert the next morning. . . . Having a love affair makes one very remote and useless to one's friends. I didn't care much at that time what happened to any of them.

I slept better the nights I knew he wouldn't come. Another trouble was the thought of his having to leave in the early hours and go out in the dark and cold right across London to his own home. It worried me more and more. We hadn't thought of that side of it; only of the peace and relief of his being able to stay late. Now that he did, I saw it was bad for him, it meant short broken nights, nervous strain. . . . I began to dread it for him. I thought he did too. I'd start quite soon saying, "You'd better go . . ." I'd follow him in my thoughts all the way, picturing his journey, timing it till I could imagine him home. It wasn't till I saw him undressed and in his own bed in that dressing-room that I could relax, and try to sleep. He caught a bad cold going back in a snowstorm one night, he gave it to me and it went on my chest. I couldn't shake it off. . . . Oh, God! There's no solution for a situation like ours. Whatever we try out, the clock defeats us, complacently advancing acknowledged claims, sure of our subservience, our docility. . . . Why should she be so protected, pitied? Why shouldn't she have one pang, one wet lace handkerchief? . . . Why shouldn't she lose him, why not? What's she done to deserve to keep him? Let her stand on her own; why not? It's what she needs. Make her grow up. Make her get out of bed and pull herself together. Shirker! Upper-class parasite! Hysterical little vampire! . . . *Stop!*

Once after lunch, taking me back to Jocelyn's in the car, he stopped at a flower shop in the Fulham Road, he'd seen some pink lilies in the window he wanted to get me. He says it with flowers all right. . . . White lilac too. He picked it out, branch by branch, and the girl packed it up, and the lilies too, in cherry-coloured paper. My arms were full. He wandered round as he always does, and then stood looking at some sprays of stephanotis, precious-looking, in a glass on the shelf. "I'll have these too," he said, curt. She lifted them out to wrap up and he said, "I want them sent, please. Give me a card." He scribbled down Mrs. R. Spencer and the address, no message. "See they go at once, will you?"

Outside he said, a little apologetic, "It's her favourite flower."

"It *is* heavenly," I said, cool and bright. My arms were crammed with lilies and lilac, I shouldn't have minded. I wanted to throw them all away. I thought of her thanking him for the charming thought when he got back—wearing them in her dress that night . . . little guessing who'd given them a dirty look before they reached her. It's the only time he's ever been obviously tactless. It must have been he hadn't quite got his grip after rather a heavy lunch.

One night the bell rang late; about midnight, down I flew thinking Rollo had come unexpectedly. I opened quickly and there on the doorstep was an unknown young man. As he saw me his expectant smile faded abruptly. "Is Jocelyn in?" he said uncertainly. He was hatless, with rough brown hair, he wore a shabby overcoat with the collar turned up. He had large brown shining eyes with clear-cut lids under a broad jutting forehead; and that worn look of dignity, stress, youth which sets the maternal instinct working, wanting to look into the question of his food and underwear.

"I'm so sorry," I said when I'd explained.

"It doesn't matter a bit." His voice was gentle. "I just looked in."

.I wanted to do something about him, ask him in—but I didn't. He looked as if he'd walked a long way. He smiled in a friendly and charming way, and said good-night and went away. I don't know why the incident made such an impression, but it did. It still haunts me. I wonder who he was, what he's doing. . . . He was so different from the person I'd opened the door to let in. He should have been there, he should have come in—not Rollo. . . . I don't know. . . . It was wrong that he had to go away again.

I suppose I was there about six weeks altogether. I know it was April when the two things happened. One was, I got 'flu badly, the other, his trip to America. Two months; on the firm's business: alone, that was something. I think he told me the day I started to be ill. Anyway, when I try to think the two things are mixed up: a waste of waters, a liner, the New York sky-line churn in my mind with shivering and aches and throbbing and trying to get up and falling back in bed again. When Mrs. Crisp came as usual about ten to tidy, she found me. Her appearance was wrong for illness, but she went out and got me some more aspirin, I'd run out; then she did a bit of dusting and clattering and went away again. After she'd gone I managed to ring up Rollo at the office and tell him not to come; he had to sail in ten days. The day wore away, parched, dazed. I dozed and woke and poured down aspirin and dozed again. Late in the afternoon the bell rang. I staggered down and it was pink lilies and grapes and peaches with a note from Rollo. After that no one came or rang up. The night was terrible. Next morning was Saturday, Anna was away, Rollo away, I couldn't face the week-end alone in the flat. I didn't know, but I thought I must be pretty ill. When Mrs. Crisp arrived I told her to ring up Etty, and she came, and the doctor came, and I was bundled in blankets and taken back to Etty's in the doctor's own car. He was nice and good-looking, a personal friend of Etty's of course. I'd managed to scrawl a line to Rollo while Etty was ringing up Mrs. Banks to order my bed and hot-water bottle. I gave it to Mrs. Crisp to post. So that was the end of living in Jocelyn's room. I suppose Mrs. Crisp took away the lilies and peaches. When Etty kindly went back next day for the rest of my belongings they were gone.

Etty looked after me, and the doctor went on coming and I went on having a cough and temperature. I'd been in a low state for a long time, I suppose. The struggle to keep secretly in touch with Rollo was too much. I gave up, and let on in an airy amused way to Etty after the second load of hot-house blooms. . . . I suppose he thought flowers were uncompromising. . . . Of course she was enchanted, and after that brought me up bouquets even when they weren't from him—Simon sent some, and Anna—in a roguish triumphant way—and when he rang up once to inquire had a little conversation with him which she enjoyed very much.

"He's fearfully solicitous, darling. *Too* perfect."

I said, "It's only because I happened to be going to lunch with him—his wife's away—the day I got ill, and had to put him off. He's very prompt with little attentions— lavish. The kind of gentleman-friend who gives one prestige in nursing homes. I suppose he's well broken into it—his wife's ill a lot. . . . I don't wish to belittle," I said. "It makes a nice change for me, and I do appreciate it, but after all, sending flowers is an easy way to get people off one's mind."

"There's an easier way," she said. "Sending none."

"Not always," I said. . . . "You know, even if I hadn't known him nearly all my life," I said, "I don't think I'd ever have found him terribly attractive."

Luckily she agreed about that, he's not her type, she likes small un-English-looking dapper men.

"But, my dear, *some* women *rave* about him, I believe. Iris Mountford was *tremendously* smitten once—and that Hungarian

wife of Ronnie Arkwright's. Ronnie had to take her round
the world."

"When was that?" I said.

"Oh, *before* he married—years ago. I believe he's *most*
circumspect and domestic now, isn't he?"

"Oh, yes," I said. "At least, as far as I know."

"You take care," she said, shaking her head archly. "Those
virtuous husbands can be awful traps—*far* more insidious than
the obvious flirts."

"Oh, my dear!" . . . I shrugged my shoulders, entering into
the spirit. . . . "Not a hope." An utterly dreary feeling came
on, thinking of the Hungarian wife, of his reputation as a
virtuous husband, of Etty's typical light assumption that all
married men were up to no good on the sly.

After a week I was much better, but the doctor made me
go on staying in bed. I was thankful—I dare say my subconscious was seeing to it—it was easier to hide in bed; it
meant I needn't face the business of living over the time of
good-bye. He came to say good-bye one evening about six. I'd
been having visitors the last two days, so it didn't seem too
odd. Etty went out, arch and tactful. He brought a bottle of
champagne, which saved the situation, suppressing the ghastly
cobwebs and sawdust feeling in my inside, not to speak of the
tears I'd felt sure I'd shed. I got quite cheerful and made him
laugh, he was so relieved and pleased with me. I expect he'd
dreaded a scene. He said I looked prettier than ever—much too
tempting. I took his big blue and green silk handkerchief out
of his pocket, to have something of him to take to bed every
night. I did, too. He debated what to take of mine that would
be intimate yet not compromising. My toothbrush, I suggested.
Finally he took the ribbon off my nightdress and put it in a
compartment of his manly note-case.

"One plain white satin ribbon, an inch wide, without
laundry mark or initials," he said. "Non-identifiable in case
of loss, accident or theft. . . . It's safe there. I shall take a peep

at it every night and morning . . . and possibly sometimes at
midday as well."

We kissed, he held me close; it isn't for long, we said, write
often, cable. . . . "A family dinner party to-night," he said.
"I shan't be able to ring up. Besides, you must go to sleep
early." There didn't seem one particular instant of his going,
but he'd gone. . . . And then he was gone. It was rather bad
then. . . . Late that evening half a dozen bottles of champagne
arrived of course. I must say they helped my convalescence. . . .
In the morning, before Etty was awake, I crept down to the
sitting-room and rang up his house: the first time of breaking
the rule. "Hallo!" I thought for a moment it was him—the
butler must imitate his voice. "Could I speak to Mr. Spencer,
please?" Everything was swimming. I shook all over.

"Mr. Spencer left for the United States, madam, twenty
minutes ago. Mrs. Spencer has accompanied him to Southampton and will be back to-night; would you care to leave
any message, please?"

Very nicely said; efficient, concise, polite. "*I* see . . ."
Emphatically casual. "No, no message, thank you. It doesn't
matter a bit. Thank you very much."

When I was better Anna told me she'd decided to give up
the studio, anyway for the summer, and try to do some painting again instead. She wasn't paying her way, she was sick of
it. She'd felt lately she must take to the brush again. She had
ideas about changing her technique and getting on better.
Simon was going to be in France all summer, he'd offered her
his cottage for two guineas a week. Why didn't I come too?
She wouldn't let me share the rent, but I could share other
expenses. She was worried, I knew, having to cut off my pound
a week, but also she wanted my company. So I said Yes. With
Rollo not there London was awful, anyway. Time enough
when he came back to see how he felt about my being out of
London, but easily reached by car. I thought myself I might
see him for longer times with more peace and leisure . . .

country summer evenings, I pictured, perhaps nights together in country pubs. Mother highly approved my leaving my unhealthy London life. . . . A year ago she'd have tried to make me come home and be looked after, but now with Dad and nurse to supervise, she seems to dismiss me more easily. She has enough. Violet and Ada have enough trays and hot drinks to see to. The last times I'd been home she'd only wanted me to gossip and amuse her. She'd seemed almost detached about James and his walking tours in France and his suddenly announced decision to take a room in Paris. As if she'd decided to say at last, "Oh, what the hell! Let them rip. . . ." She's tired. Home is narrowed down to an unalterable invalid routine.

May, June went by in the country. . . . There's no two ways about it, the early days are clearer—those first few weeks in the winter. . . . Now after May, right up till now, till August, there seems a slowing down of my vitality, impulse—a faint mist over every scene. Don't I feel so much? It's natural, I suppose. One can't keep up the pitch I started at, it wears one out. There comes a sharp break of separation. You feel at first it's not to be borne, but you bear it, you grow accustomed. . . . Longing sinks down and is silted over. . . . You never uncover it again in its first unearthly freshness. . . . That's what happened. Week after week of being irrevocably far away. Sitting up in bed in the nights, sending out the very utmost desperately-stretched feelers of thought quivering to find him wherever he was—I couldn't find him; though sometimes I kidded myself I did for a moment or two. . . . Perhaps one needs a mutual effort for successful telepathy; I'm sure he never tried. Of course there were letters. But as usual his letters were sketchy, they didn't make a lot of difference, though if they hadn't come, I suppose I'd have gone mad. . . . On the whole it was easier than I expected; being with Anna was what really helped, and in the country, and in Simon's house.

Simon's house is one to love, it's important, like a being with its own life and idiosyncrasies. It filled up a little of the emptiness, it got to be in some way a substitute for a part of Rollo: a channel for emotion. . . . Simon's house is poetic. Not pretty, sweet, quaint, old-world, anything like that. . . . When I think of it, I think of it as standing back a little from reality, like a small Victorian engraving of a house—a tail-piece in a book; or like something seen through the wrong end of a telescope. Yet one can pass dozens more or less like it on a motor drive; small white houses, prim, rather narrow, straight-fronted, green-shuttered, two pairs of windows, the lower pair longer, larger than the upper, a steep-sloping, slate-tiled roof, with two miniature dormer windows in it. I wonder who built it and when. . . . It's by no means an architectural gem—yet it's entirely special; I suppose it's the setting and the feeling of isolation. . . . And because it's Simon's. When Billy came down he said haunted, but he would. . . . The lay-out of garden is what's so queer. No flowers or flower-beds; all grass—trees—water. In front, the narrow length of rough lawn, edged all round with a ragged stout hawthorn hedge. . . Two rosemary bushes under the lower windows. Half-way down the lawn, a bit to one side, the pear-tree, tall and old, flings up with an astonishing sideways curve and lift—a dancer's pause. . . . Three elms at the end of the grass. The front door's in the right side; no gate, a gap in the hedge, a bit of grass and you come to it, painted green. Opposite it, the other side of the rutty cart-road leading to it, is a perfectly round black pond ringed with fine chestnut trees; and beyond, half-hidden by them, a barn, some cow-sheds, old brick and lichenous tile, tumbling down, disused this many a year. If you stare into the pond, the black mud basin goes down sheer —bottomless they say. The surface never stirs, but just beneath it goes on a myriad stirring of infinitesimal wriggling black pond life. . . . The cart road winds off at an angle through the field to join the hedgy lane to the village; and the way to the river is over a stile by the elms at the bottom of the lawn, over a flat green meadow, another stile, another meadow, willow hedges—then the river, with shallow broken earthy banks just there, rushes, flags, meadow-sweet, willow-herb; a sort of little beach in one place, where we picked up mussels when we bathed.

Anna does love that house. She says one could paint all one's life within a two-mile radius from the door. Morning, afternoon, evening, she scuttled out with her easel—whenever she wasn't cooking, in fact. She likes cooking, she did more of it than me, I'm afraid. She had depressed times about her painting, and scrapped two-thirds, but she thought she was getting on better on the whole. All the rooms smelt of turpentine and wet canvases. She was preoccupied at meals and forgot to comb her hair, and had streaks of paint on her face. Dear Anna, I do like her so much. She's so quiet. . . . She's independent, her judgment is right, just on the sour side. Though she's not at all serene or confident underneath—quite the reverse—she makes no demands. When she's very low she just gets quietly drunk. She lives an intensely concentrated inner life of thought and feeling, but never highbrow, priggish or pedantic; and when she's enjoying something—a picnic, a drive, a party—she's almost ludicrously irresponsible, as unselfconsciously extrovert and simple as a child. A grotesque element comes up in her—something there is in her of the clown of the world. . . . The most unvulgar woman I've ever known. . . . Colourless. . . . Unperspicacious people think dull, insipid; they're wrong. If you break up white, there are all the colours. . . . I wonder if she'll ever marry again or get properly fixed up. . . . Poor Anna, she doesn't have much luck, she will choose the most unlikely people. . . . I suppose the truth is, she doesn't in her inmost heart want anybody to supplant Simon. . . . He's absorbed her emotion . . . although I suppose whatever the relationship once was—nobody seems to know exactly, she never tells any one much—it's all quieted down now, worked itself on to some sort of possible permanent friends basis. It can never have been very satisfactory for her. It must always be partly painful to love Simon. . . . I'm proud that Anna's fond of me. It's not only her being so much older makes me rely on her. . . . Integrity has become a debased word, sentimental, like purity, or I'd say Anna has integrity.

May, June. . . . May was wet and cold, June sunny from end to end, my legs and arms got brown, Anna's dusty hair bleached in stripes, her eyes looked brilliant blue in her dusty-brown face. In May the hawthorn hedge was soaking; after a windy night the elm flowers came down in drifted heaps at the end of the garden. How pretty they are; I'd never noticed: clusters of green discs with a clear, red stain in each. Being with Anna is what makes me remember such country details so precisely. Her visual sense is so sharp and penetrating, she helped me to see too; not just look and dream, half-remember, half-overlook and forget. Country walks with her make an experience in themselves, not an excuse for day-dreaming; or for banging along blindly, like Jocelyn, fiercely considering literature and the proletariat. She sees into hedges, seeing leaves and moths and beetles; she sees how a tree grows in a landscape.

In May there was a frost; it made the evening strange. The full-sailing, torch-loaded chestnuts were caught, islanded in the pale blue-green Arctic fields of sky. All over the earth was the flowering spring growth; in the sky was frail winter light. . . . *A dream of winter, sweet as spring.* . . . The living green, the fruit-blossom enclosed in a cold transparent lucent shell of light—brittle, perilous. . . . The cuckoo was strange, an icy note. I wanted Rollo terribly that evening. We were threatened.

After that frost, the weather softened out, the warm days came. The doors and windows stood wide open from morning to night, people came every week-end to stay; in the evenings we went down through the buttercups and willows to bathe in the river, and afterwards played darts and had drinks at the Dog and Duck. Or if somebody had a car, we motored in to Oxford. . . . It sounds an ideal life . . . it should have been. . . . I don't remember much apart from the sun, and waiting

for the post; and swimming in the river. . . . I was writing
a bit, but it didn't get on much; I planned three stories, each
with a different background of water—a river, a lake, a sea.
It sounds a good idea, but it won't get done. I took some jolly
fine notes though; all my writing energies went into doing
that—and into my letters to Rollo. Every three days I posted
off a fat envelope, a diary really. He loved them; so he ought.
Every single one of his letters was disappointing and precious.
. . . He seemed to be having such a good time; he said how he
missed me, but I don't see that he had a moment to miss me.
Parties, week-ends, gorgeous American girls. . . . Loads of
peaches, he wrote, nobody who's taken my fancy, darling. I
didn't always believe it. I saw him open to onslaught on every
side—flirting as he always must, saying the things he said to
me, starting an affair for the duration. . . . There'd be plenty
willing, and he loves sleeping with people—and what was to
stop him? Me? Nicola? Unfaithful to her with me, why not
to me with someone else? Ce n'est que le premier pas qui
côute—and he'd taken that with me. Why shouldn't he embark
on a career as lover, one affair within another, each secret, in a
water-tight compartment? . . . Perhaps he had already. . . . Of
course he had. I had bad moments. . . . Jealousy coming like
a bank of poison gas out of a clear sky, corrupting the face of
the earth. After one letter about a week-end on Long Island
I lay on my bed and tore his blue handkerchief, and hit my
head again and again on the bed-rail. I did. . . . I can't believe
it, but I did. . . . It was after that I couldn't stand it any more,
I told Anna that evening that he was my lover. That made it
more real, a load rolled off, I was happier. We talked about
him till very late, she said everything just right and cheered
me up. For one thing, she took it all for granted, accepted it
with her cool sympathy as a live, working relationship. And
she seemed to understand why it was, how it was; she illumined
the situation all over again for me, asking questions that
showed me him and myself. Trying to describe with absolute
sobriety and precision what he was like, what had happened,

made me detach him from the amorphous emotional fog and observe him more objectively, as I did for a brief moment before this started. She understood I was jealous. . . . I asked her had she guessed what was going on and she said quietly, Yes, but didn't like to ask questions. She *is* nice. I'm glad I told her. I can trust her to be silent, and she won't criticise or give advice. . . .

He sailed for England early in July. But he didn't land in England; Nicola met him at Southampton and they went to Cherbourg and landed, and spent a week in Paris. A reunion, a holiday away from everybody; her idea, he said; he personally would rather have come straight back. I wonder what . . . I wonder why . . . He didn't refer to Paris much to me, except to say it had been looking nice, they'd had quite an amusing time, but it was her idea; she hadn't been in such good form for years, full of impulsive plans like that. I said Good, I was glad, she must be feeling better. I wondered to myself if she had a lover. . . .

It was the middle of the month when he got back and rang up. I wanted to dash straight up to London, but he said better not, he was so busy; he'd slip off the first moment he could and get down for the day, anyway. He'd come home to a perfect whirl. . . . He sounded busy and *distrait*. Two days later came the telegram—meet him in Oxford, the Mitre, one o'clock. It was a Friday, hot and sunny. I went in by the morning bus, in my clean coral-pink linen dress, and the peasant straw hat from the south of France, with a wreath of poppies and daisies round it. I walked down Long Wall and the Broad, trying to observe the architecture, looking into shops, but I was too flustered. I shivered, my hands were icy-cold, sweating. At one I walked into the Mitre. He was a quarter of an hour late, he looked hot and Londony. . . . We had a couple of iced gin fizzes, then it was better, we could look properly at each other and smile. He said. "Oh, darling, you look about seventeen in that hat!" He kept saying: "I *am* so pleased to see you,

darling. . . ." But he was—what was he?—a bit preoccupied . . .
not evasive exactly, but skimming about on the surface, a
shade imprecise, facile, hard to pin down. He didn't seem to
be able to describe much of what he'd been doing all these
weeks . . . but he never can give a clear account of his activities.
He forgets, he says. . . . He told me it had been awfully difficult
to get away—he'd had to tell the most complicated set of lies
to get out of a family fixture that evening; there'd been considerable sickness; he'd had to invent something about seeing
George off to the Continent, and he didn't see how he could
stay the night; she'd accepted for a week-end party for him,
they were due to drive down in the morning. . . . Yes, it wasn't
just the natural awkwardness of re-meeting in a public place,
he was different in some deeper way. . . . Perhaps I was too.
. . . Perhaps it was simply the break and neither of us was the
same—or ever has been since. . . . Naturally, relationships
can't stand still, they must develop. . . .

We drove back to the house after lunch, I showed him
everything. We had it to ourselves; Anna had gone out with
Colin and the others on the river, we were to join them after
tea for a bathe. The house delighted him, specially inside—
the light bright mixtures of colour, the decorations on the
walls and doors, the whole flavour of the house that is so
strong and individual I can almost taste it in my mouth;
every object, every bit of stuff chosen with an unfailing
idiosyncratic eye—even to the water-jug, the salt-cellar—yet
all quite valueless in terms of money; mostly faded, chipped,
worn. . . . And the rooms in themselves aren't a good shape or
size. He said he hadn't realised what one could do with a
cottage. I don't think it was just the desire to be agreeably
enthusiastic; Rollo's very quick and sensitive to places, he
takes in a lot. He said, which is true, that though it's stimulating, there's something not quite cheerful. . . . He wished
Marigold could see it. But she wouldn't like it, really—none
of those people would; any more than Kate would. As for
Mother, she'd deplore it. The fittings are distinctly casual;

queer mattresses, and a stormy, capricious plug, and a rough
little bright-green bath in a blistered bathroom so small you
soon can't see for steam. Personally, I like it—cosy and
secretive—hardly able to see one's own legs. Back to the
womb with a vengeance. Anna says if I could sublimate my
bath-lust I might become adult. She's sublimated hers all
right, if she ever had one. I had that bathroom practically to
myself.

Alone together all the afternoon. Oh, at last! . . . It was so
still, we heard the hot bees burning in the rosemary. The blind
knocked, knocked. Through it the violent afternoon light was
purple, almost black. "No, truly, darling," he whispered,
coaxing, "I didn't find anybody else. . . . Not one. . . . I couldn't
forget you. . . . I did miss you. . . ." I still can't help wondering
sometimes though. . . . About five we came down, had tea
and bread and honey in the kitchen where it was cool. Then
we walked down across the field with our bathing things. . . .
I'd been nervous about producing Rollo; all they knew—except
Anna—was a friend down for the day; but now I didn't worry
any more. I suppose it was because of feeling released, slack,
peaceful after the afternoon. He was rather nervous. He kept
saying: "What'll I talk to them about? I don't know about
books and pictures, darling."

That evening was a riot. What fun it was! . . . A bathing
party breaks ice among strangers quicker than anything else
I know. Something about swimming together makes immediate intimacy. By the time we were out of the water, we
were all old friends. Adrian had turned up with a German
young man from Berlin, to whom he'd been showing Oxford.
His name was Kurt, and he was very decorous-mannered,
anxious for information, determined to be equal to any mani-
festation of English behaviour. He wore an amethyst ring and
a stylish light cloth overcoat, elegantly buttoned in to his
waist, never taking it off—except for bathing; and a few spots
apart, he was attractive. Adrian had got bored with him and
was neglecting him shamefully; and Anna was being nice to

him. He was a beautiful swimmer, and justly proud of his torso. He added a curious, slightly unreal element.

The westering sun was spilled all over the water. A pleasure steamer went by, crowded, people were dancing on board to the gramophone. They waved as they passed. On the opposite bank some little girls, skirts pulled up to their waists, were dipping and splashing each other with shrieks; and two fat middle-aged couples in black clothes came and sat down close to where we undressed, and took off their boots and drank ginger beer, and ate out of paper bags and stared, munched, stared at us in silence. They must have been on an outing. Like a picture by Rousseau, they looked; all in a stiff row; the bourgeoisie under the aspect of eternity.

Colin and Rollo hit it off together from the word go. Colin was happy that day—giggling, cursing the horseflies, trying to turn somersaults and dive off Rollo's shoulders. They made such an odd contrast; Rollo, tall, broad-backed, narrow-loined, white-skinned, ruddy, giving out that sense of harmonious effortless privileged existence; Colin, small, thick, sunburnt, muscular, with his thin hair plastered down long, lank with wet, over his forehead, his face rough-modelled like a head in clay, all broad steep planes, thumbed into hollows at the temples, beneath the cheek-bones. Such a contrast. . . . But that evening Colin had thrown off the thoughts that furrow and corrode him. His face was alight, enjoying the moment, his voice quick and laughing, without its echoing, heavy note of melancholy. I longed to keep him like that always, bathing in sunny water, not thinking at all, just being. Afterwards, dressing, they stood in the sun by a thorn bush, towels round their waists, lighting cigarettes for each other, slipping their shirts vaguely over their roughened heads, their clear, hard, square-breasted chests—deep in talk, not hurrying, forgetting the rest of us. I see them now, so absorbed, so idle in the sun. . . . "What a fascinating character," said Anna quietly to me, as we sat on the bank. She never says anything she doesn't mean, so I was glad. She watched him, I could see she was delighted by his physical ease and charm. We went back and had supper.. We needed more eggs for scrambling, and Rollo dashed me to the farm for them in his car. That was the only moment we had alone all evening. He was so cheerful, enchanted to find highbrows were quite ordinary and easy to get on with. He said Colin was a marvellous chap, wasn't he? What did he do? Studying nervous diseases at the moment, I said, and left it at that. The word psycho-analysis starts stubborn resistance in Rollo; the only time I tried to explain, he would go on saying surely people ought to be able to get themselves straight by themselves, and isn't it an excuse for gutlessness? . . . He didn't know anything about it, and he supposed there was a lot in it, but personally he couldn't imagine himself ever wanting to go and pour out his troubles to a perfect stranger. Why not be a Roman Catholic and go to confession once a week, and be done with it? In fact, he got distressed as well as fogged. . . . So I gave him quickly a list of all the jobs Colin has had in the past. "By Gum!" he said. "He must be versatile." It sounded so schoolboyish, I got a shock—admiring Colin for all the things he's tried and got sick of—teaching, translating, being a journalist, being secretary to a gallery, doing woodcuts, masks, hand-printed stuffs, market-gardening—none of which expresses Colin in the least—or rather only the crack right though him which makes everything sooner or later equally distasteful. "Too much in the brain-pan, I expect, to settle down," said Rollo comfortably—the silly. For the first time I realised it's no use telling him *really* what people are like. He doesn't care to inquire. . . . If I weren't in love with him, would this matter rather? Might I get irritated? Bored?...

"I *am* enjoying myself, darling," I said.

After supper we piled into his car and went rushing to a pub Adrian knew about, a few miles up the river. What was it called? . . . A pretty name. . . . The Wreath of May. Picturesque is the word for it—old, thatched, whitewashed, sagging, full of beams. We sat outside on a bench against the front of the house. The garden is quite big, long, running down to the river. The light was rich and still, standing in simple gold shapes among the shadows. Groups sat about on the lawn under apple trees, and the grass was brilliant, thick; there were a good many beds of cottage roses, red, white, pink, carefully tended. Two swans lurched up the path from the river. From the bar just behind our heads came men's laughter and clinking of glass. Chaps with Oxfordshire voices kept roaring up their motor-bikes and going away on them with ugly girls in crinoline straw hats and flowered frocks and high heels and twisted, peaky expressions in their calves, genteelly riding pillion. We drank ale out of mugs. Colin began to get drunk and talk about trees. . . . Staring at a grove of poplars, alders, willows, growing up high all together the other side of the road, picking out the variety of shape, colour, texture, depth in them. "Now why can't painters do anything about them? . . . Anna? You just scratch them in all exactly alike and think you're painting trees . . . even Simon . . ."

Anna just smiled. It began to grow dark, stars pricked the blue-iris air, a white owl swooped from the poplar out towards the river, and Colin leapt up excited, waving his arms, saying:

"Did you see? Did you see? That *meant* something! . . ." Kurt said, interested, "De oil is ein English symbolism, yes?" and down sat Colin, punctured; and then giggled. After a bit he sighed, and said:

"It's the first sign of madness when every object appears to contain a hidden meaning—that nothing's what it is. . . . In another moment you'll grasp what's going on behind the scenes, what everything's up to—but you never do. . . . Those children paddling this afternoon—they were tremendously significant, important in some cosmic scheme or other I thought I had a glimpse of. . . . It's wrong, it's bad. Mystic. . . . I find it extremely painful."

And he was silent, we all were. . . . We went indoors and had more drinks. We found an ancient piano in the bar, and Anna played, and we yelled songs, and Adrian did a mad dance with Colin. Kurt suddenly began to sing to himself; his voice was beautiful, he sang louder, alone, soon, German songs, and everybody came round to listen. Adrian borrowed my hanky to wipe his eyes, and wrung my hand with feeling too deep for words. . . . By the time we left we were all fairly drunk, with varying results. Anna seems to whisk, fly about on her thin legs like a cat, very quiet and amused. Nothing happens to Rollo except that he gets more so . . . seems to give out double strength, like an electric radiator switched on full from half. He beams and towers and is very much in control of his wits . . . luckily that night; it was a crazy car load, tearing through the lanes. The roof was open, and Colin stood up in the back, hailing every passer-by with free courtly gestures. Adrian found our straw shopping bags we'd brought stuffed with bathing things in case of another dip, and he put one on his head, one on Kurt's, the handles under their chins. God! they looked funny. . . . We had to stop once for them all to get out; Adrian made a wild rushing leap at a quick-set hedge and landed on top, stuck fast, his long limbs waving. We tried to drag him off, and he kept shouting, "I'm an eagle! I'm spread! I'm an eagle!" And Anna and I gave up hauling on his ankles and sank limp, tortured with laughter, on the bank. . . . Rollo seemed to assume the rôle of host or manager, I remember that, and looked after everybody, giving sudden bursts of laughter now and then to himself, shepherding them into the house. He started off for London about midnight with Adrian and Carl; they had to get back, Kurt was travelling back to Germany next day. They were getting subdued and sleepy, but Colin, who was with us for the week-end, was still going strong. I kissed Rollo good-night and he was embarrassed till he realised kissing going on all round, and then he gave me a kiss and Anna one too, and Colin and he shook hands, both hands, for a considerable time.

"One *last* favour, my dear," said Adrian. "The gin." And he took the bottle and climbed into the car beside Kurt. They started, we waved . . . and suddenly Colin went off at a gallop down the road after them, took a spring on to the running-board and went head first in on top of them. We saw his feet sticking out as they rounded the corner, and that was the last of them. . . . He came down again by train next afternoon rather morose and yellow, and merely said the journey back had been successful. Rollo had upper-class charm, he said. . . . "Obviously madly neurotic. . . ." I was furious.

I suppose I saw him about five times in all the rest of that month. There wasn't any more fun. He snatched times and drove down. Never a night. I ate my heart out rather, as they say. . . . We sat in a cornfield once, and once or twice took a punt on the river. . . . It was towards the end of the month he was always moody, his high spirits were gone. He pretended not—but catching his face in repose, it was heavy, his mouth drooped; though when I asked, he said immediately, no, nothing. . . .

It was an absolute surprise, the sudden plan to go abroad together. I'd been thinking he and Nicola would be sure to be going off somewhere in August, wondering how I could possibly bear it, but I never mentioned it—dreading what I'd hear, I expect—deciding to scrape the money somehow and join Jocelyn, rather than stay alone, gnawing away, always being the planless left-behind one. Anna was going to the south of France for a bit with some others, she wanted to be near Simon. . . . She's still there, I suppose. . . . I'll hear when I get back. . . .

Why shouldn't we? He said, Why not? I'd never heard him speak like that—defiant, bitter-sounding; more as if his motive was to do something against the world than with me. Nicola wasn't well again, the brief improvement was over, I wasn't too shattered to hear, she wanted to go down to Cornwall, instead of the trip to Ireland they'd tentatively planned. "And I'm damned if I see why I should go with her," he said. I felt half-thrilled, half-alarmed, hearing him say it. He could only be away a fortnight, so we decided to fly to Vienna and pick

up George's car and drive about in it. Dear George, always
coming in so useful. He'd left his car in Vienna and wanted it
driven home. We thought we might do that. It seemed too
good to be true, coming unexpectedly like that, I hardly knew
myself for joy. The only snag was telling Mother, I dreaded
searching questions; but there was no trouble at all. When I
went home for a night, she was busy preparing for Kate's
children's visit, touching up the nostrils of the rocking-horse
with red paint, and beyond a momentary attempt to arrange
I should stop in France and see James and a warning about not
losing my passport, she seemed quite satisfied I should be going
out with friends to join friends. She likes people to go abroad
and broaden their minds. She rummaged in her wardrobe and
dug out for me a little canvas bag you're supposed to strap
on round your waist under your skirt and keep money and
valuables in. She'd worn it the time she went to Italy with
Dad, twenty years ago. It was astonishingly obscene. I sent
it to Anna with instructions. . . . She gave me five pounds,
which was sweet of her, and I bought this nice coat in the sales.

It's strange I don't remember more deeply, vividly about
this time. . . . Perhaps I will a bit later when the images have
taken their place in the gallery, and I can stand back and look
at them. Oh, what a beautiful holiday! . . . Will it ever happen
again? What's going to come next? Nothing stays without
development, growth or decay. The pause has gone on too
long, the immobility. . . . Like August, the sinister pause in
the year. . . . But August will go over, the year tip imperceptibly
towards inevitable change. . . . I feel the change ahead, it must
be, I know; I don't see what or when. . . .

My first flight, sitting beside him, among the other quiet,
somehow ghost-like passengers turning their heads, raising,
lowering papers; sun on the huge wings, our shadow far
below us on the water; sun, heat all the way; coming down
outside foreign towns, sweeping off again; the journey so
smooth, sheltered, easy with Rollo—the unmistakable depend-

ably-tipping English gentleman. A night and a day in Vienna; but it was too hot, and we found the car and motored off into the country where we could feel lost and safe. . . . Oh, it was peaceful. . . . We stayed always in little inexpensive places for fear of English tourists; not that we didn't see plenty, but not the ones he'd know. Never more than one night in any place. . . . The super-romantic obvious landscape—peaks, pinewoods, lakes, waterfalls, bright-green villages—not Anna's taste, or Simon's, I was sure—rivers rolling their turbulent, thick, grey snow-waters through Innsbrück, Salzburg; spacious white peasant houses with their painted fronts and shutters and rich wooden balconies covered with vines and geraniums; churches set high, with those white towers and green bulbous domes; the bare clean pinewood floors and furniture of our nightly bedrooms; the smiling, sociable Austrian faces with their open uncomplicated look of innocence and equability, their bursts of laughter and music in little cafés, their soft grüss gotts, bitte schöns, mahlzeits. . . . We did enjoy our meals too. I got plump in a week on eggs and meat and creamy vegetables, and coffee mit schlagen. We walked in the woods, we picked blueberries, we bathed, we got bitten by horseflies, and drank from mountain brooks. . . . Lord, what a rustic idyll. . . . The smell of the pines in the hot afternoon, while I read poetry aloud to him. Housman was what he liked best, and Wilfred Owen. . . . He bought me a peasant dress in Innsbrück—nice stuff, silver buttons on the bodice. I wore it every day, he liked it; it gave me a touch of disguise, of novelty and excitement for him. . . .

It wasn't long. Only ten days all told. It seems much longer—and yet nothing—a pause without even a breath. We never had a quarrel or an argument. More tender, more dreamlike every day, not in the world at all.

One night we drove late, up in the mountains. No moon, but starlight made a muffled incandescence. . . . When I was a child I had more sense of infinity, of the universe, than I have now. I'd stare at the stars till gradually they began to be worlds

to me, spinning immense in space, and under the awe and
terror of them I'd sink away, dissolve. Now I don't generally
bother to look at them, and when I do they remain points of
light in the sky. . . . But that night the feeling came back.
"Look, *look* at the stars!" They hung enormous over peak and
valley.

"Good Lord! They are bright!" he said. "What are they
so big for?"

He switched off the headlights and drew in to the roadside.
It was cold in the mountains, he wrapped me in the rug, I put
my head on his shoulder. What stillness it was. . . . I listened.
How many sounds? Rollo, whistling softly, intermittently.
One frog, very loud. The wind, a light gust, now and then.
Cowbells, in the distance. A brook, striking a tiny, rapid
chime. A little waterfall hush-hushing somewhere. The
number of sounds was surprising; they seemed to help make
up the enormous silence. . . . He sniffed up the air, and said:

"I wonder where we are? We can't be near the lake. I don't
smell water."

I giggled. "Rollo, can you really smell water?"

"Of course," he said. " Can't you?"

It got too cold, we drove on. Round the next corner was
the lake, big stars aching over it, breaking in it, misty. "There
now, you *can't* smell water!"

And I remember, of course, the evening before the last.
Stopping in the evening at a small gasthaus, set a little back
from a narrow, dusty road edged with apple trees, leading to
the village. There were tables and white chairs set about under
chestnut trees, and a band was playing in a corner of the yard
—three yellow-haired youths, that is, in leather shorts and
green jackets and hats with feathers—two violins and an
accordion, playing slightly ludicrous merry tunes, and sometimes singing. After a while they packed up and Rollo gave
them some money, a good deal, I should think, from the way
they beamed and bowed to us, and wished us luck; and then
they took out their instruments and played us one more tune

to honour us before they went away. We felt moved by that absurd sentimental little band. After a while, we were the only people left; we sat on under the trees, drinking a bottle of ice-cold yellow wine. . . . Oh, let me think about it all again, let me remember. . . . His eyes looked into my eyes, he was utterly in love with me then . . . at last . . . I knew he was.

"Listen," he said, "let's not go back. Why should we ever go back? I don't want anybody any more but you. Let's just go on being together—anywhere—round the world if you like. There'll never be anything so good as this again and why should we miss it?—break it off? Let's not go to Salzburg to-morrow for our letters. . . ." His voice, different from any voice of his I'd ever heard. . . .

"We must," I said.

"Listen," he said, "you can do anything with me. Only say. You choose. You say." Urgent, insisting almost harshly, throwing the onus on me, like in the beginning.

"Let's not think to-night," I said. "Let's wait. We may see what to do." Putting him off, he seemed so wild, so unlike himself. His voice was reaching to my marrow, I must keep my head. I felt such a glorious new burst of confidence I was able to counsel patience, prudence. Thinking: I've won! . . . Not caring much beyond that. "We'll go to Salzburg first and then see," I said.

"No, don't let's go," he said. "I don't want to, I don't want to be bothered with any damned stuff from England."

"You said this morning you'd have to get your letters," I said, gentle and reasonable. "Besides, I rather want mine." . . . Feeling we must go back to the world and touch it for luck, if only for an hour, in case some blow was being prepared, had been launched in the world against our unlawful, reprehensible life outside of life. . . . Feeling always Dad might have died, with me lost, ungetatable, condemned for ever. . . . He said no more, he was silent on the drive back to our *pension*; but at dinner he was the same as ever—more loving if anything that night. No more insistence on reckless schemes. All that was

as if it had never been. Next morning we drove in to Salzburg
and went to the post office for our letters. The streets were
crowded, one saw *Tatler*-familiar faces there for the Festival,
and a good many smart English cars. I had a letter from
Jocelyn giving me his new address in the town, one from Kate,
one from Mother. All was well. Nothing from Anna. Rollo
had a great packet, he didn't open them then. We didn't dare
stay and have a look round, we got into the car and went out
to the Wolfgangsee. After lunch I went to my room to lie
down, my head ached, there was thunder in the air. From my
window I saw him sitting on the terrace by the lake at the
table where we'd had coffee, under a scarlet sun-umbrella,
reading his letters. I watched him a long time.

I must have dozed off. He came in at tea-time, and sat on
my bed and took my hand, and said he must go back to England
to-morrow. It wasn't a surprise, I knew it. . . . Some muddles
about dates, he said, another partner wanting to start his
holiday, he couldn't feel justified in taking more now, specially
after America; besides, he wanted some of September off to
shoot in Scotland. . . . We said never mind, it had been perfect,
more than anybody could reasonably expect in a lifetime. . . .
The best days of our lives, we'd never forget them. . . . I didn't
feel any great pang of misery. . . . So brimful of contentment
and satisfiedness, it seemed enough and to spare to keep me
going through even a long separation. We considered for a
moment whether I should drive back with him, it was very
tempting, but he didn't urge me, and I didn't want to be back
in England yet—Etty's house closed, Anna away, Kate and her
family making too much work for the maids at home. I
wanted to see Jocelyn—to have a week or so of a different kind
of time while I was about it. . . . We looked out Rollo's route
on maps, I wired to Jocelyn to expect me, we were quite cheerful
and serene.

That night, just before dawn, the thunderstorm broke. I
was afraid. I shall always be afraid of thunder. At the first
tremendous peal he came in from his bath next door, saying,

"Don't be frightened." I did love him then. It was what one had always longed for, never expected to have—someone appearing quietly at need, saying that—someone for oneself. . . . The storm went away, the sun came up over the lake behind banks of shimmering splitting mist, the air was fresh and cold. We went to the window and looked out. He turned me to him, holding me by the shoulders, and said: "Remember I love you."

Remember I love you. . . .

I packed, and helped him pack. He made me take some money and come home comfortably, with a sleeper. God, I'm glad I did. . . . The dark smiling waitress brought us a bunch of dahlias and gladioli as a farewell offering. We drove on to Salzburg and left my suitcase at the station; I got out by the fountain of the horses, and said good-bye, and saw the car move on, out of the Platz, and then I was alone in Salzburg. I strolled about a bit and sat in the Mirabelle Gardens, and then I went to Jocelyn's hotel.

He was banging away on a typewriter in a cell of a bedroom, with a thick smell of cooking and drains coming up from the court, his clothes all over the bed; and he was pleased to see me. He was leaving that very afternoon to join some friends on the Attersee. We went out by the bus, it seemed to take hours. He sat hugging his typewriter and talking about his plans for starting a new review. I could hardly take it in, I suddenly felt exhausted; and I kept on seeing Rollo rushing away, farther and farther away, over strange roads, alone, my place beside him empty.

What a contrast, these last ten days. Jocelyn, everything he stands for, the whole colour and temper of his mind—politically indignant and convinced, bigoted, really, so much the reverse of complacent: Europe not England his country, his point of departure in argument and discussion; his rabid class-consciousness, his ill-fitting clothes, just clothes—necessities—unrelated to him inside them, his earnest, midnight-oilish,

physically arid look, his unemotional affection for me. . . .
What a contrast! . . . A kind of life I've never shared in before;
anti-luxurious, a bit antiseptic, a bit humourless . . . but cheerful, friendly, smoothly regulated. A life of belief—that's the
true difference. Jocelyn and his kind believe in themselves, in
their work, in a future they must contribute to. There's no
principle of belief in Colin, Anna and those, nor in Rollo. . . .
In Simon it's different again, an unconscious power, without
direction, or this awful moral fervour. It was a frugal life,
funds barely eked out, drinks and expeditions carefully communal. . . . No one got on anybody else's nerves. . . . Johann
and Willi, the Austrian friends, so neat and spotless with one
change of linen, so easily happy, sensitive, delicate-mannered;
so much the antithesis of what is coarse or oafish. . . . Willi
three years without work, Johann's elder brother shot in the
Vienna rising. . . . I should think more about such fates and
struggles. If I were free I would, perhaps. . . . Willi taught
me some German. He's charming, with his lazy blue eyes and
ravishing teeth. Pale Johann played in the evenings on the
café piano. Willi's plump Lisel from the village came boating
with us and fell in. . . . The tow-headed child at the villa where
we lodged, with his page's haircut, his white cat, his passion
for Jocelyn's typewriter. . . . Our long swims in that heavy
peacock-blue water, the pert, theatrical little steamers, the café
on the jetty, the moon on the water. . . . Rollo's heavenly
letter coming, far the nicest he's ever written, a poignant
letter. . . . I read it again and again, almost incredulous.
Jocelyn lent me books; I began to think again about writing.
. . . Took some notes for my lake story. I should have done
more if I hadn't begun to get worried. . . .

What are they all doing now, I wonder. . . . Sound asleep
beneath their *plumeaux*. . . . Good-bye, Jocelyn, Willi, Johann.
. . . You were good to me, I was happy . . . till I got worried.
Even after that of course; because, of course, there's no need
to worry. Six, seven days late . . . I'm worried. But it's happened
once before, the first year Ivor and I were married; over a

week then, I was beginning to be sure—but it was a false alarm. . . . That was in August too—so I expect it's the time of year, I'm sure I've heard it does happen sometimes; or all that long cold bathing, lake water's very cold, that might easily account for it . . . I'm worried. Falling for one, Mrs. Banks calls it. "When I fell for our Doris . . ." I feel a bit sick. Train-sick, I expect. I've never been train-sick in my life. This morning when I got up, suddenly retching as I began to wash. . . . Nerves. Lying down like this I feel fine. Be all right to-morrow. Sleep. Thank God for lying down, a sleeper to myself. Supposing I'm sick when I get up to-morrow. . . . That would clinch it. No, it wouldn't. A long journey like this often upsets people.

Switch on the blue light. No, off again—too mournful. The water-bottle rattles. Is the stopper out? The cupboard door unlatched? My hands are dry, I feel the smuts in my nails. . . .

Queer, how a train journey throws up images, applies some stimulus to memory and desire. . . .

The story unrolled from the beginning in a kind of rough sequence; like when a person's drowning, so they say. . . .

Ai, what a screech. . . . Into a tunnel, my ears thicken . . . out again. Nearer home, nearer Rollo. To-morrow, come quick . . . don't come. . . . Slowing down now. . . . Through a station, lights on the blind, under it, sharp flashes; rumble and clank; a man's voice calling out, what does the French voice say? . . . Cut off. . . . On again, faster now, gathering speed. . . .

Relax, go with the train's speed, give to its swaying. . . . Breathe, breathe easily. . . .

Sleep. . . .

PART THREE

I

DRIVING AWAY from Victoria, she thought: I can let myself
in, put cool sheets on the bed, be hidden, sleep for a few hours
anyway. Face facts to-morrow, see what to do . . . Get hold
of Rollo. But I don't want to . . . I don't want to see him or
think of him. How can this be, in twenty-four hours? Is it
a symptom, does it seal my fate? . . . The female, her body
used, made fertile, turning, resentful, in hostile untouchability,
from the male, the enemy victorious and malignant . . . Like
cats or bitches. . . . Ugh!

London in the scorched irritable airless end of day was an
extension of the mind's loathing and oppression. Petrol fumes
were nausea; the traffic a fatuous, reluctant, laborious progress
towards a pointless destination; the picture-houses, with mock-
oriental fronts, proclaiming within a blend of cool darkness
and hot passions, were tawdriness, satiety, cynical sham and
cheapness. The main thoroughfares looked empty and dis-
couraged. Only in the by-streets, where mews and slum just
touch, just unaggressively nudge the more classy residential
quarters, groups of children, submerged in the fuller season,
had come up and overflown upon the pavements: London's
strident August undergrowth, existing like cactuses in water-
less stone; shouting, running, taking communal licks at ice-
cream cornets; deprecated by the charitable passer-by, wish-
transferred with spade and bucket to the seaside, where it
would be better for them to be. . . . But they look tough,
cheerful enough, perhaps some Fund is sending them soon,
one really should contribute. . . .

Outside the pub on the corner, a yellow mongrel lay
stretched on the stone in the shade, tongue dripping, teased by

flies. A couple of urchins in ragged bathing-suits were water-
ing one another out of a watering-can. . . . Oh, to be under a
fountain, sprinkled from head to foot with fresh reviving
spray; to be dissolved in the crisp break of a cold salt green
wave! . . .

Lifting heavy weights is a good thing to do. She dragged
her suitcase to the second landing. Etty's bedroom door flew
open, and who should appear but Etty, in her dressing-gown.
"*Darling!*"
"Etty! I didn't expect you'd be here." She pulled her face
together to smile a delighted greeting. "I was just going to
creep in for the night and collect a few things and go on home.
What are *you* doing in London?"
Etty had come back, she explained, for two nights on the
same errand: to refurbish her wardrobe before joining Mona
and some others on a Mediterranean cruise.
"My dear, *Greece*! Isn't it too marvellous? I shall really *see*
all that. I've been most *studiously* informing myself about the
Acropolis and *all* those temples. They have *lec*turers on board,
too—I shall come back a perfect *blue*-stocking."
"Etty, it is nice to find you."
It was: a comfort . . . possibly salvation. Etty'd be sure to
know of someone, in case. . . . Everything would be all right.
Of course. Already the nausea had let up a bit, retreated to
manageable distance.
"Come and sit down and tell me *all* about it. I was just
having a little rest." She went back and lay down on her bed
again, and Olivia sank in the arm-chair, her back to the light.
"Did you have a *mar*vellous time? Austria *is* a divine country,
isn't it? There's something so *ador*able about it. You're
*mar*vellously brown. Oh, how I *en*vy you!" She glanced in the
mirror at her own white cheeks . . . which she would perish
rather than permit to tan. "Look, over there, darling,
there's some letters for you. I didn't know *where* to forward
them."

Among a mixed lot, one fat one from Anna. Nothing from Rollo . . . though I told him to write here . . . I don't care.

"Darling, it's *too* unfortunate I'm dining *out* and there isn't a *bite* in the house. I never *dreamed* there was a *soul* left in London, but *Jack* rang up this morning, he's *stuck* in an office all this month. What *can* we do? It would be *too* unkind, wouldn't it, to desert him at the *last* minute? Shall I ring up and sug*gest* bringing you *too*?"

"God forbid! . . . No aspersions meant, darling, I'm sure he's divine."

"Well, he's *not* actually. He's quite sweet, but I'm afraid you *might* be rather bored."

" Is he mad about you?"

The expected formula of reply—familiar since the far days when Etty had dazzled her cousins with a flapper bow of black taffeta, high-heeled patent-leather slippers and corsets— tripped blandly, deprecatingly from her tongue.

"Well, *rather* enamoured. . . . He's not awfully *scintillating*, poor sweet, but he's a good *friend*." She added, in the new line of tart self-mockery which was growing on her: "And how we superfluous women do value that!"

Disquieting in Etty, unsuitable . . . as if nowadays something led her to consider, in secret, with distaste, the passage of time, and with dissatisfaction her own part in it.

"As a matter of fact, Ett, I think I'll go to bed. I don't want any food—except perhaps a biscuit. I'm a bit done in after the journey."

"Darling, what a *shame*. Of course you must be. Those sleepers always *finish* me."

"It's the heat. It was fearful."

"I can imagine! Too *ravaging*. I can't tell you what an *oven* London's been to-day. I'll make you a cocktail. Luckily there's a scrap of gin and grapefruit in the cupboard. I was just about to indulge in a di*min*utive doleful orgy on my own, just to *strengthen* me for Jack. Stay where you are."

She rolled busily off the bed. Olivia, on the point of saying, out of habit, "Let *me* . . ." gave it up, stayed where she was and opened Anna's thin French envelope. Anna's handwriting, small, nervous, spidering, half formed, her style, child-like, vivid, ingenuously eccentric, her punctuation, a few capricious commas, made up an obscure yet revealing commentary on her character.

Darling Olivia (she wrote) here we are in Villefranche now, and I personally never want to leave, although needs must shortly, having spent £100 what with one thing and another. That is the Last of the Profits of Photography and shortly comes the Winter of my total Beggary. It's gambling that's chiefly done me in, Simon's so reckless in every way, running the gamut of sensations and passing money like water. He's mostly in very good spirits and has collected a lot of remark- able friends. Arthur Menzies for one—do you remember the one his discarded mistress shot at and wounded?—poor man, he's more or less in hiding in his sumptuous villa, and has more or less persecution mania, which, of course, makes him persona grata to Colin. It was Peter Cunningham who dis- covered him; he took us all to call, and we won him round at once quite unintentionally by saying we'd come by bus. The result is we have the car sent round daily, in case we need it.

There are a few monsters with sketching utensils in the hotel we don't speak to, and one lovely Frenchwoman who looks like a South Sea Islander—I would like to paint her, but of course don't dare ask and anyway would make a muck of it. Besides, there hasn't been time to touch a brush. She has a superb two-seater roadster, she and her husband sit in the front in white linen motoring caps with clip-on ear-flaps. We sit in the dicky and drive at terrific speed to Juan-les-Pins, drop husband at the gambling rooms and go and dance rumbas with lovely negroes under the palm trees to lovely negro rumba music.

Our last evening cost the poor husband 9000 francs,

as we rushed from Juan to Cannes and completely forgot about him till 4 a.m. He'd gambled it all away waiting for us—made it during the first part of the evening, put it in his pocket and sat down to wait for us, when we didn't appear he got so bored he started to play again and lost the lot. We had a glorious drive back in the dawn, eating hot dogs from an American bar. I wish you could see some of the negresses in beach pyjamas, yachting caps and monocles.

I'm having a mixed time as regards emotion, but I am determined to go with the wind, bathe, drink and *not brood* till I get home. That will be soon for Mrs. Cunningham's turned up and is having an Effect on Peter, though she's in a different party, living in a fragrant literary ethereal upper-class way with Gil Severn, and not interfering. We met her walking in Cannes the other day with her hot-water bottle in a pink plush cover full of tepid water instead of her bag. She only seemed mildly surprised when we pointed it out, and what's more, even that didn't make her in the slightest degree a figure of fun, we all felt just as respectful.

Cora's turned up too, and haunts Simon night and day, which he suffers with patience unruffled. However futile my own predicament . . . (here two lines were barred and cross-barred out in thickest impenetrable black) I will let you know directly I get back. Simon says we can go on having his house for September, so I hope you will come there too. I do hope all is well, I do think of you. Personally I don't think I could be happy in Austria, I didn't like it when I went, it seemed awfully thick-skinned and uncivilised visually—no good—but I suppose this is a narrow exacting professional view. I can't remember any Austrian painters, but I suppose they say look at our music. Love A.

She folded away the letter, amused and depressed. It wasn't quite like Anna : so glib, external. She must be in a bad state over Peter. . . . How are we all to make the change-over quietly into winter ? To what shall we look forward ?

Etty came back with a glass of yellowish liquid in each hand.

"I just *popped* some sheets on your bed while I was about it," she said. "Then you can *cast* yourself between them whenever you feel like it."

"You are an angel, Ett."

She took up her glass. The chunk of ice from the frigidaire clinked temptingly, but the fumes of gin came up, overpowering. This is a test now: if I can swallow this . . . She sipped, and her mouth twisted. Sticky, sickening, unclean . . . Her jaw muscles tightened, fighting down nausea, hard-pressed . . . Thank God for the ice. She fished it out and sucked at it, said smiling:

"This is what I was longing for."

"Darling—you don't feel *sick*, do you?"

"Good lord, no. Just thirsty and sort of unfresh—you know how a journey makes you feel. I'll have a bath unless you want the bathroom, and sip this later in bed to cheer my solitary evening."

"It's rather a *me*lancholy little programme." Etty looked distressed.

"Far from it. Bed, book, drink—perfect."

Etty sighed.

"It's a *com*fort to think if the worst comes to the *worst* there *is* always bed and the bottle. I often feel I shall end my days in a *stupor* of debauchery."

She took her drink in little nips, throwing her head up between each, like a canary.

"Now have a bath, darling, and I'll tuck you into bed. I'm not dining till nine. I felt so *wilted* I wanted to do my packing quietly and have plenty of time for *collapse*."

Protesting against protest, she helped Olivia to carry up the heavy suitcase, straining her puny arm and shoulder with ineffectual stubbornness; then tripped down again and turned on the bath.

She got into bed and lay flat. That's better. The room was almost cool, the sun had left it hours ago. The picture looked back at her from above the mantelpiece—cool people sitting at peace in chequered shade. Rollo's cigarette burn on the table beside her. . . . Oh, be abolished, all signs and reminders of him, till I'm out of this mess. Rollo, I've started a baby, what shall we do. . .? No, I won't. Not yet, anyway.

She dozed for a few moments, lapped immediately in confused and violent half-dreams; was roused by Etty coming in with a plate of vita-wheat biscuits.

"Darling, *but* for these the cupboard is *bone* bare. I just had these and some orange juice for breakfast and I've been out *all* the rest of the day. I feel so *mortified*. *Do* let me run out and get you some fruit or eggs or something."

"No, my dear, thank you." (Eggs—fearful thought.) "This is just what I want."

She nibbled eagerly: good taste, dry, crisp, slightly salt.

"Ett . . . I've had a letter from a friend . . . Where is it? . . . Oh, I put it in my bag, never mind. She's in the most awful hole."

Etty, sitting on the end of the bed, presented a face of expectant sympathy.

"She's been having an affair with some man or other, married, I believe, and to her horror she finds she's started a baby."

"Oh, my *dear*, how *shattering*. . . ."

Was it imagination—one rapid, questioning glance from Etty?

"She wants to know if I can help her."

Etty reflected, serious.

"Has she tried pills?"

"She doesn't say. There are pills, are there? That really work? She'd try anything, I'm sure. Do chemists sell them?"

"I know of one who does. But I've never heard of them working if it's really the worst. . . . They may, of course."

Etty fell silent, adding, "They give you the most *stup*efying diarrhœa, that I do know . . . Still, she might try."

"She sounds pretty desperate. You see, she's an actress, on tour. It would simply do in her career."

"Where is she?"

"Weymouth or somewhere—touring along the south coast." If Etty'd had suspicions they must surely be allayed: the story comes so pat, so plausible. "She says she could get up to London if she had to."

"Has she got any money?"

"No. . . . But I think . . . she says she could get some—a little—I don't know how—from the man perhaps."

"I do know someone . . ." said Etty uncertainly.

"In London?"

"Yes. Let me think . . . His name . . . It's ages since I . . . Tredeaven—that's it."

"Is he in the telephone-book?"

"Oh, yes. He's a what d'you call it—manipulator or something. . . . He's got a more or less respectable practice. This is a *side*-line."

"How could I get hold of him? Could I ring up and make an appointment for her? Or take her to see him?"

Etty was silent.

"He won't take any one unless he knows who's sent them," she said at last. "You see, it's *fear*fully dangerous for him. If you're caught it means prison . . . In spite of his being, of course, a public *be*nefactor really. I suppose he's saved *reg*iments of unfortunate *err*ing women from *ru*in . . ."

"You mean," said Olivia, "he might refuse to do it—if she just went out of the blue?"

Silence again.

"You could give my name, I suppose. . . ." Etty stirred. Her slightly protruding eyes between curly doll's lashes became fixed with a certain wild blankness on her cousin. "Only it was so long ago. . . ."

"Did you go to him, Ett?"

"My dear, *once*. Wasn't it *shat*tering?" The colour came up in her fragile egg-face, painfully, from neck to brow. She laughed, rather shakily. "The *wa*ges of *sin*, darling."

"Poor Ett."

Amazing. A shock, definitely. That narrow miniature body, that, too, trapped, subjected to the common risks and consequences of female humanity. It only showed, for the hundredth time, how little one knew about anybody, particularly one's nearest. . . . Seeing only Etty's marionette surface, allowing one's intuition and mere circumstantial evidence to decide that never—however much she might dally with preliminaries—would she have brought herself to face ultimate physical issues.

"I've never told a *soul*," said Etty, wiping her eyes. "I nearly *died* of it. *Never* breathe it, will you?"

"Of course I won't. When was it?"

"About five years ago. Oh dear! And he was *married* too. . . ."

"Were you awfully in love?"

"Well *no*, darling—*low* be it spoken—that was the *crowning* shame. It was just *once*. He was so impor*tu*nate . . . I never *dreamed* . . . Oh, how *sordid*! . . . I *couldn't* tell him. I simply *loathed* him the *mo*ment after. I never wanted to *see* him again."

"Yes, I can imagine . . ." But, of course, not the same with me and Rollo: not sordid. I love him so much. I always wanted to have his child.

"Really," sighed Etty, examining her face in Olivia's hand-mirror, "these physical processes are too *treach*erous. *Why* should wretched females be so be*leag*uered? . . ." She dabbed on a little powder, came back and perched herself on the bed again; sitting there with her look of pathos, as if the sudden emotion had exhausted her. "I *swore never* again would I stray from the path of virtue." She glanced at Olivia, arch, faintly sly. "But one *does* forget, *doesn't* one?"

"One does."

"I must say it's a *com*fort to feel he exists. . . . Not that I *ever* intend to require his services *again*. . . ."

"Was it awful?"

"Not *really*—not too shattering. He was *divine* to me. He's a *lamb*. But of course I did feel *too* squalid."

"Did you go alone?"

"Well, *no*. Mona was a *saint*—she simply arranged *every*-thing. You see, *she'd* been to him *just* before, poor darling."

"Oh, had she?"

Mona too! Well, well . . . She began to feel fatally cosy and consoled, the seals of arduous secrecy, of solitary endur-ance melting, melting. . . . Not such a catastrophe after all: quite a common little predicament, distressing, of course, but soon over and no one the wiser. . . .

The fact is, Ett, it's me—I'm properly in the soup. I've been having an affair with Rollo Spencer. . . . Darling, how distraught you must have been feeling. But don't worry any more. You'll get put right in two twos. . . . Enter into the feminine conspiracy, be received with tact, sympathy, pills and hot-water bottles, we're all in the same boat, all unfortunate women caught out after a little indiscretion. Give up the big stuff. Betray him, yourself, what love conceived. What's love? You're not a servant girl, bound to produce illegitimately, apply for a paternity order, carry a lifelong stigma. . . . You can scrape up the money and go scot-free. Go on, go on. . . . She bit into her thumb. *I won't.* I can lie and lie; I can be alone.

"Do you know what he asks for doing it?"

"I'm not sure. He's not *cheap*, I'm afraid . . . but then he's safe. And I believe he varies according to what he thinks you can afford. I'm sure if your friend told him she was hard up he'd be kind."

"Could I really ring up and ask for an appointment for her, and say you sent me? . . . I'll have to see her through."

Etty considered.

"I know *what*. Give Mona's name. It 'ud *sound* better, as

she's married. I'm sure she wouldn't mind. It's at second-hand, so to speak, but I suppose you can *vouch* for your friend being *mum*. I'll look up his number before I go to-morrow, if you remind me. He's in one of those little streets off Welbeck Street—I forget which." She listened to a clock striking. "Nine. I must go and do one or two *last* things. Good-*night*, my pet. *Bless* you, sleep well. Drink up your drink. I'll be back early, I've got a *bar*barously early start to-morrow. See you in the morning. Ma Banks will be in, of course. Don't *stir* unless you feel like it."

"Oh, I'll be fine to-morrow. I'll go home by the midday train, I expect. Good-night, Ett, bless you. Have a nice time. Give Jack a break."

Perhaps she will too. . . . Nobody thinks of anything else in this beastly world.

She smiled at Etty, smiling in the doorway, kissing all her carmine finger-tips. . . . Dear pretty Etty, familiar, mysterious creature, unfailing girl-friend: ready to keep a secret, or console by giving one away; amiable feather-pated rattle— yet saying, knowing what?—to herself only, alone at night or sitting by herself? Cool, brittle Etty, untouched by heat, fresh to one's sick, contaminated eye and nose; comfortably detached, yet known from the beginning. Saviour Etty.

Chemist's outfit first: probably work, I'm always lucky. If not, Tredeaven, divine to one, a lamb, special terms if you're hard up. . . .

When bell, voices, slam of the front door, departing car successively had died away, she got up, poured the cocktail down the wash-basin, went to the telephone. Giddy, bemused, the motion of train and boat still swinging and spinning through her, she lifted the receiver and gave the number of Rollo's house; for the second time. . . . She heard the bell cawing over and over again at the other end. . . .Not in, then. Wait a little longer, just a little. . . . At last a voice . . . "*Ull*-oah!" By no means the bland male voice of last time: female, hot, cross, offended . . .

"Could I speak to Mr. Spencer?"

"E's not in." Under-housemaid or such, reluctant from the back door or the upper regions: Rollo living in a small way with depleted August staff.

"I suppose you don't know when he's likely to be in?"

"'E didn't say. 'E called back for 'is dog before dinner and went straight out again."

"I see. It doesn't matter. Thank you so much."

Down clapped the receiver at the other end. That settles that one, and D.V. no more of 'em to-night.

It doesn't matter, doesn't matter . . . Just as well. Somewhere, a mile or so away, Rollo's walking with Lucy.

She went back to bed, sank through another sharp trembling fit into heavy sleep.

She dreamed of green waves that never broke. Swinging, swinging, from one cool glassy bell of silence to the next, up and down, up . . . down . . . In her dream she cried to someone shadowy beside her, "Oh, this is *bliss*! I'm in bliss! . . . bliss. . . ."

II

THE bath-chair bowled briskly over the lawn. Grandpa sat in it with his eyes shut, carefully dressed in his old-fashioned light grey summer suit, his Panama hat placed by Grandma on top. Grandma was at the helm. Jane, aged six, Christopher, three and a half, dragged at the handle, steering a jerky erratic course from rose-bed to shrubbery, from shrubbery to walnut tree; over and across, up and down, as fast as possible, giving Grandpa a little airing in the cool of late afternoon. Grandma was tireless. In a blue linen frock, trimly belted, a little tight behind, she swung along at a girl's jaunty pace. She beamed and marched, occasionally shouting directions, warning or encouragement. The bath-chair amused the children. All was well.

Kate and Olivia sat under the walnut tree in deck-chairs.

Now and then Kate said, "Where's that child?"—got up, extracted the lurking baby from some nook, brought her back, sat down again.

"How old is she, Kate?"

"Nearly sixteen months."

"Surely she's very forward?"

"I don't think so." Kate let out a long sigh: almost one of mother's old sighs: certainly of the same genus. "They were all much of a muchness. They could all walk at a year —except Christopher, he was slow. . . . But he was the first to talk. In fact I never remember him *not* talking." She looked across the lawn at her son, narrowing her eyes, frowning faintly. "He's enough to drive anyone dotty."

"His style seems rather eccentric."

"Oh, he's a freak." Kate rubbed her eyes. "I don't know where he came from."

"I expect he takes after some of our side-lines."

"Yet he looks more like Rob than any of them."

"Only on the surface. There's something pretty tricky looking out from beneath: nothing Rob's responsible for, I'm sure."

Kate's frown relaxed: her nostrils dilated in half-apologetic amusement. It was nice talking to Olivia about the children. She was sensible. She treated them as curious specimens, was delighted when they quarrelled or were rude; and this caused a sense of lightening of one's responsibilities. One did forget to be scientific enough. . . .

"He really is rather extraordinary," she admitted, succumbing to pride.

"He reminds me of James," said Olivia, "though he couldn't be more unlike."

"I hope he won't go sour on us like James," said Kate, depressed by the comparison.

The likeness was generic, the unlikeness partly a period one. Little girls were women in embryo; little boys frequently seemed not fathers of themselves but some totally separate, unaccountable, disconcerting kind of animal. She attempted to explain this.

"Perhaps," said Kate. "I suppose what you really mean is boys don't play to the gallery. They don't care about making a good impression." She followed the bath-chair with her eyes. "His brain's too active," she said, worried again, abandoning theory. "It's quite a relief to see him gambolling and squawking round that bath-chair."

"He's all right," said Olivia.

"There's one thing," said Kate. "He's never been afraid of the dark. They're all quite tough in those ways. Jane's the only one who ever had to have a night light—after being frightened by some animal masks at some idiotic party Rob's mother took her to. It was only for a short time though."

"I think you manage very well."

It was one's rôle as childless aunt to replenish Kate's maternal confidence.

"As for the period question," said Kate, leaning back, "if you mean they don't know the meaning of the words filial respect, they don't. They cheek Rob and criticise me—at least not Priscilla so much, she's always been soppy about me—but Christopher even goes on about my clothes—can you imagine? . . . He can't bear me in brown and he can't bear me in a taffeta frock I've got, and I'm not allowed to wear stockinette bloomers and I don't know what. Rob says he's bound to be one of those cissy dressmaking young men. He won't have a speck of dirt on his hands and the fuss that goes on about what he's to wear! I wish Jane and he would swap a bit of each other, she might be a tramp's child—— What's that you've got in your hand, Polly?" She broke off sharply, seizing the baby's paw in a firm and gentle grip. An unripe greenish-pink half-squashed mulberry lay revealed. "You haven't eaten any, have you?" She prized her jaws apart and investigated. "No, I don't think so. Polly not eat, good girl. Nasty, Polly, ugh!"

The baby attentively examined the mulberry upon her

cushioned palm. After a moment of trance she cried, "Away!" and as a bowler towards the wicket, plunged immediately into a gallop, swept her arm up and back, and hurled it from her. "Gone!" she announced. She began forthwith to search over the grass, croaking "Where? Where? Where?" in urgent reiteration.

"There it is," said Kate languidly, pointing with her toe.

"Dere tis," she cried rapturously. Knees flexed, she bent forward from the hips to examine it once more, then fell on it, stamped it to pulp, her face contorted with disgust, an eye on Kate. "Ach! Ach! Ach!" She was hoarse with loathing.

"She's very good about not putting things in her mouth," said Kate.

"She's terribly engaging." Olivia watched the legs, a couple of burstingly stuffed pegs, start off once more towards the mulberry tree.

"She's a bit overweight," said Kate, also watching. "I'm sure my clinic would condemn her. I can't see that it matters. Those weight charts are all bunk."

"She'll be the most attractive," said Olivia. "The crooked smile."

"That's like you!" cried Kate in triumph. "I told you she was like you. And the eyes too. Everybody says so—except Mother for some reason."

"I see what you mean." Deprecatory, flattered . . .

One could go on for ever. It was a drug, a substitute for thinking. *I can have a child too.* I'll take a cottage somewhere near Kate and have it without any fuss and bring it up with hers. I'll look after it myself, and plant sunflowers and hollyhocks in my garden, and have a wooden cradle on rockers, and sing it to sleep. Kate and I'll sit under the trees when they're all in bed and talk about them . . . She's going to light a cigarette. Don't do it, you brute, don't do it, why must you, you don't want it; who wants to smoke in this heat? . . . She turned her head away, receiving the first penetrating nauseous whiff, closed her eyes. The blood began to push up thick and scorching in her cheeks and neck, behind her ears. Getting on for the bad time of day; have to crawl upstairs soon and surreptitiously be sick: continue the interminable slow-motion struggle with Laocoön.

Kate stole a look at her. Hollow-cheeked, inert. . . . A ghastly colour, greyish beneath the make-up. Thinner than ever. Blast her . . . and she'd been looking so much better, so happy: in love obviously: somebody with money it seemed like—those silk stockings, those expensive flowers, that handbag. Who is he, has it gone wrong? Damn. Damn.

She said sharply:

"You haven't told me much about Austria. Did you enjoy it? What did you do?"

"I did enjoy it," Olivia opened her eyes, tried to think, to speak briskly. "It's so difficult to describe a holiday, isn't it? Unless you know the country."

"God knows when I shall get abroad again," said Kate bitterly. "Never, I shouldn't think. . . . Not since my honeymoon. And even then Rob didn't like it." She brooded.

"Some day we'll pop off together somewhere. We've always said we would. Not that I believe you'd ever bring yourself to leave the family."

"*Wouldn't* I!"

Perhaps when Christopher's gone to school. . . . When Priscilla's stopped minding my being out of reach. . . .

After a while Olivia said:

"Getting this blasted food-poisoning on the journey has sort of spoilt it all."

"How d'you feel now?"

"Oh . . . better . . . Only it still niggles on."

"Gripes?"

"M'm. Can't seem to keep much inside me. Still, as Mrs. Banks says, a good turn-out never did nobody any harm."

"Don't be idiotic," said Kate crossly, worried. "You've said that the last five days—ever since you've been here. You ought to see a doctor."

"Good God, no! It's nothing. Etty's doctor gave me some stuff. He said I'd be all right."

Time for the next dose . . . When will it work? "We've never had any complaints," said the rat-faced young man in the white linen coat, knowing, smooth, reassuring among the jars and bottles. "Of course, you must persevere." I'm persevering. Per ardua ad astra.

"For Pete's sake don't say anything to Ma about a doctor." Not Dr. Martin saying, "Well, young lady . . ." and peering through his glasses, grunting, saying, "Now are those cheeks your own, or are they not?"—remembering me as a child, when I was jollier. . . .

But Kate was looking round for Polly, and shouting at Jane and listening to Christopher. Her non-parental, undiluted moment of attention was over. She was dispersed again, split up with nervous alertness among them all.

No danger there.

"Now me!"

"No, *me*!"

"Get him out, Grandma."

"Please," said Kate.

Grandpa, a non-magical effigy, without the sinister power of a guy or a ventriloquist's doll, was hoisted out of his conveyance and placed in a *chaise-longue*. He opened one eye, closed it again. Christopher climbed into his place, Jane seized the handle, away went the bath-chair at a spanking pace, Christopher jigging and squealing inside, Jane rushing with a crimson face and grimaces of mad exertion.

"It's much better without Grandpa," shouted Jane.

"Look out for Polly, don't run her down," called Grandma indulgently. Really, the bath-chair was the greatest blessing; it kept them happy for hours.

"Now, Christopher, it's my turn. Get out, I want to try by myself down this hill."

The chair and Jane launched themselves from the top of

the mildly sloping terrace and, gathering impetus, ran down to the very end of the lawn, coming to rest with a bump against the kitchen-garden wall. Grandma started forward.

"Leave her alone," said Kate sharply. "Don't shout at her. She's much more likely to crash if you make her think she will."

"My border," said Mrs. Curtis doubtfully. "Still . . ." She sat back again. "Her nerves seem very strong. It's curious how much more fearless girls are. You and Olivia were just the same. James took twice as long with his bicycle."

They said all the things, it all went on and on. They were handed over lock, stock and barrel to the young.

"Kate, dear," said Mrs. Curtis smoothly, "I've asked Miss Mivart and Miss Toomer to look in for tea on Saturday. They're so longing to see the children."

"That'll test their nerves," murmured Olivia.

Kate groaned. But not now, as in the old days, did she object with scorn, argue with acrimony, make herself difficult. The old scarecrows could see the children if they wanted to.

"Well, keep Dad out of the way," was all she said. "You know Miss Mivart *will* try to shake hands with him and pass him the bread and butter and generally bring herself to his notice with tender tact and solicitude."

"Dad doesn't bother," said Mrs. Curtis comfortably. "He doesn't take any notice. She likes to do little things for him. She always admired him so very much."

"I wonder if she sees now why God in his infinite mercy didn't see fit to let her marry Dad."

Mr. Curtis lay back without stirring in his chair, pale, his jaw sunk, his lips blowing in and out as he lightly dozed.

The bath-chair stood abandoned in the herbaceous border beneath the wall, half-hidden in August perennials. Jane and Christopher were hurrying back.

"We're very very sorry, Grandma," began Jane from some distance. "We accidentally snapped off this." Flushed, anxiously honest, she held out a head of pink hollyhock.

"Oh, dear!" said Grandma, "what a pity. Poor hollyhock."

"We don't call them that," said Christopher.

"What do you call them?"

He considered a moment, his eyes blank, false.

"Mountains," he said casually.

Polly also had returned.

They stood in a row before their elders—the two solid, mouse-haired, unproblematic little girls, the frail-legged dangerous little boy.

"I wish we had our Priscilla here," said Mrs. Curtis, trying again, sparing a thought for her eldest grandchild, on a visit to her other grannie.

Jane and Christopher exhanged sly glances. "We don't," said Jane. They doubled up, cackling with laughter. "We don't! We don't!"

"Not want Priscilla? Oh, come now, why not?"

Christopher went on squawking, but Jane looked troubled, sighed, turned a negligent somersault before replying:

"Well, she's rather rude. She bites."

"She bites," said Christopher, "but she's not *rude*. I've met rude people. They smash flowers." He also turned a somersault, a poor one, continued: "I've met them in Scotland."

Grandma raised inquiring eyebrows at Kate, who shook her head.

"This is rude," said Christopher. He ran a few steps forward, stopped and stuck his bottom out towards them.

"What could be ruder?" said Olivia faintly. She covered her face with a handkerchief and her chair shook.

"Mabel said it was rude. Pip's rude sometimes. D'you know who Pip is? He's our dog. I call him Poodle. D'you know which he wears, fur or fevvers?"

"Fur, of course," said Jane with scorn. "Only birds wear feathers."

"Genklemen wear fur on their legs," said Christopher, rolling aimlessly on the ground. "Daddy does. Mabel does too, but she's not a man, she's a nursemaid."

"Mummy, Polly's got something in her hand, she won't give it up."

"Polly, show Mummy."

Another unripe mulberry. Jane pounced on it, and Polly shrieked. "It's a mulberry, Mummy."

"Throw it away," said Kate, rubbing her eyes.

"Can't I eat it?"

"No, it's too sour."

Jane bowed her head over the mulberry, murmured to it regretfully, "You're too sour," and threw it into the bushes. "It *was* a shame to pick it," she said regretfully.

Grandma started to croon, tossing the tearful Polly on her knee. "*There was—an old woman—tossed up in a blanket, seventeen times as high as the moon*," she sang. Marvellous how the old rhymes came back to one. James had been the one for nursery rhymes. Ceasing to toss, starting to jig, she continued, "*Polly put the kettle on, Polly put the kettle on. . . .*"

"I don't care for your singing, Grandma," interrupted Christopher. "So please stop."

Mrs. Curtis stopped abruptly . . . No, *not* an attractive child. Spoilt, tiresome. His father spoils him. James was inclined once to have a phase like this, I soon got him round . . . It wouldn't do to appear to be noticing him. She started singing again, but in a suppressed way.

Christopher sat down on the arm of Grandpa's chair. The effigy behind him put out a hand and touched him, smiling faintly . . . the faintest hovering flicker . . . But all passed unnoticed. Christopher didn't even wince or wriggle. He seemed dreamy, gazing at the grown-ups each in turn with melancholy hazel eyes.

"What a nice smiling face you've got, Mummy," he said gently.

"Have I?" Kate shot him a sharp glance behind her smile.

"I like smiling faces. Daddy's got the best smiling face."

"Hasn't Grandma got a nice smiling face?" coaxed Mrs. Curtis, rushing as ever upon her fate.

"You've got a cow's face," he said casually. The pause was too long, nobody did anything whatever. He added, "You've got the best smiling cow's face."

"Mummy, Polly's wet," said Jane.

"Never mind," said Kate. "Here comes Mabel. Get up, Christopher, bed-time. I'll see to you. Mother, will you keep Jane? Mabel'll come for her after she's bathed Polly. Polly, say night-night, Grandma. Christopher, say good-night, give Grandma a kiss."

Jane sat in the swing, wound herself up and unwound again rapidly.

"What a pity they've all got such straight hair," said Mrs. Curtis to Olivia. "You had such lovely curls, every one of you. I believe it's all in the brushing. However, don't mention it to Kate." To Jane she said: "Don't make yourself giddy, dear. Wouldn't you like me to read?"

"No, thanks."

"It's funny they don't care to be read to. You all loved it so." To Jane: "Well, what about a little game then?"

"Yes, shall we climb the potting-shed roof?" Jane got down rapidly.

"Very well. Olivia, you'll stay by Dad, dear, won't you?" She took Mr. Curtis's handkerchief from his pocket, wiped his nose, tucked it back again. "Come then, Jane."

They went away hand in hand.

"How much can you do on it?" Olivia heard Jane ask. "Can you get to the top?"

Grandma was Jane's favourite person. "She's just what I was," said Grandma. Jane alone received Grandma's tomboy confidences: how when she was six she'd fallen out of an apple tree and left her skirt caught on the topmost bough; how she could jump high hedges and had beaten all the boys once vaulting a five-barred gate. . . .

"And when we were children," said Kate aggrieved, "she was so on her dignity she practically pretended she had no legs."

Was it Jane's influence, or the withdrawal of Dad's? . . .
Was a load lifted now she was freed, in all but elementary
impersonal ministrations—freed in her mind and speech—
from that ever incongruous-seeming union?

There he lay. Sometimes he knew one, sometimes he didn't.
On and off he muttered, mostly he was silent. Uncle Oswald's
visits seemed to revive him a little, but Uncle Oswald didn't
come so often now: Mrs. Curtis had never liked the little man.
He'd got quite fat too. His bird's face had a pouch beneath the
jaw, like a pelican's in embyro. Miracle: his asthma was gone.
Not a trace of it since his mind began to go to sleep. There
was a lot to be thankful for. He was obviously quite comfortable.

Only when he did those things . . . like putting his hand
out to touch Christopher . . . it was a bit upsetting. Otherwise
one took him for granted. After all he hadn't said—whatever
it was he should have said, had been on the point of saying.
He'd given up, let it slip; and now it didn't matter . . . even
to me . . . any more. What was left had gradually, imperceptibly lost power to disconcert, to move to love or sorrow.
. . . Only pity and a somewhat weary patience. . . . After he
dies I'll remember him again and weep . . . remember that he
said: I want you to be happy; and I said: I will be happy,
I promise.

His eyes were open now. He was leaning slightly to one
side, studying a small patch of sun that moved and flickered
on the grass, shadow-crossed in the light breeze. After a while
he looked at her, cocking one eye, amused.

"Never try to take away his bone," he said quite clearly.

"Not I, Dad. I wouldn't dare."

"Get your foot snapped off." He chuckled.

Simpkin the Pekinese, a handful of bones this many a year
beneath the mould and the primroses in the hazel grove at the
bottom of the garden, still revisited his master in glimpses of
sun or moon, as a shadow on the floor by the chair, a hump in
the eiderdown at the foot of the bed.

He closed his eyes again. Almost she leaned forward to say: "Dad, are you pretending?"—the notion was suddenly so strong that he was still there, that it was all assumed, out of perversity, laziness, disillusionment: as people decide to be deaf. But the moment passed. He was far out of earshot.

The loud deep voice of Jane floated over the garden from the potting-shed roof. She got up and crawled languidly over the lawn, down into the kitchen garden. She saw Jane's strong brown legs and scarlet-suited rear vigorously ascending the slope of the tiled moss-grown roof. Grandma on the path was adjusting a ladder and preparing to follow her.

Olivia called:

"Mother! I'm going in now. Dad's all right. He's dozed off." What an effort to raise one's voice. . . . Nearly fatal.

"Very well, dear."

"Do take care on that roof, Mother. Your skirt's too tight for climbing."

"I'm quite all right. I shan't go all the way up . . . Go on, Jane, Grandma's coming."

Vigorously Mrs. Curtis launched herself upon the ladder.

Olivia went briskly indoors, spurred on by the rising nausea. Thank God . . . That's over for a bit.

Now I must, I really must force myself to write to Rollo. Probably he'd been ringing up Etty's every day, poor boy; and getting no answer. Sitting on her bed, she scribbled a note in pencil.

Darling, no word from you—or have you written and it's got stuck in this cul-de-sac of a month? I got back and thank God for your sleeper, for I began to feel ill on the journey and illish I've been ever since. So not wishing to show you a glum green face I made tracks for home to give my family the benefit. My plans are vague. Please let me know here, darling, if you're in London. I want to see you. Your O.

She put it in an envelope, sealed and addressed it; then

opened it again and scrawled under her signature: I *must* see you.

Something must be done, something . . .

Tell him, or not tell him?

I don't want to say it to him. I don't know him. . . . Far in the back of her mind persisted a loved, an almost abstract image, free of taint. Not to hate him she must think of him thus, by himself, unrelated to her, impersonal.

She took two pills, washed ; summoned the bare energy to make her face up carefully. I mustn't let myself go. If nobody else suspects, that damned nurse soon will. . . . She went down and slipped her letter into the middle of the pile—Kate's and mother's—lying ready for post on the pantry table. She began once more to think about prune juice, to yearn for it. Prune juice, prune juice . . . I must have it . . . She took a glass from the pantry shelf and went softly to the larder door. No one about. She heard the wireless going in the kitchen where Ada was cooking dinner. She went noiselessly into the larder, saw the basin of prunes, poured out a glassful of juice and drank it greedily. More. More. Must leave some . . . just a little. She stole out again, washed the glass under the pantry tap and put it back.

Kate called over the stairs.

"Liv, they want to say good-night. Can you be bothered?"

"Of course."

She went up with a show of alacrity. Jane in the camp-bed, Christopher in the old cot with headrails, sat up in Aertex sleeping suits, their bath-flushed faces tense and shining with self-conscious expectation.

Olivia sat down on Jane's bed and looked at her animals: a monkey, a teddy bear, a Doleful Desmond, and a rabbit in a suit of pyjamas.

"What are their names?"

"They haven't got names." She looked troubled. "They're my Annies."

"Short for animals," said Christopher.

"Have you got anything of the sort?" said Olivia.

"No, I wouldn't have *Annies*. I call everything names."

"He's got a *doll*," said Jane. "She's called Barriecasie."

"May I see Barriecasie?"

"I haven't got her to-night. I wanted something else instead." His hand crept under the pillow, his eyes, fixed on her, looked dangerous: *If you laugh I'll hack you up.*

"His new shoes," said Jane, bouncing in bed.

"May I see them?"

He drew forth a pair of scarlet sandals.

"How beautiful. No wonder you wanted to sleep with them."

"He always has to sleep with anything new," explained Jane, without scorn. "Last Christmas Father Christmas brought him a porter's hat."

"A real one," interrupted Christopher, making a quick peak-expressing shape with his hands.

"And he had to have it on to go to sleep. He went right to sleep with it on."

"It wasn't on when I woke up," said Christopher.

"I think we ought to lie down now," said Jane. They lay down. "But you needn't go yet," she added.

"What a blue sky," said Christopher, gazing out of the window. "Blue as bluebells. Blue as Percy's eyes. D'you know who Percy is? He's Mabel's friend."

"He mended my wheelbarrow," said Jane.

"Once we had tea on the lawn when Mummy was away, and Percy came to tea. He had tea with all of us. Did you think Mrs. Eccles had tea with us too? Well, she didn't. She was having a barf."

"Mrs. Eccles was a cook," said Jane. "She's gone now."

"Percy's very funny," said Christopher. "He said Mabel Mabel under the table." He burst into shrill laughter.

"He's got a motor-bike," said Jane.

"He said another thing. He said I'll have a shave and go to my grave." Christopher doubled up, convulsed.

"Do you ever make up poetry?" said Olivia.

"No," said Jane.

"I do," said Christopher.

"You don't."

"Do tell me one," said Olivia.

His face froze in an agony of concentration. A poem should come. He willed it. He said rapidly:

"The clouds pass and pass. Willy's lying in the grass."

"Very good," said Olivia. "Any more?"

He turned away his head, let his lids fall, muttered:

"I can't answer any more voices."

"I think we ought to go to sleep now," said Jane politely. "We've said our prayers. Will you pull down the blind?"

Speculating on Kate's reasons for bringing up her children in the strict letter of orthodoxy, Olivia did so, kissed them and went to the door. Jane said out of the yellowish twilight:

"If we go for a picnic to the woods to-morrow, will you come too?"

"Would you like me to?"

"Yes."

"Then I will."

"We didn't remember you very well," said Jane. "We thought your face would be like Auntie Ruth's."

"Are you glad it isn't?"

"Yes," said Jane.

Christopher sprang violently inside the sheet, and lay still.

"Kate, shall you ever have any more?"

"More what?"

Kate lay on her back in the copse, relaxed, staring into the beech tops. They had brought the children in the car to the old picnic wood.

"Children."

"Oh . . . No . . . Too much sweat."

"I suppose it is an awful sweat."

"I don't mind them once they're there—but it's the hell of a performance to go through four times. *Nothing* to be said for it."

"Did you feel awful when they were coming? I don't seem to remember."

"I felt sick at first, of course. Most people do."

"How long for?" I must know.

"Oh, I forget. It varied. Six weeks—eight weeks."

Kate rubbed her eyes, bored, on the verge of irritation, as always when her health was in question. Why go on about feeling sick? . . . She added with a sort of sour triumph: "I did everything just as usual, of course. Nobody ever knew I had a qualm. You don't want to go giving it away to everybody."

She can't have felt like me, she can't have. . . .

"But after the beginning, did you feel well?"

"I felt all right, more or less. One doesn't feel one's brightest."

I mustn't go on.

A little way away the children ran about, hunting for the initialled tree-trunks. Occasionally one or the other shouted, "Is it tea-time yet?"

"Yes," called Kate finally, sitting up. They came tearing back and she unpacked the tea basket, and spread out interesting white paper parcels.

"We call this jelly red," said Christopher, parting his sandwich. "Sometimes we call it pink. I call it a mixture."

"We had doughnuts when we went to tea with David," said Jane. "And do you know what his daddy said? He said: If I catch you calling your sister pig any more I'll spank you with a slipper, so he called her horse. David's older than me, a whole year, but I can lift him as easy as anything."

Christopher belched. He said in pride and surprise:

"Did you hear me make that turn?"

"When Mabel does it, she says beg pardon," said Jane.

"Do you know why I do it? It's because I'm a windbag."

He looked dreamy. "Men think it funny, but ladies don't care for it. . . . Mum?"

"Yes?"

"What man of all the men you know would you choose to make that noise for you?"

"You, I think."

He smiled secretively, flattered, self-conscious.

Replete, they ran about, each with an empty paper bag.

"Christopher, Christopher, there's a little baby in here."

He took a frantic peep.

"Shut it up! Shut it up!"

Screwing it tight at the mouth they rushed with it and poked it into a hollow place among beech-roots.

Christopher peered into his bag. His face was wild.

"Jane, there's a *giant* in mine!"

"A GIANT! . . . Shut it up, shut it up."

"Hide it so he can't see us."

"No, bury it, bury it, so he can't get out."

They ran about in a frenzy, squealing.

"What a remarkable game," said Olivia.

"Idiotic," said Kate.

She lay on her back again, unaware of the dropping around her of ripe plums for analysts. Suddenly she said in a different voice, a voice for Olivia:

"God, I wish they were all grown up! If I could have a wish that would be it. Grown up and—all right—independent —off my hands. . . . It seems such *years* before one can hope to feel they're all safely through . . . Perhaps one never will. . . . Supposing they're not happy . . . Sometimes when I get back from London or somewhere and smell eucalyptus coming from the bathroom *again* and know they'll *all* catch it and Christopher'll have a temperature and Priscilla a cough—I go quite . . . I feel what's the use, why not leave them out on the grass all night or something. . . ."

"I can imagine . . ."

Kate, darling, this is you, I know you, you're too vulnerable. Does Rob know you are? . . . I must have a child, to share this with her.

I'm going to have a child.

It was real for the first time, it was love and truth, she saw it with joy. A son, mine and Rollo's . . . Now I'll tell Kate, and then it will be irrevocable. Kate, listen . . .

She turned her head and looked down at the figure beside her—the pink, soft, firmly-modelled lips, slightly parted now, young-looking, the clear-water eyes looking up, abstracted, the wavy hair swept loosely backwards, the long supple body that had borne four. . . . Beautiful still; but where were those lyric lines, that astonishing grace really like a flower, a young tree? . . . She was the wife of Dr. Emery, living an ordinary middle-class family life, valued, successful, fairly contented. One saw her life running, peacefully, unsensationally now on its course, right on to the end: and why did this make one want to cry? Kate isn't wasted. But there should have been something else, I alone know her, some exaggeration. . . .

Kate, listen. . . . Madness. . . . Kate, I'm . . .

Staring up into the glowing black-ribbed roof of beech boughs Kate said suddenly:

"Who d'you think I saw when I went to the village this morning? Tony Heriot. Coming out of the post office as I went in."

"Speak to him?"

This was important. Their small cool voices betrayed them.

"No, I didn't. . . . He looked at me and sort of just lifted his hat-brim and went on and got into his car. Directly I saw that car I knew it was his. . . . I wonder how long he's home for. . . ."

"Was he embarrassed?"

"I don't know. . . . A bit, I think. Neither of us knew whether to stop or smile or what. . . ." She rolled her head sideways on the dead beech leaves, away from Olivia. She said with the ghost of a smile, "I nearly fainted."

"Kate ... What did happen?" For not a word, through all those old hot-eyed, heavy days, had passed Kate's lips. Locked behind her stretched, harshly contracted, resigned, incredulous forehead, she had resisted them all. . . . Imprisoned me, too, far away from her. . . .

"Nothing," said Kate finally. "It wasn't anything. He was going to come to Paris and see me—it was all fixed up—and then he never came. Never wrote. Absolute fade-out. By the time I was back he'd gone off to India. . . . Oh, I don't know —it was all quite idiotic. I suppose he just thought better of it. . . . Or sometimes I feel certain his beastly parents interfered —thought he was getting involved . . . God knows."

"He married, didn't he?"

"M'm. About five years ago. I saw it in *The Times*." She relapsed into silence. The reversed angle of her head on its flat leaf pillow narrowed her eyes to shining slivers of green glass beneath the dropped lids. After a bit she said:

"I'm glad I've seen him again. It's always been something to get over. I've dreaded it." She turned her neck again and looked straight upwards. She said simply: "Whatever happens, nothing can be as bad as that again. The endless blankness and suspense . . . One can't put up any defences. . . ."

"You don't mind any more ... do you, Kate?"

"No, I don't mind any more. One gets over everything in time."

Christopher came hurrying up from where he had been, out of sight somewhere. He sat down quickly beside his mother. After a bit he said:

"This wood's rather big, isn't it?"

"Fairly big, but not dark, is it? A friendly kind of wood."

"M'm." He leaned against her. "When will it be time to go home?"

Kate sighed, inaudibly.

"Now, I think," she said cheerfully, getting to her feet, holding his hand.

This before-dinner bout was the worst yet. The drive perhaps . . . or the emotion in the wood. It was all gone, the good feeling. Nothing now but the black miasma. The cold sweat broke out all over her. Faint . . . Get out of here. She found the lavatory door, unlocked it feverishly, got out along the passage—to the head of the stairs.

She cried out with all her strength:

"Mother!"

Mrs. Curtis was there at once, flying out from nowhere, her face opening with alarm, amazement. Olivia fell down with a crash at her feet.

Then she was lying on her bed with Mrs. Curtis holding smelling salts and nurse feeling her pulse.

"Hallo!" she said, "I feel fine." She pushed away the salts.

"That was a silly thing to do," said nurse, her eye cool, sharp, professional.

"It was . . . The heat always lays me out."

"Lie still," said her Mother.

"Like a drop of brandy?"

"No, thanks, I couldn't . . ."

"Cup of weak tea?"

"That would be lovely."

Nurse went away.

"Sorry, Mum. I don't know why I bellowed for you like that. . . ."

"Are you unwell?" Mrs. Curtis shook out eau-de-cologne on a handkerchief, and dabbed her forehead.

"That, and the tag-end of this rotten upset."

Kate came in with a cup of tea.

"You needn't have sent nurse," she said. "I'd got it already. Here, can you hold it? . . . A nice lump you were to carry."

She heard their voices bright and casual, saw their faces preoccupied, concerned. She repeated her explanation.

"I've never known you go off like that before," said Mrs. Curtis. "Kate used to be the one for faints."

"Oh, mayn't I too, please? Kate can't always have every-thing." She sat up and sipped the tea.

"I think I'll just ask Dr. Martin to look in." Come to think of it, she'd been a bad colour again lately . . . Tiresome girl . . . Eating well though. . . .

"Yes," said Kate sharply.

"Oh, Mum, don't be absurd. Just for a little faint. Besides, the poor old boy'll just be sitting down to his supper."

"Well——" Mrs. Curtis weakened. Dear old Dr. Martin, his well-earned rest, it did seem a shame. "If you're not better to-morrow . . ."

"But I shall be. There's nothing really wrong. I feel a king now, as Mrs. Banks would say."

"Well, stay where you are. I dare say a good night's rest is all you want. I'll send you up some nice fish and the sweet."

"She'd better get to bed," said Kate. "I'll see to her."

"Yes, do. I must give Dad his supper."

Mrs. Curtis went away; Kate stayed, keeping a rather silent fierce lookout while she undressed and got into bed. She rattled on, absurd jokes and tags of mimicry running glibly from her tongue: to make Kate laugh, to take that look off her face. . . . She was successful. By the time the gong sounded, Kate had relaxed, was wreathed in smiles.

When they were all safely in the dining-room, she got up, took the pills and the bottle from the back of the drawer—where I used to hide face powder, that other deadly secret—went to the bathroom, ran the basin tap and poured away everything. There, thank God. Those brews were poisoning me. I'll be better now.

I must go away to-morrow, say Anna's back, asks me to join her. They won't miss me. Not safe to stay here any longer, now they've all begun to watch . . . Send Rollo a telegram in the morning. She composed it in her head.

Leaving to-day, ring up or write London please. Liv.

III

"Is that Mr. Spencer's house?"

"Yes, madam."

"Could I speak to him, please?"

"Mr. Rollo—Mr. Spencer is out of town."

"Oh, is he? Could you tell me when he'll be back?"

"I couldn't exactly say, madam. Mr. Spencer has gone to Ireland. I fancy he goes on to Scotland until the middle of September."

"I see. . . . I suppose letters would be forwarded. . . ."

"Oh, yes, certainly, madam. Anything sent here would be forwarded at once."

"Thank you very much."

Third time of ringing up Rollo's house: third time unlucky. These voices speaking for him made him mythical, removed him far out of reach, guarding him like a public personage in an artificially important world. This time it was a different voice again: the muted voice, benevolent, of an old retainer . . . Familiar somehow, surely. . . . Who could it be?

There was nothing to do but wait for a letter. Surely he must write. Why hasn't he? . . . He'll write the moment he gets my letter, or, anyway, my wire. . . . Who forwarded that? Uncomfortable thought . . . signed *Liv.*

It doesn't matter.

His letter came the last day of August, by the same post as Anna's.

He wrote, darling, he wrote one page, saying sorry you've not been well, I got your wire and letter. I did ring up but got no answer, thought you were still enjoying yourself abroad, thought safer not to write till I knew you were back. London was so awful I couldn't stick it, he said. A pleasant house-party here but not exciting, some duck-shooting, Dickie Vulliamy and his new wife are here, she's a nice amusing woman. Not

at the very top of his form, he said, but all right really: he'd
be all right with some fresh air and exercise. Scotland next
week, this is my Highland address, back about the middle of
the month. Take care of yourself, darling, he said. You know
I'm no good at letters, but I love you, darling.

He didn't mention Nicola.

Anna's letter was a scrawl on a torn-out page of a note-
book, almost illegible. She'd been on the point of leaving, but
now Simon wasn't well, a bad chill and to-day a temperature,
and feeling awful. She was staying a few days longer, till he
was better. She'd let Olivia know the moment she was back
and they'd go down to Sallows. Simon sent his love.

To be alone, sick, in London in this dry, sterile, burnt-out
end of summer, was to be abandoned in a pestilence-stricken
town; was to live in a third-class waiting-room at a disused
terminus among stains and smells, odds and ends of refuse
and decay. She sank down and existed, without light, in the
waste land. Sluggishly, reluctantly, the days ranged themselves one after the other into a routine. Morning: wake
heavy from heavy sleep, get up, one must be sick, go back to
bed; nibble a biscuit, doze, half-stupefied till midday; force
oneself then to dress, each item of the toilet laborious, distasteful, the body a hateful burden. Tidy the bedroom more or less,
dust a bit in the sitting-room, let in what air there was: for
Mrs. Banks was on holiday, there was no one to keep one up
to the mark, no sharp eye and sharper tongue to brace one or
contend against. Prepare to go out for lunch. Rouge, lipstick,
powder . . . do what one might, it wasn't one's own face, it
wasn't a face at all, it was a shoddy construction, a bad disguise.
Walk down two side streets to the Bird Cage: morning coffee,
light lunches, dainty teas, controlled by gentlewomen; blue
tables, orange chairs.

She maintained in one compartment of her handbag a
supply of salted almonds and these she chewed on the way . . .
She kept on at them steadily till the mob-capped lady waitress
set before her the first delicacy of her two-shilling three-course

ladies' lunch. At least there was no particular smell in the
Bird Cage, nobody smoked much or drank anything stronger
than orangeade. There was nothing to remind one of men.
The china was sweet and the menus came out of *Woman's World*.
She ate greedily through the courses, reading the *Daily Express*.
The waitress had a wry neck below the mob cap, and a check
dress with short puffed sleeves and a dainty apron. The
depressed angle of her head suggested mild suffering, feminine
patience and resignation. After the pudding she inquired
meekly, " The usual ?"—and brought with a sad smile a portion
of mousetrap cheese, extra charge threepence, saying sometimes, not always, " You never get tired of cheese, do you?"
With answering deprecatory smiles, Olivia thanked her; and
when she had retired, ate a morsel, then secreted the remainder
in her bag. Necessity makes one cunning: she was never
surprised in the act. Such fellow fowls as patronised the Cage
—never more than two or three, every one was out of town—
appeared both cowed and famished, concentrating glassily upon
the food card, repudiating their helpings with light throat-
clearings and refined, difficult, swollen-cheeked pauses in
mastication.

Women eating by themselves look shockingly greedy.

After lunch, a bus to the park. She travelled on top, and
began to think about cheese. Cheese. *Cheese!* CHEESE!! The
lump in her bag seemed to shout it at her, her salivary glands
began to ache. Sometimes she mastered the craving till she got
to her bench in the park. Sometimes it was all gone before he'd
taken her penny and punched her ticket. And then, more . . .
more . . . MORE . . . began the clamour of her gnawing, perverse
palate. Once or twice it couldn't be endured, she went on up
as far as Selfridge's and bought some more.

She walked as far as one of the benches near the water; for
this was her one actively remaining pleasure: to see water.
This, too, was a craving, a demented appetite; not an æsthetic
pleasure. If not to be in sight of it, to dream of it by day
and by night, seeing it cool, willow-shaded, still at twilight;

or slipping polished, smooth-necked, obsidian-coloured over weirs to rise again beneath in a shudder of unearthly green-lit beaten-up whiteness. Oh, to lie in such waters of life, to watch the smooth column sliding down, down over one for ever, drowning one, dissolving all in that pure winnowed effervescence. . . . Fresh, fresh . . . to be fresh; to be washed clean, light as air. . . . To be a fish, cold in ribbony weeds. To swim far out, to cease from swimming and be rocked, cradled in soundless waves.

> *I come from haunts of coot and hern,*
> *I make a sudden sally,*
> *And sparkle out among the fern*
> *To bicker down a valley.*

Nice . . . nice . . . light and fresh. Brook: a nice word.

Dark brown is the river, golden is the sand . . . Dark brown good, merciful, washing the golden, sterile sand. *Pure ablution.* . . .

They fed her on pancakes of yellow tide foam. Oh, delicious. Airy mouthfuls, crisp and tasteless. If only I could taste them. . . .

She wore every day a plain dress of bluish-green crêpe. Red and yellow were lurid, scorching. She must be clothed in a colour like water, like the sea.

In the park the grass was brown and sere, the leaves dry, like leaves cut out of metal. Apart from the children, and the obvious but unaggressive foreign element—tourists up from the provinces, bareheaded student bands from Northern Europe—the park seemed populated by seasonal derelicts and eccentrics: muttering, bearded men, emaciated elderly women tripping on matchstick legs, in long full skirts with braid, Edwardian jackets, perched toques with Parma violets, fragments of feather boa; beings leading antique barrel-shaped asthmatic dogs; bearing parrots and cockatoos upon their shoulders; bird-headed creatures feeding the birds.

Sometimes she found an empty bench, sometimes she and the others sat side by side in silence, occasionally someone spoke to her, and once started was unable to stop; the dam of isolation down, the spate let loose.

One day it was a middle-aged man in a grey serge suit, stiff collar, black boots with bulbous toecaps. On his watch-chain hung some kind of club badge of brotherhood. His forehead was graven in savage furrows, and beneath its ploughed prominence a pair of small, deep-set, panic-stricken grey eyes scurried and hid under shuddering lids. He looked feeble, ill. After a few furtive blinks and glances he put his feet up violently on the bench and seemed to doze. Soon he jumped up as violently, sat down again, began to talk. A dead monotone poured compulsively, impersonally from his lips. After some time it became clear that his topic was motor-cars. Cars. Cars. Oil consumption, tyres, steering, accelerator, plugs . . . On and on he muttered, blinking, shuddering, glancing at her sideways, saying Riley, Wolseley, Austin, Ford, Vauxhall, saying engine trouble, saying . . .

"My nerves are bad," he said suddenly. "I've been advised to take a sea voyage. Now could one take a car to Egypt, for instance?" He stared at her in wild surmise. "But then," he said, "what about the passport difficulty?"

The passport difficulty. . . . She saw it looming mountainous, insuperable in his head, a mystic menace, blocking the light of reason. "Behold me!" implored his frantic eye. "Allow me to cast myself upon you."

After a while he became easier. His rigid lids relaxed, his voice took on a normal variation. He spoke of the bad times, deploring unemployment.

"One needs something to lean on nowadays," he said.

"I suppose one does."

"You look as if you'd had a lot of trouble."

"Oh, no, I don't think I have."

"Your face is young, but you've got some grey hairs, if I don't mistake; my sight's not very good." He moved closer.

Now I must get away, remove his spar.

"Personally," he said after a silence, "I've found religion a great consolation."

"Have you?" Now, at once . . . another second and it would be too late. She got up. "Well, I must be getting on."

He drew something swiftly from his pocket. "One moment," he said. "Please accept this. Yes, really. . . . I'd be pleased . . . I've plenty more. I frequently carry them about. . . . They're a great help, I find."

Half expecting some token of an embarrassingly symbolic nature, she looked at her palm and found a gun-metal penknife, thickly embossed with lettering and devices. Upon one side she read: *The Word of God is quick and powerful and sharper than any two-edged sword. Heb.* 4-12, above a representation of an open Bible. Upon the other side: *For what is a man profited if he shall gain the whole world and lose his own soul. Matt.* 16-26, and a picture of a globe.

"I came up to go to the Motor Show," he said, relapsing. "But I find I'm previous. I shall go next week. I shall look out for you there."

Another time a woman leading by the hand a pale child came and sat down beside her. He carried a little basket with some toys in it, and he was dressed in his best: a miniature coat and cap over a white pullover and white shorts, all homemade, neat and clean as a pin. He sat in silence beside the woman, holding the basket on his lap, not investigating it. From time to time the woman stooped forward and kissed him. He remained unresponsive. Only child, doubtless, one of those crushed into early apathy by the excessive embraces, bouncings, loud, wild crowings of relations: by the oppression of the crease in his pants, the damp brush concealed in a bag, whisked out at the corner to brush up his pretty curls; finicky over his food, segregated from common people's children. . . . There she was, taking off his cap, touching up his fine silvery curls with her fingers: just as I thought. At this he turned his head and looked up at her, but blankly. His large blue eyes travelled on and rested without inquiry on Olivia. Delicate-featured, beautiful almost. The woman watched him eagerly, looked at Olivia, smiled.

"How old is he?"

"He's three. . . . He doesn't know it, but he's going to the hospital." Composed, pleasant, superior, parlour-maidish voice. "He's got something the matter with his brain. Yes. Fits. Yes. Two a week he gets. Oh, yes, he suffers. He screams something cruel in the fits. Ever since he was fifteen months. The doctors are very interested in him, they want him in for observation. Only a miracle can save him, the doctors say. They say unless there's a miracle he can't live more than another year. Talk? Oh, yes, he can talk—says anything. But he doesn't care to talk. He's so good. When he's going to have one of his fits, he says to me, ' Mammie, I'll be dood.' Yes, he's taking his toys, but he doesn't care to play. He wants to be working all the time, if you see what I mean. He's too forward, that's his trouble. Oh, yes, he's my only one." Her voice continued conversational, her pleasant face seemed without stress or grief. "I'd like to have him home for Christmas," she said, "but I don't know . . . Oh, yes, thank you, of course, we hope so too."

Custom? Lack of imagination? Indifference? A noble reasonableness? Christian resignation? Was that it? . . . A little martyr in the home—soon to be a little angel in heaven? Not lost, but gone before, gone to the Better Home . . . A first-class cross, one with particular prestige attached. . . . And then, the doctors were so interested. . . . But then that way she had of watching him, of suddenly kissing him, not emotionally, but protectively: a helpless half-automatic gesture, it seemed, expressing—what?

Well, let's hope the doctors . . . Well, what can I do anyway? Offer a card, my address, do drop me a line. . . . Send a wreath later, *with deepest sympathy*? . . .

Nothing to be done. Merely one of millions of atoms,

doomed a little sooner than some millions of others . . . that
was the way to look at it. It doesn't really matter. Human
beings are all in a bad way, we are in a bad way. . . . It's to be
expected.

"Good-bye."

"Good-bye, miss. Say bye-bye to the lady, dear."

To and fro near where she habitually sat passed a young
man every day. Tall, gaunt, fair; shabby grey flannels, shirt
unbuttoned at the neck, books under his arm. On he drove in
a shambling, unconscious way, the wide world in his head
confusing him, causing him to trip on the edges of pavements,
to knock up against chairs and people. His fierce excitable eye
poured unfocused light. A trial to friends, an anxiety to
parents. He talked too much, he trusted everybody, incurably
expecting from human nature some behaviour that would not
occur; crying then, "Traitors! Swine!"; next turning cynic,
thanking God with mirthless barks of laughter for a sense of
humour. . . . Losing his way five times a day, forgetting
errands; trying his eyes till the small hours in a wretched
light; frying himself a sausage a day on the gas ring, his
digestion suffering; tossing sleepless on his lodging-house
bed. . . . When winter came he caught a bad cold. He drank
the smutty milk out of the bottle on the doorstep and turned
his face to the wall. When it was night he felt lonely. He got
up, and having no dressing-gown wrapped himself in the plush
tablecloth and looked out of the window at the lights of
London. He thought about being unloved and about the
sufferings of humanity, and wept. She bought him a muffler.
"You must wrap up." So he did. He wore it always, right
through the summer. She befriended him and he liked her,
but soon he passed on, away from her: she was not what he
sought. Nobody would be that. There was no comfort in him.
He was of the breed of Jocelyn; of that one who came one
night to Jocelyn's door. James was turning into something
like that, walking through France, secretively filling up his

copybook. . . . There seemed to be a good many of them striding about Europe, looking thin. Not safe, conformist young men. Perhaps more important than Dickie Vulliamy . . . or Rollo.

About five she left the park. On her way home she stopped at a snack bar and bought sandwiches for her supper. Sometimes she had a glass of ginger beer. Oh, delicious! More, more . . .

The evenings were bad, were very bad. She had a bath, washing with the cake of Wright's Coal Tar Soap she'd bought, because she remembered from childhood its pungent unsweet smell. The Martins had used it and smelt of it when they didn't smell of indiarubber, the guinea-pigs or bull's eyes. She went to bed, her sandwiches beside her. Ham was food. She never sickened of it. Oh, for a long savoury dinner! . . . Game . . . Welsh rarebit . . . If only there were someone to bring me iced soup; or one lamb cutlet. . . . Impossible to face cooking for oneself. . . .

She was no longer so thin: it must be growing, getting enough nourishment. Her breasts hurt. She fancied her figure changing perceptibly. When do one's clothes begin to get too tight? . . . She remembered Kate unfamiliar and touching in a grey maternity frock with white ruffles. Such dignities will not be for me. To be rid, to be rid, to be rid of this. . . . To be not sick . . . I should be hanging on doors, lifting wardrobes and pianos, trying to fall downstairs, doing everything I can. . . . Instead, day after day, inert, she rested, strolled, sank down in chairs, crawled to the bathroom, fell into bed again: protecting herself against her own designs against Nature, lowering herself unresistingly to a vegetable standard: A maggoty, spoiling vegetable. . . . I don't weep, I don't fret. I regulate my life; I hope only as a marrow might hope for sun and rain: a dull tenacious clinging.

In bed she read her old Oxford copies of Victorian novelists. *Vanity Fair, David Copperfield, Mansfield Park, Villette*—on, on . . . The characters so out of date, so vital, lived in her with a feverish, almost repellently heightened activity and importance, more real for their remoteness.

Sometimes a flash pierced her: I bear Rollo's child. Soon gone again. Or a good dream woke her exultant, haunting her with shapes and sounds of transcendental beauty. Nightly, the dreams crowded: voluptuous, or straightforwardly sensual dreams about Rollo—but not always Rollo; faces and fears from childhood or adolescence, long forgotten or suppressed; dramas in sequence, intricate conspiracies; those water images with swans and water-lilies; and a host more cloudy symbols. . . .

A fortnight went by alone in London. The telephone never rang, and Rollo didn't write again.

IV

A BAD afternoon. The park was airless. The sky was clouding from the west, saffron-tinged: the fine spell would have broken before night. There would be thunder and then the rain would come down. She was restless, waiting for the change, unable to breathe. Figures passing to and fro, or sitting on benches in the distance looked diminished, flat and lifeless in a sinister way, like figures in a nightmare. She left the dry railed spaces, the lurid trees, and hailed a taxi. Thank God, I needn't stint yet. Taxis, ginger beer, ham sandwiches— the remainder of Rollo's journey money supplied them all.

Too limp to climb as far as her own room, she lay down on the sofa in the sitting-room. *Alas, alack, my aching back is near to crack I feel so slack* . . . The tag rang in her head, over and over again. Invented hundreds of years ago, when we had measles, when I was ten. . . . The room looked unfresh, neglected. No flowers. Smuts on the window-sill; to-morrow I must pull myself together and dust properly. Must make a resolution to be more energetic. Another ten days and Etty would be back. Anna too, surely, soon. Anna'll be appalled at this fix. She never wanted a child. Even to discuss childbirth in a physical way upsets her. She's neurotic; she'd drown herself rather than face it. I must avoid her, or she'll avoid me. There was a gulf fixed, and on one side of it were women with child; on the other, men, childless women. She was alone on the one side. On the other, Anna, Simon, Colin, all of them, walked away from her with averted heads, estranged. . . .

The sharp ping of the front-door bell went through her, twisting in her chest like a probe. . . . Who? . . . Was he back, had he come? It rang again. She went down and opened the door, and there was Lady Spencer.

"Lady Spencer . . ." Come for me.

"Ah, Olivia. . . . Something *told* me I should find you in."

Yes, there she was . . . looking just as I've always known she would some time or other on my doorstep. A large hat of thin black straw swept with grey ostrich feathers was attached to the summit of her coiffure; her gown of black flowered chiffon, broken up with chains, ruffles, pearls, flowed about her ankles. Lavender kid gloves, a grey silk parasol. Her eyes were steady, ice-blue: dictator's eyes, fanatically self-confident, without appeal.

"Do come in." In spite of herself the conciliatory smile beginning. "How lovely to——" No . . .

"*May* I come in? Just for a very short time." The tone was pleasant, but all-concealing; the old cordial note one's ear was tuned for absent.

"I'd no idea you were in London." Her guilty voice trailed off. Unable to look anywhere, she led the way to the sitting-room. Lady Spencer lowered herself in a stately way upon the sofa. Olivia sat down on the edge of a chair. . . . Keep my back to the light.

"Will you have a cigarette? Oh, I'm afraid there aren't any. I think there are some upstairs. I'll just go. . . ." And be alone for a minute, compose myself, dash a bit of rouge on.

"No, no, I never smoke, thank you."

"Nor do I much." One whiff, you know, in my present condition and I'm finished. . . .

"What a charming little house." Peeling off her lavender gloves, Lady Spencer looked about her.

"Yes, isn't it? Etty's abroad."

"Are you alone then?"

"Yes, for the moment. I'm going away in about another week, I expect."

"I suppose your work kept you?" For the first time a note of sympathy crept in: Lady Spencer's respect for the bread-winner.

"No, I'm not working really. . . ." Trapped, trapped. . . . She said rapidly, "Are you in London for long?"

"It's a little uncertain." Lady Spencer folded her gloves, looked away. "I brought my poor John up three weeks ago— for treatment. It's a horrid time to be in London, but we so *hope* it's doing him good—he's *such* a clever, charming man, we have such faith in him—and then it will be *well* worth while, won't it?" There was perceptible uncertainty behind her emphasis. She's really as muddled as Marigold. . . . She doesn't know how to begin. But she will, soon.

"I'm so sorry. I do hope it's nothing serious."

"Thank you, Olivia, we *hope* not. We don't know yet . . . but there seems *every* prospect of alleviation if not *cure* . . . so that's a lot to be thankful for, isn't it? Besides, we're *very* comfortable where we are. Rollo's so very sweetly lent us his lovely house."

"Oh, has he?" So that's who it was on the telephone: of course: the family butler: who used to give us pink throat pastilles when Marigold took us into the pantry.

"Rollo is away till the middle of the month."

"Is he? . . . They both are, I suppose."

"Yes, they both are."

"How's Marigold?"

"Marigold is well. She's just gone to Venice." Lady Britton basking on the Lido. . . .

Silence fell. The noise of her pulses seemed to Olivia to

drum in the room. Lady Spencer loosened a gold chain round her throat, as if oppressed.

"I came to see you, Olivia——"

"I suppose *not* a friendly call?" Olivia offered her a small weak smile.

"Friendly, I hope, Olivia. I do hope you will believe friendly. . . ."

That's as may be. I won't say anything. I won't be bamboozled: a good word that.

"I've hesitated a long time," said Lady Spencer, her clear eyes gazing ahead into space, heroic, calm, "before deciding to come. . . . You may think the fact of my being Rollo's mother doesn't warrant my interfering . . ." Olivia was dumb, and she added, still with the same alarming faith: "I must risk that."

"Has he told you then?"

She said quickly, with all her trenchancy: "Rollo has told me nothing."

That's something—that's a lot. Just guesswork. I must keep my head. She knows she can terrify: she counts on that, and worship.

"How did you know?"

Lady Spencer turned a curious expression on her for a moment . . . complicated . . . partly apologetic?

"You sent him a telegram."

"Oh, did you open it?"

"Yes. It was brought to me. Naturally," she added quickly, "it was sent on to him at once."

God, what bad luck, what a half-witted thing to have done. . . . with that silly intimate signature too—*Liv*—read, sent on by her. He must have been annoyed, fussed when he got it. His letter hadn't said so. . . . Sooner or later the criminal will be careless over a detail and betray himself.

"But of course," continued Lady Spencer, "I had known for some time."

Olivia stared at her, hypnotised.

"I should say—had guessed . . ." Lady Spencer looked down, ever so slightly flustered.

"How?"

"It's hard to put in words. . . . I'm his mother. . . . Naturally one is sensitive to . . . He was changed." She coloured, very faintly.

"Happier," said Olivia.

She paused.

"He was different," she said. "Unlike himself. At least I thought so."

"You're very quick."

"Not particularly."

"He didn't feel ashamed—guilty. Why should he?"

Misplaced defiance, useless. . . . Its only effect to make one feel coarse-mannered. Lady Spencer said quietly:

"I never ask my children for confidences. But needless to say, I knew there were difficulties—in his married life, I mean." She went on with a touch of acerbity: "People of my generation may seem to you very ignorant and old-fashioned. You like to think we all wear blinkers and live in cotton-wool, but some of us know something of the world. I had long expected Rollo would take a mistress."

The sudden plain speaking and downright tone startled her, almost brought a blush. Unexpected . . .

"And after you came to dine with us that night at Meldon" —Lady Spencer nearly smiled—"I expected it would be you." She paused reflectively. "That sounds a little crude. I don't mean to imply there was anything in your behaviour. . . ." That means there was. I was more than etiquette expects: I knew it then . . . "You are an unusually attractive woman, and, well!—call it an intuition. . . ."

"Does everybody know then?"

"I don't know who everybody may be," she said sharply, "but as far as *I* am concerned, I have not discussed the matter."

"I wonder if Marigold knows. . . . She has intuitions too. Besides, she wanted it to happen."

Misplaced again. . . .

"I have no idea," interrupted Lady Spencer sharply again, "what Marigold wanted. In this case her wants are not of the slightest interest to me."

As if focusing headlights upon Olivia, she turned towards her, and summoning all her powers, said intensely:

"Olivia, do you love him?"

"Yes." Icy sweat burst out on her forehead. . . . Brutal. . . . Stop it, I'm ill. . . .

"I'm sure you do. Of course you do. Forgive me." She made a slight, rapid movement, as if suppressing the impulse to put out a hand, to show affection. She said gently, "Then will you give him up?"

"Why should I——?" Olivia shrank back in her chair, rigid, panic-stricken.

Lady Spencer sat still, giving them both time.

"I think he's unhappy," she said finally.

"Unhappy——?" A wave of blackness came over her. What do you know, you fiend?

"Lately, I have thought so. I'm sure of it."

"Why, has he complained?" . . . *Mummie, I'm so unhappy. . . . Tell me all about it, dear.* . . . The blackness kept on coming in waves. . . . The thing is, she's always right. . . .

"I've told you already he hasn't said one word. He never will." She fidgeted with her gloves, smoothing them. "I realise I am taking a lot upon myself. . . ."

"You are. Too much, I think." Insufferable, unwarrantable interference. . . . But I can't say that, I can't keep it up. She was trembling, breathing in long-drawn shallow breaths. I mustn't faint.

Lady Spencer allowed the rudeness to pass. She said simply:

"Something tells me he wants to bring it to an end." In the silence she added, "I don't think I'm wrong."

Not you. . . .

"If he did—he'd have told me. He's not a coward. We trust

each other. We know we can say——" We do, don't we, Rollo? . . . Do we? . . . He said by the window: Remember I love you.

"Yes. . . ." Lady Spencer looked a little embarrassed. "Only you can judge of that, of course. I'm sure Rollo would never —er—— He would never be selfish . . . light . . ."

Olivia laughed.

"I suppose you think I snared him."

"No, no. Why should I?" She does too. "I'm sure—I don't doubt—— But we won't enter into that."

The room had grown suddenly dark. Outside a thunder-shower broke sharply, rattling on the pavement. They listened to it for a few moments.

"If you think I don't know about *her* . . ." said Olivia. "I know he loves her. In fact, she's much the most important— I know that. He told me. I understand. . . ."

"Yes, he does love her," agreed Lady Spencer, unshaken, considering quietly.

"I know he'll never leave her for me, if that's what you——"

"No. No, never. . . ."

"I expect monogamy's a tradition in your family. . . ."

A show of it at least. . . . Façades of virtue and principle, as an example to the lower classes. Anything may go on underneath, because you're privileged. That Marigold's no good, she's a drunken tart. And what about old Sir John in his day, I wouldn't be too sure . . .

"Any break up in his marriage is unthinkable . . ." continued Lady Spencer, once more scoring for dignity. "Although of course things have been most unsatisfactory. . . . She is very much to blame . . . she and her . . ." Now she was a little flustered. "But I have every hope—that they—that their difficulties . . . that there may be adjustments . . . her health will improve . . . that she will make her duty her happiness . . . I'm sure she will. She is a dear child really. . . ." More than flustered, actually floundering; the *de haut en bas* im-pressiveness gone. Her hands moved restlessly on her lap.

She appealed: "You know him. You know that what he needs is a real home."

"Yes." Children . . . I won't say that for her.

"Olivia, will you be generous? Will you make a sacrifice for him? Will you give them a chance?"

Another blackout, a bad one. Don't give in. . . . She burst out with violent weakness:

"What's all this? What are you . . ." Her lids closed. "Has something happened I don't know about?" Rollo, where are you? How could you? . . . Tortured, and you don't care. . . .

Lady Spencer was silent. Outside the rain redoubled for a moment, then suddenly sighed itself out.

"Rollo is weak," continued the voice implacably. "I know it. . . . He can't bear to hurt. . . . Any—any sensitive man is bound to be weak in such a position. . . . Believe me if you can, Olivia, I am here as your friend. . . ." Rot. Here as a blackmailer, here to smell out my game, see how dangerous I am . . . to buy me off with sentiments: pity for you you can't suggest a cheque. . . . "Olivia, will you help him?"

"I do help him. I give him everything I can. I've made him happy—he said so. . . . You ought to be glad."

Silence again. And the furniture listening. . . . This is the room it began in. Can she see our kisses?

"Perhaps," said Lady Spencer with sorrowful rebuking gentleness, "we must agree to differ on that point. Perhaps our ideals of happiness . . . *true* happiness . . . But we won't embark on such a wide question. . . . I only wish to say that I think Rollo at least will never find peace—shall we say—in a divided allegiance? That if you continue this—this"—intrigue she'd like to say, doesn't quite dare—"you will do him a terrible injury. There, I've spoken plainly. It's the least I can do. That is my view. I may be mistaken. . . ."

But you're damn sure you're not.

"Well, there's nothing more to say, is there?"

Stalemate? Not a victory for her, anyway. I haven't given her much change: managed to keep my end up. . . .

Suddenly she said in a cross voice, as if irritated by a bit of bad management:

"You appear to have been remarkably indiscreet."

"How do you mean . . . ?" She heard her own voice weak, guilty, apprehensive. What's she going to spring now . . . ?

"I should have thought it would have been wiser to avoid a town populated by half London for the Festival."

Good God!

"Were we seen?"

"You were."

"We didn't think we had been." This is awful. . . . "Who saw us?"

"I don't propose to mention any names," said Lady Spencer crushingly, pressing her lips together, looking like a headmistress.

"We were so careful . . . we never stayed in towns. . . . It was only about a week. . . ." Feebler and feebler: excuse, apology, embarrassment. . . . Oh, God! It was in ruins. It had seemed so beautiful—such pure escape and flight. Oh, God! Toad faces, rat eyes of the world. Where had been the eye bulging in the crowd, the gloating nostril? . . . We thought we were so wary, going about always as if with feelers all over us, back and front and sides, quivering, on the lookout. . . . Except when we said good-bye in the square, by the fountain of the horses . . . that was the only time I forgot the crowds, forgot to be on the alert. . . . Was it then?

"Luckily," said Lady Spencer, "my informant is *unimpeachably* discreet." The emphasis had come back. "I can *count* on its not going any further." She jerked her head, looking both imperious and complacent. . . . Somebody under her thumb. . . . A relation. Suddenly, in a spasm like a flashlight photograph, it was Mary Denham . . . who hated me so that night— my enemy. . . . It would be. She would go to Salzburg for the Festival. . . . It was the right thing to do this year. . . . She would spot us, and gleefully post off to Aunt Millicent with the news, importantly vow absolute eternal secrecy, for the sake of the family. What a break for her. . . . Pure supposition, of course, utterly illogical, probably nonsense. . . . But the image of that face, trivial and gluttonous, peering and pouncing unseen from a car? a café? from the sidewalk?—was fixed now.

"How beastly. . . ." She sighed deeply.

"I merely wished to point out that you don't go about wearing a cloak of invisibility," said Lady Spencer. Her voice rose, hardened. "Rollo must have been mad to—Think of the risk! You might at least. . . . The scandal! Did you ever think of that—for *him*? What right have you—even if you're prepared to sacrifice your own reputation—to endanger—other people's? Supposing it had come to *her* ears. . . . It's a miracle it didn't. . . . I hardly like to think——"

"Oh, don't you? *I* can think of it without swooning! Why shouldn't she have a bit of trouble like everybody else? Do her good!"—Coarse, hostile, scolding like a couple of scolds, me and Lady Spencer, how awful—"What's the matter with her? What's this thing about her? Is she dying? Just because she hasn't even the guts to put her own stockings on—she's to be treated like a Ming vase. You think it's all right to behave like her—she's so well-bred and ladylike—she must be protected. And it doesn't matter what happens to inferior people like me—we can be ill—we can be worn down—and badgered and attacked—and dropped overboard—so long as *you're* . . ."

The blackness came over again, and settled. Now I needn't hear any more. Needn't answer. What a relief. This isn't a faint, am I pretending? She was aware of herself slumped down sideways in her chair, her head on the arm. Quite comfortable. Can't move.

From far away she heard an exclamation, rustling movements. A voice said:

"Olivia . . ."

"It's all right," she said earnestly, not moving.

"Shall I get you some water?"

"No, thank you."

Presently she sat up. Lady Spencer was bending over her, rather red and anxious. Their eyes met, dwelling full, searchingly, on each other. . . . Time started again. Lady Spencer straightened herself.

"How do you feel?"

"Better. I'm sorry. I haven't been feeling up to much." Two tears ran down her cheeks. She brushed them off and two more ran down.

"You should have told me."

"It's the weather, I expect. Thunder always does me in."

"Are you having proper meals? Who's looking after you?"

"I look after myself. There's nobody left in London— except you and me." She smiled. "I'm all right really. This is enough to upset any one, isn't it?"

"I'm so very sorry to have upset you. I feel so distressed. . . ." Her voice faltered, a spasm twitched her face. She didn't think I was so sensitive. . . .

"Please don't be. I'm sure you came because you felt you must."

"Some day you may feel more inclined to believe I have acted for the best." She looked away, a wrinkled old woman. "So far as I could judge of it," she added.

"Yes. . . . I just think families are too awful, that's all."

She stood erect, gazing towards the window. After a while she said:

"This is not perhaps the time to speak of one's own feelings, but I've always been fond of you, Olivia." Her voice was unemotional but convincing.

"And I of you. More than fond." In love with the whole lot of them.

"I've always so admired you and Kate. It seems such a pity—I felt so grieved when your marriage—I should so rejoice to see you with a happy home of your own."

"I should be less of a menace, shouldn't I?"

"Don't be bitter," she said with mournful dignity. "After

all these years I hoped—you would have been able to judge less
cynically of my motives. I have been fortunate myself—happy
in my marriage—but I don't for that reason suppose marriage
is the solution for every woman. But for you—it's what should
be. . . ."

"That's what he said too. . . ." She got up and stood with
her elbows on the mantelpiece and her chin propped on her
hands.

"Don't waste yourself," said Lady Spencer earnestly.

The old feeling came surging up. Lady Spencer, I'm in
trouble, help me. You know everything. Beloved benefactress,
infallible . . . Punish and forgive me, approve of me again.
Say: I knew my Olivia wouldn't fail me.

"I can't give you any promise or anything. . . . When I
see him, if I really think he wants . . . I'll know when I see
him."

"Truth is all that matters. We see eye to eye there at least,
don't we?" She smiled sadly, encouragingly. "Make it easy
for him. You're not weak."

"I am."

She began to draw on her gloves.

"I can rely on you—not a word to him of this conversation?"

"No. I promise."

"You needn't fear that I shall trouble you again, Olivia.
Think of me as out of the picture *definitely*, for ever. Unless,
of course, you should wish to see me. . . . I shall always be
glad. . . . Otherwise we may not meet again."

Never again the cordial greeting, the warm kiss, the sympathetic inquiry. . . . How sad. . . .

Settling her chains and ruffles, giving a touch to her hat,
she pronounced:

"People must manage their own lives."

"I always knew you'd come," said Olivia. "I've been expecting you for nearly a year."

As if wondering what to make of this, Lady Spencer shot
her a dubious glance, paused; decided to let it pass.

"I must be getting back," she said. "He frets if I'm away too long."

They went down the stairs together.

"I'm so sorry about him. I do hope he'll get much better."

"Thank you, my dear. I'm afraid we can't really hope for very much. But so far he's had no pain. If he can be spared that, I must try not to complain." Olivia opened the front door, and she stood on the threshold, her strong, noble profile lifted towards the street. "He has a full, happy life behind him," she said. "We both have. It shouldn't be too hard to find oneself at the end."

How sad, how sad: they had come to the end. . . . His full, happy life must close in peace; she would fight for that, see to it: no breath of doubt, no shadow of distress about his only son should trouble his last days.

"The rain's over, isn't it?" She peered out, short-sighted.

"Yes. The air's fresher, I think."

"Delicious. *Blessed* rain." She turned, holding her hand out. "Good-bye, Olivia. God bless you. Take care of yourself."

Her gaze dwelt on Olivia standing at close range with the light full on her. Suddenly the smile froze, the blue eyes flew open wide, fixed in unmistakable panic. "You don't look at all well," she said. The dusky red came right up to her forehead.

She's guessed.

"Why . . .? I'm all right." Steady now, steady. . . .

"Are you in any trouble?"

What it cost her to say that, in a level voice, was written all over her. She had turned as white as the handkerchief she held to her lips. Her eyes were sunk to tiny black pits.

"No. Why should I be? . . . What do you mean?" I do sound guilty. . . . She summoned a laugh. "Do you mean—like kitchenmaids?"

"I think you understand me." Her voice dragged.

"You're very suspicious." Try icy dignity.

"I don't mean to be. I . . . After all, such things do happen."

She pressed her unsteady mouth with the square of lawn. "I should be so sorry. . . . It would be so terrible for you. . . ."

"I'm not going to have a baby, if that's what you think."

She went on as if she hadn't heard:

"Rollo could never. . . . An illegitimate child would be quite out of the—quite unthinkable. . . ."

"What would he do? Would you think he ought to marry me?"

"Please say no more. I'm very sorry to have—— It was a sudden—— You must forgive me. I must——" In agitation she looked up and down the street. "I'd better take a taxi."

"Shall I ring up for one?"

"Thank you, no; I'll walk and pick one up."

"There's generally one just round the corner."

"Yes——"

She started off down the street, hurrying, her back erect, yet with a look of strain. . . .

She was gone.

She didn't look at me once after that look. She didn't dare.

How did she guess? Is it so plain in my face? A kind of telepathy, or intuition? Did I convince her?

Well, I've seen her once knocked cock-eyed, utterly reduced to chaos. . . . The oddest likeness to Marigold had slipped out in her disarrayed face: Marigold's look of being cornered, of desperate shift and stratagem.

What an awful thing, what a shattering way to part.

I'm not going to have a baby, if that's what you think.

I'm not going to have a baby.

She went upstairs and was sick and then lay down.

Now, let's face facts.

He said, Remember I love you. That was after he'd read his letters: because of something in one of the letters? . . . meaning: remember what I meant at best? . . . meaning: in case from now on there's a falling-off? . . .

The words tolled now with a dirge-like note.

And he hasn't written, he didn't wait in London for me.

It doesn't matter. I don't feel anything whatsoever.

Only I'm in the hell of a mess.

Rollo, where are you? Help me.

No, I must get out of it by myself. Because he's not going to say: Oh, *darling* . . . tender, pitying, comforting, overcome; he won't say, like in books, "Our child." . . . Of course he won't. He'll say, "Christ! Are you sure? How awful. What are you going to do?"

An illegitimate child would be quite out of the question.

I must get out of it before he comes back. *All be as before, love.* . . .

She got up and went down to the sitting-room, and looked up Tredeaven, W.P., in the telephone book.

"Mr. Tredeaven's secretary speaking. Mr. Tredeaven is away on holiday."

"Oh. . . . When will he be back?"

"He's expected back next week. Did you want an appointment?"

"Yes, I did."

"May I make a provisional appointment for you? Tuesday next at twelve? What name is it, please?"

"Mrs. Craig."

By the last post that night came a letter from Rollo: a scrawl, one side of a big thin sheet, from a Highland address.

Darling, I do hope you're better. Your letter didn't say. This is a pleasant party, and eight hours of fresh air per day have blown some of the cobwebs away. (He always says that.) I'm staying in an old castle—walls feet thick—everything panelled in oak—no curtains or papers. Secret doors leading to secret passages—just what romantic you would love. Life is simple, drink and eats plentiful, and sport consists of a few grouse, partridges, black game, snipe, etc.—the usual rough Scottish shoot. It is all so feudal, all I need is a bonny lass to

share my couch—I know who, in fact. I feel so fit. I think I
could retire here and be a hermit for the rest of my days quite
happily. Perhaps I couldn't. Anyway I can't! I'll be back about
the 15th, darling, and hope to see you soon after that, or will
you be at your cottage? It was lovely our day there, wasn't it?
I loathe the thought of coming back, except for seeing you.

Next day Anna's letter said Simon was still in bed. His
temperature swung up higher every day, he was feeling ill. It
might be something worse than a chill. She'd got worried
thinking she wasn't nursing him properly and she'd called the
doctor who'd had him moved to the British hospital, but
wouldn't say anything yet. She went to see him every day.
She couldn't come home yet. He said to send his love.

v

"No, my husband's not here, he's abroad," she said. "He sailed
for India last month, and I'm to join him at Christmas. So
you see, it couldn't be more unfortunate. I *can't* undertake
that long voyage alone in this state. I'm being so awfully
sick, otherwise I wouldn't mind so much. But anyway, the
sort of life we'll be leading the next year or so—quite in the
wilds—I don't see *how* we could cope with a baby."

"Quite. Quite," said Mr. Tredeaven, folding his hands.

She sat in his arm-chair twisting the ring on her marriage
finger: Rollo's emerald, unearthed from the back of the
drawer . . . to look a person of consequence.

"It would upset all our plans."

"Quite."

"Of course, we want one later . . . when we're settled. It's
only just now——"

"Quite. These accidents will happen. Nature's a wily dame.

"No, no. You need have no fears. My treatment is absolutely harmless—absolutely simple."

He leaned back, tapped his fingers together. The light from the window gleamed on his egg-bald pate, trimmed round with an unprepossessing semicircle of lank, sparse mousy hair. He wore a morning suit and a high stiff old-fashioned collar with broad wings. His face was broad, bland, hairless, secretive, with full eyelids and a slight puffiness about the jowls, the eyes opaque, set on the surface and widely spaced, the lips long, pale, stretched-looking. There was something about him of a Methodist preacher; something of a professional conjurer.

"Don't worry, Mrs. Craig, we'll fix you up."

"Thank you so much. . . ." She fidgeted with her bag. "And about—I'm not quite sure—what it is you charge—about your fee. . . ."

"My fee is a hundred——" Mr. Tredeaven crossed his knees. "Pounds, not guineas," he added with a reassuring smile.

"I see."

Silence fell heavily. . . . A body blow. . . . Mr. Tredeaven took up his fountain-pen from beside the blotter, unscrewed it, turned it about, replaced the top.

"It's a bit difficult," she said. Her heart beat thickly. What did I imagine? Twenty at the outside. Has the emerald put my price up?

He tapped his nose with the pen.

"Well, I don't want to be hard on you," he said at last. "Say eighty."

Her straining ears caught or fancied the faint cooling-off in his voice, the slightest withdrawal of affability. Disappointed in me.

"I can manage eighty. . . ." If I bargain he'll throw me out. What'll the emerald fetch?

"That's agreed then."

"Thank you very much." For his tone suggested magnanimity. "When do you want it? Before? Now?"

"No, no, no." He chided gently. Come, come now, tact, dear lady! . . . "There's no such desperate hurry." He opened his appointment book. "Suit you to bring it with you when you come?"

"Yes, I can do that."

He said sauvely:

"Preferably not a cheque, if you don't mind."

"Notes?"

"If it's not giving you too much trouble. Just in an envelope, you know."

"All right, I'll do that. On Friday at three, then." She got up.

"Friday at three." He, too, rose. He held out his hand; strong, plump, manipulative fingers with cushiony tips.

"Is it painful?" she said.

"What a lot of worries!" He shook his head, chiding again paternally, half playful, still holding her hand.

"I'm not afraid. I only wanted to know."

"You needn't worry," he said. "Don't think about it. A few days taking it easy afterwards and your troubles will all be over."

"I'll be glad."

"I'm sure you will." He nodded, sympathetic, understanding. "Poor dear. . . If you ask me, Nature hasn't given women a square deal—I've always said so—not by any means a square deal, poor things." He patted her shoulder. "Now cheer up, Mrs. Craig. My advice to you is: forget about yourself. Get hold of a pal and fix up something cheerful. What about a theatre—eh?"

Conducting her to the door he paused by the mantelpiece and said: "Care for pretty things?"

"Yes." . . . Oh, rather.

"I thought you did. What do you think of these?" He indicated a couple of bronzes—female figures, semi-nude, with drapery, holding torches aloft. "I picked them up the other day. Nice, aren't they? Empire . . ."

"Lovely." She looked at them. Meaningless, expensive, repulsive objects. "It's not a period I know much about."

"I like to pick up a piece here and there when it takes my fancy." He fingered them with his notable white hands.

Whose envelope paid for those? What'll he buy with the next one?

"I don't go in for being a connoisseur," he said, relinquishing them, opening the door.

VI

THE gentleman in the morning coat with the pearl tie-pin came back, ring in hand, from the inner sanctuary and leaning across the plate-glass counter, said confidentially:

"We should say seventy."

"I see. Thank you. I'm afraid I couldn't possibly let it go for that." She took the ring from him and held it up, staring at it. Green, glowing, flawless. . . . A bit of green stone. "You see, I know it's worth a great deal more than that."

"It may have cost more, madam." He shrugged. "The market for this class of stone fluctuates. It *may* have—I don't say it didn't—but between you and me if it *did* . . . I should be inclined to say . . . well . . ." His shoulders expressed regret, discreet contempt. "Perhaps just a *litt*le more was paid for it than *we* should have felt justified in asking. . . ."

Rollo, darling, I'm sorry, what a shame—your gorgeous present . . . I can't help it, Rollo.

"I suppose you wouldn't know where it was purchased?" he asked, drumming lightly with his fingers on the plate-glass. He wore a handsome signet ring.

"No, I don't." She went on staring at it. "It's a perfect emerald, isn't it?"

"It's a good stone . . . quite a good stone." We are always scrupulously fair here. "I shouldn't go so far as to say *perfect*. The colour's just a trifle harsh. Now, if you'd like to compare it . . . let me just show you a few. . . ."

"Well, no, thank you. I won't bother." Slowly she pushed

it back in its red morocco case. I must try somewhere else. I must get eighty. . . . Supposing no one will give me that?

The jeweller picked up the case and examined the ring again.

"Say seventy-five," he said.

"All right, then . . . seventy-five."

I can't bother any more, too ill. . . . I want to get home. To-morrow I'll pawn the cigarette case, it ought to fetch a fiver.

Baleful, reproachful upon its black velvet pillow, the green eye stared at her for the last time. He snapped down the lid of the box.

I wonder how much I've been swindled. Never mind. Value is only relative.

She touched the ring on her little finger. Still there. As long as I have that. . . .

Ten pounds for the cigarette case: a pleasant surprise. Obviously a very superior article. Handing it over was quite painful.

Eighty pounds in an envelope; and five pounds over. Very acceptable: Rollo's journey money had come to an end.

VII

"STAY where you are, Mrs. Craig," he said softly. "There now. Quite comfy? That's right. Don't worry. All over. Wasn't too bad, was it, eh?"

"No, thank you."

He put a cushion under her head, threw a light rug over her. She lay flat on the hard surgical couch and closed her eyes. Several tears ran down her face and dried there.

"Relax, Mrs. Craig."

"Yes." She smiled blindly, obedient, behaving meekly, a good patient. He slipped a hot-water bottle under the rug, close in to her side.

"Thank you." I'm cold—funny in this weather—glad of it.

He moved about softly, busy with something the other side of the room, his natty back turned to her. She opened her eyes. In spite of the September afternoon sun the room was in twilight. The buff blinds were lowered; and besides this, curtains of wine-coloured net across the windows diffused a lurid murkiness. From where she lay she could see an arm-chair upholstered in purple brocade, a black-and-gold lacquered screen half-concealing a two-tiered surgical wheeled table; his big desk with papers on it, one or two silver-framed photographs. There was a smell of antiseptics.

Presently he came back.

"All right, Mrs. Craig?"

"Yes, thank you." She smiled up at him faintly, meekly. His face loomed over her, broad and bland. The high-winged old-world collar carried on the motif of his pointed prominent ears.

My deliverer. Your victim, here I lie. . . . "Bit shaky still, though."

He went away, came back with a glass.

"Drink this."

She drank. It was sal volatile.

"I might be sick."

He placed an enamel kidney bowl beside her chin; and soon she was sick.

"Tt-tt-tt. . . ." Sympathetically he removed the bowl. "Poor dear. You won't be troubled with this much longer."

She sat up, swung her legs slowly over the side of the couch, did up her stockings, combed her hair.

"I'll tell my man to get you a taxi." He touched the bell.

"I don't like your man." Black eyes with a cast, memorising her face in one sharp furtive glance, taciturn, noiselessly showing her up. "He frightens me."

He glanced at her as if he thought she might be wandering; laughed.

"Why? He's quite harmless. A most trustworthy chap. Been with me for years."

"I expect he's all right." She sighed. "I don't like his face."

"We can't all be attractive young women," he said casually.

There seemed to her to be a dreadful intimacy between them: sexual, without desire: conspirators, bound together in reluctant inevitable loyalty. She bent down to look at the photographs on the desk: a rather good-looking women in evening dress, with a pre-war plait of hair round her head; two children, girl and boy, grinning, in party socks and pumps.

"Those are my two," he said, picking up the photographs.

"They look very nice." The sights those kids must have grinned at. . . .

"Jolly little pair." He scanned them with an indulgent eye. "That was taken some years ago. The boy's just gone to Harrow." He can afford, of course, to give them an expensive education. "That's my wife. . . ."

"Charming. . . ." Does she know where the dough comes from?

He picked up an enlarged snapshot: a man in waders, with a tweed hat, holding up a dead salmon.

"Recognise that?" he said rather coyly. "Me. . . . That was in 1928. Biggest I ever landed, he was: thirty-pounder. Game old boy, too: gave me the tussle of my life. Played him for four hours. Between you and me I thought I'd pass out before he did." Simple pride and pleasure warmed his voice. He put down the snapshot, sighed: not sinister at all, rather wistful; playing salmon more to his taste than performing abortions. "Fishing's a grand sport," he said. "Ever do any?"

"Not often," she said regretfully. "I don't often get the chance."

She opened her bag, extracted the envelope and gave it to him.

"Oh, thanks, thanks very much." He whisked it into a drawer.

"When will it begin?"

"Oh—sometime within the next twelve hours."

"I see."

"Good-bye, Mrs. Craig." He shook hands. "Best of luck on your travels."

"Thank you so much. Good-bye."

They stood and looked at each other. Never to meet again, please God.

"I should trot home now and go straight to bed with a book. Something cheerful. There's nothing to worry about. If you *should* want to ring me up, you can. But you understand—no messages. . . . You quite understand?"

"I quite understand. I won't ring up."

He put an arm lightly across her shoulders and led her to the door. On the other side of it, in the dark hall, waited the manservant. He opened the front door for her, and there in the quiet sunny street waited the ordinary taxi.

She went to bed and read *Pride and Prejudice*.

About eight she got up again and dressed and went out and took a bus to Leicester Square. An hour or so of oblivion at the Empire, and all may be well.

It was an American crook film, not first-class, but snappy enough, absorbing. . . . Packed humanity weighed down the dark above, below her. She felt a tingle of consciousness: as if someone she knew were somewhere quite near in the darkness. . . . I don't seem to mind the smoke smell so much: a good sign?

She leaned back and plunged into a film-trance.

It was before the end that the discomfort hoveringly began. Pain? Yes, surely. . . . But I'll sit it out. Just before the lights went on she slipped away, avoiding "God Save the King." A few others were straggling out too. In the glare of the entrance hall she saw Ivor ahead of her, walking slowly through one of the doors into the street.

He was held up at the first crossing and she came level with him and stood beside him. He was looking at the traffic.

"Hallo, Ivor."

He turned his head and saw her.

"Hallo!"

"I saw you come out of there."

"Oh, were you in there?"

"Yes." He didn't seem surprised: but he never did. "Not really quite good enough, was it? I suppose our palate's jaded."

"M'm."

He looked pale and puffy, his eyes without lustre . . . the way they always went when his digestion was out of order. His white shirt, grey flannels and navy blue jacket had a seedy look. . . . Down on his luck. . . .

They walked along side by side towards Piccadilly.

"What are you doing in London, Ivor? I thought you were abroad."

"I have been. I was in Brittany all summer. I'm just back."

"With what's-her-name?"

"With Marda," he amended with dignity. "She's got a house near Quimper. I've been writing a book."

"Finished it?"

"Not quite. I got stuck, and Marda thought I'd better put it aside for a bit and have a change. She thought I'd been overworking."

Got sick of him probably and kicked him out. . . .

"Besides," he said, drawing up his shoulders and frowning in an important, theatrical-ferocious way she remembered, "I've got a new job in the offing."

"What?"

"Well, nothing's fixed yet. I'd rather not say too much about it." However, after a few moments of walking shoulder to shoulder in silence, he said: "As a matter of fact, Halkin's half promised me something in films."

"Who's Halkin?"

"You must have heard of Halkin. He's one of our biggest directors."

"What are you going to do—act?"

"No—on the production side. Halkin's got ideas. It ought to be interesting working for him. I know if I once got a break in films I could do something. . . . I've always wanted to get in on them."

They waited together on the edge of the Circus, then crossed towards the Criterion; then across again into Piccadilly.

Extraordinary, depressing, how the old relationship re-established itself at once pat and neat, without a moment's embarrassment or uncertainty: oneself aloof, caustic, and cool, pricking every balloon as fast as he blew it up: a sadistic, conscientious governess; he resentful, aggressive, feebly jaunty, making a stand against yet wishing to collapse, to receive protection.

"Had supper?" He looked at her out of the corner of his eye.

"All I want."

"Where are you making for now?"

"Home. If you want to come along and forage in the kitchen you can. I can't offer you much—but I think there's a tin of tomato soup and some bread and cheese—perhaps a bit of ham."

"Thanks. I will if you don't mind."

His voice brightened. He's hungry. . . . He stepped out more jauntily with his short, cissyish, sideways-veering gait, one shoulder up, one down.

"Well, I can't walk any more," she said presently. "Get a taxi, will you?"

He hailed one opposite Burlington House. Pain. . . . The lights, the traffic swam and snapped in her head as she waited. *Pain.* . . .

In the taxi she huddled in a corner. After a bit she burst out laughing. "This is a rum start," she said.

"I suppose it is," he said absently. He was leaning forward to watch the clock.

"It's all right, I've got half a crown."

"Though I don't know . . ." he said. "It doesn't seem outstandingly odd to me. Rather pleasant . . .?"

She didn't answer; and presently he noticed that she seemed to have been taken ill.

VIII

SHE turned over and saw him standing by her bed.

"How are you now?" he said.

She said through clenched teeth:

"Pain. . . ."

"Was it you making that noise just now?"

"What noise?"

"Calling out or something. . . ."

"It might have been. There's no cat."

"Where's the pain?"

"In my stomach."

"Got any brandy?"

"No."

"What's wrong, do you suppose?" He looked perplexed, bothered.

"Nothing. I'm very ill." The vice temporarily slackened and she said, "Have you had enough to eat?"

"Yes, thanks. I enjoyed it. Hadn't had any dinner."

"You might fill my hot-water bottle."

"I will. Where is it?"

"Hanging up on a hook behind the kitchen door. . . . Kettle on the stove. . . ."

He trotted off, noiseless, glad to be of use. He was always a good nurse . . . tactful, deft. He poured out my medicine five times a day when I had 'flu, and changed me twice the night my temperature came down with a whizz. I was always seeing him shaking the thermometer. . . .

She heard Ivor moving about below in the kitchen. After a while he came running up.

"Here you are," he said.

She didn't move, and after a startled pause he slipped the bottle between the sheets, stood looking down at her, at a loss, then took up her wrist and felt for the pulse. At the bottom of the pit she had a twinge of amusement, thinking: wrong place, anyway. . . . He said loudly:

"Olivia!"

She heard herself say clearly:

"I'm having a miscarriage."

"Shall I get a doctor?"

"Yes. . . . Quick."

He went hurtling down the stairs. She cried out on a tag-end of breath:

"Don't be long!"

He wouldn't have heard.

From some unknown level deeper than sleep she floated up, and saw Ivor looking down at her.

"Hallo!" she said. "How long have you been away?"

His face altered in relief.

"I don't know. I had to tear up and down streets knocking up people with brass plates. Then I couldn't make him hear."

"Who?"

"The doctor."

"Has he gone?"

"No, he's gone down to his car for something."

"What's he been doing?"

"He's been holding something under your nose."

"Oh. . . ." That's all, is it? "Well, I'm better." Pain only a faint dying echo. "What time is it?"

The doctor came in rapidly, carrying a small case. He had a black beard trimmed to a point, and steel-rimmed pince-nez. A beard—good gracious! . . . She smiled winningly. He put an arm under her head, gave her something in a medicine glass, laid her back. Sal volatile again. This time I'll keep it down and that's just the difference.

"I'm all right now."

He took her pulse.

"Well, young lady," he said, "you gave your husband a fright."

"Sorry."

She caught Ivor's eye; they exchanged rather sheepish smiles.

"She'll be all right now," he said to Ivor.

"I bathed too long yesterday. I must have caught a chill."

"You must be more careful at these times," he said severely, refusing to be melted. "Athleticism is all very well, but you young women should have more sense. If you're not more careful you'll ruin your health."

"I know," she said meekly. "I will be."

When she looked at him she wanted to laugh. He'd got out of bed in a hurry, and one long pointed prawn's-whisker eyebrow was pushed rakishly over one eye. He had a stiff collar on, but no tie or waistcoat, and this informality combined with his beard, glasses, black suit and paunch, gave him an invented appearance, like the distressed bourgeois character in a Rene Clair film. He looked far from young: a locum probably, unearthed from his retirement. What a shame to get him out of bed.

"I'm terribly sorry to have dragged you out," she said. "I feel an awful fraud."

She couldn't stop smiling. Serenely, weakly, she floated at her ease in the pellucid element of resurrection.

"Don't worry about that," he said, less grudging. "All in the day's work. Any pain now?"

"Just a niggle only."

"These will help." He took a pill-box from his case, and sent Ivor for a glass of water. Directly Ivor was gone, he said evenly, rearranging and closing his case with slow rather fumbling movements:

"You haven't been taking anything, have you?"

"Oh, *no*. . . ."

Too quick, too emphatic, understanding too well. . . . But he was old, tired, he wanted to get back to bed. All he said was:

"That's right. Never monkey about with yourself. Your heart seems a bit flabby. Been overdoing it?"

"I have been doing a good deal lately. I've had to be very busy. . . ."

"How long have you been married?"

"Not very long——"

"You'll want children later——"

"Oh, yes."

"Well, don't be foolish. Don't overstrain yourself. You can't play about too much with Nature without paying for it."

Been hearing a lot lately about Nature's character: nothing to her credit. . . . more spiteful than God. . . .

Ivor had come back with the water. She swallowed the pill. The doctor said:

"Give her another of these in four hours' time if the pain goes on. She'd better stay where she is for a few days. Keep quiet and eat plenty of nourishing food. You're thin. Been going in for this slimming craze?"

"No. It's just natural. . . ." It's no good, he doesn't like me. . . .

"Well, don't. If you want me to look in again, give me a ring."

"Thank you so much. I don't expect it will be necessary."

Ivor started to follow him out; she pointed violently towards her handbag on the dressing-table.

"Pay him," she whispered.

Swiftly he took out the notecase and ran downstairs after the doctor.

"Well, that's that." Ivor came back and sat himself down in the little oak arm-chair. He stroked his hair back into position. He was always very particular about the set of his thick soft wavy dark hair.

"I'm sorry, Ivor. I've been a hellish nuisance."

He said cheerfully:

"That's all right. Rather a good thing on the whole I ran into you, wasn't it?"

"It certainly was. . . ." She added casually. "What did you tell him?"

"I said you had a pain."

"You didn't say anything else . . . ?"

"No, I didn't."

"I seem to remember yelling out something in a mad way. . . ."

"Yes, you did. I didn't know what to make of that, so I left it alone."

He spoke apparently with perfect simplicity, incuriosity. Typical.

"I suppose you said I was your wife."

"Well, yes. It seemed less trouble than stating the exact position. Besides, it's true, I presume, isn't it?"

"I suppose it is."

They laughed.

"His *beard*," she said. "I thought I must be dreaming."

"I know. Superb."

"I should have thought a beard like that would interfere with his practice."

"Not in his heyday—I dare say it was an asset."

"It's very odd: he's *exactly*—in every respect—how I always imagined Dr. Fell."

They laughed again.

"Comfy?" he said.

"Yes, thanks."

"I think I'll sit up here for a bit in case you want anything, and read the paper. If I'm not in your way."

"Not a bit."

"I bought it hours ago and I was going to take it home to read in bed." He pulled the *Evening Standard* out of his pocket.

"Where are you staying?"

"Well, Marda's lent me her flat for a week or so—just till I can find something of my own. She's still abroad."

Scenting danger, he rapidly unfolded his paper, and concealed himself behind it.

"Move the light if you like. . . ." It's not for me to pry into his parasitic little arrangements.

He turned his chair round, pulled the lamp—Anna's lamp that always amused Rollo—closer to him, tilting up its shade.

"Anna do this?" he said.

"M'm."

"Rather witty. . . ." He jerked his head in the direction of the Park chairs picture. "Not unpleasant to see that again. It doesn't wear too badly." He screwed up his eyes professionally.

"I like it still. I always shall. Partly for the wrong reasons, I suspect—literary ones. And then it helps me to preserve the line of continuity. . . ." She closed her eyes, sighed with fatigue. "Which is sometimes hard to hang on to when one looks back. . . ."

She fell into a light doze, thinking of Rollo: nebulous thoughts and images, not sad. Ivor sat quietly, reading, rustling the paper now and then.

"Mind a pipe?" he said presently.

She woke up and said no.

He lit it. The first whiff she caught smelt odd—not quite right yet, but not nauseating. The sickness is over. I shan't be sick any more. I can go about anywhere, talk to people, look at them with nothing to hide, eat, drink, smoke. Oh . . . how wonderful! It's over. . . . Really the things one goes through. . . . But it's over. I always just manage somehow. . . . Lucky Livia. . . . I can be human and have thoughts again. My face will come back, I'll get a new frock with the money left over, to look pretty for Rollo. . . .

She turned her head towards Ivor. There he sat again, puffing at his pipe: clenching it between his side teeth, occasionally stretching his mouth and drawing in a hissing breath, exactly as he always used to. . . . She studied his profile. Oh,

Ivor, you've changed, how sad! . . . The lines of nose and lips had coarsened, the sweetness was gone. There was a fold of flabby flesh beneath the soft, full curve of his chin. . . . Did he drink? What's going to happen to him?

She dozed again. When she reopened her eyes, Ivor's head was sunk on his chest. She stirred and he roused himself, started up.

"How d'you feel?" he said half-mechanically, confused with drowsiness.

"Grand. That pill seems to have done the trick. I wonder what it was. I should have thought he'd set himself against any form of female alleviation. . . . What time is it?"

"Two o'clock."

"I'm hungry." Ravenous: not the morbid lugubrious craving, but real fresh elementary hunger. "I could eat the *Evening Standard*."

He jumped to his feet, alert, excited.

"I could do with a bite myself. Shall I make some chocolate? I saw the tin."

"Hot chocolate! Oh, yes, and there's some milk." She had bought a pint on the way back from the purple room that afternoon, vaguely conjecturing she might be glad of a hot drink in the night. "But that won't be enough." She sat up straight in bed. "I want something solid. I tell you what —a mixed grill—— Oh!" She yearned at the thought of it. "Is there *nothing* in this blinking house? Some bread, I suppose. . . . Would any shops be open?" *Fool* not to have replenished the wretched store cupboard, got in eggs, bacon, cream, every sort of thing.

"I know what I did see: a tin of beans."

"Baked beans!—are you sure?"

"Yes—alongside the soup."

"And I never knew! Oh, God bless Mrs. Banks! She always has one in reserve for when Etty goes to bed early with a tray. It's Etty's favourite delicacy. Baked beans would be *perfect*." She laughed with excitement. "Do hurry, there's a good chap."

"I'll be as quick as I can."

Off he trotted, delighted; a midnight spread! . . . He's awfully willing and domesticated. He'd be happy if he could live like this always: with someone or other for company—someone just in practical control but shelved as an exacting aggressive individual—someone being agreeable, not picking on him. He'd be a treasure to a lady invalid with cultured tastes. He'd push her chair round and round the garden, and take an interest in the bulbs, and they'd have hot scones for tea.

He came back with a loaded tray.

"I made myself a cup, too, while I was about it," he said.

"Good. Have a few beans as well—just a few."

"Well, I don't mind if I do."

"Go on."

Perhaps he also had days of lean fare to make up for. But he was always greedy. She recalled his questing eye over other people's tables; his furtive glance round always, as the next course came in.

He had arranged the beans nicely on squares of toast: a tempting dish. The chocolate was rich, steaming hot. Oh, good, *good*! . . . Moment of sharpest pleasure of my life.

"Sorry there's no beer," she said.

"I prefer chocolate," he said simply.

"What was the name of the man who did the detective in the film to-night? I've never seen him before."

"Harry Wallace? You must have."

"He's jolly attractive. The girl was good too—hideous figure, but good. I call it the phenomenon of the age—the brilliance of the acting in these wise-cracking American tough pictures."

They chatted about films.

She finished her drink, lay down again. She began to whistle, repetitively, rather flat, lackadaisically: *We won't go home till morning*. . . . Not getting further than the second line. . . .

"We'd better go to sleep now," she said after a bit. "Where do you propose to extend your limbs?"

"Anywhere you like," he said amenably. "I can sleep anywhere."

"I know you can. There's Etty's bed. I suppose you could have that. Only it isn't made up or anything."

"I don't mind sleeping in blankets. I'll hop off back to the flat if you'd rather, but I think I'd better stay in case you want anything."

"I shan't—but all right."

Impossible not to be ungracious. He was so jaunty, so unaware of undercurrents. He's lit on a free lodging, he'll dig himself in, I know he will. . . . He'll hog away in Etty's bed all to-morrow unless I kick him out. . . . Remembering his capacity for leaden sleep stirred up an old wave of exasperation.

"You can stay just to-night," she said, turning over, composing herself for sleep. "The maid'll be back to-morrow or the day after to clean up against Etty's return, and I don't want her to find me harbouring you. She's a tigress about Etty's belongings—she'd send for the police. Mind you take your shoes off and don't knock your pipe out on the electric fire or anything."

He said amiably:

"I won't. Good-night."

"Good-night."

Contrary to expectations, he appeared by her bedside before ten—just as she began to wake up. He must have made a terrific effort: must have had me on his mind.

"How are you?"

"Very well." Exhausted, peaceful, clear-headed.

In the light of the morning, he looked a trifle squalid—unshaven, pale, swollen-lidded.

"I'm hungry," she said.

"So am I."

She gave him money and sent him out to buy coffee, rolls, eggs, marmalade, butter.

About eleven he brought up a delicious meal on two trays. They ate it, in silence, concentrating on food.

He went out for a walk and she slept again.

The day trickled by, languid, animal—sleeping, eating.

It was evening again.

"I've been trying all day to find Brian," he said, sitting in the oak arm-chair, lighting a pipe. "He more or less promised he'd run me down to see Halkin."

"Who's Brian?"

"Carruthers. You remember. . . ."

"Oh, *him*. . . . D'you still see that lot?"

"What lot?" His voice was stubborn. She made no answer, and, deciding not to press the point, he went on placidly. "I thought he might be in the old Café. He often is. I looked in about lunch-time and again about six, but I couldn't spot him."

"Perhaps you ought to look in again."

"I might. . . . a bit later perhaps. He often turns up about midnight."

He sat and smoked his pipe.

"Do you ever write poetry now?" she said presently.

"Now and then." He sounded evasive. "I did a thing last year—a sort of satire. Marda liked it. I showed the beginning of it to Beckett Adye—he liked it very much. He said when I finished it he'd publish it, but you know he's left the *Clarion*. It was rather bad luck. I've been meaning to polish it off and send it to *New Poetry*. . . . Don't know if they'd take it."

"Do try. I'd like to read it." He might write quite a good small-scale satire. He had some wit, and a shrewd detached turn of his own.

"I'll send it along to you to look at when I've finished it," he said, looking pleased. "I wouldn't mind having your opinion."

He unfolded his *Evening Standard*.

"This is a curious situation," she said, after a long silence.

"What?" he said, looking over the top of his paper. "You mean us being here?"

"M'm."

"Rather amusing, isn't it? Still, I don't see why not, do you? I mean—we never quarrelled or anything, did we?"

"No, we never quarrelled."

"I don't really see any reason why we shouldn't occasionally see each other, do you? As a matter of fact, I've often felt I'd like to ring you up, or drop in. . . . I didn't quite like to."

His manner was wary, tentative, waiting for a lead.

"Well—it's a bit squalid, the whole thing, really." She whistled a few vague rather dreary bars. "It would be best as a satire. . . ."

Everything seemed to be on a knavish, rotten level. The seamy side. . . . Reaction, I suppose. Him turning up again, cool, unperturbed, to cap it all. . . . As if the past we shared wasn't worth, to either of us, even one moment's tremulousness, tenderness, remorse. . . . There is no health in us.

Ignoring or missing any implication, he added:

"I presumed, of course, you were perfectly friendly disposed——"

"Of course, Ivor."

"Still, one feels a bit chary of butting in."

A marvel he hadn't done so on one of Rollo's nights. . . . He puffed away at his pipe. Presently he said, looking at her obliquely, a funny look:

"Marda's always asking me why I don't get a divorce."

"Has she asked you lately?"

"Well, not very lately. Last year she was always on about it. I remained non-committal. It didn't appear to me to be really her business."

Still the edge of cautious propitiatory inquiry . . . combined now with a most peculiar hollow pomposity: like a parliamentary candidate attempting a declaration of policy upon a subject insufficiently studied and of no interest to him: yet upon which a strong opinion is obviously expected of him.

"I suppose she wants to make it her business."

"She seems to think I ought to be free . . ." he said dubiously.

"Oh, she does, does she? Does she propose to marry you?"

"I'm not sure."

"Do you want to marry her?"

His mouth dropped slightly open. He looked perfectly blank.

"I don't altogether think I do," he said at last.

"I wouldn't. It's not my business in the slightest degree, but honestly I wouldn't."

"No, I don't think I will." She detected relief; though his manner continued lofty and judicial.

"She's too old, Ivor. I don't mean that's necessarily fatal, but I think in this case it might be. Besides, that black varnished fringe would get on your nerves. I don't mean to be rude. . . ."

"No, no, I know." He brooded. "She's an intelligent woman, you know. Got a mind like a man's. . . . Sympathetic too. She was awfully kind after——"

"After what?"

"Well, the bereavement," he said, embarrassed, jocular. "You know—Mamma. . . ."

"Your mother?"

"Yes. She died nearly a year ago. November last to be precise. You didn't know then?"

"Good God! I'd no idea." She broke out into a sweat. I can't stand shocks in my weak state. . . .

"Well, I thought if it *had* happened to catch your eye you'd probably have written me a line. . . . As a matter of fact, I nearly wrote to you—just to let you know—but then I thought I wouldn't bother you."

"I'd like to have known."

Might have been spared some bad, guilty dreams. . . . Or would the dreams go on just the same, till I die too? . . . Last November: about the time it started with Rollo. . . . She remembered the conversation at Meldon about mothers-in-law: "Has yours passed away?" "Far from it. . . ."

"I'm so sorry, Ivor."

"It was pretty bloody," he admitted, sheepish. "She didn't have too pleasant a time. Cancer."

"You were living with her, weren't you?"

"Yes," he said in the familiar defensive-aggressive way. "She took a little flat in Knightsbridge after—after we separated. I had my own room—quite independent, but of course it wasn't an ideal arrangement from my point of view. Still, it seemed the easiest thing to do for the moment. . . . I'm afraid she didn't particularly like living in London. She was lonely . . . though I tried . . ." His voice trailed off, flat, dejected. . . .

All at once Ivor's mother lost her power, her venom; appeared as one of hundreds of harmless elderly middle-class widows dying with resignation of cancer. . . . In a minute I shall boo-hoo because I was a beast to her and she hated me and we weren't reconciled on her deathbed.

"She loathed me," she said shakily. An enemy's death is simply awful.

Troubled, at a loss, he drummed on the arms of his chair, looking blank.

"She never mentioned you afterwards," he finally ventured, uncertain. "She knew I wouldn't stand for any—well—you know what she was—attacks." He added resolutely: "I made her understand that once and for all, the first time she started."

"That was nice of you." More than I did for him. . . .

"She wasn't an outstandingly rational woman." He relit his pipe. "As you know, I was the only person who counted. I dare say that didn't do *me* much good. Still . . ."

"I'm glad you had Marda."

"Yes, it was something," he said meditatively.

Ivor an orphan. . . . It wasn't quite suitable. Somebody ought to be responsible. But somebody would be; he'd be all right; if not Marda, another mother. The world was packed

with them. He was tenacious and he still had some looks; and
that charm, with its curious, cold, somehow diminutive, somehow abstract flavour.

After a silence he said cautiously:

"What about you—as regards divorce?"

"Oh . . . I don't really mind one way or the other. It seems
perhaps a pointless extravagance—unless one were proposing
to remarry."

"And you're not?"

"No, not at the moment. Had you heard I was?"

"Oh no. . . ."

Had he or not? You could never be sure with Ivor. Might
he be up to some funny business on the sly?—as Kate had once
suggested. He was tricky. A dark horse. If Marda decided on
detectives, and put up the money—would he need much
persuading? She said, her voice rising a semitone:

"I'm afraid I can't oblige with any evidence just at present."
As she said this, she suddenly saw light. "Besides, even if I
could, it would be no go now, would it?"

"How do you mean?"

"Well, you see, we've just spent a night under the same
roof. That's what's known as condoning, I believe. You've
condoned anything I might have done up till now."

"Oh, have I?" he said simply. "I see."

"With Dr. Fell as witness."

"That's torn it, then," he said . . . humorously? . . . His
face was totally expressionless, as it frequently was. You
couldn't quite put anything past Ivor.

"I don't wish to stand in your way," she said.

"You don't," he said. "Not in the least."

He took his pipe out of his mouth and examined the bowl.

"I'd very much rather you didn't tell Marda about last
night," she said.

"No, no, I won't."

"Is she jealous?"

"Apt to be . . . I'd certainly better not mention it."

He could be relied on there, anyway.

He eyed her, looked away again, straight ahead of him. She was conscious of his turning some scheme or other over in his mind. Presently he said:

"I don't know about you, but it seems to me remarkably natural being together again."

"Everything seems to me remarkably natural," she said. "My eye's right out."

"We never got on too badly, did we?"

"Not badly enough, really."

He hesitated: passed that over.

"When two more or less civilised people have roughly the same point of view they ought logically speaking to be able to hit it off."

"The hypothesis seems sound. . . ." She sighed. "But I feel there's a flaw."

Puffing away, looking perfectly blankly towards the opposite wall, he said:

"What would you say to another shot?"

"What, you and me?"

"Yes." She was silent, and he went on, warming to the proposition, "I take it you're more or less a free agent. . . . We might try it out, anyway. Of course, it would cause a certain amount of back-chat and gossip, but I don't suppose either of us minds that. I'll get this job—at least I see no reason why I shouldn't. . . . I ought to get quite a decent screw—these film people are rolling. And I suppose you've got just a bit. It wouldn't be penury like the last time—that's what got us down, to my mind. . . . What about it?"

She said painfully, apologetic but vehement:

"I couldn't, Ivor. Not possibly. You see, I've made my own life. I don't want to change."

"Right," he said immediately, in a hearty voice, not a flicker on his face.

She lay still, feeling upset. Just what I expected. . . .

"Sorry," she said.

He said equably:

"It was merely a suggestion."

What does he see, know, feel? Anything? . . . Impenetrable as agate. . . .

"You'd better go now, Ivor," she said. "I'm afraid you truly can't stay to-night. Mrs. Banks turns up to-morrow at eight. We don't want to be compromised any further, do we?"

"No, rather not." He got up briskly, folded the paper and rammed it into his pocket. "Mind if I take this? I haven't quite finished it."

"No, take it."

He set his hair with careful touches.

"I couldn't touch you for ten bob, I suppose? Just till I get this fixed up. I'm rather low."

"How much do you want?" He saw the notes in my bag.

"Well, if you could make it a couple of quid. . . . I'll pay you back."

"Take them," she said. "Leave me the rest. I may have to live on it for a considerable time."

"There's over two pounds left," he said after inspection, closing the bag.

"I had a little windfall."

"Lucky."

"It was."

"Well, so long. I might look in to-morrow to see how you are."

"I'll be all right. I shall get up to-morrow. Good-night, Ivor. Thank you for all you've done."

"Not at all." He paused by the door. "We might have a meal together occasionally . . . if you're going to be in London."

"I expect I'll be going back to the country soon. Still, we might."

"Good-night."

"Good-night."

When she heard the front door close, she got up and went down to the floor below to remove all traces of his occupation.

The kitchen was beautifully tidy. He'd washed up, hung up the cups, the jug, ranged the plates, put away the food in the cupboard. On Etty's bed the uncovered pillows looked faintly dented and disordered. . . . Oh, the queer little man, he'd lain there all last night, bounded in his stone nutshell. . . . We fell in love, we told ourselves to each other, kissed, shared a narrower bed than this. . . . Unimaginable. What did we tell each other? . . . Surely he wasn't agate then? . . . Have I done something to him? . . .

She plumped up the pillows, smoothed out the blankets and bedspread, went upstairs again and got into bed.

Depressed.

Soon I'll be out of this slough, I'll live again.

The slow blood goes on passing away . . . cleansing me. I shall look at Rollo with clear-washed eyes, I shall see truth.

I shall be washed whiter than snow.

Not next morning, but the one after, just before twelve, he came round. She was packing a suitcase to go down to Kate: Kate surprised, excited, on the telephone, almost emotional in her pleasure. . . . The door bell pinged. Mrs. Banks called huskily up the stairs:

"Expectin' any one?"

"No."

"Well, are you in, or aren't you?"

She slipped down to Etty's room and peeped out through the gold net curtains. There he was on the doorstep, looking down the street, his hands in his coat pockets. She could see his blunt, pale, puppyish profile.

She called down softly:

"Say I've gone away to the country. If he asks for how long, say you don't know."

She heard the front door open, voices, the latch clicking shut again. Now he'd be going away down the street, disappointed, jaunty, feeling snubbed perhaps. . . . Oh, bother!

Presently Mrs. Banks came creaking up.

"'E's gorn," she said. "I don't know what 'e came after. 'E arsked when you'd be back so I told 'im what you told me to. I said would 'e leave his name, but 'e said no, it wasn't of no consequence, 'e'd call again."

"I wonder who it was. . . ."

"Not a bad-lookin' young chap. Long 'air. Ar-tis-tic lookin'—you know. Un'ealthy. I should say 'e suffered from 'is stomach. Or it might be drink." She gave a flick to the lamp with her duster. "Anyway, if 'e does come again 'e does, I suppose." Hoping he will. . . . More inquisitive than usual. Concerned about him. And she's no sentimentalist.

Oh, he'll be all right.

PART FOUR

I

THEY motored down from London in the early afternoon, called at the Dog and Duck for the keys, and drove on to Simon's house.

The moment she opened the door, the new smell met her; not the familiar one of Simon's house—penetrating, exciting somehow, earthy, like ferns or mushrooms—something different—damp, sour, pervasive; something that had taken possession; a threatening smell. . . . She threw back the shutters in the sitting-room, opened the windows. Standing behind her shoulder, Rollo was silent. They looked out at the stretch of lawn, the elms, dry looking, shrivelling up, the pear-tree already shedding pale brown and grey leaves. The weather was dull, gusty, with clouds and wind coming up.

"What's the date?" she said.

"The twenty-fifth of September."

"It's autumn."

"M'm. Depressing idea." He gave a rapid start and shiver, as if suddenly chilled.

"The grass needs mowing. I wonder if I ought to get somebody to see to it."

Extraordinary how neglect could encroach in less than two months. It seemed abnormal. Simon's house had become an empty house. . . . It doesn't feel as if anybody would ever live here again.

"It looked awfully different last time," he said. "That *was* fun that evening, wasn't it, darling?"

"Oh, *wasn't* it fun?"

"This Simon's a myth to me. You all talk about him, and I'm told this is his house, but I don't really believe he exists."

"That's his portrait."

314

He went slowly over to the fireplace and looked at the head of Simon hanging above it. Billy had done it years ago, in black outline, and tones of green and yellow.

"It's not really the kind of portrait I understand, darling, but I'm sure he's a fascinating chap."

"It's exactly like him." She crossed the room and stood beside him and stared up at it. "He's ill," she said.

"Badly?"

"Yes, very badly. Typhoid fever. Still, he's better. I had a card from Anna yesterday—they're in the South of France. She says his temperature's gone down. As soon as he can travel, she's going to bring him here to convalesce."

An exciting thing to look forward to—living in his own house with Simon, helping to look after him, getting to know him better. He would be the necessary, the sufficient focus, the stepping-stone over into autumn. He would shift this deadlock, this meaninglessness. *After he comes, I shall see what to do. . . .*

"Will you be here?" said Rollo, looking away.

"I expect so—for a bit, anyway." The thought of Simon always made him oddly sulky, depressed, suspicious. "It's *some*thing to look forward to." He was silent, staring at the window, his mouth moodily pouting. She added: "But I suppose I must think about trying for another job soon. I'm sure I don't know what."

He looked miserable.

"What shall I do, Rollo? Try for a job in the chorus? Too old—and I can't sing or dance. I might be a mannequin perhaps—if I had any influence. . . . I suppose you don't know any smart society dressmakers with a vacancy?"

Where is the crystal element we were to bathe in without fear? Rollo, look at me! . . . I planned it to be beautiful and simple: a night together in this house where we were once so happy; the last perhaps; but that was to be revealed to us. . . .

"Or I might get a walk-on in a film. I saw Ivor about a

fortnight ago—did I tell you? He seemed to think he was in with some film magnate. He might give me an introduction."

Propped on top of the long, low, yellow-painted bookshelf was a picture of Anna's, unfinished; hay-cart, field, elms, the spire in the distance; a summer landscape. A long time ago, an old story. . . . Will she finish it in the winter? She never can finish things.

He was wandering about all over the room. Restless. Something on his mind.

Remember I love you.

"Rollo darling, if you'd like me to be in London I will be. I needn't be here when they come back. I'd rather be near you than anything, of course. But it's not as if you—as if we managed to be together very often, is it? And I haven't much life of my own in between—now—to fill up." I've given up seeing most people; they all think of me as remote now, under a glass case, not mingling with them. They're bored with me. "At least," she added, "if Anna and Simon weren't there."

But less than a year ago these fragments flowed over from such richness and fullness that no emptiness existed, not one empty cranny.

He went on pacing about, not coming near her.

"Darling, you must do as you like," he said heavily . . . *as if I were badgering him.*

Oh, stop walking about! . . . She straightened herself with a jerk, said briskly:

"Let's go up and open the bedroom windows. Try and get this stuffiness out."

She slipped her hand through his arm as they went upstairs. *Melt, melt, come close, look at me, give me one kiss, then I can speak.*

A high, thin, street-corner soprano started again in her head, going on as if it had all day: *Let our affair—be a gay thing. . . .*

"Oh, my precious," she said rapidly, "I have missed you."

"Have you, darling?" He gripped her close to him for a second. "So have I."

But when they got upstairs he loosened his arm, her hand dropped down . . . or I took it away.

They went first into her bedroom. She threw up the window, looked about her. In the corner was the low, narrow, rather tumble-down bed with its red and white cotton patchwork quilt. She said, smiling:

"We couldn't share it all night with much comfort. You'll have to have the spare room next door."

"I don't mind where I sleep," he said agreeably.

He said that. The accommodating guest.

She said quickly:

"It doesn't seem so stuffy in here."

"No, I don't think it does."

"Why does everything look so bleak? Is it just a mood?"

She leaned her elbows on the window sill and looked out. Anything rather than see this different room with the different person standing in it, dejected, unresponsive; where we stood, in the dark light, that hot afternoon, blind tapping, bees burning in the rosemary. She lowered her eyes to the straggling grey bushes growing under the sitting-room windows. Two blue-tits were threading noiselessly in and out of them, pecking and flitting.

"It's a rotten sort of day," he said. "Liverish, I think."

A peevish weather, hostile to man. . . . I'm back in the blind alley again, where the fresh air can't blow; where vagrants nose in the dust-bins, drag out the cods' heads. . . . What's to be done? How can we stay here?

"What about a walk?" she said, turning round to look at him.

He exclaimed under his breath, took a sudden step towards her, and said:

"Why are you pale?"

"Am I? I'm always pale."

"No . . . you're different."

"I'm sorry I don't look pretty for you." She rubbed her cheeks, laughed shakily. "I meant to . . . I haven't been feeling too lively."

She felt him stiffen, refusing a demand on sympathy—suspecting blame attached.

"But you're all right now, aren't you?"

"Oh, yes, I'm fine."

"Please to be."

He has enough illness with that creature. . . .

"Everybody seems to be a bit sickly. It's a sign of the times."

"Oh, don't be biblical!" he said plaintive, irritable. "I can't bear that sort of thing."

An ordinary plain-thinking chap. . . . She laughed briefly, saying:

"*You're* all right, anyway, aren't you? You haven't lost your Austrian tan. I suppose all the open air you've had since ground it in nicely."

"Yes, I feel remarkably fit, I must say. I've had a jolly good summer, really . . ." He broke off, added, "As regards——" Stopped uncertainly.

"Look," she said. "You can just see the river. I don't think we'll walk that way, though, do you? It looks so chilly."

"It does, rather."

"Do you remember that night on the mountains when you could smell water?"

She smiled at him.

"Yes." He smiled too; put his arm round her. "That was a lovely night, wasn't it, darling?"

He aims at tenderness. . . . They leaned together. Now . . . Rollo, don't go away again. She tried to speak. Rollo, listen. . . . Her throat closed, aching. Not a word would come. He gave her a little pat and dropped his arm again. Lady Spencer who had momentarily dwindled, presided once more, as she had all day. . . . He didn't let me know he was back for nearly a week.

"Shall I make a fire in the sitting-room? That would make it perk up, wouldn't it?"

He loved a blazing fire.

"Olivia . . ." He looked round the room, as if trapped. "Let's not stay here."

"All right," she said quickly, quickly. "D'you mean—go back to London?" A pit seemed to open in her diaphragm.

"No. No. I want us to be together. At least if you do. Only not here. It's so incredibly uncheerful. There's something wrong with it."

"How do you mean wrong?" He feels it too, then. . . . But it's nonsense—Simon's getting better.

"It's got a funny sort of feeling, hasn't it? I noticed it before—a sort of feeling I wouldn't like to be alone in it. I suppose it's all bunk, but one does get like that sometimes about places. I'm sorry, darling, if it's a disappointment. Let's go somewhere not gloomy. D'you mind?"

"Where would you like to go?"

"I can't think of anywhere. Can you?"

"No. I can't think of anywhere not gloomy."

She began closing the shutters.

"What about that little pub place where we went and had drinks that night—where that German chap sang? That seemed nice, didn't it? Shall we go and see what it looks like to-day?"

"The Wreath of May," she said. "Yes, it seemed cosy. All right, let's try there."

She fastened the green wooden shutters. The little square room sank into sad monochrome. They went downstairs, locked up the house, went out. The car was under the chestnut trees by the pond.

"That's not a very appetising bit of water," he said.

They got in, backed and drove away down the rutty track. She looked back. It was a small white house with green shutters and a leaded roof, set in a piece of neglected lawn: dismal, unwelcoming. Nothing special about it except the ragged thorn hedge all round. The shrine was broken, the genius had departed.

There was nobody about at the Wreath of May. They went into the garden by the wooden gate. Ghosts of the summer evening haunted her: motor bikes roaring up, stopping, roaring away again, the groups beneath the apple trees, the cheerful, loud, male voices from the bar. Now all was deserted. There was a ladder set up against the apple tree, three or four mongrel chickens pecking in the damp grass, a blue-painted, peeling garden table with a pool of wet on it; still a few roses on the neat standard bushes. She looked across the hedge at the tall plantation of poplars, alders and willows growing all together—where the owl had flown out; and Colin held forth about trees. . . . When she looked at the house, she noticed things she hadn't noticed before: only one wing was old, the rest was shoddy pseudo-old-world, with thin, poor thatching. Rollo pulled open a glass-panelled garden door in the side of the old wing, and stooping they went into a dark musty parlour with thick sagging beams in the low ceiling. He was just able to stand upright on the hearth.

"But I couldn't anywhere else," he said. "Look."

He went and stood under the middle beam, his head bowed; he seemed to be bearing the weight of the ceiling on his nape. They laughed.

"What a smell! . . . Damp? Mice?"

He strolled about with his head down, set a tiny child's rocking-chair rocking, tapped on the oak panelling.

"Seems solid," he said. "Fearfully old, I suppose. Shall we have tea, darling?"

"I don't think tea would be very nice here, do you?"

"Plenty of seating accommodation, anyway."

The tenebrous space was choked up with hard-looking brown arm-chairs; probably a cheap lot bought up all together in a sale. He pulled two forward in front of the fireplace. A sallow, thin woman wearing a white blouse and a choker of large pink pearl beads appeared suddenly in the doorway from the garden, looking startled and suspicious.

"Do you want anything?" she said.

"Bring me twenty Player's, would you, please?" he said in his easy take-your-orders way. "And I'd like this fire lit."

She looked stubborn, hostile.

"We don't generally light fires at this time of year. Not unless visitors ask specially."

"I am asking specially," he said slightly raising his voice. "Will you please have this fire lit? We may be staying the night or we may not."

Without another word she disappeared. Now we've antagonised her. A horrid beginning.

"Bloody woman," he said. "God, these British inn-keepers. . . ."

Presently a large plump country wench in bedraggled black uniform and cap appeared from another door with cigarettes. She knelt down, put a match to the sticks, blew on it, her hips and haunches swelling out immense as she bent forward. When she got up again, Olivia said, smiling at her: "Thank you so much." Somebody here must be on our side. . . .

She said huskily in broad Oxfordshire:

"Please would you like tea?"

"No, thank you."

She continued ploddingly, carrying out instructions:

"Please, will you be taking dinner?"

"What could you give us if we did?" said Rollo, amused.

"Don't know, sir."

"Could you catch us some nice trout?"

"No, sir." She began to wriggle and squirm, her face congested, dementedly coy. "She says you can 'ave a chicking roasted if you arst now," she whispered.

"We'll stay for dinner," said Rollo, lighting a cigarette.

"Shall we, darling? We'll have a chicken. Mind it's a nice fat one."

She vanished with a sidelong lurch.

Olivia met his smiling eye, and smiled. He'd had to win over the girl, to right the balance. He must have friends around him, devotion, eager service.

The fire burned up brightly. He put on a few lumps of coal from the scuttle.

"This isn't too bad, is it, darling?" he said. "We'll have a drink soon."

They could hear the girl loudly singing and stumping about in some room the other side of the wall. He got up and locked the garden door, drew a short checked cotton curtain across the glass, opened a narrow inside door, saw that it led into a brick-paved bit of passage, shut it again.

"There," he said. "If anybody wants to come in they'll have to come that way and we'll hear their fairy footfall."

He came back, sat down, pulled her out of her chair on to his knee.

"Oh, darling, this is nice," he said, sighing. He began to kiss her.

Was it all to be as before then, after all? Dismissing, agreeing, accepting . . . the apt, familiar, responsive bodies smoothing all out, lubricating the stiff opposing heads? . . . Would the block of misery begin to dissolve into rich slackness, to drain away like noiseless smooth dark water into a tunnel? . . . All as before, the recipe unfailing, as before. . . . She murmured:

"Rollo, there's so much to say."

"Don't say it now."

"You do know what a lot there is to say?"

He sighed. "Yes," burying his face against her breast. "Perhaps. . . . Is there? I don't know. Oh, darling, I have wanted you."

But presently he stopped kissing her. My fault, I can't. . . . She slid down from his knee on to the dirty black wool rug in front of the fire, fed the flames with another coal or two.

He felt in his pocket and drew out a little box.

"Darling, I saw this somewhere yesterday. I thought you might fancy it. . . ."

It was a platinum bracelet watch with a minute oblong face set in diamonds.

"Oh, how exquisite!" another present for Nicola. "Rollo, you shouldn't . . ."

"You haven't got one, have you, darling?"

"No, indeed." She slipped it on. "It's much too grand for me. I don't know myself."

"Don't be silly."

She stared at it, elegant and expensive on her wrist. What would this have fetched? . . .

"Is it a good-bye present?" she said, staring.

"What do you mean?" His voice was flat, guarded.

"I don't know—it looks like one. . . ." But she laughed quickly, as if laughing off a foolish slip of the tongue. It wasn't the right way to begin.

"Now," she said, "I'll tell you the time by my beautiful new watch. It's just on six. What about a drink? You go and have one—and bring me one back. A gin and lime. Double."

He got up and unlocked the door, and went away.

She sat on by the fire, and was clear in her mind.

We mustn't remember *Remember I love you*—we mustn't speak on that scale. When we were in that world we were not in the world. When he spoke such truth, under the chestnuts at the Gasthaus table, standing by the lake-watching window, seeing light and water mingle, then he was not true to himself. We all say things at times we don't mean: or even if we mean, can never manage to adapt to our fixed arrangements: unwieldy shapes, looming too large, impracticable, best put away entirely. . . . It would be a shame to hold him to all that. We must face facts: he was beyond himself: we were translated. Life in the world is what must go on; not that other life. If we went back we wouldn't find the rocket, but the sodden end of burnt-out stick.

He's an ordinary chap, he insists, and he likes a quiet life. He's afraid of me now, because I had a victory. I got too far . . . like taking advantage of a person when he's drunk. He's been thinking the best thing to do is to avoid me for a bit, till things have settled down. *All be as before love* . . .

Perhaps an evening, even a night, together now and then, when it's not too difficult. Because that's turned out a most satisfactory arrangement. . . .

We don't live by lakes and under clipped chestnuts, but in the streets where the eyes, ambushed, come out on stalks as we pass; in the illicit rooms where eyes are glued to keyholes.

Well, that's how it is.

Lady Spencer, your son. . . . I mustn't let you down.

He came back with a whisky and soda in one hand and her drink in the other. He looked much more lively.

"Sorry I've been so long, darling. There was a comic commercial traveller bloke in the bar, and we had one together. Funny life these chaps have—rather interesting—I wouldn't mind it at all. . . . The old girl's quite amiable now. Once she got a double gin inside her she cheered up no end. She's not so bad, really." Genial, expansive patronage. . . . Why not be jolly? "Drink up your little drink, darling, and have another. You'll feel better."

He sat down, leaned forward to stroke her cheek and neck. Presently he said, coaxingly: "We *were* morbid this afternoon, weren't we, darling? I was in rotten form—I'm so sorry. Fancy spoiling our first time together after such ages. . . . What do you say to staying here? Let's! I slipped upstairs just now and had a peep into one or two bedrooms. They might be a lot worse."

"Oh, good. Let's stay then."

It was all to be as before. Leave out one or two moments of recklessness and indiscretion and carry straight on. . . .

She sipped her drink.

"I like this funny room," he said. "What a lot of funny rooms we've been in together, haven't we, darling?"

"Yes. . . . The unlikely fires we've lit! . . . Do you realise it's nearly a year?"

They began to say do you remember—remembering the first week-end, the night of Cochran's revue, other times: not the lake and the chestnuts. She moved closer, clung against his knee. . . .

Everything's all right, what was the fuss about?

"How's your father, Rollo?"

His smile faded, he looked troubled.

"Oh, poor Daddy—he's no better. He's having injections and things, but they can't cure him. If he'd let 'em operate six months ago he might have had a chance, but he wouldn't. And now they can't, his heart's too dicky. They've been in London."

"Oh, have they? For treatment, I suppose."

"Yes. I lent them the house while we were away. But he wanted to get back to Meldon, so they've gone. He's restless."

"Your poor mother."

"Yes, isn't it wretched for her? She's marvellous of course." He brooded. "You ought to have looked them up—they'd have been pleased. You were always a favourite."

Look them up! . . . Take it easy; keep things comfortable all round; what people don't know about can't worry them. Cover your tracks and what's the harm in anything? It's a little deception here, a little there, that makes the world go round.

"I couldn't see them now. I can't keep things separate like you. I suppose I've got a worse conscience. I should want to break down and confess all." She added vehemently, emotionally, "I'll never see them again—never!"

So be off with you, Lady Spencer, Goddess of Morality, sententious, interfering old woman. . . . Don't you listen to this—this is between somebody you don't understand—as usual—and another person you know nothing about. If you only knew what I'm going to tell him. . . .

He had glanced at her, startled, saying mildly: ·"All right, darling." He put his fingers through her hair, lifting it lightly back, caressing her. She buried her eyes against his thigh.

"Rollo, darling, shall I tell you what happened?"

He'll be so tender, so sorry for me; think me so brave. We shall be so close. . . . Nobody was as good as he at comforting words.

She began to tell him about what had happened.

He seemed too dumbfounded, too appalled to speak; that is, except for exclaiming "God!" under his breath, again and again.

"But it's all right now. It's over . . ." She caught him by the arm, insisting, trying to make him look at her.

"Why didn't you tell me . . ." he said at last. But not reproachfully, with indignant love and distress for keeping herself from him, not allowing him to help, to share; more as if—yes, as if trying to suppress the extreme of revulsion and dismay. And quickly he took away his hands.

"You seemed so far away," she said, panic-stricken, struggling for words to explain, to put it right for him. "I couldn't get near you. After a bit—almost at once really—I felt so awful—I didn't want you to see me like that. And then I got into the state where you *can't* make any effort, not even to write a letter. The only thing that mattered was to get through each day somehow and go to sleep again. And of course not to let anybody know. . . ."

"*Does* anybody know?"

"Not a soul—except the man who did it. I didn't see anybody at all, so as to make sure. I lived in a wilderness—on a desert island. . . ."

"Christ!" He propped his head on his hands, ruffled his hair up wildly. "Was he awful? Didn't he want the hell of a packet? They always do, don't they?"

"It wasn't too bad. I had enough. I borrowed a little from Kate. . . ."

"You should have let me—you must let me pay for it. . . ."

"No, no! Don't let's *think* about it even any more."

"Please! For God's sake! Surely it's the least——"

She cried, stopping her ears:

"*You did!* . . . I sold your ring."

He was silent at that, then said quietly:

"What, the emerald?"

"Yes." She burst into tears. "I'm sorry. I did mind. What could I do? I couldn't go on. He sprang it on me—I had to find the money at once. I couldn't write to you for it—I've never asked you for . . . And I couldn't explain why in a letter, I couldn't. I couldn't bear to bother you. I thought I'd better get through it by myself as quick as possible. Because you see, I *knew* . . . it was no good—we couldn't have it. . . . You'd never—you always said never, it wouldn't do. . . . I *knew*. . . . I thought—well, it'll make it a little better to do it by myself —it'll redeem it a little—because *I'm* the one to mind—I wanted it. . . . You didn't. For you it would be just a tiresome mistake, but for me it was a grief . . . so I must bear it by myself. I told myself—all through the worst, it was for *you*. . . . I said your name. That helped. Something to do for you. Not sordidly getting rid of something not wanted. Oh, I *did*! I did want it. I wish I'd never told you now. I'm sorry about the ring. I minded too. And I'm sure I didn't get nearly enough . . ."

"Hush! *Stop!*" He took her by the shoulders and shook her, not roughly, but not gently. "As if it mattered about the blasted ring. I'm glad it's gone—if it was some use. . . . Only it's the idea of you——" His voice failed. ". . . Going through that by yourself. . . . I feel such a——"

"You needn't feel anything—anything. It's finished."

"But are you sure you're all right?"

"Quite all right." She dried her eyes, blew her nose. The storm of tears had eased her, and she felt calm now, clear-headed. "Perhaps it wasn't quite like I said. I didn't mind with the whole of me at the time—far from it. My chief idea was to stop being sick—and the *relief* when I did! It's really since—I've never stopped minding—and longing for it. I suppose it's Dame Nature's revenge; one's body cheated. . . ."

"What a shame," he said helplessly. "Oh, darling, what bad luck."

"Sometimes I laid the craziest plans for going through with it—going away somewhere abroad to have it, and then coming back in a year and presenting you with the finished article. I thought you'd get such a thrill when you saw it, you'd be glad after all, you'd . . . I don't know. I suppose it would never have worked out."

He shook his head slightly, plunged it in his hands again, drew in his breath.

"I don't honestly think it would. I'm rather glad you didn't. . . . I should have been awfully——"

An extraordinary sound burst out of him—a kind of groan —almost a laugh.

"I know it was a wonderful ring—but I didn't love it like this one." She turned the cat's eye on her little finger. "As long as I've got this. . . . This is our ring, isn't it?"

He smiled briefly, took up her hand and kissed it, let it fall again. He said nothing.

Steps sounded on the brick passage. The woman in the white blouse came in, amiably smiling, carrying an oil lamp with a white glass shade. She set it down on the table in the middle of some green plush and woollen fringe, and struck a match.

"Thought this would brighten things up a bit," she said. "It does get late early and no mistake, as the saying goes. This room's no artist's studio when it comes to light at the best of times. Still, visitors seem to like it. It's old, you know— genuine—that's what appeals to them. That's why we didn't have the electric light put in this part—more in keeping like. I don't care for antiques myself—can't see the point. You don't go to make a show of a lot of senile old crocks in bath-chairs, so why anything else old? It doesn't make sense to me." She uttered a high, harsh thrill of laughter. "Oh, dear! Winter's coming on. I'm rheumaticky already. Last year we had the floods right up the garden. It's enough to give any one the pip. . . . There! Quite comfy? Fire all right? What time d'you want your dinner? Eight? Righty-ho."

He suggested a stroll before supper, and they walked arm in arm along the willow-bordered road as far as the lock. They leaned over the parapet of the bridge and watched the weir plunge dizzily and boil below them. The sound of it bemused them, breathing its eternal monotone into the noise of the wind and the rainy murmur of the poplars behind the lock-keeper's cottage.

"Why is water so fascinating?" he said. "I could watch it for ever."

They said it would be nice to be a lock-keeper. They admired the old bridge of rose-coloured brick with its long smooth-curving span and Gothic arches. They strolled back again, down through the inn garden beneath a straggling pergola to the bank of the river, where there was a raft, and a skiff tied up, and a punt with a green canvas shelter over it. On the farther bank, opposite them, the bank rose abruptly into broken knolls clothed with woods and crowned with a square grey church tower: an un-English looking outline. With sunset a deep glow had come into the sky. Dark fire-fringed masses of cloud raced along the west, splitting around a perilous intense green core of light. Earth, sky and water reflected one another in one unifying, clear, liquid element. A short way out a fleet of white ducks lay at anchor, bobbing and dipping with soft, creaking, gossiping noises. Two swans sailed out round the bend heading for the middle of the river, taking the full, living and dying, light-and-wind-shaken, mid-stream current with round full breasts of peace. They stood on the bank watching the swans float away downstream.

"Look!"

It was seeing too much. She turned away her head and looked at him instead.

What's to come next?

Oh, I see! . . . An illumination went through her, sharp, piercing and gone again; what I've been waiting for. All the pieces fell together . . . like the broken-up bits in James's kaleidoscope we used to look through, exclaiming at the patterns.

"Oh, I see. . . ."

She was scarcely aware of saying it aloud until she saw his unconscious lips move, murmuring some vague word of query or endearment.

But it's nothing to do with him. . . . We are born, we die entirely alone; I've seen how it will be. To suffer such dissolution and resurrection in one moment of time was an experience magnificent enough in itself. It was far above the level even of the lake, the chestnuts. It should have no sequel.

Everything went away again. . . . There it is: a fact in the world that must be acted on. . . .

"Look at those creatures," he said presently.

She strolled with him to the fence and looked over. On the step of a thatched cottage an old woman in a black print dress was setting down saucers of milk for three ginger cats.

"I've always wanted a ginger cat."

"Shall I give you one, darling?"

They strolled up again, arm in arm, beneath the ramshackle pergola.

The transfiguring light was gone, and it was dark and cold now, blowing up for rain.

The dining-room was in the new wing: a long, dreary, pallid room with curtains of pink casement cloth, and big tables with white cloths, and a number of palms in stands. It was lit by three electric lamps hanging from the ceiling beneath ornamental orange-tinted shades of bogus marble. Built doubtless to accommodate summer parties from steamers or charabancs, it contained that evening only one other couple, silently masticating at opposite sides of an expanse of table at the farther end. A youngish, flat, pinched pair of weather-beaten holiday makers. The male wore grey flannel trousers and a blazer, the female a royal blue stockinette frock with a crochet neck. Both had long indefinite noses and brownish eyes set close together.

"Campers; out of that punt with the shelter, I bet."

"Come in for a hot meal and a night's lodging, I suppose."

"That means it *must* be going to be a dirty night. I'm sure they're very nearly waterproof."

Tinned apricots followed the stringy, over-roasted chicken, and then a sour and tepid cup of coffee. Afterwards the sallow and now servile woman conducted them to a narrow brittle-looking bedroom with an art frieze of black, blue and orange leaves, and narrow twin beds with orange art bedspreads. The fireplace had a fan of paper in it. It was too meanly proportioned and grudging to hold a fire worth lighting. After she had left them he made a wry face.

"I'm sorry, darling. I must have been tight when I saw it before. The sun was streaming in and it didn't look too bad."

"These beds look a close-fisted respectable pair, I must say. . . . Made for people like those campers. Of all the art specimens this frieze takes the cake. . . ."

"The walls are made of cardboard. The campers are next door, I'm afraid. I saw the chap prancing in with a haver-sack."

"We shall hear them brushing their plates."

"I don't somehow feel we'll hear much else, do you?"

"What do you suppose he says to her?"

Flippancy, foolish jokes had never come easier; she'd made him laugh all through dinner. We're hollow people, and our words are so light and grotesque. . . . Clown's patter. I could always make him laugh. . . . The laugh's on me. . . .

"I *am* sorry it isn't nicer, darling. I feel I've let you in for it."

"Never mind. It doesn't matter."

Because I suppose I shan't sleep here with him, after what's going to be. How, where shall I go? Will I stay out all night somewhere, walk about or lie in a ditch or get a lift in a lorry to London or what? It's all very awkward. It's a cold night. Could he possibly make it unnecessary for me to go away? . . . If only he could. He's so ingenious. . . .

"We'll try and manage to forget about it, won't we, darling?" He put his arm round her. She twisted herself lightly away, moving as if to look at herself in the glass above the dressing-table. He glanced at her. She felt him shrink under the snub, taken aback, puzzled. He's so sensitive in those ways. What's he thinking? "Is she going to turn touchy too? . . ." That look on his face—somebody else caused it long ago, has seen it often. . . . It was so immediate, it must come from an old wound.

"Have you signed the register?" she said brightly, powdering her nose.

"Not yet. Who shall we be this time?" His heaviness lifted; anxious, as always, to be comfortable. . . .

They giggled, remembering or inventing names.

"Shall we go down for a bit by the fire, darling? I've booked the old oak parlour:" Thinking, "She'll soon come round. . . ."

"Oh, good!"

He thought of everything.

The room was overpoweringly close, its former complex smell submerged beneath the single smell of oil lamp. She threw open the garden door and drew the dark plush curtain across. Now if I must I can get out that way. They stood together on the hearth lighting cigarettes. Now it was like the first time, in Etty's house—standing up side by side saying thank you for matches, stubbornly resisting the pressure, like grindstones, that was already irresistibly bearing in on them, forcing them together. Already they couldn't see each other any more; their eyes were blank, too close.

Olivia said:

"Where is she?"

"She's still in the country. But she'll be back morrow."

"How is she?"

He said in his rueful half absent-minded way:

"Well, apparently she's all right now. Never been better. I went down last week-end."

"Some people do feel their best at these times—specially quite often the delicate ones."

He seemed to grow heavier, blanker where he stood; and he kept his eyes fixed on a point above and beyond her head,"

She said:

"She's going to have a baby?"

He said yes, and then it was said. It had long been a fact. There was no change between the moment before and the moment after saying it. Nothing could have been simpler.

"Who told you?" he said.

"Nobody. . . ." Your mother told me clear as a factory whistle. I didn't listen. . . . "When?"

He gave a kind of stifled groan under his breath—as if saying, must we talk about it? . . .

"Sometime next spring. I'm not quite—April, I suppose." Let's see. . . . Last July then. . . .

"But how exciting! I suppose everybody's thrilled . . . all the friends and relations? . . ." Guarding her, cherishing her so carefully now that she was justifying herself: the precious vessel for the heir. Imagine any scandal coming to her ears— at such a time. . . . Unthinkable.

"I suppose so," he said sullenly. "They haven't said much to me."

"I do hope for everybody's sake all will go swimmingly this time." Talking like in a modern play: slick irony: almost enjoying it—feeling nothing. "Let's hope it's a boy."

He turned away. His broad-backed figure blocked the garden exit, the escape. He said:

"How did you guess?"

"Oh. . . . I have visitations, you know. . . . Messengers from the beyond to lay bare mysteries. . . . Voices and great lights."

"Was it when we were down by the river?"

"Yes, it was." So he'd been aware of that much.

"I thought something happened," he said. "I couldn't think what."

Sometimes he did get on to a thing quick like that. . . . Intuitive. . . . Secretive too—not giving a sign. . . .

"I can't explain," she said. "Everything fell together." The moment when the catch slips at last and the jack-in-the-box flies out. "Watching water always makes me psychic. . . . There was a sort of annunciation—by proxy." She laughed. "Most extraordinary. Women do sometimes seem to appear in a sort of foreshadowing aura of pregnancy. I've never known it happen to an expectant papa."

His shoulders went up. After a silence, she said:

"Were you going to tell me? Or was I to have a glorious surprise?"

"I did mean to tell you," he muttered, still with his back to her. "I was going to—of course. But when I saw you I didn't know how to. Especially after you'd told me——"

"About my own little attempt. Very awkward for you, I do see." She was shaken with a moment's violent laughter. "Poor Rollo! A bit more than you'd bargained for."

He turned round on her with a furious suppressed shout: "Don't!" And again there was silence.

"You must admit I'm making it easy for you," she said. "I always hoped I would."

He sat down suddenly in the arm-chair, put his head in his hands, looked helpless; got up again. She said:

"It's not my business, but did you know before we went abroad?"

"No, I didn't."

"But you knew the day you left me."

"Yes."

That, of course, was the letter he'd read by the lake, under the red sun-umbrella. . . . What did she say? How did she put it?

"So you felt you must hurry back to her."

"She didn't ask me to." He hunched his big, heavy shoulders in sullen defensiveness like an animal. "She said not to think of coming home on her account. . . . She'd got to be in bed for a bit as a precaution—it would be so dull for me. . . . She did hope I was having a lovely holiday. . . ." The harsh struggle in his voice shocked her: self-contempt, bitterness, rage, appeal. . . . Poor Rollo. . . . It's not my place to pity him. . . .

"What a good thing you took my advice and went to Salzburg for your letters."

He said stiffly:

"It was."

"How wonderfully you mask your emotions! What did you actually feel when you left me?"

"I don't know. I just felt I'd got to get away."

She burst out laughing.

"Hurrah! It's a safe bet—men feeling they've got to get away." Women prefer to stick around and make something happen next. "What *did* you do? Dash to her bedside?"

He waited before answering. He'd like to strangle me.

"I went to see her, yes. I left her down there at her home— she wasn't allowed to move for a bit. . . . Then I came back to London." He sank down again in the chair, pushing his hair up with both hands. In contrast with his usual well-groomed appearance he looked startlingly dishevelled. Everything's comparative: Simon's always dishevelled. "I meant to stay in London," he said helplessly; "but I couldn't. I went off to Ireland. I tried to write to you. . . ."

She sat down too, leaning forward in her chair, staring at the fire. The scene looked cosy and domestic. She said:

"Well, it's all worked out like they tell you in *Woman's World*. A husband may stray, but home ties are strongest, and if you hang on he'll come back. It's the Other Woman who gets had for a mug."

He drew in a painful breath. He's really in torture—almost more than he can bear. . . . Though I'm not making a scene.

"I must tell you another funny thing," she said. "That night I told you about—I ran into Ivor. He was with me all the time. Wasn't it killing. I didn't actually explain the situation, but he was tremendously tactful and helpful. And at the end of it all, what do you think? He suggested setting up together again."

He got up violently and strode two steps to the window. Feeling he must get away. . . . He pulled apart the curtain. . . . He's going to . . . dropped it again. He came back, and said flatly, utterly embracing his inadequacy:

"I'm sorry."

"Don't apologise. It's so much better to get things straight. It's been so ludicrously pointless for ages, really, hasn't it?"

"Has it?" he said in the same voice.

"Well, I mean the only point was——" Her throat closed. What was swelling in her frightened her—so black, so boiling and gigantic. "The only point for *you* was—wasn't it?—difficulties which one must presume are over." She went on more and more rapidly, in a high-pitched voice: "It'll be rather a relief, don't you think? One does prefer to be blameless—it's so much less trouble. It gets so wearing, always the worry of being found out. It isn't worth it—honestly, is it? I'm sure you agree. You never know who'll find out and start a bit of blackmail or something."

He stared at her, his eyes fixed and bright, dangerous. But he can't stop me. "One would simply hate her to find out in her present state. Supposing somebody sent her an anonymous letter or something——"

"Oh, rot!" he said angrily. Making a bid for temperance

. . . not liking sweeping statements ever, always pulling me up. . . . She cried furiously:

"It isn't rot and how dare you say so! The world's full of blackmailers and don't I know it! I'm going to steer clear of you!"

He made a blind, bull-like half-turn again. He's off—I'll stop his game.

"Good-bye!" she said insanely. She pushed past him, pushing him roughly with all her weight, made a dash for the curtain, and was on the dark slippery path, running.

Where shall I go? Which way shall I start off? This way was the river . . . and that . . . and along there, beyond the field. The river was everywhere. He'll think I've gone to throw myself in, what a predicament for him. . . . How dark, I can't find the road; the wind, what a wind, a gale, I hadn't noticed; the wind from the Atlantic, the equinoctial gale. When it died down for a moment a sound came after it like giant tumbrils rolling and snarling in caverns in the sky. What a night to be out, how pathetic, a heroine's night in a film: *Way Down East*, Lilian Gish to the rapids. . . . Well, I might. . . . Into the boiling plunge of the weir pool. . . . But I won't. Do I walk all night or what? I've got no money, will he stumble after me, shouting my name? . . .

She started to walk along the road. Growing accustomed now to the moonless dark she began to distinguish outlines of objects—the lines of pollarded willows bordering the road, a five-barred gate in the hedge. She climbed up and sat on the top bar. The wind rushing against her blew her head clean and empty, clean and thin as a sieve. She jumped down from the gate on the farther side, and set off across the meadow, but aimlessly now, knowing that after a bit she would go back. A dark object loomed up in her path. It moved sideways. A horse. Good gracious. I can't go running into horses. What's it like to be a horse, standing up and breathing in the dark for hours? The field grew full of large quadrupeds advancing unseen upon her. She turned and hurried back towards the gate, lost it, went up and down in panic along the hedge looking for it. Her foot slipped, she went down heavily, sprawling in the ditch. Icy water gripped her ankles.

I've fallen down in a muddy wet ditch, I've twisted my leg, my stockings are soaked, the mud's on my knees, in my nails. . . .

She thought she heard a shout. My name. . . . Or did I fancy it? . . .

Next moment she found she was an arm's length from the gate. She got over. Rollo was on the other side.

"Is that you?" he said.

"Yes."

He took her by the shoulders, holding her hard, not lovingly. He said hoarsely:

"You shouldn't have done that." He was trembling. He took out a handkerchief and wiped his face.

"I don't know what to do. . . ." She began to weep.

"Come back."

"I ran into a horse. . . ."

He put his hand through her arm. Bending their heads forward against the wind, they began to walk back together down the road.

The woman in the blouse came out from somewhere and met them at the foot of the staircase, saying:

"Been for a blow?"

"Yes," they said, smiling.

"Not an extra special night for a stroll. Still, it freshens you up. . . . Could I trouble you to sign the register, if it's not troubling you. . . ."

"Oh, yes," he said; and to Olivia: "You go on up."

She went upstairs and down the passage. He caught her up by the bedroom door.

"What name did you sign?"

"Smith," he said. "Disappointment for her."

She sat down on the bed and he took off her mud-caked

soaking stockings and rubbed her feet. She examined the dirty hem of her frock and took it off and hung it up.

"Better let it dry and brush it off to-morrow."

She went over to the washstand, poured out warm water from the can and washed her hands. The water became stained pale-brown and she stood and held her hands in it, staring at them, stock-still, her head sunk over the basin.

He went on sitting on the bed, bowed forward with his palms propping his forehead. After a bit he looked up and saw her standing the other side of the room, bowed over the wash-basin, in her white slip, with bare legs and arms. He got up quickly, with a stifled exclamation, and came over and led her away.

"You'd better get to bed," he said.

"All right."

"Where's your nightdress?"

"In my suitcase."

He got it out and slipped it on over her head. He said not to bother about her teeth, and turned back the bedclothes, and she got into the cold bed and lay down.

"Could we have separate rooms?" she said.

He was silent; then said miserably.:

"All right—if you like. Only it's a bit awkward now going and asking. . . . Still, I will. . . ."

"No, don't, never mind, you couldn't. . . ."

They spoke very low, because of the noiseless couple the other side of the wall.

"Do you mind too horribly me being here?" he said in a broken voice.

"No."

"Anyway, we've got separate beds." A brief laugh came out of him.

"Yes. It's all right."

He sat down on the other bed, facing her. Dead beat he looks; poor Rollo.

After a while he said bitterly:

"Well, I always told you I wasn't any good, didn't I? I told you I'd let you down."

"I'll get over it. It's my own fault for taking things too seriously. And for believing what you said. I just feel a fool. If I'd had the sense of a mouse I'd have known it couldn't be true."

"What couldn't be true?" he said hesitatingly.

They went on speaking very quietly, not raising their voices at all.

"I suppose I had no business to ask, anyway—and you thought a lie would be easier. Keep me quiet. Anything for a quiet life!" She smiled. He was looking at her in an uneasy, doubtful way. . . . *He doesn't even know what I'm talking about. . . .* "I mean when I asked you if you and she . . . and you said, no, never now."

He exclaimed again under his breath, in that helpless hard-pressed way.

"But it was true," he wrenched out. "When I said it, it was true. I don't think I'd have told you a lie about that. . . . I was always more or less honest when you asked me things. . . . Only how could I come panting up to tell you——" He stopped, struggling painfully. "I mean—when it stopped being true, I couldn't exactly come posting to tell you. . . ."

"When did it stop being true?"

"Oh. . . . I don't know. . . . After that . . ."

"About the time I went to live in Jocelyn's flat?"

"Yes—perhaps. . . . I suppose so. About then."

About the time he was in such tremendous spirits—so loving to me in that new way I noticed: more spoiling, more attentive. And yet, somehow remote. In fact, just as husbands are supposed to behave to their wives when they're up to no good on the sly. Probably the way he'd behaved to Nicola when he started the affair with me. Playing a double game both ways: a ticklish position. Only an equable voluptuous non-moral temperament such as his could have coped with so successfully.

"I see," she said.

"I couldn't very well come dashing along to tell you," he repeated.

"I see it was awkward for you." Poor Rollo, what an embarrassing conversation for him, really in ghastly taste. "I know what you feel about telling being indecent. And then I suppose your maxim came in useful—'what people don't know about can't hurt them.'"

He shook his head.

"You see . . ." he began, stopped, his breath sighing out slowly.

"What?" This was the third time he'd begun like that and stopped. It had always been when the talk turned on Nicola.

"I don't know," he said. "She changed. When we married," he said with a great effort, "she wasn't in love with me. I knew it. She'd always been in love with another chap."

"Archie?"

"Yes, Archie . . . how did you know? . . . He went all out after her and then . . . he sort of backed out. It's a favourite little trick of his." His voice grew harsh, as it had at Meldon, talking of his cousin. "She had the hell of a time. . . . She takes things terribly to heart . . . and she can't sort of express herself. . . . She agreed to marry me on the understanding—I'd sort of be there—you know—she could rely on me. . . . As long as she wanted me about I wouldn't snap out of it. It worked fairly well for a bit . . . and then——" He stopped, swallowed. "Then there was this baby business. It sort of upset her, you know. Everything seemed a failure all round . . . she got into a sort of state——"

"Poor girl. . . ." Yes, I see. . . . Now one must accept her as real, as human and suffering.

"Well, then—I got a bit gloomy myself. I'd sort of hoped she'd. . . . I didn't see what to do. . . . And then I met you, and all that started. . . . I thought it wouldn't make any difference to her one way or another, whether she knew or not. I

honestly didn't. But I don't know . . . gradually it did seem
to make a difference. . . ."

"You mean she knows?"

"No, no. At least—you know—sort of subconscious business perhaps. I was different, I suppose." He looked embarrassed. "She may have felt I was—sort of moving away from
her and that made her—sort of want me not to. I suppose
she'd never thought I would. . . . Anyway," he said, horribly
uncomfortable, "she began to want to try again. . . ."

"She fell in love with you."

"I suppose she did—a bit. It sort of seemed like it." His
embarrassment was profound. He added: "One does sort of
hear of it happening, doesn't one?"

"It was what you'd always wanted and longed for."

"Yes." But that was tactless, he saw. He tried again. "But
. . ." He gave it up.

"And that's why you were so happy last spring?"

"I wasn't happy. At least——"

"Didn't I tell you you had a lucky life?"

Once during that time he'd said in soft, grateful amazement: "*Everything* seems to come my way. . . ." That's what
he'd meant. Two women in love with him. Two separate
intimacies not overlapping at all, both successful: it was what
he needed—what suited best his virility and secretiveness. It
was all quite clear.

Well, that's how it is, there it is. . . .

"Then things suddenly went wrong again—with her," he
said. "At least I thought so—but the reason was this thing
starting—the baby. You know, it sort of makes women close
up inside themselves, doesn't it? I didn't realise, and she
wouldn't tell me till she was sure. . . ."

That was when he'd been so moody and dispirited.

"When she wanted to go home instead of going to Ireland
with you?"

"Yes."

And that's why we went to Austria. . . .

"I didn't know what to do," he said, ruffling his hair up, sighing heavily. "You may not believe it, but I loathed playing this sort of double game. I couldn't give you up, I simply couldn't. I knew I ought to. . . . A year before—I'd have said it was the only thing I wanted—to get things right with her. . . . But you went and got so terribly important. . . ." His voice shook.

Well, that's something, of course. . . .

He said, overcome:

"And all I've done is to muck you up."

"Oh, well . . ." she said. "It can't be helped. It's just one of those things. . . . As a matter of fact, I really did have it in mind to suggest to you we'd better—bring it to an end. I couldn't see any future for us—it seemed to be a blind-alley after all—and I didn't want it to get messy and fag-endish. Only it seemed so difficult to say it. . . . I meant to have a different kind of parting. I'm sorry about that. I didn't mean it to be hideous. I really do want you to be happy—and have a nice baby."

"You mean, you don't want ever to see me again?"

She said in a light, simple way:

"I really don't think I could, you know." What with Nicola having him and a child, and a home and everything. . . . The contrast would be too denuding; I should behave badly.

After a long time, he said slowly:

"I see. . . . Very well, then."

There was nothing more to say in quiet voices in this bed-room. She turned over and lay with her face to the wall. He undid his suitcase and got out his pyjamas and sponge-bag, and undressed and switched off the light, and got into bed. Everything he did was done in a resigned, noiseless way like a child who is in disgrace and attempts by obedient, unobtrusive behaviour to reinstate itself.

They lay quietly in their beds, not hearing each other breathe. He stirred one or twice, then turned over on his side. She knew he was turned towards her.

He'll soon be asleep.

But she listened and knew he was going on being awake. He was usually such a quick, peaceful, easy sleeper. It brought home the fact that he was unhappy, and she felt distressed. Finally she whispered:

"Go to sleep."

His hand came out, feeling over her bed to find her. She pushed hers out from under the bedclothes, and he grasped it and held on tightly.

"I love you," he whispered. "You don't believe me, but it's true."

"I do believe you."

Yes, it was true. It was only that the word love was capable of so many different interpretations. It could perfectly well be nothing to do with exaltations, with the lake and the chestnuts, or with going up the darkening cliff-face stopping to kiss, seeing the mauve sea below. hearing the gulls. For another person it could just as well be I do love you, you're so sweet, such a delicious person to be with and so attractive. We do make each other happy, don't we, darling? . . . It was what he'd always said, from the beginning: Let's make each other happy. There'd been no deception: only two people.

Soon after, she heard him fall asleep.

They got up early next morning. He drove her to Oxford Station and left her there; going back to London together was too much to face. He bought her a ticket and the morning paper, and then he went away, and got into his car, and drove off.

In the afternoon she went to a cinema. She sat the programme twice round, and then she went back to Etty's house. Etty had just come in, with a copy of the *Evening Standard*.

"Oh, darling," she said. "Isn't this horrid? I didn't know if you'd have seen it."

This was a headline saying, Baronet's Son in Car Crash. There wasn't much other news that day, so they let themselves go over it. Mr. Rollo Spencer, only son of Sir John Spencer, Bart., had been injured that morning in a collision with a motor lorry on the London road, between Henley and Maidenhead. He had been removed to Maidenhead Cottage Hospital, suffering from grave leg and head injuries. His car had been completely wrecked, and the lorry seriously damaged, the driver escaping with a severe shaking. The exact cause of the accident was not yet known, but eye-witnesses including the lorry driver state that Mr. Spencer, apparently miscalculating his powers of acceleration, passed another private car just before a deep bend in the road, and subsequently found himself unable to cross completely to his left side before the bend, where he met the lorry—also travelling somewhat too close to the crown of the road—in a head-on collision. The surface of the road appears to have been somewhat slippery at the time and this was undoubtedly a contributive factor.

There followed a brief biography.

"Isn't it too *dev*astating?" wailed Etty. "I was so afraid you'd see it before I could *break* the shock. It's on some of the *placards* too. I know how devoted you are to them *all*. Oh, dear, let's *hope* for the best. I ex*pect* he'll be all right. It's *mar*vellous how people *do* recover. . . ."

The telephone rang. Etty answered it and after a moment said:

"Yes, *would* you hold on, please? . . . Darling, it's for *you*. I don't know who."

She handed over the receiver and went discreetly out of the room to change for dinner.

"Is that Olivia?"

"Yes, Lady Spencer. Yes—yes——?"

"I thought I must get in touch with you—in case you've seen these tiresome evening papers." Strong, crisp, invigorating voice, unimpaired.

"Yes. I just have——"

"He's all right."

"*Oh! . . .*"

"*Quite* conscious and as comfortable as can be expected. We can't *altogether* say he's out of danger, but we *hope* and *believe* with his splendid constitution he'll pull through."

"How bad——?"

"A broken jaw, poor dear, and a rather horrid smashed leg, I'm afraid. . . ."

"Pain?"

"Well—he's under morphia. . . . Everything's being done that can be done. We got hold of Slade-Murray at *once*—you know he's such a brilliant surgeon. . . . And he's in a nice room, and they all seem so capable and anxious to do everything possible."

"Can I see him?"

There was a split second of silence. Shocked. . . .

"No, I'm afraid that's out of the question." The voice was firm, on the indignant side. ". . . At present," it added, less uncompromisingly.

"But I must. Don't you see? It's my fault."

"What do you mean?" The voice froze alarmingly.

"I'd just said good-bye to him. . . . I upset him. He was being careless, I'm sure, he'd *never* have . . . He's such a good driver. . . ."

Nothing occurred in the receiver; until at last the voice said in a new, muffled way:

"I wondered where . . ." But almost immediately resuming sharp control. "Pull yourself together now, my dear. What nonsense! As if there were the *slightest* reason to blame yourself. . . . It seems to have been one of those *unfortunate* accidents when the fault, if you can call it fault, was on *both* sides. Rollo insists on taking most the of blame— he told me at once it was his fault, but you know what he is— so generous."

"He does talk then?"

"Well, of course we don't allow him to—more than a few words. I was going to tell you that the lorry driver called *personally* to inquire this evening—most distressed, poor man.

I thought it was so nice of him. It's always so horrid when there's bad feeling afterwards. . . ."

"Is she with him?"

"Yes, she's with him now."

"How is she?"

"She's being quite splendid—so quiet and sensible. I'm *delighted* with her. We were a little afraid for her—the shock —but I don't think we need have been. She's pulled herself together wonderfully and thinking *only* of him—I've just driven up to collect a few things and then I shall go straight down again. Now listen, Olivia. I shall keep you informed— do you understand? Every day. I will ring up or write you a line *without fail*. You can trust me. . . . I will also take the first opportunity of telling *him* you have inquired and that I *myself* spoke to you."

"Thank you. . . . He might worry. . . . Thank you. . . . If you just mention me along with a lot of other names —he won't think anything. . . . I mean . . . naturally I *would* inquire, wouldn't I? Being friends, that is, we *were* friends. . . ."

"Of course, my dear, *such* old friends. . . ." Kindly, pitying. . . .

"Thank you, Lady Spencer."

"Good-bye, Olivia." Wishing to cut off as quick as possible.

"Good-bye. Thank you more than I can say. I'm so terribly grateful. . . ." Don't cut off, don't leave me alone in outer darkness. . . .

But the receiver had been hung up. She didn't want my thanks, or any of my emotions. It was not to pass beyond the limits she imposed. Her magnanimity, her perfect behaviour made subjection a moral obligation.

Oh, she's wonderful! . . . Lady Spencer, you've won. I am beholden.

She went upstairs. Etty was in the bath, and called through the door that she must fly, she'd be half an hour late.

She went on up to her own room.

This is what I always knew would happen, this is the punishment. I foresaw it—an accident, his relatives round the bed and me outside. What I didn't foresee was the clemency even of one. . . .

She's sitting by his bed, so quiet and sensible, thinking only of him, I'm delighted with her, let's hope she won't have a miscarriage. He's bandaged, he's under morphia. He's not out of danger. If he dies, I did it. He wouldn't mean to kill himself, but I meant it. I corrupted his confidence and destroyed his happiness. I accused and condemned him; I put death in him.

Where's that handkerchief. . . . She began to search frantically, terror-struck, pulling open drawers and throwing things about. There it was, at last, in the place where she'd looked first—the blue and green silk handkerchief crumpled and neglected—torn too, where I tore it. . . . She wrapped it round her wrist and tied it tightly. There. And never take the ring off for one moment day or night. Charms. And I will keep awake all night, holding on to him, without one moment's relaxation. . . . I'll save him. . . . I shall do it—not her, or any of them. . . . Will he know . . . will he think of me? . . .

Start now.

Anna! If Anna where here I could go and be in the same room as her. If I could see Simon. . . .

It's no good, they're far away.

Start now.

II

MRS. CUNNINGHAM's November party for Amanda was an outstanding event. Amanda herself was supposed to have selected her guests, but as it turned out the ingredients were fundamentally the old familiar ones, with a sprinkling on top of Amanda's contempories—the word friends would give the wrong impression, she had none—striplings and virgins still obscure and folded in the bud: a decoration or flourish, like the nuts and cherries on top of a pudding.

To be Mrs. Cunningham's daughter was to be situated from birth upwards in a paradoxical position—concealed yet public, beneath a responsible wing of sorts, yet so overpowering and magnificent a one as rather to dazzle and dismay than shelter its peering infant object. It might be that Amanda, like other little English girls of gentle birth, had received the attentions of a reliable Nannie, had hung up her stocking, learnt to ride a bicycle, worn a school hat and a gymn tunic, done fractions and the exports of Australia, played lacrosse, been taken to the pantomime—gone, in short, with the throng; but if it were so, it had not interfered with Amanda's development. To be Mrs. Cunningham's daughter set a problem in comparison with which all other interests and activities were negligible. She had solved it by being what nobody considering her parentage could logically have expected: a tricky, doubtful proposition, take it or leave it; the antithesis incarnate of the Victorian-heroic-statuesque; a nymph, tall, willowy, graceful, capriciously fascinating, with a cloud of ash-blonde hair floating to her shoulders, describing an aureole round a pale, indefinite smudge of a face with slanting half-shut eyes; not so much of delicate appearance as downright ill-looking; melancholy, emotional but unaffectionate, self-centred but disorganised, with a taste for art and theatricals and for inventing æsthetic gestures and poses to unlikely modern music. No doubt the heritage of will and shrewdness from her parents was greater than superficially appeared.

At seventeen her future as unpredictable. She'd lead them a dance, was the expression which, looking at her, rose to one's lips. How she herself would emerge, if at all, from the mixture of Celtic twilight and Aubrey Beardsley décor which at present enshrouded her, was another question.

Meanwhile, putting a dab of vermilion on her long mouth to heighten the greenish pallor of her complexion, she chose to attend a school of acting and miming; and to celebrate her

coming out by a festival which was to include charades, and
three original dances by Amanda.

The entertainment, charming and touching though it was,
designed and executed entirely by Amanda and a tender troupe
of associates, chiefly from the Slade and the dramatic school,
rather interfered with the free development of the party spirit.
After the clapping and cheering had subsided and Amanda had
reappeared among her guests, gliding sidelong, rapt and
speechless, in a dress of white brocade with a hoop—her great-
grandmother's—and a nosegay of moss rosebuds in her bosom
—the crowd began to overflow the two connecting classical-
cum-contemporary rooms which had hitherto congestedly
contained it. Mrs. Cunningham stood in the double doorway,
in black velvet with a deep fichu of cream lace, receiving with
a smile of the lips, but not of the hollowed *mater dolorosa* eyes,
congratulations upon Amanda. Not far off stood Mr. Cunningham, florid, Roman, stockbroking, incongruous; as usual
an unaccountable addition to the party: yet there he was,
always, at every one of the parties, quite affable and imperturb-
able; and no one knew what to say to him; and what the
position, what the relationship was, no one could do more than
conjecture. He provided the money, some said, and was proud
of his artistic wife and children, and discreetly looked after his
own interests by keeping a mistress in a little house in John
Street. They were a devoted couple, said others; she relied on
him absolutely, there had never been any unfaithfulness. . . .
But she was worn, white, this evening; she had aged. In
her heart was locked away the image of Simon. She would
never speak of him again. She had loved him for eighteen
years. . . .
Now we shall get on without him, we shall make do with
imitations of him. Peter, she thought, watching her son across
the room, was an imitation. At twenty-five he had something
of the look Simon had had as a young man: the merest superficial resemblance though: the quality wasn't there. There was

nobody left in the world like Simon, who had died in September. Naturally one would go on giving parties, going to the ballet, the opera, going abroad, filling the house, filling the days. Life was perfectly full, one saw to that; one could manage without Simon who had never been a practical part of any of it. There was scarcely anything tangible—scarcely a letter or a snapshot —to remember: anything, that is, of a private nature. His pictures hung on the walls. She had started buying them on Desmond Fellowes' advice when Simon was unknown and twenty-one. She now owned the best of them. These would shortly be lent to a memorial exhibition. He wasn't a great painter, but he might have been. It was in his nature, she thought, to be great; never to narrow or to crystallise in mediocrity. It was the richness and variety of his temperament which had hindered a straightforward development; so that at thirty-eight he was still half-promise, half-fulfilment. He hadn't entirely found himself. A painter of charm, of intense individuality, not a great painter. . . . I helped him, I gave him a splendid start. . . . Oh, Simon! . . . You've left me nothing for myself. My portrait by you wasn't done for me, it didn't spring from our intimacy; which existed only by my will to which you were never subject. . . .

"Clara, my dear, it was charming." Gil Severn came up and took her hand and kissed it. He stuck his monocle in and sighed.

"It was rather moving," she said, smiling faintly.

"Touching," he said. "Lyrical creature. . . ."

"She hasn't much talent," said Mrs. Cunningham, in the way that caused her friends, her children especially, to consider her severe, alarming, cold. "Just that she's got youth, and there's a grace . . ."

"Exquisite," he agreed with enthusiasm, suppressing, his private emendation: no talent at all.

The fact is I don't know what to do with her, thought her mother, gazing beneath marble lids towards where Amanda was, unfortunately, dancing with Jasper, handsome and swarthy, bending his magnetic eyes, his wide, square brow upon her, exerting wizardry. Successfully or not? Amanda looked fugitive, innocent. . . . Well, she must look after herself. The death of Simon had been her first grief. She'd known him all her life. It had disorientated her, made her distraught, rebellious for a day; vowing never, never . . . crying out why, why? . . . Spurning comfort. Then she had put him away from her. At least it seemed so. In youth these things go over. . . . Though I know nothing about her. She was undoubtedly at her best with Simon; happy and unaffected. She'll miss him.

Olivia joined Adrian downstairs in a small back room, a kind of study.

"Hallo, darling," she said. "Who are you prowling after?"

"My dear, the relief of finding you." . . . He seemed tearful.

"You haven't found me. You weren't even looking. Adrian, will Anna come, d'you suppose?"

"I think so. Colin rang up from Sallows about four. He said she'd practically decided to appear—and if he could manage to keep her to it he was motoring her up almost at once."

"It's time she was here."

Her heart turned over in her chest. The first time since Simon died. . . . When I see her it'll be true. Nobody had seen her so far, except Colin: she'd suddenly asked him down to Sallows last week to help go through Simon's things. Simon had left her his house, and she'd been there ever since she came back after burying him.

"My dear, a word to the wise. I have a strong feeling the whisky will run out before long. It's apt to at these respectable festas. Should we make sure of more than our share?"

"Upstairs again?"

"Yes, upstairs." He was looking about him in a vague yet preoccupied way. Something on his mind. . . .

They emerged into the hall, and met Anna and Colin, just arrived, at the foot of the staircase.

"Hallo! . . . You've missed the performance." Olivia gave Anna a hug, speaking with off-hand brightness. For one must be natural, deny any change, any ghost in attendance. . . .

"Should we regret it?" said Anna, quietly smiling, just like herself.

"Between ourselves," said Adrian loudly, "it was the most witless, arty, boring performance I've ever attended. Never was such a lack of any idea of anything paraded."

"Amanda looked rather divine in her tunic," said Olivia.

"Did Peter perform?" said Anna.

"Peter was very good indeed to my mind as the front part of the bull in the charade—or was it the back part?"

"The back," said Adrian. "I've been trying in vain to discover the front ever since they doffed their disguise. Does anybody know who he is?"

"I didn't notice him," said Olivia.

"He was one of those absolutely charming pug faces. . . . Don't you remember, Olivia, when he peeped out through the hole in the neck at the end?" His eye roved anxiously round. "I distinctly saw him come downstairs, but my pursuit was impeded and he vanished. I wonder if he's slipped up again."

"Take care you don't slip up," said Anna, just like herself, starting to ascend the wide, shallow, curving staircase. But just at the turn she stopped, seemed to shrink back. "I suppose it's a respectable party," she said uncertainly.

"On the well-conducted side. There's a perfectly devilish array of young. Hurry if you want a drink."

"I love your dress, Anna," said Olivia. It was made of stiff, dull, rich prune-coloured stuff, high in the neck, with long sleeves and a fitted waist, perfectly plain.

"Oh. . . . It's French stuff," said Anna, still hanging back. "Simon gave it to me. I don't like it on me. It's too important."

"Nonsense!"

"I've never seen you in such a good dress," said Colin.

"I quite agree, my dear Anna," said Adrian.

"It ought to be yours," said Anna, gripping Olivia's arm. "I shall give it to you." Her eyes started to fix, in panic and revulsion: seeing through and opposing the attempt to support her upwards into the throng with a show of bright normal behaviour. They all stood still, unnerved, guiltily meeting each other's eyes; Olivia by her side, the others behind her. It was one of those moments in a party when there is no coming and going; when, arriving late, listening in alarm, you think you have mistaken the night, for the house seems deserted.

But next moment, as if they had been momentarily deaf and hearing was now restored, voices, movement, laughter opened out on them above. Two or three young people came bounding down the stairs, brushing past them without a look. Anna went quietly on, saying in a murmur to Olivia:

"How is he?"

"Better. Much. Moved to London. I get only an occasional bulletin now."

"His mother?"

"M'm. . . . I'm to be allowed to see him soon—just once, when she can arrange it."

"Good!"

Wanting to say: But none of that matters, for God's sake don't think of me, don't sympathise—it's not of the least importance. . . . Forgive me for my letter. . . . The letter dashed off in frenzy the night of Rollo's accident had crossed the one from Anna saying Simon died peacefully at two this morning. Hers was so calm, restrained, and when she got my yell she sent a pre-paid telegram saying so distressed wire news at once. She'd behaved too well. Oh, Anna! . . . If she wouldn't look at us as if we were shadows.

They reached the broad first-floor landing and met the hubbub and the brilliant light. Peter Cunningham appeared on the threshold, pale, handsome, his blue crystal eyes burning, slightly drunk, holding a plate and a glass. He cried, "Anna!" with such warmth of welcome that his cry seemed to draw her forward to join him. He encircled her with the arm that held the glass and made her drink. They heard him say: "This was for old Cora, but we'll get her some more perhaps. Don't leave my side. Anna darling, you look marvellous and I am so pleased to see you." They drifted off together.

Yes, he was a bit like Simon—the colouring, the shape of the face. If he was going to make a fuss of her, she'd be all right. He wasn't of intrinsic importance, she'd see that now: but one went on feeling emotional about people long after one had seen through them; and he might help to link her on to living again—blow up a spark in her perfectly indifferent, faintly smiling face.

"You managed to get her here," said Olivia to Colin: for one *must* force oneself to speak of her and Simon sensibly, without this anguished chest; discuss ways and means, what's best to do for her; practically, dispassionately. It's not my tragedy. I'm right outside. It was my day-dream, loving Simon.

"Yes," said Colin, staring at the party. "She was acquiescent. Agreed it was time to start seeing people again—and a party was the easiest way. I made her tight after tea and dashed her up and took her to the Palladium. She enjoyed that. I've never seen her laugh more."

"Does she talk about him?"

"Yes. A good deal. She's been going through old papers of his all day—burning a lot—and sorting his clothes and things. She wants to distribute them and be done with them. She's quite calm. I don't think she sleeps. But last night I made her take a drug."

"Good. . . ." Well, we shall all get used to it in time. . . . "Come and find a drink."

Adrian had disappeared. Soon Colin, acclaimed and surrounded, vanished too. One thing about having had a lot of trouble—I don't mind any more being stranded at a party.

The tide's going away from me, carrying them all on its crest;
my dress is an old boring one; I can't say I care.

At the buffet in the farther room, a large young man in a
dark suit that needed pressing, elbowed her in an effort to
reach the galantine. He turned out to be her brother James.
She said:

"I was wondering where I'd seen you before."

He looked at her under his eyelids. She noticed he had that
look of a bird of prey . . . a wild or untamed version of Dad's
and Uncle Oswald's look of a queer bird. A notable young
man, alarming.

"Have some of this," he said. "It's remarkably good."

"When did you get back?"

"A few days ago."

"Been home?"

He looked at her quizzically.

"Not yet. I'm going to-morrow perhaps—or next week.
It depends."

His voice was cool, slightly ironic. You leave me alone, it
said. I'll go home when I like.

"It seems very odd to find you in this galère. How did you
get here?"

"Through the back door," he said. "I'm friendly with the
second footman."

He doesn't trust me. . . . I don't blame him. . . . He used
to trust me when he was a child.

"It's terribly nice to see you, James. You look awfully
well."

"So do you," he said. . . .

I don't. . . . But he wouldn't notice.

"You seem to have grown enormously and filled out, or
something."

"Yes, I have," he said. "My chest measurement's a good two
inches up on last year."

"Splendid. . . . Thank you for all your post cards."

"Can't thank you for yours," he said.

"I know—I'm a hopeless correspondent. I did mean to . . ."

"You might have sent me one line, I do think."

He sounded injured. She thought: Can I win him then?

"I've thought of you a lot. Only I felt out of touch. . . . I thought anything I wrote might seem unreal . . . or unwarranted." Taking the plate of galantine from him, she added quickly but casually: "Any plans?"

"Nothing definite. I shall go back to Paris soon, I think, for the winter, and then do a bit more wandering. I want to go to Central Europe, and then perhaps eastward a bit— Russia—Persia."

"I see." It sounded an impressive, expensive programme. But one must be careful to take it for granted he was sole master of his movements. "You like living abroad?"

"I do."

"Got friends?"

"Some."

Among that young, unknown group, perhaps, swarming in and over the settee, looking confident and lively.

"Have you been writing?"

"Yes." He glanced at her; then seeming suddenly to decide to trust her, said: "*New Poetry* has taken two. Look out for them if you're interested. I've got a sort of play in verse too. . . . I'll show you some of the stuff one day. If you like."

"I should indeed like. How exciting."

She thought: He'll do something, and I never shall. Achievement-to-come sat on his brow, it seemed to her, as it had in his childhood. He had his eyes again, and they were the same but different; he'd struggled a good deal, suffered. . . . He looked twenty-five rather than eighteen: twenty-five and five years old mixed. Something's happened to him that didn't happen to his sisters. . . . He's broken the mould entirely which we were all cast in. Kate might have but she wouldn't— doubting herself and her rebellion, deciding the discipline of ordinary ways was best. I might have, but I couldn't: meeting everybody half-way, a foot all over the place, slipping up here and there; in a flux, or thinking things funny. But he won't do that.

"How's the old man?" he said.

"Just the same. There he sits. Sometimes he makes a remark and Mother marvels at his brilliance and quotes it to everybody—like a parent with a child just beginning to talk."

He brooded.

"I rather wish I'd known him," he said.

"I wish you had. He was . . ." No good going into that now. Still, it was curiously consoling, James saying that.

"Is Mother still sore about the mill?" he said.

"No, I'm sure she's not. She's changed, I think—or gone back to something. Now she's alone so much she seems to turn things over in her mind. She makes pronouncements which fairly make one sit up; about education being no use and one can overdo self-control, and there's a lot in this new psychology, and trying to direct other people's lives is unpardonable. . . . All the old manner but such different matter I feel quite shocked. What d'you think she said last time I was there? Out of the blue: ' Your Grandpapa lived much too long—he ruined his children's lives.' Think! *Grandpapa!*"

Smiling together, seeing in mind's eye Grandpapa's imperial expanse of waistcoat and watch-chain, his magician's beard and dome of baldness guarding the sideboard, they were brother and sister.

"Poor Mother——" he said regretfully, well disposed but detached, unfilial sounding. "I'm glad she feels like that about the career question. Because I don't intend to settle down and be a credit."

"How about money?"

"I'm all right."

"A hundred and fifty doesn't go very far," she said, carefully casual.

He looked at her under lowered lids, debating within himself. "Of course," he said, colouring, looking youthful, "I hope to be able to earn a trifle by my writing. But apart from that. . . . I tap another source, you know."

"No, I didn't know," she said mildly.

"Uncle Oswald."

That was a startler and no mistake. But she managed to say with no more than the slightest lift of the eyebrows:

"I'd no idea . . ."

"Isn't it amazing?" he said, appeased by her equable front. "He started it about a year ago—just before I was packed off to Fontainebleau. He just wrote and told me he'd made arrangements for me to have a hundred a year from him—to help me do what I wanted—so that I needn't be pushed into anything for lack of funds."

"But he's got nothing himself. . . . Two or three hundred . . ."

"He said he had enough—more than he needed. Anyway, when I saw him just before I went, and said he mustn't, he got into one of those moods—you know, when he whisks down all the blinds and shrinks up to a little monkey-nut."

"I know."

They both fell silent, contemplating afresh the fact, which had been from the beginning, of Uncle Oswald's secretive nobility about possessions. All my life he's worn the same threadbare overcoat; frayed linen, grease spots on his suit; he lives in one dark room and hasn't enough to eat and gives his money away in the streets. Once, on my birthday, I put my hand out to shake hands and he slipped ten shillings into it, pretending not to know he'd done it. . . . The only purely disinterested character I've ever met. . . . Not quite right in the head, the freak of the family . . . a bit sinister, too—not altogether attractive. . . .

"It never occurred to me he knew what was going on," said James. "He never appears to register, does he? He didn't say one word to me. For some reason I couldn't stand the sight of him just then. I tell you what. I've an idea he pinched the key of my desk one day and read my journal. I knew somebody'd been at it." He laughed. For a moment his expression had the oddest resemblance to Uncle Oswald's: knowing, ambiguous, humorously sly.

"Please, it wasn't me." Though I wanted to. . . .

"I never suspected you," he said, "of as much interest in my affairs as that."

Now, was that meant to be a crack?

He put his plate down and said pleasantly:

"Why don't you come out to Paris for a bit this winter? I could show you a side of it you probably don't know."

"I might, James." She was gratified. "I'd like to."

"Well, think about it," he said.

He's not a bit interested in me, doesn't wonder what my life is. Not that I mind at all, it's rather a comfort. We might manage to get on, I shouldn't wonder. He'd be delighted to show me round, instruct me. . . .

He was scrutinising a picture of Simon's hanging just above their heads; a Provençal landscape.

"Is that by that man Cassidy?"

"Yes, Simon Cassidy. Those panels are his too—and that portrait." I can tell him something too.

"Extraordinarily competent," he said after a pause; "but on the sentimental side, isn't it? Nasty pink." He had the kind of dominating nose and curling lip that seem to scorn whatever they observe. "He's dead, isn't he?"

"Yes, he died nearly two months ago. He was a great friend of mine."

He nodded, not interested; strolled away—by design?—as Adrian bore down upon them.

"My dear," said Adrian, "between you and me, I feel profoundly uneasy. The younger generation's fairly hammering at the door—what do you feel? Who was that eagle you were engaged with?"

"My brother."

"Good God! I didn't know you had one. Is he nice?"

"Not exactly. He rouses pride in me, but also dismay."

"Why?"

"Well, I don't know. . . . Something to do with feeling his principles might oblige him to shoot us in the revolution."

"Good God! How beastly." Adrian had become a good deal tipsier in the last half-hour. "He looks to me an absolutely cold-blooded beast. I'm sorry—he's your brother, Olivia—but I must say it. Now, don't let's think about him any more. I come to you, my dear, with a personal request." He took her hand. His lower lip trembled.

"What, Adrian?"

"You *are* my friend, aren't you, Olivia? There's nobody else I can turn to. The only being besides myself who believes in disinterested affection." He burst into tears. "You're not laughing at me, are you?"

"Of course I'm not."

"You see that boy over there? The one who took the front part of the bull. . . ."

"Yes?"

"I *know* it's no good. I simply *know* he'll dislike me and be disagreeable—but to avoid the humiliation, my dear, of being an instantaneous object of suspicion—because *all* I want— which I *know* he won't believe, or his parents won't—is to offer him my friendship and affection . . . which at *my* age, my dear, is absolutely all one wants. . . ."

"I know, Adrian. Shall we go and talk to him?"

"That's precisely what I was about to suggest. If you'd support me, my dear—break the ice with a few light friendly words— I leave it to you. . . ."

They crossed the room, went out on to the landing and approached a fair-crested, attractive youth with a natural look of dissipation. He was standing alone upon the landing, lean-ing against the headpost of the banisters. She said to him with all the light amiability at her command:

"Do tell me, were you the front part of the bull or the back part?"

"The back part," he said simply.

"There, Adrian!" She looked encouragingly at Adrian; adding to the youth: "We've been having an argument about you."

Nervous, wistful, a bowed column of wincing, tender susceptibilities, Adrian uttered a hollow laugh, and said:

"I was absolutely convinced you were the front part."

"Were you?" said the youth. He seemed very sleepy, and didn't look more than fifteen. He looked vaguely away, then at his feet. Silence fell.

"You were frightfully good," said Olivia, losing ground.

"Did you think so?" he said politely.

"Wasn't it awfully hot under those great thick rugs?"

"Not particularly; I had a little hole to breathe through."

"It was frightfully amusing," said Adrian. "When you suddenly emerged at the end. . . . U—uh—huh—huh—huh—huh!" What a laugh—he oughtn't to attempt it. . . .

"Did you think so?"

Well, I can't do any more. . . . She slipped away. Out of the tail of her eye she saw Adrian take a feeble step forward, saying with an unnerved swallow:

"*Which* was it you said you were—the front part or the back part?"

"The back part."

Jasper kissed her hand with old-world courtesy, gazed deeply beneath his brows upon her, said intensely: "Yes . . ." nodding his head with slow and cryptic significance. But soon he passed on. I can't be bothered to-night and nor can he. He's other fish to fry. Fresh, palpitating young virgins to mould and subjugate. I'm in a black dress, drab and sober, unalluring; an old stager with a totally undistinguished walking-on part. . . . It's Rollo's fault, and Simon's. . . . Something with resentment, defiance, bitter, stirred inside her. I must be attractive again. I shall find another lover, Rollo. . . . Simon, I shall stop weeping for you. You make my face as dead as you are.

The party was splitting up and evaporating. One room was

now almost entirely occupied by a noisy huddle dancing and
stamping in a ring—Lancers, judging from the shouting of
contradictory orders, and the passing and repassing in different
directions. Colin's face flashed up, sharply defined upon a
background of more or less amorphous entities: frantic, he
looked, with dilated eyes, one arm round the waist of Amanda,
and the other encircling a plump, appealing young creature
with a mop of dark curls and a dewy skin. Amanda was
flushed, laughing—enjoying herself; she looked peaceful,
dissolved into the noise and rhythm.

"Grand Chain!" shouted someone; and Olivia flung herself
forward to join them, seizing and seized at random, whirled
round, carried off her feet. . . . Mingling at last . . . for the first
time this evening: laughing back into laughing faces. . . .
But only for a few minutes. Soon it all petered out, broke up
and drifted away . . . as if I'd broken it up. . . . She was left
among a mixed group of drunken acquaintances, secondary
figures; and David Cooke said:

"I hear Jocelyn's gone to China."

"Yes."

It would have been a drop of comfort to have Jocelyn in
England.

Then he said:

"My dear, how's Rollo? It was too shattering, that accident.
Marigold was beside herself—I happened to be dining with her
that night."

"Rollo Spencer? Oh, he's all right now, I think. I heard
he'd made a marvellous recovery."

She moved away and went downstairs.

In the small back room on the ground floor she saw James
leaning up against the mantelpiece deep in conversation with
another young man, absorbed and grave. Something clicked
in her head, photographing them: James on his own, in his
own world. He didn't see her, and she went upstairs again.

She saw Anna sitting quietly in a corner talking to her old
friend, Desmond Fellowes. She was all right still. Everybody

was looking after her, being kind and tactful. . . . She doesn't look well: faded, parchment-coloured, not a bit young any more, not pretty at all. She hadn't bothered to have her hair washed or properly cut; it looked dull and ragged. . . . Was it merely one's own knowledge of her suffering which seemed to remove and isolate her; or would a stranger also see her as it were behind a veil, scarcely in the room at all?

Colin came up with a tankard in his hand.

"Smell this," he said. His lock of hair was over his eyes.

"Gin."

"It smells of thyme. Do you notice? Did you know gin smelt of thyme?"

He went away, carrying the tankard round the room, holding it under people's noses, saying, "Did you know gin smelt of thyme?"

Presently he came back, and said:

"There's been a mistake. Have you noticed?"

"What mistake?" He looks quite mad.

"He's not dead, I've discovered. He was in this room a moment ago, didn't you see him?" He gave a sudden loud shout of "Simon!"

She stood paralysed.

"No, Colin, no . . ."

"A resurrection," he said. "I must let them know."

He went on, but next moment his purpose seemed to desert him. He turned on his heel and disappeared down the stairs.

Adrian joined her. The anguish left by Colin began to relax, and she said, smiling:

"Well, was it any good?"

He said a little mournfully, amused at himself:

"Not an unequivocal success, I must admit." He wasn't nearly so drunk now. "The distressing thing is, my dear, he was really very boring as it turned out. A moron. I've noticed it goes with those eyelids."

"The young seem to have taken charge to-night, don't they? Although they're in a marked minority. I feel like a chorus of elders. I keep on wanting to say things like, Gather ye roses, and si jeunesse savait. . . ."

"I'm renouncing parties," he said. "I'm thirty-three. It's time to think of one's dignity."

"We're in an awkward patch again, I suppose. Just on the turn. . . ."

He looked across the room at the ebullient group still swarming on and over the settee or reclining upon the floor.

"How extraordinarily self-centred they seem," he said, with a note of indignation. "Does that strike you? Entirely wrapped up in themselves."

"They're beginning to fall in love and get biffs on their egos, and that sort of thing. . . . It *is* very absorbing." . . . She watched them. "I don't know if it's a delusion, but they seem much more vigorous and confident than we were. Happier."

"I loathe the young," he said grumpily. "Selfish, silly little beasts. I'm damned if I see why they should make one feel inferior."

Amanda came swimming up to him, her head on one side, holding her arms out towards him—affected, ingenuous, coaxing.

"Adrian, dance with me. . . ."

"With the greatest of pleasure, my dear Amanda."

I never knew Adrian could blush.

He put his arm round her and side-stepped off with her. Olivia heard her say in her sweet, fluting voice:

"I like dancing with you, Adrian. You're just the right height for me."

"Yes, my dear, yes, it's perfectly charming."

"I adore dancing, don't you?"

"I adore it, my dear. Just a second . . . I can't quite catch the tune. . . . Ah! . . . Here we go."

Bashfully smirking, holding her gingerly, he lunged into the stream of dancers; gradually assuming a softened bland expression, on the foolish side, but happy. A nestling look stole over them, as a couple.

Desmond Fellowes touched her arm, and said:

"Anna sent me to fetch you."

He disappeared, and she went to Anna: still sitting smiling in her corner. Anna said:

"I'd like to go now. I'm a bit tired. Will you come back with me?"

"To the flat?"

"No. To Sallows. I don't want to stay in London. I must go back. Colin said earlier on he'd drive me, but I doubt if he's fit to. . . . I'll drive. Could you come?"

"Of course, Anna. I'd love to. If you'd stop a second at Etty's and let me pick up a thing or two."

"Pick up several things, in case you feel like staying on some time. . . . Would you try and collect Colin? I must say a word to Mrs. Cunningham."

She went away to find Colin, her heart lifting in relief and anticipation, in spite of dread.

Now I shall be made to feel again. . . . An operation without anæsthetic is going to take place. Going back to Sallows. You're quite tough enough, you can stand it. . . . Anna's asked something at last.

After the first shock, there'd been no forward movement, nothing to disperse the element like a pea-soup fog that had come down and covered all. When the news came, like ghosts they had all drifted together for a bit, wandering about from place to place all over London, keeping together so as not to be alone, now and then letting fall a word, casually, about Simon, more often saying ordinary things. In fact, we talked a lot—even more than usual; not wishing to be too long silent. There wasn't any difference in the things we said. . . . I only had one collapse, when Colin came round. . . . Clinging to each other. . . . After that we blew our noses and went out to join Adrian at a pub for lunch. . . . Out of kindness, Colin had rung up old Cora Maxwell, and asked her to join them. They'd sat in the pub, and Billy had joined them

too, and then Ed. In the evening they all went on in a party
to the Plaza.

The next few days had rather overpoweringly starred Cora
and featured Billy—Cora bedraggled and shaky, her orange
hair flaunting incongruously above her ruined hulk of a face;
Billy outstandingly drunk, making intricate symbolic maps
and diagrams in red and blue chalk on the tablecloth. But Cora
went on the water wagon for two days as a gesture to Simon.
Her grief was tremendous and grotesque. Having to deal with
her and Billy added a surrealist dream element, and sometimes
they laughed a lot.

A few abnormal days and they then settled back. Everybody
made careful preparations for managing without Simon.
After all, he'd never been very close to any of them, never a
familiar figure in daily life, so there was no great wrench or
necessity for practical reorganisation. Colin wired to Anna
should he come out, but she wired back, No. He had the key
of Simon's studio, and he went and looked through the unfinished canvasses and stacked them tidily. Nearly everybody
remembered owing Simon money.

III

ANNA drove, and Adrian, who had turned up and jumped into
the car at the last minute, sat beside her. Olivia and Colin
were in the back. The more the merrier. We'll break in all
together on Simon's house.

A cold sleety rain began to fall as they came out of London.
Colin's old car was draughty. Adrian was now in bubbling
spirits, at the height of talkative amiability. Olivia saw Anna
glance round at him once in affectionate amusement, grateful
to him for being exactly the same as ever. Probably that was
one of the worst hardships of her state—everybody putting on
a behaviour for her. Even not to do so, which was one's own
aim, involved something of effort and self-consciousness,

obvious to her no doubt. But Adrian remained himself, whether Simon was in the world or no. He'd do Anna good.

"I see *no* reason, my dear," he was saying, "for not falling in love with her. She's attractive, intelligent, amusing—and obviously pretty keen on me, my dear. She simply came up to me and made the most charming, graceful, spontaneous advances—didn't she, Olivia? Olivia can bear witness."

"She's a fascinating character," said Anna, quietly smiling.

Adrian said she had one of those ravishing slightly pug faces, if you know what I mean, my dear. . . . As for her figure! . . . they went on talking about Amanda.

Flattened in a corner with his coat-collar turned up to his nose, Colin woke perfectly clear again in the head from a brief stupor and broke in:

"Can't you *see* she's no good? Can't you see? Doomed. In despair already. No hope for her." His deep musical voice with its echoing note seemed to toll Amanda's fate. "Now, that other one," he continued, "Pamela, Desmond's niece—do you *understand* how wonderful she is?—do you? I suppose you don't. . . ."

"Did you give her a kiss, Colin?" said Adrian.

"She does look a pet, I must say," said Olivia soothingly.

"*Pet!*" He snorted. "Now *there* is a really happy character! . . . Something developed without a trace of damage in the process. A freak, if you like: but what a miracle! Don't you see it? Don't you admire it? No! How sweet, we'll all say, what a nice friendly girl. . . . And we'll all fall in love with that grisly Amanda, designed to hate us and make us wretched."

"She doesn't hate me," said Adrian tenderly. He went on: "The point is, my dear, my conception of love differs from that of most people, and I should very much like to explain it to her, because I've a feeling I should strike a kindred chord. 'Amanda, my dear, I'm different.' . . . Rather a ticklish thing to say. . . ."

"In the gentlemanly style," said Anna. "but perhaps just

a shade banal." One could tell her broad delighted grin was stretching from ear to ear in the dark.

"Now, my dear Anna, you mustn't laugh if I say my conception is idyllic. What I should very much like to do, my dear, is to offer her my friendship and affection. I'll tell you roughly the kind of thing I had in mind. To begin with, a light but delicious lunch, possibly at the Ritz, my dear—then hire something absolutely slap-up from the Daimler hire and simply motor out into the country. Possibly holding hands under the rug. . . . Tea, my dear, at some country house with charming friends—possibly *your* house, Anna. In fact, I think almost certainly. . . . Then towards evening we should undoubtedly arrive at some Cathedral town——"

"I did that once," called out Olivia.

"If you did, Olivia, I dare swear your experience was not what ours would be. We'd stroll in the Close, Anna—look at the west door, I dare say—possibly sit down on a bench, and have just a little quite ordinary conversation. Between you and me, my dear, I'm not absolutely sure conversation's her strong suit, but I shouldn't mind that in the least. For instance, I might say: Look at that funny old woman with a string bag, Amanda—remarks of that, to reassure her."

"I see," said Anna gravely.

"What does she need reassuring about?" said Colin.

"Supper," continued Adrian. "Well, you can imagine supper. I dare say we would wash it down with a bottle of burgundy, or something of that sort. . . . After that we'd begin to feel deliciously sleepy from the long drive. We'd go upstairs. I'd have quietly booked an excellent bedroom for her and a small very uncomfortable dressing-room for myself. ' Amanda, my dear, good-night, God bless you,' I'd say, raising her hand to my lips. . . ." He paused: added uncertainly, "What do you suppose she'd say?"

"Adrian, don't go," pleaded Anna.

"In the event, my dear, of her saying that, I'd simply say, ' Oh, Amanda. . . .' and slip into bed beside her without another word. We should fall asleep almost as soon as our heads touched the pillow."

"Like two children."

"Exactly, my dear."

Suddenly Anna gave a choke, a snort; her shoulders shook; she burst into a deep, prolonged chuckle. Peals of laughter went up all round the car, Adrian joining in after a moment.

We can still laugh, still have good times.

They were far into the country now. The cold rain was left behind, and they travelled under a high travelling sky of intense freezing starlight and dark cloud patches edged with incandescence from a waning brilliant moon. An Arctic sky.

"Another twenty minutes and we'll be there," murmured Colin.

"Yes."

He put out his hand and took hers in a reassuring grasp. She moved closer to him.

"It'll be all right," he said. "It's just the same."

She nodded, unable to trust herself with words. *Dying's a part of living, Colin had said when he came round to find me: remember that. Not its utter cancellation. . . . Besides, see things in proportion, do: another trick of time and our dust, ours too, will be blowing away with his.*

They lay back silent, leaning close together; and soon Anna turned off the road down the winding lane; then the halt while Adrian got out and opened the white gate; the awkward turn through on to the cart road, the bumpy quarter of a mile. Anna drove the car into the barn, and they got out and went into Simon's house, where everything was exactly the same.

IV

ANNA knelt down and blew up the embers in the sitting-room grate. The logs came to life in a moment.

"I told Mrs. Woodley to come in and see to it as late as possible," she said. "*Also* to stoke up the boiler."

"D'you mean I can have a bath?" said Olivia. "Good egg."

"I knew you'd want to stew yourself before you got into bed," said Anna.

Then she'd planned it, I was expected.

"My dear," said Adrian, "would it be etiquette to ask one favour?"

"Gin and whisky in the usual place," said Anna. "You might put the kettle on. I'll make a hot toddy. What about you, Olivia? I'm chilly."

She whisked out of the room upstairs; came down again with an old coat of Simon's over her shoulders—a shepherd's jacket, lined with fleece, he'd brought back years ago from Palestine or somewhere.

They sat in front of the fire and ate bread and cheese and nuts and bananas and drank their drinks and talked about the party.

He was there and not there, for everybody, for nobody, as he always had been.

It was past five o'clock when they went up to bed.

Anna got sheets and Olivia helped her make up the camp-bed for Adrian in Colin's room. Olivia's own bed was already prepared, with the stone hot-water bottle in it. She had a bath in the tiny green-blistered bathroom in the middle of the steam, among the hissing, snorting pipes and the towels frayed and yellow with age and bad washing, and the cracked shaving mirror with the frame made by Anna of South of France shells.

She went to her own room, drew aside the thin linen curtain —Colin's first attempt during his far-off hand-blocked fabrics period—and looked out of the window. There was the pear tree, quite bare, its wide, curving aerial leap silhouetted dramatically in moonlight. A wind of the upper air, hollow-sounding, vast yet without menace, swung all the elm tops together. A queer night. . . . Where the uncut grass lipped the patch of shaven lawn was a line of light, like phosphorus from a breaking wave. We stood here and Rollo said, "Let's go away, there's something wrong": the day Simon was dying. Was it Rollo's mood or Simon's death that had made the dark oppression that day, the sense of virtue draining away? It wasn't so any more, in spite of cold and darkness: all was restored.

What he gave us can never be taken away. He so enriched us that we can but be the happier. We must value life more because he lived. Think that. . . .

There was a tap on the door, and Colin came in.

"Are you all right now?" he said.

"Yes, thank you."

"Do you see it's all right?"

She nodded.

Since that time when Colin came round he had been solicitous for her. They had shared a new intimacy. It was impossible to imagine being closer to a human being. I'll never be uneasy with him any more; he won't ever say again with hostile bitterness and contempt: "Olivia laughs at us all." . . . This is the best one can have probably: affection, confidence, understanding like iron; this willing, exact, unemotional giving of oneself away. Yet we shall never particularly want to be together. . . .

He came over to the window and stood beside her, looking out.

"Dying's so insidious," he said, speaking softly out towards the night. "It's so easy. Death's catching. We must steer clear of it. . . . Look at us all going about breathing it in at every pore because he caught it. . . . Carrying death about with us."

This is a lecture. He thinks I'm pretty rocky still—need watching. It's because of what I said when he came round— the thing he said was unpardonable, which he made me swear to unthink . . . that Simon was the sacrifice. . . . Meaning all the guilt and corruption, the sickness. . . . Dad, Rollo . . . me. . . . We didn't die—not us: it was Simon, the innocent one. . . . I was overwrought.

"We've all got too much death in us," he said. "A sight too much without him helping."

"He was more alive than any one, wasn't he?" she said eagerly. "Nearer the source. . . ."

He brooded, his face dark and bony, marked with pits of shadow in the light of the one lamp.

"He was," he said at last. "But not of life. Though they're so mixed. . . ." He fell silent again.

She waited for what he would say next, hearing the shriek and rumble of a goods train from across the valley, the other side of the river.

"He separated himself," said Colin, "long ago. I don't see what went wrong, but he chose the other thing. That's why he'd never have been a great man—only a person of genius. There was always something hectic about him, wasn't there? . . . hunted. To me he was like a being rapt away in an endless feverish dream. . . ."

He said that in his slow mournful voice; and all at once her resistance began to slacken. Was that the clue? . . . She saw Simon threading so light and swift through crowds, as if direct towards some narrow mastering purpose; as if impatiently saying to himself, "Is it time? It must be time now" . . . stopping dead on the pavement's edge, flitting back then to the room's threshold, peering out of the window, standing alone in the throng, chain-lighting another cigarette; sitting on the chair's edge, his eyes brilliant, vacant (with that look that made people say, did he drug?—but he didn't), checked again, thwarted in his flight.

"He was more completely remote than any one I've ever

known," said Colin. "*Nobody* was to know him. If you tried
to get near him he hated you . . . as I found out. He was very
dangerous—surely you could see that. . . . He was·only interested in being loved. . . ." He added, "Anna knew it. . . ."

Was that why he knelt on the floor beside ignoble Cora,
supporting her, binding her cut forehead, holding water to
her lips . . . compassion itself. . .? Was that why he released
that warning, delicate current of happy stimulus?—lent people
money that would never be paid back?—clowned, as he sometimes did, in that inimitable way?—and all the rest? . . .
Surely one couldn't explain him away with text-book statements. Things were more mixed than that—motives and
results—inextricable. Colin himself said so. One could lay out
all the ingredients one could think of, yet still the vital element
was missing, and Simon as himself eluded one.

"Wasn't he happy, then?" she said.

"Happy?" he cried as if astounded; as if no one in their
senses could have asked that. "Simon?"

He thinks it's better for Simon to have died.

He turned away from the window, said affectionately:
"Good-night, Olivia," kissed her cheek and went to his own
room.

Adrian was in bed, asleep already, but Anna was still
moving about below in the kitchen. Olivia called over the
banisters: "What are you up to?" and she came running
upstairs again.

"I was just laying breakfast," she said. "Then we can all
sleep on. Everything's done now."

"You would steal a march. Why didn't you call me?
You're a thoroughly hostile character."

"Well, I wasn't sleepy."

She went on into her bedroom, which was Simon's, Olivia
following her.

A ramshackle old trunk stood open in the corner, piled with
his clothes. They stood and looked at them.

"I don't know who could wear them," she said. "He was so long and slight. . . . What shall I send back to his mother?"

"Has he got a mother?"

"Yes. She came out. We spent quite a lot of time together."

"What's she like?"

"A little grey body with glasses and wrinkles." Anna smiled. "Nice. She'd never been abroad before."

"Does she want his things?"

"She said she'd be glad of any little odds and ends." She smiled again. "She said he had his grandfather's gold watch but I can't find it. I'm awfully afraid he must have popped it—or just lost it. There are some rings and coins and things in this box . . . studs: Woolworth. She doesn't care much for his pictures, and she's not one for book-reading. Perhaps some of the photographs I took last year. . . . Only I don't think she'll like them." She picked up a Moroccan belt sewn with blue, white and red beads, dropped it again. "You must have something," she said, sighing vaguely. "What would you like?"

"Not now, Anna—please. Later, perhaps. . . ." Thick tears began to drip down. It was this sort of thing that took advantage of one—legacies, relics and mementoes of the departed.

"I know he'd like you to have something," said Anna.

She was so self-possessed standing there looking around at his things. The person who's been by the deathbed always is, they say.

"Simon was very fond of you," she said, looking at Olivia with blue fatigue-sunken eyes. "He said one day when he was ill he wished you'd walk in. You were refreshing."

"*Oh!* . . . I loved him. . . ."

Anna knelt down by the trunk and folded a mulberry-coloured shirt, not looking at her, giving her time to recover. After a minute Olivia managed to say:

"Did you know he was going to die?"

Anna considered.

"I'm not quite sure. Perhaps half-way through he had it

on his mind. . . . But not at the end. He tried very hard for quite a long time to live—and then he just didn't try any more. He got too weak."

"Did he talk much? Say anything?"

"Not very much." Anna sat back on her heels. "At first he liked being read to, but later on he couldn't concentrate—it worried him. We used to play word games, very simple ones—and invent names and conversations and life histories for his nurses—really ludicrous games. He made up rhymes too, and said over poetry to himself . . . He joked a lot. The nurses were mad about him. . . . He didn't ever seem distressed in his mind—although he had so much discomfort—except once when he said he'd never been able quite to understand how the telephone worked—and I couldn't remember either." She smiled.

No last words then. . . .

"I've burnt all his letters—letters to him, I mean," said Anna, still sitting on her heels. "I know he'd have wanted me to. There wasn't much. He never accumulated."

"What are you going to do, Anna? Have you made any plans?"

"I shall stay on here. I suppose you know he left it to me?"

"Yes, I do know."

"He actually made a sort of will last spring before he went abroad. I can't think why. Just on a half-sheet of paper—but Colin happened to come in while he was doing it so he told him, and showed him which drawer he was putting it in, so everything's all right and there'll be no trouble."

"That's lucky. . . . I'm so glad he left you the house."

"I often wonder," said Anna meditatively, "whether he had a hunch he was going to die."

"Did it seem as if he had?"

"I don't know. He never said anything. I've never seen him in such tearing spirits as he was this summer: enjoying everything quite extravagantly. Of course he always did, but . . ."

She pulled the lid of the trunk down slowly, and got up. "Have *you* any plans?" she said.

"Well, no. I'm a bit nebulous still, I'm afraid." Say it cheerfully, don't bother Anna with your totally blank future. "I've had an invitation to Paris. But I'm not sure if I'll go."

"I hope you'll come here tremendously often. I hope everybody will."

"Thank you, Anna, how lovely. . . . I must think about a job, I suppose. Turn a penny somehow."

"Oh, about that," said Anna. "I meant to write but I didn't: Simon left me some money—wasn't it angelic of him? Four hundred a year. It's more than I want and you're to have half. I'm arranging it. I know he'd be pleased. The letter said I was to do exactly what I wanted with it, but keep half anyway —so that means he knew I'd rather share it." She began to unbutton her stiff silk dress.

No words came.

"Get along to bed," said Anna, looking up, smiling. "You look like nothing on earth."

She held out her arms and gave Olivia a quick hug, saying: "It's nice to have you here."

She let her arms drop again; stood a moment staring in front of her.

"After he died," she said. "I made him a wreath of bay. He looked so triumphant."

V

As she rang the bell of number two, she thought she saw the family car, with Benson at the wheel, disappear round the corner at the far end of the square. Imagination, of course. Lady Spencer would never have cut it so fine. "Calling at two-forty," she'd said, "to take Nicola for a drive and a little shopping. Be there yourself at three," she'd said, "not before:

that will be safe. Be gone by four at the latest. I depend on
you. . . ." "Thank you so much, Lady Spencer, it is kind of
you. . . ." "Good-bye, Olivia." She hung up briskly, having
kept her promise: you shall see Rollo once. (Alone. But under
my auspices. I need say no more, I'm sure: you are on your
honour.)

The front door was opened.

"Oh, I called to inquire for Mr. Spencer."

"Mr. Spencer is going on very nicely, thank you, madam.
He's up—in an arm-chair, that is. We hope to get him downstairs and out for a drive next week." Owner of telephone voice
number one: young, pleasant, reassuring, disillusioned-
looking.

"I *am* so glad. It's been a terribly long time, hasn't it?"

"It has, madam. A very nasty time indeed for all. But
Mr. Spencer he's a wonderful patient. So cheerful. That's
what's helped him most."

"I'm sure it has. Would you give him this note, please? If
I might wait for an answer. . . ."

He ushered her into Rollo's study. She stood on the hearthrug—where I saw Rollo standing that night—looking at
nothing till the door opened noiselessly and he returned.

"Mr. Spencer says would you please come straight up,
madam."

Up they went on the chestnut-brown carpet, past the shut
drawing-room door, round, up another flight, next landing,
up two little steps and second door on the right.

Rollo said, "Come in," and he held aside the door for her
and shut it again noiselessly after her.

The afternoon was dark, inclined to fog. At first it was
difficult to distinguish much more than the outline of Rollo
sitting in an arm-chair by the fire with his back to the light,
one leg propped up on low stools and pillows.

"Darling!" he said softly.

"Hallo, Rollo." She saw her note open on his lap. He was
wearing a stylish navy-blue dressing-gown. Then she saw a

crumpled white fur head pop up shrewishly from a basket by the chair: Lucy.

"Darling, it *was* a glorious thought to come." He put his hand out, and when she gave him hers, held on to it. "And the most incredible luck—I'm quite alone. How did you know?"

"A little bird told me." She sat down in the arm-chair opposite him. "As a matter of fact, she added, "I didn't see why anybody should look at me old-fashioned if I did come to inquire after such a discreet interval. After all, I'm an old family friend, aren't I?"

"You are, but thank God the family are out. They've gone shopping or something."

Gone to look at cots or baby clothes perhaps, or to be fitted for her special tea-gowns, with tactful saleswomen to offer chairs in the right departments, and relatives to say take care, holding her arm down awkward steps or on slippery pavements. All the pleasantly important flags and garlands would be hung for her over the rooted, the appalling, the ultimately-unshroudable rock.

She sat and smoked and asked the proper questions. He felt as fit as a fiddle, he said—pretty bored, that's all. Only the leg hadn't quite mended according to plan. However, next week he was to start massage. He had a nurse still, a boring woman, quite pleasant, he didn't really need her, but they insisted. . . . Now she could look at him less waveringly, she saw scars on his nose and forehead. He was thinner too; not pale, but the ruddy look was gone. His present complexion suited him.

Silence fell.

"I didn't bring you anything," she said apologetically, looking round at the stacks of fresh library books and weeklies, the bowls of flowers, the plate of fruit—everything for the sick-room. His bed with its quilted dark-patterned cretonne head was turned back and piled with pillows all ready for him to get back. Nurse would support him, and Lady Spencer would call out injunctions, and Nicola would plump up the pillow if she hadn't gone to lie down—and he'd hop back and rag the nurse and heave himself on to the mattress and say thank you darling to his wife. . . .

Go on thinking of things to say now. Carry it off with a high hand. It was bad luck to be the one facing the light. She bent down to pat Lucy, who winced away.

"She's still there, I see."

"Still there. And I'm completely at her mercy. Who said the monstrous regiment of women?" His eyebrow went up ruefully. "You've no idea how awfully well looked after I am."

"There's nothing like family life," she said.

"It's a funny thing," he said, gazing at her with embarrassing warmth, "when they—when I knew I was going to be alone this afternoon I as near as anything—I wanted terribly to ring you up and ask you. . . . I didn't like to. . . ."

"It must have been telepathy," she said smiling, aloof.

"I've wanted to so often. Only I didn't know if you were still angry with me." He lowered his voice, coaxing, plaintive.

A feeling of unreality began to float her away. Really, the things he said! . . . She made no answer, and he went on with a sudden emotional break in his voice:

"I thought I was never going to see you again."

"I had to come once." She swallowed nervously. "I had to ask you—I had to know if it was my fault you—had the accident——"

"*Your* fault?" He was astonished. "How could it be your fault?" She hadn't seized the wheel or been the driver of the lorry or anything. . . . Or did she mean . . .? "If you mean was I trying to bump myself off, I wasn't," he said with that rough, almost brutal contradictory note. "It I ever wanted to do anything of that sort, I'd chose a less messy way and not drag poor innocent lorry-drivers into it." He was quite indignant. "Good God, what an idea!"

"I only meant—perhaps you weren't being so careful—you'd been upset—and that was my fault. . . ."

Oh, give it up, what's the use, we don't understand one another. . . . The unreality was encroaching everywhere, blurring every outline. She was conscious now of nothing but him sitting there, bulking so large, almost touching her: Rollo, his face, his hands, his voice again. . . .

"What's the time?" she said.

"Half-past three."

"Will any one else come?"

"No. Don't worry. I told William not to show any one else up."

He always thought of everything.

"I must go in a minute."

"Not yet. They won't be back till four, they said so. Sit back and relax. Tell me what you've been doing, darling."

He will go on saying darling—as if everything was the same.

"Nothing very interesting. I've been in the country lately —with Anna. Simon's dead, you know. He got typhoid and died in September."

"Good God, he didn't really, did he? Poor chap—I'm most awfully sorry."

He looked away, with a funny sort of petulant sigh: meaning, I know it's awful and you've had a beastly time, but I have too, I'm not quite fit, I oughtn't to be made to dwell on miserable things.

After a pause he said softly:

"You've got it still then."

"What?"

"Our ring."

"Oh, yes." She looked down at it as if in surprise. "It's got to be such a part of me, I couldn't not wear it."

"I'm glad." He looked at her with meaning, trying to make her meet his eyes.

"I've got the wrist-watch too," she said. "But it doesn't seem to keep very good time. I think it must need regulating."

"Oh, send it back to me," he said, "and I'll get it over-hauled."

"Oh no, don't bother. I'll see to it."

Lucy scratched at the cushion, turned round three times and settled down to sulky sleep with her nose tucked into her flank.

"Darling, you do look sweet," he said softly.

She got up.

"I must go now. I'm nervous about people coming."

"Will you come again if I ring up?" His voice hardened, obstinately pleading.

"No, Rollo, I can't."

He held out his hand, stretching it so that the fine familiar lines of wrist, palm, fingers, showed startlingly.

"Come here."

She put her hand in his and took a step closer.

"Kiss me," he said.

She bent down and he kissed her on the lips, a long kiss. He held her face down and whispered in her ear:

"I'm you're lover, aren't I?"

She raised herself, flushed, the blood gone to her head, feeling dismayed, acutely self-conscious. This isn't what she meant—what I had leave for. . . . Breaking my trust. . . .

He said with determination:

"We're going to see each other again, aren't we?"

"I shouldn't think so."

"One day!"

She shook her head.

"Say perhaps!"

"Perhaps." No harm in saying that. He'll forget again. It's only that he's feeling hemmed in, bored, over-domesti-cated. . . .

"I think we'll see each other again," he said, staring at her fixedly.

"Rollo, you are an awful man. . . ."

"Let's not be final and desperate, darling." Coaxing, stroking her palm. "It's so silly, isn't it? We've had such lovely times, haven't we? Life's so short. When two people get on so well together, it's so stupid to say never again. Don't you agree?"

"Yes . . . perhaps. . . ."

So stupid, to make a fuss. A little rift, an unfortunate misunderstanding—over now. One must see things in proportion.

"I should so terribly miss our lunches," he was saying with soft persistence.

So should I. They were so pleasant.

"Our drives. . . ."

Oh, yes, the drives, they were so pleasant. Why not a lunch, a drive, if he wanted to, very discreetly, now and then? . . . It was all so pleasant. . . .

"Do you remember our drives in the mountains?" he was saying. "And the heavenly places where we stayed? The little inns? Do you remember that queer one under the chestnut trees?—with the funny little band? . . . It *was* fun, wasn't it, darling?"

THE END

Also by Rosamond Lehmann

With New Introductions by Janet Watts

INVITATION TO THE WALTZ

'Miss Lehmann has always written brilliantly of women in love, of mothers and daughters, of suffering'
— *Margaret Drabble*

'She looked in the glass and saw herself . . . It was the portrait of a young girl in pink. All the room's reflected objects seemed to frame, to present her, whispering: Here are You'

Groping through thick waves of sleep Olivia Curtis wakes to her seventeenth birthday. Within the bosom of a family at once lovingly familiar yet curiously remote, she stands poised on the brink of womanhood, anticipating her first dance with tremulous uncertainty and excitement. For her poised elder sister Kate the dance will be a triumph, but for Olivia, shy and awkward, what will it be?

First published in 1932, richly evoking the texture of rural middle-class England, in the charm and sensitivity of Olivia's personality Rosamond Lehmann perfectly captures the emotions of all young girls on the threshold of life.

A NOTE IN MUSIC

'No English writer has told of the pains of women in love more truly or more movingly than Rosamond Lehmann'
— *Marghanita Laski*

'She was fairly comfortable, she told herself (putting in the last hairpin) – quite comfortable really, embedded thick and flat now in her life. Nothing mattered, nothing would ever happen for her again'

In a grey manufacturing town in the north of England live Grace Fairfax and her dull, conventional husband Tom. At thirty-four Grace is settled and childless, inhabiting an outer world of dreary routine, sustained by an inner world of lush, wistful dreams. Her only friend is Norah, energetic, chaotic, equally resigned in marriage to the irritable university professor Gerald MacKay. Then Hugh Miller and his red-haired sister Clare descend upon the quiet town. On all four the hypnotic charm of these two visitors exerts a different spell, conjuring up what might have been: the lost dreams of youth, the hope of new passions to come. With their departure life thus violently disrupted will be the same, but never *quite* the same again . . .

THE BALLAD AND THE SOURCE

'I cannot doubt that this is Miss Lehmann's best and most permanent book' – *Raymond Mortimer*

'I could not get rid of a vision of her . . . Her glittering face blazed in the firmament, savage, distraught, unearthly: Enchantress Queen in an antique ballad of revenge'

Ten-year-old Rebecca is living in the country with her family when Sibyl Jardine, an enigmatic and powerful old woman, returns to her property in the neighbourhood. The two families, once linked in the past, meet again, with the result that Rebecca becomes drawn into the strange complications of the old lady's life – with her husband, her errant daughter and her grandchildren. Through the spellbound eyes of the young Rebecca we enter into an intricate and scandalous family history and slowly the story of the passionate, stormy life of Mrs Jardine unfolds. Bewitching, hypnotic, sibylline – both sweet and savage, both saint and sinner – Sibyl Jardine is Rosamond Lehmann's most formidable literary creation.

A SEA-GRAPE TREE

'Full of her sensibility, her funniness, her own particular acumen. It is also beautifully devised and written'
– *Elizabeth Jane Howard*

'Love, concern, still draws us back to earth. Thoughts directed to us, strong thoughts, urgent, seek us out, call us, touch us: we are connected, we respond. That is the law of love'

In 1933, we meet Rebecca the heroine of *The Ballad and the Source* – but in a different world, on many levels. Betrayed by her married lover, Rebecca arrives alone at a small Caribbean island. Here she meets the splendidly eccentric members of the British expatriate colony, and then the former ace pilot Johnny, crippled now, a misanthropic recluse in his beach hut: for both of them their passionate love affair demonstrates the powerful life force love can be. Here too she encounters voices from the past, and the vibrant spirit of Mrs Jardine – voices which remind Rebecca of the girl she was and the woman she could become.

THE SWAN IN THE EVENING
Fragments of an Inner Life

With a new epilogue by the author

'Combines something of the earthiness of Colette with the imaginative insight of Virginia Woolf' – *Cyril Connolly*

This is all we have of Rosamond Lehmann's autobiography and it is a perfect piece of work, recreating first the child she was and the experiences which made her the woman she became, then moving on to tell of the birth of her beloved daughter Sally and the tragedy of her early death. Then, tentatively and persuasively, Rosamond Lehmann relates the totally unexpected, overwhelming and scrupulously recorded psychic and mystical experiences she underwent after that terrible loss. First published in 1967, this is both the personal testament of a great writer and a rare and important spiritual autobiography. Rosamond Lehmann has expanded the latter sections of the book for this, its first paperback edition.

Also of interest

A PARTICULAR PLACE

Mary Hocking

'Mary Hocking's wry straightness makes posher novels about marital unfaithfulness seem arch, pretentious and overdone by comparison' – *Observer*

'Mary Hocking is an undisguised blessing' – *Christopher Wordsworth, Guardian*

In this, her most memorable and triumphant novel to date, Mary Hocking is confirmed as the successor to Elizabeth Taylor and Barbara Pym.

The parishioners of a small West Country market town are uncertain what to make of their new Anglican vicar with his candlelit processions. And, though Michael Hoath embraces challenge, his enthusiasm is sapped by their dogged traditionalism. Moreover, Valentine's imperial temperament is more suited to the amateur dramatics she excels at than the role of vicar's wife. Their separate claims to insecurity are, for the most part, concealed and so both are surprised when Michael falls in love with a member of his congregation: a married woman, neither young nor beautiful. In tracing the effects of this unlikely attraction, Mary Hocking offers humour, sympathy and an overwhelming sense of the poignancy of human expectations.

TORTOISE BY CANDLELIGHT

Nina Bawden

'An exceptional picture of disorganised family life . . .
Imaginative, tender, with a welcome undercurrent of
toughness' – *Observer*

With the ferocity of a mother tiger defending her cubs,
fourteen-year-old Emmie Bean watches over her
household: her amiable drunken father, her gaunt,
evangelical old grandmother, her beautiful, wayward
sister Alice and, most precious of all, eight-year-old
Oliver, who has the countenance of an angel and the
ethical sense of a cobra. But with the arrival of new
neighbours, the outside world intrudes into the isolated
privacy of family life and Emmie's kingdom is no longer
secure. Combining the guile of a young child with the
desperation of adolescence, Emmie fights to stave off the
changes – and the revelations – that growing up
necessarily brings. Powerful, heart-rending, but never
sentimental, *Tortoise by Candlelight* is a captivating
excursion into the landscape of youth.

Also by Nina Bawden

A LITTLE LOVE, A LITTLE LEARNING

'A nearly tragic novel that is yet a work of such radiant vitality that the people walk off the page into the room' – *Punch*

In this poised and attractive novel Nina Bawden reveals the fragility of happiness. It is the year of the Queen's Coronation and Joanna, Kate and Poll, who are eighteen, twelve and six, are living in a riverside suburb of London with their mother Ellen, and their stepfather Boyd, the local doctor. Accepting unquestioningly his wise, unstinting love, they are incurious about their vanished natural father; their lives appear safe, protected – but that safety is tenuous. The past arrives to upset the present in the person of Aunt Hat, a gossipy old friend whose husband has been imprisoned for assaulting her and who seems to bring news from a different world of chaos and drama. The real danger, however, comes not from Aunt Hat's indiscretions but from the girls themselves . . .

Perfectly balanced between pain and laughter, *A Little Love, A Little Learning* combines a touching and convincing family portrait with the lively evocation of a small community.

VIRAGO MODERN CLASSICS

The first Virago Modern Classic, *Frost in May* by Antonia White, was published in 1978. It launched a list dedicated to the celebration of women writers and to the rediscovery and reprinting of their works. Its aim was, and is, to demonstrate the existence of a female tradition in fiction which is both enriching and enjoyable, and to broaden the sometimes narrow academic definition of a 'classic' which has often led to the neglect of a large number of interesting secondary works of fiction. In calling the series 'Modern Classics' we do not necessarily mean 'great' — although this is often the case. Published with new critical and biographical introductions, books are chosen for many reasons: sometimes for their importance in literary history; sometimes because they illuminate particular aspects of women's lives, both personal and public. They may be classics of comedy or storytelling; their interest can be historical, feminist, political or literary.

Initially the Virago Modern Classics concentrated on English novels and short stories published in the early decades of this century. As the series has grown it has broadened to include works of fiction from different centuries, different countries, cultures and literary traditions, many of which have been suggested by our readers.